P9-BZW-008

FOUR PASSIONATE GENERATIONS

From old New York, where a frightened young orphan gives herself to a lover who is too perfect to be true . . . to high-rise Manhattan of the 1990s, where a fierce old matriarch matches her will and her wits against sharklike opponents in a bitter business battle . . . from a picture-book suburban home, where a wife desperately tries to keep a shocking secret from a tyrannical husband . . . to an exotic Greek isle, where a free-spirited, independent woman finds her match in an international financier as magnetic as he is ruthless . . . from the experience of age that teaches a woman how rare true love is and how easy it is to make a terrible mistake . . . to the innocence of youth that exposes a beautiful teenager to the dangers of fame and fortune . . . through passion and heartbreak, trust and betrayal, four generations of women help each other, hurt each other, and ultimately turn to each other to try to save their youngest and their best . . . .

BLISS

SIGNET ● **ONYX** (0451)

LOVE, ROMANCE, AND ADVENTURE

☐ **THE PALACE AFFAIR by Una-Mary Parker, best-selling author of *Enticements*.** Three women of Society in London are caught in a web of deceit, desire, blackmail, and betrayal in this novel of Life in Royal Circles and a world of pomp, power and privilege. Scandal and intrigue only royalty can create.... "Delicious!"— *Sunday Telegraph* (173090—$5.50)

☐ **TEXAS BORN by Judith Gould.** Jenny and Elizabeth-Anne were opposites in every way—except in the fiery force of their business ambitions, and their overwhelming desire for the same man. Theirs was a struggle in which the winner would take all—and the loser would be stripped of everything.... (174216—$5.50)

☐ **MARGARET IN HOLLYWOOD by Darcy O'Brien.** In this extraordinary novel, the irrepressible actress Margaret Spencer tells her millions of fans all about her outrageously intimate experiences—on camera and off. (170776—$4.99)

☐ **NOW AND FOREVER by Claudia Crawford.** Nick Albert was the type of man no woman could resist. Georgina, Mona, and Amy were all caught in a web of deceit and betrayal—and their irresistible passion for the man that only one of them could have—for better or for worse. (175212—$5.50)

Prices slightly higher in Canada

Buy them at your local bookstore or use this convenient coupon for ordering.

PENGUIN USA
P.O. Box 999 — Dept. #17109
Bergenfield, New Jersey 07621

Please send me the books I have checked above.
I am enclosing $_____ (please add $2.00 to cover postage and handling). Send check or money order (no cash or C.O.D.'s) or charge by Mastercard or VISA (with a $15.00 minimum). Prices and numbers are subject to change without notice.

Card #_____ Exp. Date _____
Signature_____
Name_____
Address_____
City _____ State _____ Zip Code _____

For faster service when ordering by credit card call **1-800-253-6476**

Allow a minimum of 4-6 weeks for delivery. This offer is subject to change without notice.

BLISS

by

Claudia Crawford

A SIGNET BOOK

SIGNET
Published by the Penguin Group
Penguin Books USA Inc., 375 Hudson Street,
New York, New York 10014, U.S.A.
Penguin Books Ltd, 27 Wrights Lane,
London W8 5TZ, England
Penguin Books Australia Ltd, Ringwood,
Victoria, Australia
Penguin Books Canada Ltd, 10 Alcorn Avenue,
Toronto, Ontario, Canada M4V 3B2
Penguin Books (N.Z.) Ltd, 182-190 Wairau Road,
Auckland 10, New Zealand

Penguin Books Ltd, Registered Offices:
Harmondsworth, Middlesex, England

First published by Signet,
an imprint of Dutton Signet,
a division of Penguin Books USA Inc.

First Printing, September, 1994
10 9 8 7 6 5 4 3 2 1

Copyright © Jeannie Sakol, 1994
All rights reserved

REGISTERED TRADEMARK—MARCA REGISTRADA

Printed in the United States of America

Without limiting the right under copyright reserved above, no part of this
publication may be reproduced, stored in or introduced into a retrieval system, or
transmitted, in any form, or by any means (electronic, mechanical, photocopying,
recording, or otherwise), without the prior written permission of both the copyright
owner and the above publisher of this book.

PUBLISHER'S NOTE
This is a work of fiction. Names, characters, places, and incidents either are the
product of the author's imagination or are used fictitiously, and any resemblance to
actual persons, living or dead, events, or locales is entirely coincidental.

BOOKS ARE AVAILABLE AT QUANTITY DISCOUNTS WHEN USED TO PROMOTE PRODUCTS OR
SERVICES. FOR INFORMATION PLEASE WRITE TO PREMIUM MARKETING DIVISION,
PENGUIN BOOKS USA INC., 375 HUDSON STREET, NEW YORK, NEW YORK 10014.

If you purchased this book without a cover you should be aware that this book is
stolen property. It was reported as "unsold and destroyed" to the publisher and
neither the author nor the publisher has received any payment for this "stripped
book."

For Audrey LaFehr
Past, Present, and Future

"Follow your bliss and don't be afraid and doors will open where you didn't know they were going to be."

—Joseph Campbell
The Power of Myth

Part One

CHAPTER 1

December 1991

Bliss

Insomnia?

"Baloney!" To hear Rachel on the subject, insomnia was a scam dreamed up by the pharmaceutical boys to sell sleeping pills. Create the disease and market the cure! Far from having sympathy for anyone who had trouble sleeping, including her secretary, she dismissed insomnia as a character flaw, a pathetic weakness of will.

Mind over matter was her guiding principle, whether it applied to diet, exercise, or the ability to digest complex business data faster and more accurately than the lunkheads who worked for her. And she was her own best example of self-discipline. Over the years she had trained herself to fall asleep at will. On planes, in limousines, under the dryer, whenever and wherever—all she had to do was push her mental sleep button and she was out like a light. Adding further insult to those with circles under their eyes was her boast that at bedtime she was fast asleep the instant her head hit the pillow.

But not tonight. Tonight the city slept; she could not. Tonight she was a nervous wreck, so charged up with anxiety she could barely sit down, much less lie down. Mind over matter? She did mind and it did matter. Her entire life's happiness and fulfillment were at stake and there was nothing she could do but wait until morning.

She turned off the lights. She turned on the lights. She turned on the TV. Turned off the TV. Fluffed the pillows. Plumped the duvet. Turned on the radio. Turned off the radio. Talk shows! Child molesters, space aliens, perverts, crybabies and freaks. Where did they find these people, under a rock? Her daughter Hannah the Intellectual said there was a farm in Wyoming where they bred them.

She creamed her elbows. Did a few neck rolls. Rearranged the silver-framed photographs atop the baby grand and tested it for dust. Too bad she couldn't play. One of these days she would take piano lessons. Not that lessons did her granddaughters Eleanor and Jessie any good. All that money, all that time, and neither one of them could play chopsticks.

Back to the radio. More dirt on Kennedy's sex life. She had half a mind to call in. If JFK wore a back brace and was in such pain all the time, how did he have the energy to fool around? Oh, but what was the point; she'd sound just like all the other morons who called in.

She tried to divert her mind by planning what to give Bliss for lunch. It was nearly a month since she'd seen her. The sweet anticipation of an afternoon with her great-grandchild cheered her, but not sufficiently to induce sleep.

Finally she gave up and passed the remaining hours of the night prowling the vast penthouse from room to room, touching her cherished possessions for comfort and reassurance, until at last she heard the familiar thud of the *New York Times* on her doormat.

She closed her eyes and crossed her fingers. Would it be in? Would the years of time and money and social maneuvering at last be paying off with the recognition she so passionately desired?

At last night's ceremony, the doyenne of New York's

upper crust, Brooke Astor herself, had presented Rachel with the prestigious Gotham Charities Award as Woman of the Year. Flanked by such notables as Mayor Dinkins, Senator Moynihan, Kitty Carlisle Hart, Pauline Trigère, and Estée Lauder, Rachel had thanked God for her bone structure and her excellent digestive system.

"Tough ole birds," a photographer quipped as Rachel and Brooke air-kissed. Brooke had stiffened noticeably. Rachel had grimaced and pretended chagrin while being tickled pink. She was proud to be a tough old bird. God help anyone who dared to pull a fast one. God help anyone who tried to clip her wings. God help that *Times* photographer. First she would see if his photograph had made it into the paper. Second, it if wasn't in, she would call Punch Sulzberger personally and say the photographer had insulted Brooke Astor.

In her short acceptance speech, Rachel had thanked Brooke and the entire board of Gotham Charities for permitting her to serve the community. She had acknowledged with becoming sadness the loving encouragement of her dear husband, whose illness had kept him from being at her side. She had also silently thanked Julio Vasco for her makeup and hairdo and Robert, her personal trainer, for helping her maintain her lithe and slender body.

At eighty-nine, she was younger than Brooke. Standing together amid the applause and flashing cameras, she wondered how Brooke maintained her youthful looks and energy. Genes, people said. Choosing the right parents. Rachel didn't know who her parents were but thanked them anyway. Perhaps the award would prompt Brooke to suggest lunch—just the two of them, nothing to do with fund raising. Just two old birds dishing the dirt. If that happened, Rachel fully intended to learn the other woman's secrets.

In marked contrast to last night's cool self-possession, Rachel attacked the *Times* with trembling, impatient hands. Sports! Forget it. Business? No. Movies. Theater. Crossword puzzle. Obituaries. Nothing. Not a word. Nothing. Her hands were black from the ink. That's why she never read the *Times* in bed. The ink came off on her Porthault sheets. Damn the paper anyway. Couldn't they afford better ink? Would it hurt them to run the photograph? Brooke Astor was always in the papers. This was Rachel's chance at the big time. They mustn't ignore her. It wasn't fair!

Once more. She would go through the paper once more. Four sections, that was the problem. Who needed four sections of a daily newspaper? Think of all the trees that had to die! Suddenly, just when she was about to hyperventilate, there it was! Leaping up at her like a lost earring bored with playing hide and seek. Although she was alone, she hugged the folded newspaper protectively to her bosom as if shielding an infant from Cossack marauders and snuggled herself into the chaise lounge in the solarium to read it.

Evening Hours

GOTHAM CHARITIES HONORS RACHEL LAWRENCE SALINKO

Real estate tycoon Rachel Lawrence Salinko received the Gotham Charities "Woman of the Year" Award last night at the organization's annual dinner at the Plaza Hotel. Presenting the award was last year's recipient, Brooke Astor. Mrs. Salinko, known for her energy and humor as well as her generosity, wore a vintage Pauline Trigère gown, confessing to a bit of vanity "because I'm still exactly the same size as I was twenty-five years ago!"

Among those in attendance were Miss Trigère herself; the honoree's daughter, Hannah Osborne;

and her granddaughter, the photojournalist Jessie Lawrence, whose best-selling book *The World of Bliss* chronicles the adolescence of her niece—and Mrs. Salinko's great-grandchild—Bliss Calloway.

A blizzard in upstate New York prevented Bliss and Mrs. Salinko's elder granddaughter Eleanor from driving to town from their home in Riverton-on-Hudson yesterday. They are expected to make the journey as soon as weather permits for a round of holiday shopping and family festivities.

In the accompanying photograph, Rachel and Brooke looked like childhood friends. An aura of aristocracy embraced them both as they embraced each other, enhancing the superb bone structure and flawless grooming of each. Rachel's last-minute decision to wear the bib of pearls instead of the diamond and sapphire choker Marcus had given her before he took sick proved to be exactly on target, understated and absolutely right. Brooke and most of the other women were also wearing pearls, most of them probably Ken Lane knockoffs like Barbara Bush's.

Rachel's plan had been to end her triumphant evening by going dancing at Roseland. Hannah and Jessie had other ideas, however. They hustled her into the limo, took her directly home, and dismissed the driver so that Rachel wouldn't sneak back out again like a naughty teenager. Wesley, her housekeeper for thirty years had been at the door waiting, and if the truth be known, Rachel was glad she had. Once Hannah and Jessie had kissed her goodnight, the high octane of the evening had seeped out of her body like a pricked balloon, leaving her flattened and dragging.

The *Times* had changed all that. The high octane had returned despite her lack of sleep. She was flying. She felt like dancing on the ceiling like Fred Astaire. It was too early to phone anyone, and besides, if she were truly chic she would wait for people to phone her and accept their congratulations with diffident protestations of only doing her best for those in need. Unable to sit still, she stepped out on the terrace and raised her arms wide in exultation. But she had to hold onto the railing as the cold wind, rising brisk and saline from the Hudson far below, buffeted her and stabbed her with tiny icicles that stimulated her like acupuncture. "I've made it, Sam!" she shouted. "Little Rachel—the kid from the Forsyth Street Orphanage—I've made it! Oh, Sam, can you hear me? You should be here, darling! You should be here."

The tears she had held in check through the entire previous evening and through the long sleepless night now spilled down her cheeks, their saltiness freezing and sticking to her face. *Oh, no you don't, kiddo.* She didn't spend a small fortune on face creams and massage to allow sentiment to ruin her skin. Retreating inside, she determined to control her emotions. Brooke and Kitty and Pauline would never carry on like a silly shopgirl. She would take her triumph in stride. With dignity and charm. By midmorning the phone would be ringing off the hook. She'd have her secretary Daniela screen the calls and keep a list so she could return them.

Flowers. She must send flowers to Brooke. Two dozen yellow roses? No. Too ostentatious, too *nouveau*. An exquisite little nosegay would be better, delicate and pretty like Brooke herself, not obvious like roses. A charming nosegay with a charming note thanking her for her kind words and suggesting they might lunch soon. No pressure, no being pushy, just a suggestion like it was the most natural thing in the world.

Robert would be arriving at seven-thirty to put her through her paces. That gave her more than an hour to get into her workout clothes, read the obituaries, and tackle the crossword puzzle. She preened at her reflection in the dressing-room mirror. *Not bad! Not bad for an old goat!* She was still flexible enough to touch the floor with her palms without bending her knees. Her own daughter couldn't do that!

In her leotards, leg warmers, and terrycloth headband she made silly loving faces at herself as she performed the moderate exercises Robert insisted she do before he arrived. Stretching, mostly—one leg at a time for the hamstrings, neck and shoulder rolls to work out the kinks, facial isometrics to scare away wrinkles and improve elasticity, deep breaths to ease stress.

These done, she returned to the chaise lounge in the solarium with her mega-vitamin power drink. She put a therapeutic pillow under her knees and settled down once again for her morning ritual with the *New York Times*. Obituaries first. It wasn't enough that she herself was alive and well at eighty-nine. Women she'd envied or who had been nasty or cruel to her had to be dead. Preferably of a wasting disease. After being dumped by their husbands for a younger woman and left penniless by their lawyers who embezzled their wealth and looking like alligators from having sat on their duff in the sun while Rachel worked her behind off to build up the family fortune.

Alas, nobody she knew and loathed had croaked. An ad for a senior citizens' retirement village annoyed her. The very phrase senior citizen appalled her. *Old goat* was better than that. Hannah's husband Jerry seemed to understand her feelings. Just the other day he had sent her a needlepoint pillow that said,

YOUTH MUST BE SERVED
PREFERABLY ON A TOASTED BAGEL

If only he would do something about his hair. Get a rug. A transplant. If Frank Sinatra could do it, why not

Jerry! He was a good-looking man except for the bald head. Last summer on the terrace Rachel had put on dark glasses complaining that the glare from the sun bouncing off her son-in-law's bald head was hurting her eyes. Hannah had been furious but Jerry laughed. Hannah could learn something from him.

After the disappointment of the obituaries, Rachel turned to the crossword puzzle. At eighty-nine she was well aware that the vulture shadow of senility and Alzheimer's lurked overhead waiting to cover her like a shroud. The *Times* crossword was her daily personal test for early signs of mental disintegration. Today's puzzle? A cinch! The same old boring stuff. FDR's pooch? *Fala!* Nick and Nora's pooch? *Asta!* Woody's favorite? *Arlo!* Gershwin kin? *Ira!* Moray species? *Eel.* Vintage car? *Reo!* Shankar instrument? *Sitar!* Hersey town? *Adano!*

Honestly! A two-year-old could do it in five minutes. Her Mont Blanc fountain pen was another present from Jerry. He certainly knew the way to a mother-in-law's heart. Hannah was damn lucky to find a man like that to marry her. Forget the first husband, Viktor the Nazi. She'd had her say at the time. Hannah was too much of a wiseguy to listen. Rachel prided herself on never saying I told you so. Bygones were bygones. Hannah seemed happy, though you couldn't tell it from that prune face of hers, always so crabby, always so disapproving.

Tap dancing in your eighties? Embarrassing. Face lift? Rachel always denied it. She wondered what her daughter would say if she found out about the body work Dr. Petanguy had performed on that visit to Brazil. Rachel couldn't remember who said it, but she wholeheartedly agreed that life was an orange and she was going to squeeze every last drop of juice out of it.

It wasn't long before she had filled in the entire

crossword puzzle with her trademark purple ink, cheating only where necessary for neatness. At seven-fifteen her impatience got the better of her. She phoned Hannah, hoping Jessie would answer. It was Jerry who picked up the phone. "Congratulations, superstar!"

"How did you know who it was?"

He laughed, an intimate growl of a laugh. Maybe bald men were sexier, like the magazine articles said. "Who else calls at the crack of dawn? We're all very proud of you, Rachel. The picture is great. You look twenty-two at the most."

"Some nerve. I look eighteen and you know it."

Jessie got on the extension. She was staying with her mother and Jerry in the city until Clifford arrived from London. "Congratulations, Grandma! You look like a combination of Marlene Dietrich and Marilyn Monroe. Brooke Astor looks like a scrubwoman next to you!" Jessie teased, knowing what Rachel wanted to hear.

A click and Hannah was on. "Yes, Mother. I'm ordering you a new album for your press clippings," she said dryly.

"Any word from Eleanor and Bliss?" was what Rachel really wanted to know. She had nobody to blame but herself for letting Hannah bamboozle her. Eleanor and Bliss should be staying at the penthouse with her! God knows she had enough room. But Hannah's feelings would have been hurt. She had insisted her daughter and grandchild stay with her. "It's my turn, Mother. They always stay with you!" Her lower lip had trembled as it had when she was a child. It had infuriated Rachel then. It infuriated her now. It was taking an unfair advantage. But Rachel had given in.

Not that it mattered in the broader scheme of things. She would have Bliss all to herself this afternoon. And tonight at dinner she would reveal her plan for the girl's future.

Hannah was answering her mother's question. Apparently, Luke had called a few minutes ago. The blizzard had passed. The highways were clear. Eleanor and Bliss had set out at seven. All being well, they would be arriving at Riverside Drive by ten-thirty or eleven. "He said to tell you he's sorry he and Jason weren't coming. Jason's prepping for a fellowship exam in January and Luke doesn't want to leave him alone."

The old story. Luke hated the city. Period. The Great Stone Face. Rachel still didn't understand what Eleanor saw in him. Of her two granddaughters, Eleanor was the pretty one, Jessie the sassy one with the brains. Eleanor could have been a movie star, could have had any man she wanted. Rich! Powerful! Everything! So what did she do? The original shrinking violet, at age seventeen she walks out on her contract with Eileen Ford, marries this farmer, and goes to live with the cows and chickens, *two hundred miles* from New York City! She and Luke had been married nearly twenty years, so it must be working. Not that you'd ever hear a peep out of Eleanor if it weren't.

More to the point was having Bliss live so far away. This was a child of magic, a creature of ethereal beauty, sweetness of nature, and a joy in living that were evident from the first sight of her when Eleanor returned from Greece with her newborn in her arms. These were the qualities Jessie had captured with her camera and that glowed from every page of her book.

"Hey, Grandma. You still there?" Jessie was back on the phone. "I've got some hot news for you, Miss Glamorpuss."

"You're getting married!" It was about time, wasn't it? With Clifford flying in from London, Rachel's mind raced ahead with plans for a home wedding, with Brooke Astor among the guests. "A morning wedding, I think," she mused aloud. "Just the family and a few close friends. Judge Latham can perform the ceremony. And then luncheon for fifty, buffet of course. Right here."

"No, Grandma, darling. We are not getting married. When we do decide to marry you'll be the first to know, I promise."

"So okay, what's the big news? Are you cutting your hair?"

Jessie's hair was an ongoing bone of contention with her grandmother. Rachel said Jessie's hair was too long and too wild for a woman approaching forty. Jessie thought it was none of the older woman's business but humored her rather than make it an issue. With Clifford and marriage on her horizon, she resorted to the oldest rationale a woman could use. "Cliff likes it. He says he'll dump me if I cut it. You don't want me to be an old maid with a great haircut, do you?"

Outmaneuvered, Rachel returned to Jessie's original announcement. "So? The suspense is killing me! What's the hot news?"

Jessie the tease sniggered mischievously. "Oh, no, you don't. Not now. You'll just have to wait until tonight. At dinner. I want to see your face when I tell you. Bye-eeeee!"

Any other day, Jessie's sense of humor would have driven Rachel nuts. But not today. Not with her picture in the *Times* with Brooke Astor. Not with Bliss coming to spend the entire day with her—just the two of them doing what Bliss liked best, rummaging through Rachel's collection of clothes, furs, jewelry, and other mementoes of her eighty-nine years.

As she often said, she never threw anything away. You never could tell what you might want. Everything she had ever acquired was assembled in a series of mirrored dressing rooms in the sprawling 20-room triplex. Each item was catalogued, dated, and stored in temperature-controlled closets. The story of her life on hangers, shelves, and chests of drawers lined with Mary Chess paper.

Ultimately the entire collection of thousands of items would be bequeathed as a single work of art to the Metropolitan Museum for permanent exhibition in the Rachel Lawrence Salinko Wing she had endowed in her will. Her sole regret was that she would not be there to enjoy the envy of her friends, assuming any of them outlived her!

Among her favorite recent possessions was another needlepoint cushion, this one made for her by Jessie. Its message quoted Brooke Astor's famous remark, "Money is like a pile of manure. You've got to spread it around!"

Bliss was the only one of her family Rachel had ever invited to share the pleasures of her collection. Hannah was a pill. She honestly didn't see much point of hanging onto clothes, and indeed, Hannah's sense of style would fit into a thimble. Even more irritating was Hannah's suggestion that her mother's need to accumulate clothes as memories was an outgrowth of a deprived childhood, of being abandoned on the steps of an orphanage in 1902 wrapped in a tattered shawl.

"No!" she had snapped when Hannah sarcastically asked if she still had the shawl. "You've got everything else you've ever worn, Mother! It's probably hidden away somewhere waiting to be discovered, like the shroud of Turin."

If Hannah didn't understand, Bliss did. The nearly seventy-five years that separated them had somehow created a special bond. A part of Rachel was eternally young. Bliss at fifteen reminded her of herself at that age. Not in maturity. Rachel's circumstances had made her a woman at that age forced to take care of herself because she had nobody else in the world to do it.

By contrast, Bliss was sheltered and cherished in ways that would have turned any other child into a spoiled brat. The part of herself Rachel recognized in Bliss was the girl's love affair with the entire world, her curiosity and sense of adventure, and her expectation of wonder. These were what Jessie had captured in her photographs of Bliss, what one of the reviewers called "the tender incandescence of authentic innocence on the brink of womanhood." Rachel had long ago lost these qualities to experience and necessity but she knew what they were. Her daughter never had them. Her two granddaughters didn't have them. Only Bliss had them and Rachel intended to nourish them and keep them alive, to carry on her essence even after she was gone.

"Wesley!" she bellowed into the intercom.

Wesley appeared in the solarium for her day's instructions, bringing with her a Waterford goblet of hot water and lemon juice and a small lined notepad for recording Rachel's wishes.

"Bliss will be here for lunch. That means fruit, vegetables, and whole-grain breads. And tofu. Lots of tofu. Balsamic oil. Soy butter. And plenty of salad. Not like the old days, right?"

Until the health bug bit her, Bliss had been like other kids, stuffing herself with pizzas, burgers and fries, milkshakes, and mile-high bags of potato chips, the greasier the better. Not any more. It was doubtless a good idea, but Rachel missed the trips to McDonald's, the hot dogs at the zoo, the candy bars at the movies.

Tonight's menu was also a sharp contrast to the old days of pot roast and gravy and creamy mashed potatoes. "Onion tarts to start. Zucchini and tomato casserole. Brown rice and mushrooms. Homemade applesauce. Natural. No sugar. And for dessert?" Wesley had become expert at making a cheeseless cheese cake whose creamy texture and richness contradicted the fact that it contained no dairy products whatsoever.

"Congratulations, Your Majesty!" Prompt as usual, Robert strode in at seven-thirty precisely, waving the page from the *New York Times* at Rachel before stuffing it into his Armani duffle. "Now get off your ass, gorgeous. Let's get to work."

Not bad! For the second time this morning, Rachel exulted at her image in the workout room mirror. Not bad for an old goat. *A tough old bird,* the photographer had said. *I'll buy that.* She abandoned herself to Robert's manipulations, glorying in the way he banished stiffness and tension. She was a rag doll, loose and limber, a niagara of perspiration soaking her hair and coating her face with nature's own moisturizer.

Sweating buckets reassured her. She was not a dried-up prune. Her eighty-nine-year-old body was alive and well with plenty of time and triumphs still ahead of her in defiance of the calendar.

"Sweat is the fountain of youth!" she told Robert, knowing that he would purse his lips in ostentatious disapproval.

"Sweat?"

"That's what I said. Sweat."

"Ladies do not sweat!"

It was their little ritual. She joined him in chorus. "Ladies do not sweat. Horses sweat. Men perspire. And ladies? Ladies *glow!*"

Today she had plenty of reason to glow. By the time Robert finished putting her through her routines, she felt twenty-nine instead of eighty-nine. Whoever said it was dead right: Youth was wasted on the young. If she couldn't turn back the clock, she could make every minute count and also count her blessings for her genes. She had been healthy all her life, thank God. A strong body. Thick hair. Good teeth without a single cavity. Not like Hannah with the braces and the impacted wisdom teeth that had cost a fortune. Unlike other women her age or even younger, she had perfectly formed feet that had survived decades of spike heels and pointy toes. She could still wear sandals barefoot without fear of bunions or hammer toes.

"You can thank your parents!" Robert had exclaimed the first time he had analyzed her physical requirements. If she had known who her parents were she'd have done it. It was something she still wondered about even after all these years. Whoever they were they were dead by now. All that she knew was that someone, her mother most likely, had left her on the steps of the Forsyth Street Orphanage with her umbilical cord still attached and a painfully pencilled note that said "Rachel."

Any anger she felt as a child had given way to compassion for this anonymous creature. In her heart of hearts, Rachel blessed her mother for whatever passion—and, she hoped, joy!—had produced the genetic components that had taken her to this advanced age so successfully.

The only time she felt old was when she looked at her daughter. There was no excuse for Hannah's gray hair and matronly figure. She looked like an old schoolmarm. If Eleanor didn't watch out, she'd wind up looking old and dowdy, too. A slight exaggeration. Eleanor was still the family beauty—after Rachel herself of course, though it still rankled that Eleanor had thrown it all away to marry Luke, the Great Stone Face, and live hidden away in Riverton-on-Hudson.

Not a total waste. Eleanor had given her Bliss, hadn't she? From the moment fifteen years ago when Rachel held her great-grandchild in her arms, she knew the baby girl belonged to her, her true and lineal descend-

ant into the twenty-first century. Thank God that for
once Eleanor had had the guts to disobey Luke and
had gone ahead and had the baby. Others might roll
their eyes and secretly scoff when she said Bliss was
the spitting image of herself at the same age. The proof
lay in the faded photograph of herself at fifteen with
her first and one true love, a doughboy in the 69th
Regiment, later immortalized as The Fighting Sixty-
ninth. The date in brown ink was October 10, 1917.

The girl who grinned so impishly from the photograph looked like Bliss dressed in period costume for a
play. Because she had chosen never to explain the photograph to anyone she had never shown it to anyone,
prefering to keep it wrapped in the lace handkerchief
she had swiped from a pushcart for the occasion. Today, however, she had decided to show it to Bliss so
that the girl could see the resemblance, be proud of it,
and be on Rachel's side tonight at dinner when she announced her plan.

She dressed as carefully for her afternoon with Bliss
as she had for the Gotham award. Oatmeal wool slacks
with matching silk jersey turtleneck. Chocolate suede
ankle boots and matching suede belt, wide and fringed
to emphasize her Scarlett O'Hara waist. Her favorite
Hermes horse scarf knotted over one shoulder. Diamond stud earrings and diamond wedding band. No
other jewelry.

That accomplished, it was time for her usual morning call to Connecticut.

"How is my husband this morning?"

"About the same as yesterday, Mrs. Salinko."

"The Prozac and lithium carbonate haven't helped?"

"I'm afraid not. At least not yet."

"I thought Dr. Greene said we could expect some
improvement." She tried not to show her exasperation.

"I tried to show Mr. Salinko your picture in this morning's paper—and by the way, congratulations—"

"Didn't he recognize me?"

"I'm sorry, Mrs. Salinko. Perhaps tomorrow will be better."

Rachel expressed her thanks as always. "I'll see you on Sunday."

The nurse's voice brightened with professional gaiety. "Don't forget. We're having our Christmas party. Santa will be arriving right after lunch."

Christmas! Rachel made a note to have her secretary Daniela get her enough fifty- and hundred-dollar bills for the nursing-home staff. Last year her carefully chosen individual gifts of scarves and perfume and cashmere sweaters had been accepted with glacial restraint. Cash was what people wanted. Not something from Bergdorf's they didn't want and were too intimidated to return. This year she'd be Santa with a checkbook.

By the end of the morning, Daniela had logged thirty-seven phone calls and faxes, most from friends and acquaintances congratulating Rachel on her award, a few from worthy groups asking for donations, and one from Tina Brown herself suggesting they lunch and talk about an interview.

"She asked me what I knew about your affair with Rudolph Valentino!"

"Oh, that!" Rachel brushed it aside.

"But Mrs. Salinko! Is it true? Were you the real reason Valentino was in New York when he died?"

It still amazed her that people could be so gullible. More than twenty years ago a gossip reporter had followed her to the powder room at a charity affair. Angling for a juicy quote the woman had asked her to recall her most scandalous love affair. After considering the impact of George Gershwin, Clark Gable, and

Harry Truman, she had sighed demurely and murmured "Valentino! I dream of him every night."

Thinking no more about it, she was astounded when the story not only hit the scandal sheets but kept popping up in clipping files, a perfect example of how once something appeared in print, however silly it might be, it was forevermore engraved in stone as fact.

"No, Daniela. It isn't true. Rudy and I were never lovers."

"You weren't?"

Her secretary's disappointment prompted her to add, "But he did teach me the tango!"

That was a mistake. She had forgotten Daniela was a film buff. "He did? He really did? Like in *Blood and Sand*? Oh, my god. I can't stand it!"

Enough was enough. "For God's sake, Daniela. I never met Rudolph Valentino. Okay? Now calm down and call Tina Brown back. Apologize for me not coming to the phone. Explain that I'm incommunicado with Bliss and will phone her tomorrow." She would have to think carefully about what to say to Tina Brown. She would adore an interview in *Vanity Fair*—but it could boomerang. There were certain things she would not care to have revealed. She had seen other people humiliated in print, like Leona Helmsley, for instance. Once one of those research terriers got going there was no telling what they would dig up.

Publicity didn't mean beans to her, she decided, forgetting her all-night vigil for this morning's *Times*. She would just as soon do her bit for charity and stay quietly in the background. Let then write about Jessie and her photographs of Bliss. Rachel would be content to be the family matriarch, proud of her grandchild's success. Only if asked would she take credit for buying Jessie her first camera and thus launching her career.

From now on, Bliss would be her major concern.

Bliss wanted to be a fashion designer like Donna Karan and Rachel was determined to see that dream come true, whether Eleanor and Luke liked it or not. Tonight at dinner she would announce her plan as a fait accompli, no arguments permitted.

"Guess who's *he-e-e-e-re!*" The subject of her thoughts materialized before her, a spray of gardenias thrust forward as a love offering.

"Bliss!" At the sight of her, Rachel melted, her glossy facade evaporating as tears threatened her composure as well as her mascara. Like any warrior who survived and prevailed through cunning and manipulation, she was awed by authentic goodness. In Bliss, what you saw was what you got—a warm-hearted and generous girl on the cusp of womanhood, smart as a whip and original of mind.

"Gardenias! Thank you, darling. You always remember they're my favorite."

"They're from Grandma." Hannah knew they were Rachel's favorite, too.

"But you're the one who brought them. Where's my hug?"

It was less than a month since Thanksgiving yet Bliss seemed incrementally more mature. When the two embraced, Rachel could feel the firm plump breasts through the layers of winter clothes. Other girls looked like frumps in cold weather. Not Bliss.

"Let me look at you, darling."

At Thanksgiving, Bliss had shown up in secondhand jodhpurs, her brother's plaid flannel shirt that hung down past her knees, and a leather vest she had made by cutting the sleeves off a man's jacket she had found at a garage sale.

This time when she stepped back for Rachel's perusal, she was a collage of impish improvisation, combining textures and colors and shapes with such

breathtaking effect that it was hard to separate the
various parts that made up the whole. Her oversized
jeans were slashed at the knees to reveal cherry-red
tights, the jeans legs stuffed into open galoshes that
flapped as she walked. Above her waist was a BUTTON
YOUR FLY T-shirt visible through a transparent jacket
made from an old lace table runner.

On her wrists were the bracelets all the girls were
wearing, circlets made of chewing gum wrappers and
bent spoons painted with nail polish. Around her neck
was Rachel's frayed old silver fox scarf with the
crosseyed head and the latest teen rage, a baby pacifier
dangling from a pair of plaid shoelaces. Topping the
confection was a battered brown fedora studded with
political and rock-n-roll buttons and insignia. As the final touch, Bliss had fashioned a hatband out of a red
calico bandana fastened with a cluster of red plastic
cherries so that their weight pulled one side of the hat
brim down over one eye at a rakish angle.

When the lace jacket flew open, Rachel could see
that the jeans hung low on the girl's hipbones so that
her belly button was exposed. If it were anyone else,
Rachel would have exploded with outrage. Instead, she
laughed with delight.

"You think it's like—you know—too much?" Bliss
asked sheepishly.

Nothing Bliss did could be too much. She had a
Goldilocks genius for being just right. "You look wonderful, absolutely wonderful. Did Jessie get a load of
your outfit? She should take your picture!"

"Well, as a matter of fact—" Bliss stopped short, uncertain whether to continue.

"As a matter of fact—?" Rachel prompted.

"Um, I was telling Aunt Jessie about the Balmains
and Balenciagas and all that other stuff you let me try
on and she said . . ."

"She said—?"

"She said how come you never showed her your collection. She said she thought it would make a wonderful book."

Maybe Rachel had been wrong about Jessie, assuming she agreed with Hannah that saving old clothes was a waste of time and space. She knew people talked behind her back and for the most part didn't give a flying fig about what they said. Plastic surgery? None of their business. Younger lovers? Not any more. Dancing away the night at Roseland? Guilty, your honor. Having a Lincoln town car the size of the QE 2 to go down to the Fulton Fish Market at dawn when the Gloucestermen pulled into the East River with fresh lobster? What did they expect her to do, walk?

Let them talk. She didn't care. Except when it came to her collection. The clothes were her autobiography, full chapters and passing anecdotes of her life, reminders of where she'd come from and how she got to where she was now. Was there a book in it, a woman's journey through life as seen through her closets? Jessie had changed for the better since Clifford came into her life, Rachel decided. So what in Sam Hill was she waiting for? The man was nuts about her, wasn't he? Recognized her talent as a photographer, hadn't he? Published *The World of Bliss*, didn't he? Told Rachel and Hannah how *frightfully keen* he was to marry her!

Jessie was thirty-eight years old, for goodness sake. If she wanted children it was time to get a move on. Even if she didn't want children, it was time to get a move on. A man like Clifford wasn't going to wait forever. Maybe Rachel could speed things up by inviting her to see the collection and tempting her with a vintage outfit for the wedding.

Meantime Bliss was impatiently waiting for her to finish her mint tea. The girl had developed a special routine for her visits. She called the first stage her "feel trip." Closing her eyes she would feel her way through the racks, caressing fabrics and tracing with her fingertips the seams and constructions of various designers. Cutting on the bias was a revelation. As Rachel explained, "It molds the body. You get uplift without a brassiere. The problem is, it's difficult to sew."

To demonstrate, she had Bliss try on a Jean Harlow dinner gown designed by Adrian. "Cool!" Bliss gasped at her reflection. "How will I ever learn to cut like that?"

"You will, Bliss. I promise. You'll get the best training money can buy. The best schools. Apprenticeships in Paris. Milan. Seventh Avenue. That's what we're going to discuss over dinner tonight."

"But—" Bliss's exuberance collapsed like a soap bubble.

"But what, darling? Tell me."

"Dad wants me to be an agronomist. He says I love the land, which I do, and my science grades are all A's, which they are, and that people with my brains and background are going to be needed if America is to survive in the twenty-first century."

Luke again. The man never opened his mouth. The one time he did and—this! If the man had deigned to accompany his wife and daughter to town Rachel could have spoken to him personally about his daughter's future. Since he couldn't be bothered, Rachel would simply advise Eleanor, Jessie, and Hannah of her decision.

Meantime, she would change the subject. No need to ruin the afternoon. From a dark blue velour box she removed the lace handkerchief that held today's surprise. "See what's inside, Bliss."

"A photograph. A real old photograph! Cool!"

"Recognize anyone?"

"It's—I don't know. It looks like—me! But how can that be?"

"Because it's *me!* See the date? 1917! I was exactly your age, fifteen years old."

"And you're wearing a gardenia! And who is the soldier? Grandpa Will?" Eleanor had once told Bliss about the grandfather who'd died before Eleanor was born. Upon questioning, Eleanor had said Grandpa Will's life was tragic and warned her never to mention him to Hannah because it made her sad.

Rachel had pinned the gardenia Bliss brought to the shoulder of her turtleneck. She turned her head so as to inhale its heady fragrance. "The gardenia in the picture was the first I ever received. And this is the first time I've shown the picture to anyone in all the years since it was taken."

Without warning, the memory wracked Rachel with a painful sob. An alarmed Bliss patted her arm in an effort to help. "Please, tell me what to do . . . *Please.* Gransy." Bliss reverted to her baby-talk name for her great-grandmother.

Rachel's recovery was as swift as the attack. "The boy in the picture was my first love, before I even met Grandpa Will. One day I'll tell you the whole story. But meantime, I wanted you to know that this picture marked the happiest day of my life. You see the outfit I was wearing, an ankle-length walking suit?"

Bliss examined the photograph carefully. "It's so hard to see the details. I wish I could have seen the real thing."

Rachel smiled triumphantly as she removed a garment bag from a climate-controlled cedar closet and unzipped it. "Here it is." She held it against Bliss. The two of them gazed transfixed at their reflection in the mirrored walls.

"Cool!" Bliss sighed. "Where did you get it? Did they have department stores in the olden days?"

Rachel caressed the garment with proprietary pleasure. "I made it myself. I cut it and sewed it myself on an old treadle sewing machine. One of those you work with your feet! You see what I'm saying, Bliss. The talent is in the genes. It skipped a couple of generations and now it's yours."

The girl's fingers explored the curves of the seams, the shape of the reveres and the way the collar was fitted into the neckline. Bliss had made a jacket from a pattern and knew how difficult it was to set a collar in smoothly.

Rachel had deliberated long and hard about whether to show the walking suit to Bliss. It might easily have struck the girl as a silly old woman's ego trip. Pity or condescension were two things Rachel did not need at this stage of her life. She had watched Bliss for the slightest hint of either. There was none. Only admiration.

"Would you like to try it on?"

"Cool." She stripped down to her bikini briefs and bra, her near nudity reminding Rachel of how she had looked at that age. She and Brooke and Kitty and Estée and all the rest of the gang could exercise and diet until their teeth fell out, but they could never recapture the texture of youth. Still, as someone said when asked how it felt to be ninety years old, what was the alternative?

"The skirt first." She slipped it gently over Bliss's head and settled it neatly on her hips. The waistband was tight so she left the placket in the back open and fastened it with a large safety pin.

"No zipper?" Bliss protested and then giggled as she realized what she had said. "Of course, no zipper. It was 1917!"

The shirtwaist and long jacket fit as if custom tailored, changing the contours of Bliss's body from that of a blossoming adolescent to that of a stylish, dignified young woman.

"Now the hair. Bend your head." Starting at the nape of the vulnerable young neck, Rachel brushed the thicket of hair upward and outward. Gathering it loosely, she piled it on top of Bliss's head and fastened it with hairpins, tendrils flying in a manner reminiscent of La Goulou!

The transformation stunned them both.

"I'm *you*, Gransy! I'm just like you were at my age!"

Not if I can help it, Rachel vowed. Bliss would not have to suffer as Rachel had suffered or make compromises in the name of survival. Bliss would not have to learn to sew in a sweatshop; she would learn her craft at the Fashion Institute of Technology. Bliss would not have to steal remnants in order to have something decent to wear. She would not have to marry the first man who offered her security.

"Something's missing. See?" The photograph showed a blurred impression of something on the bosom that was hard to make out.

"What is it? I can't tell."

Rachel knew exactly what it was, the garnet laveliere comprised of a peacock and pineapple connected by gold-link chain, a gift from the young soldier at her side.

"Let's see how this works." Rachel returned to the velour box and fished out the lavaliere, holding it up to the light before pinning it to Bliss's lapel. "Now let's look at you."

Bliss tilted her head like the girl in the photograph.

"Perfect, darling." Rachel's voice quavered with emotion. The creature standing beside her and reflected in the mirror had become the living embodiment of the girl on the brink of marriage more than seventy years ago, the bride-to-be who never was. *Samuel!* How happy they had been that day at the photographer's.

Lost in a haze of memory, she was aware that Bliss had said something but had not heard what it was. "What did you say, sweetheart?"

"I said there's only one thing wrong."

"What? What's wrong? I don't see anything wrong." It was perfect; couldn't she see it was perfect? "It's perfect. *You* are perfect."

Bliss grinned impishly the way she did when she knew a crossword puzzle answer that Rachel didn't. "Except for . . ." She raised the skirt several inches. "My galoshes!"

Amid shrieks of laughter, Rachel crushed Bliss to her heart in an outpouring of maternal joy she had not felt for years. This was her daughter's daughter's daughter, blood of her blood unto the fourth generation and her link to immortality.

She tucked the faded photograph into its case. Some other time when Bliss was older and had fallen in love she would tell her about the Great War and how she met and fell in love with Samuel Harrington.

CHAPTER 2

1917

Samuel

It was after midnight at the Forsyth Street Orphanage. While the children slept upstairs, Rachel sat in the deserted kitchen hunched over Becky's battered Singer sewing machine, determined to finish the walking suit before morning. She sipped scalding black tea through the coarse brown sugar cube held beneath her tongue. That and a slab of rye bread rubbed with garlic and chicken fat would keep her awake and alert.

Fear might paralyze others. For Rachel it was a stimulant to activity. She was afraid of her boss, Mo Schweitzer and what he might do if he found out she was the one who stole the gaberdine. He could haul her into court one-two-three. Girls had been sent to jail for years for less. The theft had not been premeditated. She had acted on impulse after Mo tried to pull a fast one. She couldn't be sure he'd even found out about the missing length of fabric. Yet. And if he had, whether he would connect the loss with what had happened in his office earlier in the day.

It was too late to start worrying about Mo Schweitzer now. The walking suit was going to change her life. Tomorrow Douglas Fairbanks himself would be selling Liberty Bonds at a gigantic rally on Wall Street. You didn't need a ticket or an invitation. Anyone and everyone could just show up. There would be soldiers and sailors. Wall Street brokers. Uptown lawyers. Shipping moguls. Doctors. Men with clean nails who didn't reek of onions.

This was her chance to improve her life. Everyone said the war was going to change things for women. Rachel couldn't wait. She was fifteen years old. She couldn't wait for some millionaire to find her after the war was over. She needed to find a rich husband now, before she got too old to live in the orphanage and would have to spend every cent she earned on survival.

She could see herself now, all dressed up in her fancy new ensemble, sashaying through the crowds. How would anybody guess that she was a nobody, an orphan of unknown parentage and, worse yet, a sewing-machine girl at a Crystie Street sweatshop? To give herself courage, she repeated Hattie Manheim's motto again and again. *Anything was possible in America. Any young woman could rise above her station. If you wanted to be treated like a lady, you had to behave like a lady.*

Miss Manheim was one of several maiden ladies who journeyed downtown from their Fifth Avenue mansions to hold classes in personal improvement at the Henry Street Settlement House. She believed passionately in her God-given responsibility to improve the lives of underprivileged girls. While her friends might be condescending and resent the time taken away from their dressmakers and their gossipy social calls, Hattie was devoted to her charges, especially the few like Rachel Forsyth, who learned quickly and were eager to make her proud.

From Miss Manheim, Rachel learned about personal hygiene. The importance of clean hair and clean nails. The absolute necessity of washing behind the ears and the back of the neck and the arms above the wrist. The younger woman also learned that a lady always carried a clean handkerchief and that her shoes were always immaculate and never run down at the heel.

Last but not least were what Miss Manheim called the niceties. A lady always chewed food in small bites with her mouth closed. A lady never mopped up gravy with a slab of bread. Or drank tea or coffee from her saucer. Or speared food with her knife. Or licked her fingers. Or kept her elbows on the table. Or talked with her mouth full.

It was essential to know these things because you never knew when you might be invited to someone's home.

The rhythmic hum of her feet on the treadle lulled her and transported her back to the Manheim mansion on Fifth Avenue the day Hattie had invited her and the other girls to test their table manners at a luncheon. Soup. Fish. Main course. Salad. Cheese. Dessert. The dining room table itself nearly overwhelmed her with its magnificent damask cloth; its array of china, crystal and silver at each place; and the massive flower arrangement at its center.

You're as good as Hattie Manheim, Rachel reassured herself. *Some day you'll have a dining room just like this, maybe better than this.* Because she had memorized all the rules and practiced the rituals in Becky's kitchen, she soon felt perfectly at ease to the extent of enjoying herself. The serviette shaken open and draped across the lap. The right way to spoon the soup away from your body rather than toward it, being careful not to slurp. Knowing the difference between the butter knife and the fish knife. The small mouthfuls. The silent chewing. The dabbing the corners of the mouth with the serviette.

Most intimidating of all, when the uniformed servant held the platter of vegetables beside her with his white-glove hands, she picked up the serving utensils without hesitation and served herself without dropping a thing, including the green peas in butter sauce.

"Perfect, Rachel!" her hostess trilled while her other guests looked glum. "I think Rachel is really a princess in disguise!"

The same thought had frequently occurred to Rachel. A royal princess born out of wedlock to the queen of a foreign land who was passing through New York on her way to marry a king she did not love. Since there was no record of who her parents were, Rachel liked the idea that anything was possible. When, after lunch, Hattie asked if her guests would like to powder their noses, the other girls demurred, obviously from fear at the thought of using a fancy toilet.

Not Rachel. "Yes, thank you."

A gratified Hattie led the way to her own private suite consisting of her bedroom, dressing room, and separate bathroom. "I'll leave you, shall I? Don't be too long."

The overall impact was whiteness and flowers. The white carpet was so thick and plush Rachel kicked off her shoes. The double bedstead was white cane embellished with carved ivy; the matching cane chairs and chaise lounge were covered with rosebud fabric. There were frilly shades on the bedside lamps that looked like ballerina skirts. A pale rosebud pattern covered the walls. Above the door leading to the bathroom was a painting of two naked cupids cavorting in a garden.

Rachel entered and locked the door. She had been prepared for the dining room but not for the bathroom. She examined the toilet, glistening white inside and out. It took some time before she summoned the courage to use it. It embarrassed her that she could see herself in the mirror while she was so engaged and she averted her eyes and quickly finished.

Washing her hands as Hattie had instructed, she

stood rapt before the array of soaps and lotions and tiny
linen towels embroidered with more roses that beckoned from the marble ledge above the sink. Timid
about using a towel, she wiped her hands dry on her
drawers. Last but not least she gazed longingly at the
sparkling white bathtub and the faucets shaped like
swans that could fill it with hot steamy water with the
flick of a wrist. There were glass jars of bath salts,
sponges the size of her head, thick towels in stacks,
and in a corner of the room a clothes tree holding a
terrycloth robe with matching fluffy slippers on the
floor below.

What would it be like, she wondered, to sink into
hot fragrant water with a huge sponge and perfumed
soap? Rachel had never in all her fifteen years had a
real bath in a real bathtub. She had often gone with the
children to the Forsyth Street Baths for showers and a
swim in the chlorinated pool. Her only experience of
tubs was the old tin one that Becky used for the
smaller children and that Rachel had long since
outgrown.

She was considering what the consequences might
be if she took a bath in Hattie's tub—after all, they
couldn't ask her to give it back, could they?—when a
tap on the bathroom door brought her to her senses.

"Are you all right, dear?"

"Yes, Miss Manheim. Be right out."

There was one last thing she had to do. She had
never seen herself totally naked. Stripping off her
clothes, she stepped into the embrace of the three-way
mirror. Just as she had supposed, her body was creamy
smooth and as beautifully formed as the classical stat-
ues Hattie and her friends had taken the girls to see at
the museum.

Over the last year she had realized men were after
her. Men like Mo Schweitzer with their filthy nails and

smelly breath. Rude young men who stood outside the Cafe Kovno with schooners of beer, whistling and making remarks as she passed. Evil men who ran the notorious brothels on Allen Street and tried to tempt girls like herself into the "good life."

Dressing quickly, she decided to blame her tardiness on her hairpins. She had taken them out and couldn't get them back in. Another look around Hattie's bedroom and Rachel vowed to protect her virtue until she met and married a rich man and lived happily ever after.

"You're different from the other girls, Rachel," her mentor said quietly before they joined the others. "I expect great things from you. Don't let me down."

Rachel savored every detail of her afternoon at Hattie's as she continued working through the night. By dawn, the walking suit was finished, the last basting stitches pulled, the French seams pressed flat with the goose iron, the lustrous gaberdine shaken and brushed free of threads and lint.

She had made her own pattern from a photograph in a copy of *Good Housekeeping* that Hattie had brought to the settlement house. If she had to say so herself, the finished garment looked as fine as anything from Bergdorf and Goodman that Hattie and the other uptown ladies wore. Not only that, Rachel was younger and had a better shape than Hattie or any of her snooty friends.

Exhausted but happy, she hung the suit behind the door of her tiny room and slept soundly until Becky woke her at dawn. It was time to dress the children and give them their oatmeal for breakfast before sending them to school. After they'd gone, Rachel helped Becky peel the potatoes for the children's supper.

Becky was no dummy. She knew something wasn't

kosher. She had raised Rachel since the day she was abandoned on the doorstep. While she should have sent Rachel to another institution at age twelve or arranged for her to go into domestic service as a maid, Becky could not bear to part with her "little girl." She had kept Rachel with her as an unpaid assistant, giving her room and board in exchange for helping with the younger children. She hated Rachel's having to work at Mo Schweitzer's. Money or no money, he was a lecherous no-goodnik, he should only choke and drop dead! Her hope for Rachel's future lay with Hattie Manheim. The woman was impressed with Rachel's sewing skills and good manners. All Miss Manheim had to do was get Rachel a job at Bergdorf and Goodman doing alterations in a nice airy room where she'd be treated with respect.

"You're not going to Schweitzer's today?" Becky asked when Rachel didn't rush to get herself ready for work.

"Oh, Becky! I'm in terrible trouble! You've got to help me!" She threw herself into the older woman's arms and collapsed in sobs.

"Trouble?" To Becky, the word trouble meant pregnancy. "You're in *trouble?*"

Rachel instantly understood. "Not that kind of trouble. I'd never get into that kind of trouble." The story poured out with her tears. How Mo Schweitzer's behavior had sent her running for her life. How she had impulsively swiped the length of gaberdine. How she had stayed up most of the night making it into a walking suit.

"I'm wearing it to the bond rally," she sobbed defiantly. "I'm never going back to Schweitzer's. I'd rather jump into the river and drown."

Becky said she understood or at least she thought she understood. If going to the bond rally was important to Rachel then it was important to her, too. If Mo

Schweitzer came looking for Rachel, he wouldn't get anywhere with Becky. She'd think of something to tell him and when Rachel got home they'd figure out a way to hide the walking suit from prying eyes.

Meantime, her darling girl was cheerful again and getting ready for her big adventure. She watched with maternal affection as Rachel rubbed her teeth with salt to remove any traces of garlic and to make them shine. With water heated on the wood stove, she scrubbed her hands and nails and used a soft, clean rag to gently rinse her face.

A touch of vaseline on her eyelashes made them glisten. Pinching her cheeks and biting her lips deepened their naturally rosy color. With a practiced hand, she brushed her waist-length hair until it was like a silken mane and swept it into an auburn cloud atop her head, fastening it with the tortoise-shell hairpins Becky had given her for her fifteenth birthday.

Becky's one and only pair of gloves completed the ensemble. "You look beautiful, my angel. Go!"

Proud and confident, walking tall with her back ramrod straight, Rachel made her way through the crowded streets. Several men tipped their hats admiringly. Some smiled and let their eyes linger on her face and figure. Her spirits soared. Somewhere in the gathering crowd was her destiny. But then everything went wrong. The closer she got to Wall Street the more foolish she felt.

Gaily laughing groups of elegantly dressed men and women were pouring out of cabs and chauffeured cars, linking arms and effectively pushing her aside. In the spirit of the day, with bunting on every window and the band playing *Over There* and pushcarts selling water ices and candied fruit, she had thought her smiling nods would be acknowledged and that a polite conversation would result.

Not so. Unlike the love stories she read, nobody said

"Would you care to join us?" No benevolent older couple asked if she were alone and confessed she resembled their long-dead daughter. And wouldn't she like to meet their bachelor son who would be arriving presently from his downtown law offices? She felt silly and conspicuous. She was sure the walking suit looked as if she had made it herself. Tears threatened her composure. What did she expect? She was invisible. People were not going out of their way to snub her. Except for the leering men, they simply didn't see her at all.

She tried a different approach. "Excuse me. Is this where Douglas Fairbanks is selling Liberty Bonds?" She had chosen a dowdy but respectable-looking woman who seemed to be alone and might welcome a companion.

"Yes," was all the woman said and turned her back.

Her composure shattered, Rachel decided she could not stand it another minute. Here were all these shouting, laughing people, making jokes, waving flags and enjoying the wartime excitement. She felt sick to her stomach. Dizzy. Frantic to get home and cry her eyes out.

Please! She was trapped, hemmed in. The street was packed tight with people. Swimming against the tide, she tried to elbow her way toward Broadway. She needed space where she could breathe and try to collect herself. "Please! I don't feel well," she gasped. Not that it mattered. She was invisible.

Suddenly a roar went up, a raucous cheer from thousands of throats. Douglas Fairbanks had arrived, flashing his famous devil-may-care grin as he leapt onto the platform under the statue of George Washington. She was thinking how much shorter he looked in person when the crowd surged toward him. Pushed and pulled in several directions at once, like the undertow at Coney Island, she felt her foot catch on something she couldn't see. Thrown forward, her knees buckled and she could feel herself falling.

"Please—somebody—" She had heard stories of people being trampled to death in a crowd.

A khaki arm took hers and pulled her upright. The soft voice of a pale young man in uniform said, "He's only an actor, you know. A human being like you and me. No need to faint."

Her equilibrium restored, Rachel's panic changed to haughtiness. "I was not about to faint."

"I'm glad of that." His eyes smiled at her through wire-rimmed spectacles.

"It would take more than Douglas Fairbanks to make me faint."

"I'm glad of that, too."

"I tripped, that's all." She freed her arm.

"And I stopped you from falling as my dear mother taught me to do." He attempted to move away from her, but they were hemmed in by the crowd.

What was *wrong* with her? Why was she acting like a fool? Hattie had explained that a lady does not permit a gentleman to take physical liberties of any kind until they are betrothed. At the time Rachel had sniggered with the other girls but had taken the advice to heart. She was dressed like a lady; she wanted to be treated like a lady. But as Hattie also said, a lady was never rude. A lady always said thank you.

By now she and the young soldier were crushed so close together the question of taking liberties was academic. The two were about the same height. Her face was all but touching his when she smiled and whispered, "Please accept my apology. I've been extremely rude. Thank you for rescuing me."

Clearly delighted, he said, "It could happen again in this mob. Stay close to me."

Not only did she stay close, but when the rally ended

she graciously allowed herself to be persuaded to stroll down Broadway past Trinity Church to the Battery, where they could see troopships in the harbor.

His name was Samuel Harrington. "*Private* Samuel Francis Aloysius Harrington, newly enlisted in the Sixty-ninth Regiment."

"The Fighting Sixty-ninth?" Everyone knew about the famous Irish regiment and their flamboyant chaplain, Father Duffy. She made as if to swoon. "You must be very brave."

"I haven't found out how brave I am yet. See? No medals. Though my mother says I deserve a medal for wearing this uniform in public."

Pressed so close to him in the crowd, she had failed to notice how badly it fit. One shoulder was higher than the other. The sleeves were too long. The collar was uneven and gaped at the neckline. Even the buttons were so poorly positioned there were gaps where the jacket was supposed to close flat.

This sight of him aroused the same tender compassion she felt when new children arrived at the orphanage, the younger children especially, their pitiful clothes obviously hand-me-downs from older children or donated by charity groups. Her fingers itched to put things right. Give her some pins, her cutting shears, and a quiet hour at the old Singer and she would have him looking like an officer.

Prudence curbed Rachel's impulse to take him back to Forsyth Street and do just that. An old woman selling flowers approached them.

"A gardenia, I think." He chose one and held it against Rachel's lapel. "Yes—definitely a gardenia."

She wished Mo Schweitzer could see her now, walking along with a man who treated her like a lady. When she failed to show up for work today he probably thought it was because of what happened yesterday.

For days she had sensed his beady eyes watching her as he stroked his greasy beard and smacked his lips, licking halvah crumbs from the corners of his mouth.

Everyone, especially Mo, knew she was the best and the quickest of the more than thirty sewing-machine girls assembling coats and suits. Because her work brought in the orders and the profits, she didn't think he'd risk bothering her with his attentions. But a few days ago she had felt him looming over her from behind, ostensibly to supervise the neatness of her seams.

"Smaller stitches! More tension in the bobbin!" he growled into the back of her neck. His hot breath sent chills of revulsion down her spine. Thick hands grasped her shoulders. "Very nice. Very nice." He murmured incoherently into her hair as his hands slid down from her shoulders to her breasts, squeezing them like fruit on a pushcart while his pelvis ground into her back.

"Very nice. Very nice," he repeated. The girls on either side of her kept their heads bent over their machines, the treadles squeaking as they fed fabric into the needle's path. She could feel them watching her out of the corners of their eyes and could smell malice. She might have lorded her greater talent and ambition over them. She might have thought herself above them. But now she was getting a taste of what the rest of them endured from Schweitzer and his filthy hands and foul breath.

"Mr. Schweitzer—" She twisted her neck so that her face was nose to nose with his and favored him with an angelic smile. None of his victims ever smiled at him. He froze with uncertainty, his eyes riveted to hers. Fluttering her eyelids, she blithely removed each of his hands from her breasts. From the pocket of her smock she drew her shears and thrust the point into the bare gray flesh of his belly where his shirt was too tight to button. The other girls could not hear what she was saying above the *whrrrrr* of the machines. Still smiling into his face, what she said was, "If you ever touch me again, Mr. Schweitzer, I'll cut out your gizzard and throw it to your guard dogs for breakfast."

Over the following days, he took his revenge. He rejected her work, ripping open the seams and demanding she do them again. He docked her for looking out the window, for making faces at him behind his back, and for the worst crimes of all, wasting thread and breaking needles.

Yesterday when the noon break sent everyone staggering from stiffness into the side alley for a breath of air while they stretched and gossiped and ate their dinner—mostly stale penny cake and heavily sugared cold tea—Schweitzer ordered Rachel to stay behind.

"Come into the office."

She knew full well what had happened to another sewing machine girl. Sophie Lutsky, who blushed if you said boo, wound up with a black eye and a split lip. Her one and only shirtwaist that she washed and ironed once a week was torn to shreds. Worst of all, her father beat her for provoking the boss and losing her job.

Once again, Rachel slipped her shears into her pocket. "What is it, Mr. Schweitzer?"

His office smelled as bad as he did. He sprawled in his chair, his belly sagging like a sack of meal on his thighs. He regarded her with the cunning look of the bully who has trapped a helpless victim. He rubbed himself between his legs. "It's . . . my pants."

Rachel stared at him in disbelief.

He indicated his flies. "They're too tight. See?"

Did he think she was blind?

"You're good with the needle."

She was also good with the shears.

"I want you should open the buttons and measure how much they should be moved. Understand?"

She understood only too well. From what Sophie Lutsky told her cousin Minna, who told everyone else, Sophie's black eye was the result of Schweitzer trying to force her face into his lap. The same thing was not going to happen to Rachel, even if it meant stabbing him to death. Instead of showing fear or anger, she turned on the charm. Virgin she might be but she had seen enough vamps like Pola Negri to know how to flirt.

"I'll take care of it, Mr. Schweitzer. You know how much I appreciate working here. Just close your eyes and relax." His protruding belly made a tempting target. Taking up her shears she savored the thought of puncturing it while a better idea took shape in her mind. She snipped off his buttons one at a time.

"Ahhh," he sighed, his lower torso released from its prison. Opening his eyes, he reached out for her, his voice a pathetic whimper. "Come to me, *Rachele*. My *schoene maidele*. You won't be sorry."

He could say that again. Sorry she would not be. "Go to hell!" she shrieked.

Stunned for a moment, he rose to his feet with a bellow of rage. "Whore!" He lunged for her. His open pants slipped down around his knees. He tried to clutch them closed but it was too late. His legs were trapped as his fallen pants bound his ankles together and pitched him forward.

As he crawled toward her, screaming vengeance, she backed out of the office and pulled the door shut behind her. She locked him in by propping a wooden chair under the doorknob. His fists threatened to shatter the door. With a calm that would serve her well in emergencies for the rest of her life, she took her shawl from its hook on the wall and was about to leave through the alley where the other girls were waiting to hear what happened when she got a better idea.

The cutting room was deserted. Stacked high on the long work tables were lengths of beautiful gaberdine waiting to be laid out and cut to patterns. Without hesitating or losing stride, she scooped up a length of fabric, wrapped it in her shawl, and cradled it to her breast like a baby before slipping into the street through the front door. The alley was around the corner. Nobody saw her leave. Such was her fervor that when she hurried through the streets with the harried air of a mother rushing her infant to the clinic, passersby stepped aside with nods of encouragement and compassion.

"Would you care for some refreshment?" Samuel Harrington asked deferentially—an intoxicating new experience, being asked.

Over lemon ices and assorted cakes, he told her all about himself. He was the only boy in a family of nine children and had grown up in the family home just off Washington Square. His parents and sisters were living in their country place while the townhouse was being refurbished. His great-grandfather had emigrated from Ireland during the potato famine. "A barefoot lad with nary a farthing to his name," the young soldier said, laughingly mimicking the Irish accent of family myth. "Francis Xavier, his name was. He found work as a hod carrier in Brooklyn and by the time he died fifty years later of the consumption, he owned the foundry and—" Samuel stopped short in embarrassment. "I haven't talked this much in my entire life! In fact, my sisters call me Silent Sam!" With a clumsy move, he covered her hand with his. "What a dear, sweet girl you are."

He leaned forward and seemed about to kiss her. She was wondering what a real lady would do when he pulled back as if shocked by his own impertinence. The trouble was, she wanted him to kiss her, wanted to feel his lips on hers and his arms around her. For the first time in her life she felt overcome by sexual desire. Becky had warned her about such feelings since the first time she got her monthlies. According to Becky, a girl like Rachel must never ever give in to passion until after she was married, and even then must act innocent and frightened lest her husband think she was damaged goods.

Not fair, she raged silently, feeling the burning rush of desire in her cheeks. She closed her eyes and raised her face to his, her lips slightly parted. When he did not kiss her, she opened her eyes to find him staring at her with agitation.

"Please forgive me, Miss Forsyth. I beg your pardon if I gave you any cause to be alarmed by my behavior. Please say you're not offended."

"I'm not offended."

"That's a relief. Because you see, I was hoping you might allow me to escort you home, but perhaps you'd rather not. Perhaps your mother wouldn't approve your talking to strange men."

He wasn't a stranger. She felt closer to him than any man she had ever met. "My parents are dead. My father was hit by a trolley car before I was born. My mother couldn't live without him. He was her greatest love. She waited until I was born and—" Tears welled in her eyes. This could have been the truth.

"And—?"

"And she jumped off the top of the Flatiron building."

"You poor thing. And then what happened?"

She was beginning to enjoy herself. "I—I was taken to live with my Aunt Becky. She never married, you see. She has devoted her life to taking care of orphans.

She runs the foundling home on Forsyth Street and that's where I've grown up."

As tears streamed down her cheeks, he gently wiped them away with a smooth linen handkerchief. No one but Becky had ever wiped away her tears. With his face so serious and caring and close to hers, she felt light-headed with longing for his kiss. If he wouldn't do it, she would and the hell with manners. The people and surroundings faded away. It was in fact a chaste kiss, lips closed and pressed gently together, yet it sent both of them reeling.

"Forgive me, I'm sorry. I didn't mean to—" His face was flushed.

"No, no. It was my fault!" A strange new feeling suffused her. She had this man in her power. While her desire for him was strong, his desire for her was stronger. Wanting him was beside the point. She must call the tune and make him dance. "After all, I kissed you!"

Walking arm in arm was now the most natural thing in the world. "Look at us, Rachel." They halted before their reflection in a shop window. "Who is that handsome couple?" he said playfully.

It turned out to be a photographer's shop.

"I've never had my picture taken," Rachel said.

"Then today you shall."

The photographer had set up various little stage sets to accommodate his customers' requirements, whatever the occasion—family reunion, christening, betrothal. Now, with the war on, there was a painted sky framed by two American flags.

"Ah, newlyweds!" the photographer enthused.

The embarrassed protests that greeted his assumption only served to encourage him. "Not another word. Just stand the way I tell you. The camera is always in position. A few adjustments to the lights and it won't hurt a bit."

"Shall we?" Samuel grinned. "You do look very lovely in your ensemble."

"And you look very handsome in your uniform."

It seemed only natural in the circumstance to hold hands while they waited for the photograph to be developed and printed.

"It's easy to see you two belong together," the photographer said when the print had dried.

Enjoying the conceit, Rachel and Samuel exchanged loving glances and set off once again down the avenue. "It's a wonderful picture, isn't it?" Rachel said. They did look as if they belonged together. Her mind was working feverishly. Strange things happened in wartime. Couples met one day and married the next. What if he were thinking the same thing? He seemed as shy and lonely as she was. If by some miracle he proposed, she would accept. She had everything to gain and nothing to lose.

Soon they found themselves in Washington Square. "So beautiful," she murmured wistfully. She had never seen such elegant houses. The trees and fountains and the imposing arch took her breath away. "How wonderful to live here."

"Our house is just around the corner. Would you like to see it?"

"Won't your family mind?"

"No. Like I told you, the family's away because there are workmen all over the place."

Workmen? "Won't we be in the way?"

"They leave at three."

So that was it! All the sweet talk and the lemon ices and the gardenias and the gentle kisses were just his way of luring her to his lair—a Mo Schweitzer with manners!

"It's getting late. Perhaps another time." Suddenly she felt cold and tired. Her shoes pinched. Her beau-

tiful suit felt tight and shabby. Her scalp itched so vi-
olently it was all she could do to stop herself from ripping out her hairpins and clawing her head.

To her surprise, he didn't insist. "It is getting late,"
he agreed, smiling sadly. "I didn't want the afternoon to
end."

He insisted on taking her home in a cab. The
Forsyth Street address didn't seem to faze him, though
it did surprise the driver. "You're sure that's where you
want to go, sir?"

"That's what the lady said."

If the dream was doomed to be over so quickly, so be
it. She had told him she lived with her aunt and that
her aunt ran an orphanage. If he wanted to see her
again, it was up to him.

The cab was slowing down when Rachel spotted the
unmistakable figure of Mo Schweitzer at the orphanage
door.

"Don't stop!" She slid to the floor, beseeching Samuel to tell the driver to keep going.

"What is it?"

"That—man!"

All sophistication gone, Rachel cringed in fear at
Samuel's feet, her face against his knee, trembling uncontrollably. It was all over. Any hope she had of winning this fine young man had turned to ashes.

"What's wrong?"

"I—I'm frightened. He's been—bothering me."

Samuel raised her up and cradled her on his knee,
making soft crooning sounds as he caressed her hair.
"Washington Square, driver."

"Samuel!" she whispered. There was no point plotting the future. The future was now and would soon be
the past. Once, when she and Becky took the children
on the Coney Island carousel, Becky had said, "Reach
for the gold ring. Don't give up until you get it."

The house was dark and very quiet. Once inside, there seemed to be no question about what they were going to do. "Rachel. My dearest girl." He carried her up the stairs to the room he had occupied since birth. "Are you sure?"

"Are *you* sure?"

"Oh, Rachel—I want to tell you everything—give you everything—be everything you want me to be!" His face sobered. "But—"

The earlier fear returned. This was where he brought all his women when his family—maybe even his wife—was away. "But what?"

He was inexperienced, too. This was his first time. Like so many young men educated at the seminary, he had vowed to remain chaste until he married. "You're my first and only love."

"And you are mine."

"Are you afraid, Rachel?"

"Yes."

"I'm afraid, too."

She was astonished and touched. "You? A man? What could you be afraid of?"

He took her hands in his and kissed her fingers with gentle reverence. "I'm afraid of the war. I'm afraid of going to France. And now that I've found you I'm afraid of dying before I've had the chance to live."

Slowly in the half-light of dusk they undressed each other. Samuel took out Rachel's hairpins and danced his fingers through her hair. Unwilling to lower their eyes in order to see each other's nakedness, they clung together until Rachel broke free and retrieved the gardenia from her suit lapel. She pulled back the bed-clothes and scattered the gardenia petals on the pillow.

Her first gardenia. Her first love. She knew she would never be so happy again.

* * *

"You okay, Gransy?"

Rachel realized with a start that Bliss was staring at her with wide serious eyes and a concerned expression. "Of course I'm okay."

"You looked kinda funny. Like, you're not sick or anything?"

Of course she wasn't sick. She'd never been sick a day in her life. She might be eighty-nine years old but she was not getting sick. How dare anyone think for one damned minute that she was sick? Nobody was going to make an old woman out of her and that included Hannah, always trying to get her to slow down. Slow down? The day she slowed down they could bury her!

Bliss's sweet face stopped her ruminations. Furious as she might be at the very idea of illness, she was not going to take it out on Bliss. "Forgive me, baby. I got carried away thinking about the past. You look so beautiful, it took me back—what? Nearly seventy-five years. Can you imagine, I made this suit seventy-five years ago when I was just your age."

Reassured, Bliss twirled around the mirrored room, admiring her reflection from all angles. "It's in such perfect condition. Like you hardly wore it."

It was true. She had worn it but three times. The day she met Samuel at the Liberty Bond rally. The day she stood in the rain at the Brooklyn pier hoping to catch sight of him as the troopship pulled out. The day of the funeral that nearly led to her own death.

Rachel had packed the suit away in tissues, along with her bittersweet memories. Becky was long dead. She had never shown the suit to anyone until today. "It'll be yours when I croak," she said to Bliss.

"Mom says you're going to outlive us all."

Rachel liked that. "She's probably right!"

"Can I wear it tonight?"

Rachel was doubtful. "The girls may be jealous. I've

never shown it to Hannah and she's my daughter. I don't think Jessie or Eleanor would care one way or the other, but Hannah? I think your grandma's feelings would be hurt." Hannah's feelings were always being hurt. There wasn't much she could do about it.

"How were things at Hannah's this morning?" Rachel asked.

"Oh, the usual."

"What usual?"

"Oh, you know—Mom and Aunt Jessie hugging each other and dancing around like nuts." The girl looked rueful. "I guess maybe you're right. Grandma did look kinda sad—like she was left out, like she wanted Mom and Aunt Jessie to pay attention to her. Like, she tried talking to them but like they didn't see her."

"Was Jerry there?"

"He had an appointment. He's cool."

"So tell me, what were they doing when you left?"

"Mom and Aunt Jess were going to have lunch and go shopping and—" Tears filled her eyes as she sniffled and turned away—"Oh, Gransy—"

"What is it? What's wrong?"

"Well, like you were saying . . ."

If anyone had done anything to Bliss she would kill them with her bare hands. "For God's sake, tell me!"

"Grandma's feelings *were* hurt. I could tell. She really wanted to go with them but they didn't want her. They wanted to be by themselves, just the two sisters, they said. Then Jessie said, 'You understand, Mom, don't you?' And Grandma said sure she understood, but she didn't. I could tell. And then . . ."

There was more? Poor Hannah.

"Clifford called from England. He'll be arriving over the weekend. So then Grandma tried to be real cool and said did that mean there was finally going to be a wedding and then she started making plans. She knew

a judge who could perform the ceremony. Or maybe
City Hall would be better, with a big reception at the
National Arts Club. And then Jessie said to cool it.
She wasn't in any hurry and she wasn't really sure she
wanted to marry Clifford anyway and to please butt
out. It was awful."

"So then what happened?"

"Grandma suddenly remembered she had to make a
phone call."

Rachel felt a mixture of affection, pity, and exasperation for her daughter. She loved Hannah, of course.
She wanted her to be happy. Why couldn't she count
her blessings: a nice husband like Jerry after that first
disaster. A lovely home, even if Rachel couldn't stand
the decor. Two daughters, one a successful photographer, the other happily married with two terrific children.

So what if Jessie and Eleanor didn't want her along?
It wouldn't bother Rachel if they didn't want her! If you
let yourself be hurt you could always find something to
complain about. Take her own life, for example. A ter-
minally ill husband who would never recover and who
no longer even recognized her on her weekly visits. A
real-estate empire she was running by herself while the
jackals howled and tried to take over control. Her ninetieth birthday less than a year away while she still had
a whole lot of living to do. And always in her heart of
memory was the death of her favorite child. Not a day
passed that she didn't think of Samuel.

"You know Hannah misses him, too!" One of the last
rational remarks Marcus made before his descent into
oblivion was about Sam's death. "You should remember,
Rachel. Sam was your son, but he was also Hannah's
brother. She loved him dearly. Anyone could have seen
that. She's still mourning him."

"Well, so am I!"

"Yes, but you won't let her mourn with you. You've shut her out. She's totally alone with her grief."

Sam's death was a subject she couldn't now nor ever would share with her daughter. What she could do was be especially sweet to Hannah tonight at dinner and make her feel special. On second thought, she would give Jessie and Eleanor a piece of her mind. It was selfish of them to have lunch without inviting their mother to join them.

CHAPTER 3

December 1991

Eleanor and Jessie

Sisters. Relationships between female siblings can often mean gut hatred and raging competition. Not so for Eleanor and Jessie. Anyone seeing their shenanigans as they emerged from Hannah's apartment house would assume they had not seen each other in years instead of the few weeks since Thanksgiving. Eleanor was nearly forty, Jessie two years younger. Yet they cavorted like ten-year-olds, tripping each other from behind, elbowing each other this way and that, feigning anger with giggled threats and shrieks, finally linking arms in their shared delight at being together on this crisp and sunny winter day.

While Hannah watched in silent reproach from the sheltered doorway of her apartment building, the doorman hailed a cab. A final playful scramble over which sister got in first and the cab pulled away like a bucking yellow bronco.

"Free at last! Free at last!" Jessie hurled herself against her sister in a mock embrace. "Great God a'mighty, we're free at last!"

"Jessie! Don't. She'll hear you!" Eleanor turned guiltily to look out the back window before sinking down in the swaying seat with a groan of relief. Hannah could be seen talking to the doorman. Over the noisy traffic, she could not possibly have heard.

Their mother had tried to be a good sport but she

hadn't exactly made it easy for them to go off by themselves, just the two of them for lunch and an afternoon of Christmas shopping. As they explained to Hannah, they were just going to have a quick sandwich and then hit the stores, then go their separate ways before meeting up in time to go home together. As they were about to leave they were surprised to find Hannah dressed for the street and ready to go down in the elevator with them.

"Don't worry. I'm not horning in. I have my own Christmas shopping to do."

Good old Mom. Hiding their exasperation, the sisters pretended not to notice her hurt feelings. With Bliss spending the entire day at Rachel's, it was clear that Hannah had expected to go shopping with the two of them. After Bliss left, Hannah had gaily announced, "Lunch is on me, girls! Sky's the limit. You name the place."

How could they tell their mother they wanted to spend the day together? Without her. Eleanor had sputtered helplessly, her mind in a panic as she groped unsuccessfully for a way out. Jessie was more equal to the task of saving Hannah's feelings. "But, Mom. We're shopping for your present. It's got to be a surprise. It can't be a surprise if you're looking over our shoulder. I'm sure you understand. Don't you?"

Hannah said of course she understood, adding a few words about how grateful she was that her daughters were such good friends, not like other families where the children hated each other. If they didn't want her tagging along so be it, no problem. That being said, the three lapsed into an uneasy silence as the elevator took what seemed forever to reach the lobby.

"Can we drop you, Mom?"

"No, thanks! The subway's quicker." She dismissed

them grandly, pulling on her silk-lined gloves and push-ing up the collar of her coat. "And cheaper, too."

"The subway?" Eleanor's guilt persisted as their cab headed downtown. "My God, Jessie. What if she gets mugged?"

"Who would dare?"

Once more the sisters gave in to childish glee. The enemy eluded, they were once again six- and four-years-old, huddled together for mutual reassurance.

"Where to, girls?" The "girls" exchanged glances. Were they going to let him get away with it? He was a sweet old man with white hair, thick glasses, and a street-smart way of driving that bespoke decades of pushing a hack. He meant no disrespect. Given a chance, he would doubtless tell them he had two beau-tiful girls just like them and show them their pictures.

"Downtown. Head for Fifty-seventh Street while we decide."

Where to have lunch was the eternal question. New Yorkers habitually assured one another there was no-where to eat. Despite thousands of places of every known culinary persuasion, when a choice had to be made a morbid amnesia set in.

"Pastrami?" Eleanor suggested.

Cholesterol city.

"Chinese?"

MSG.

Italian? French? Indian? Tex-Mex?

Rachel was expecting them for an early dinner.

"I know! The Pasta Beanery." Jessie had read about it in the *Times*, a new place across the street from Bergdorf's. "Bean salads, pasta, capuccino. Very *Italiano*. The reviewer said the waiters have the best buns this side of the Spanish Steps!"

At Columbus Circle, the traffic was so bad they de-cided to get out and walk across Fifty-seventh Street. A camera crew was doing a fashion shoot around the Christopher Columbus statue. A cluster of models in flimsy summer clothes ignored the December chill, patiently obeying the photographer's commands.

"Let's watch for a minute," Eleanor said.

Jessie wondered if the scene reminded her sister of the career she could have had. Eileen Ford had predicted big things for her. "Any regrets, El?"

Eleanor was bewildered. "Regrets?"

"About being a model?"

"Are you out of your mind?"

A bicycle messenger snaked between them at high speed. Both sisters jumped back. Instead of being angry, Eleanor executed a tiny tap dance of exhilaration. "I love it! I love the crowds. And the traffic. And New York. I love New York!"

Forging through the crowded sidewalks to Fifty-seventh Street, they shimmied past the throngs of youngsters lined up outside the Hard Rock Cafe. Bliss would love that, they agreed. Maybe tomorrow. The Art Students League. The neon McDonald's. Carnegie Hall and the Russian Tea Room across the way.

"Jessie! Look!" In the window of Rizzoli's bookstore rose a pyramid display of Jessie's book, *The World of Bliss*, augmented with selected blowups of her photographs. "Let's go in!"

"No way." Despite herself, Jessie felt unaccountably shy. The window display was a surprise. She knew she should make herself known to the Rizzoli manager. She knew she would be welcomed and probably asked to sign books that they would sticker "Author Autographed." Her reluctance bewildered her. On the one hand, she had every right to be proud of her accomplishment. On the other, she felt somehow fraudulent, a flash in the pan, the perpetrator of a hoax based on a fluke. Being hailed as an artist mortified her. She was a working-stiff journalist, that was all.

"But, Jessie—it's your *book*!" A stranger stopped to see what the fuss was about. Eleanor grabbed his arm. "That's my sister's book! *The World of Bliss?* Bliss is my daughter—"

Jessie quick-marched her sister away. "Cool it. I'm starved."

Eleanor would not be rushed. She stopped dead in her tracks like a recalcitrant mule. "Hey, what is this?"

Jessie bit her lip. Since she could not understand her feelings herself how could she explain them to her sister? "Come on, we won't get a table."

They resumed their walk. Eleanor had always regarded Jessie as fearless, outgoing, flamboyant at times. Nothing ever bothered Jessie. Her sister's sudden shyness reminded her of Bliss and how bashful she too became when the book came out and the phone began to ring. She was worried about Bliss. It was one of the things she wanted to discuss with Jessie. She couldn't put her finger on it but she could tell something was bothering her.

"What'll we have?" Jessie held up the menu. The Pasta Beanery was crowded with that species of New York woman Jessie called The Martian Invaders, elongated creatures covered with just enough flesh stretched taut as canvas over narrow skeletal frames. They had no internal organs. There was no room. They had no hips or breasts or behinds. Because they had no pores they did not perspire.

The layered look that suffocated mere humanoids was designed by Martian Invaders as a means of recognizing each other in the alien land. In summer, Martian Invaders wore layers of cashmere, wool, silk, and leather with no sign of sweltering. If you watched them carefully you could see they did not actually eat. They ordered food. They moved it around their plates and raised it to their lips but never took any of it into their mouths.

They made Jessie feel fat and obscene as she thought longingly of old-time club sandwiches dripping mayonnaise, roast beef on rye with cole slaw and Russian dressing and a side of French fries with plenty of ketchup, and a hot fudge sundae with nuts and cherries to follow.

"I'm having the four-bean salad with tofu dressing, El. What'll you have?"

Four-bean salad? Tofu dressing? Eleanor was glad she'd had a bacon-and-egg breakfast before leaving Riverton. At tables on either side of them the Martian Invaders strained to hear her decision.

"I'll have the same." She wasn't there to eat; she was there to be with her sister. She was there to catch up on family news and to figure out what to buy whom for Christmas. Rachel as usual was Topic A. Her photograph in the *Times* was going to make her more difficult than ever. Months ago Rachel had read an article about Marlene Dietrich and how a certain makeup man had been able to take twenty years off the famed actress's face with an invisible gauze netting that compressed the flesh and firmed the chinline. It fastened behind the ears and at the back of the neck under the hair.

"She's been nagging me to find him," Jessie complained. " 'How am I supposed to find him? Am I a magician?' 'You're a famous photographer, aren't you? Photographers know how to find things out!' 'But, Grandma,' I said. She bit my head off. 'Don't call me Grandma . . .' 'Okay,' I said. 'But Marlene's famous appearance in Las Vegas was in the early sixties. Thirty-five years ago. Everybody's dead by now.' And you know what she said? 'I'm not dead!'

"And then the penny dropped, El. I figured out what she really wanted. She wanted me to tell her she didn't need gauze. She didn't need netting. She didn't need a facelift. That she was eighty-nine going on thirty-five and as we all know—"

Eleanor picked up her cue. "She nev-ver had a face lift!"

"Of course not. Everyone knows that. The time she went to Dr. Coslove's private clinic was for a—"

"—de-vi-ated sep-tum! Everyone knows that!"

They had a good laugh over their grandmother's eccentricity, but the question remained. What to get Rachel for Christmas?

Inspiration struck. "I've got it, El. By George, I've got it. A scrapbook!"

Scrapbooks were for children and new mothers.

"A very large, expensive leather scrapbook for her press clippings. Just like a movie star. Starting with the picture of her with Brooke Astor!"

One down. Next?

There was Marcus, of course. The tendency was to forget about him wasting away in that Connecticut nursing home waiting to die. Rachel rarely mentioned him, although they knew she called daily and went regularly to see him. How long had they been married? Over forty years. Right after the war, it was, right after young Samuel's death. As Hannah once explained, Rachel was inconsolable and Marcus was her strong shoulder to cry on.

Hannah never mentioned their real grandfather, Will Lawrence, who had died so tragically when she and Samuel were children. Once when they insisted on knowing what had happened, she said it was an accident, that he had fallen in front of a subway train at the Seventy-second Street IRT station.

"A gift basket of fruit and candy like last year," Jessie

decided. Marcus wouldn't know who sent it, of course. The gift was more for the benefit of the nursing staff and for Rachel's sake on her next visit. Beautifully wrapped with a beautiful card beautifully signed with love from his grandchildren, Eleanor and Jessie.

Next?

"Luke and Jason. It's such a shame they couldn't come down," Jessie said sarcastically.

Tears filled Eleanor's eyes. "Oh, Jess. I need your advice."

Was Luke still being a pain in the ass about the book? He'd raised the roof when he'd heard Jessie's pictures of Bliss were going to be published. When a CNN camera crew showed up in Riverton unannounced to capture the "real" world of Bliss, he had refused to let them in, and kept Bliss in her room until they gave up and went away. "Pornography" was what he called the shots of Bliss washing her hair over the bathroom sink, clad only in her underwear, and of Bliss washing the dog in the backyard, her wet T-shirt clinging to her burgeoning young breasts.

Time and the laudatory reviews had calmed him down. When Jessie assigned half her royalties to Bliss and Jason, he had thanked her in his stiff way. Eleanor later told her Luke was sorry and hoped Jessie understood he was only trying to protect his daughter.

"Is it Luke?"

"No. It's Jason."

Jason in trouble? It was hard to believe. If anyone had his head screwed on, it was Jason. But you never could tell. He was in his freshman year at college, away from home for the first time. Had he turned gay? Cheated on exams? Raided a sorority house? Drugs? Please God, not drugs.

"He's decided to use his middle name."

Jessie wanted to laugh but for the stricken look on her sister's face.

"*Samuel!* Don't you remember?" Eleanor cried. "Rachel will blow her top."

Jessie had forgotten what happened when Eleanor and Luke named their firstborn Samuel. Hannah had often told her daughters about her older brother who'd died in the war before they were born, how handsome and witty and kind he was and how much she still missed him. Hannah was touched when Luke and Eleanor told her of their decision and crushed when Rachel put a kibash on the whole idea.

"There will only ever be one Samuel in this family. That Samuel is my son and he is dead!"

Luke had resisted at first. The baby was theirs not Rachel's. He and Eleanor would name him what they wished. But in the end they compromised. They named their son Jason Samuel, a Samuel on his birth certificate if not in daily usage. Until now.

"Rachel won't have to know. Jason—I mean Sam—is like his father. He doesn't like coming to the city. The subject will never come up. Bliss won't spill the beans. Stop worrying."

Eleanor still had that funny look on her face.

"Okay. Let's have it," Jessie said. "Is Luke pissed off because you came to New York?"

The story poured out. After all these years, Luke still treated her like a lamebrain. They'd had an argument last night. She thought it was settled and then it started up again this morning. It was about the route she was taking into the city.

"I've driven the same route down here zillions of times, but suddenly it sounded stupid to Luke. He said everyone knew it was better to go over the Rip Van Winkle Bridge and from there to take the New York State Thruway."

"So?" What was the problem?

"So—I'm afraid of driving on the thruway. The traffic is so fast, I'm terrified of getting lost or having an accident."

"So?"

Eleanor was perplexed. Why was Jessie so exasperated?

"So which way did you come, for God's sake!"

"I took my usual route."

"And you got here in one piece, right?"

"But when he asks me, I'll have to tell him the truth."

Jessie's irritation vanished. She squeezed her sister's hand. "You got here, didn't you?"

She nodded.

"Okay. Think of it this way. You don't always have to tell him the truth, especially about something so ridiculous."

"Oh, but Jessie. We always tell each other the truth."

Jessie considered what she was about to say and then said it. "Remember Greece?"

Eleanor gasped and clung to Jessie's hand. "Oh, Jessie. You're right. Thank God you're my sister!"

"Me, too. Now let's get on with the list. We've got a million things to do before dinner."

Jerry's turn. By the time Hannah married Jerry, both sisters were too old to call him Dad, even though he was the best thing that ever happened to their mother. By every criterion, Jerry would have been the ideal husband and father if only Hannah had met him earlier. Ironically, in the days immediately following the end of World War II, he and Hannah had lived parallel lives in New York but never met. Both loved folk music and as it turned out had frequented the same night spots in Greenwich Village.

On Jerry's return from the South Pacific, he discovered that his mother had given away his collection of records: Burl Ives, Pete Seeger, Richard Dyer-Bennett, Susan Reed, Woody Guthrie. He forgave her but never got over it. Jessie fished a clipping out of her bag. "The Library of Congress has reissued the old 78s in a four-volume album. It's got everything. He'll love it."

"Done!" Eleanor checked Jerry's name. "Mom's still happy with him, isn't she?"

Rarely did they mention their real father. So far as they knew, Viktor the Nazi was still in Germany where they had last seen him as teenagers. Hannah had cauterized him from memory and covered what scars remained. She treated Eleanor and Jessie as if they had been born of immaculate conception. Only once did they get an inkling of her ordeal. A few years ago, the three had been watching a TV documentary on the Third Reich when an arrogant soldier in a Nazi newsreel sneered at a battered family of Jews being rammed into a boxcar. All three realized he looked exactly like, and possibly was, Viktor.

While Hannah and Jessie had sat tight-lipped, Eleanor had cried uncontrollably. "I hate him! I hate him."

In comforting her, Hannah was philosophical. "I can despise him for what he was but I still thank him for giving me the two of you, my two precious girls."

Her daughters had never told her the details of their trip to Germany or the reasons for their sudden and secret departure. The TV documentary had triggered the deepest feelings of loathing and disgust in Eleanor. She had been unable to control her sobs until Jessie took her sternly by the shoulders. "Keep in mind one thing. If it hadn't been for Viktor, you'd never have met Luke."

Now, the fact that Eleanor was still glad she had met Luke was evident to Jessie in the tender way she explained her problem in choosing a Christmas gift for him. He had smoked a pipe when they met but had long since given up smoking. "He looked so handsome with his pipe. A meerschaum," she sighed. Clothes were out. He ordered from catalogs and bought overalls from the local feed store.

"How about some red satin pajamas from Victoria's Secret?" Jessie suggested.

Eleanor blushed. "He doesn't . . . well, the fact is . . . he doesn't wear anything to bed," she finished in a rush.

Luke did have a spectacular body, or as much of it as Jessie had been able to see during the three months she'd spent in Riverton. Compact and hard. Strong, too, as she discovered after a heavy rain left a moat-size ditch in front of the house. He had picked her up and carried her across it as if she were a marshmallow. He did not smile when she said, "Thank you, Sir Walter."

Whatever it was, the thought of her husband naked beside her in bed or the energy-jolt of four-bean salad, Eleanor began to feel better. The two men in her life were impossible, she announced proudly. The only thing to do was head for Bloomingdale's and wait for inspiration to strike.

"Come on, Jess, why don't you get *Clifford* the red-satin pajamas!"

Jessie had already chosen his gift, an Armani leather battle jacket at Bergdorf's for Men, which they were holding until he could come in and try it on. Thinking about Clifford and bed, it was Jessie's turn to blush. In their more intimate moments, he often sang to her. Quietly and with a Noel Coward accent. *I'll seize you again whenever spring breaks through again.* As a surprise she had gone to a recording studio and had a young performer from one of the British musicals to sing Noel Coward ditties with new erotic lyrics.

"Are you finally going to do it, Jess?"

"Do what?" Jessie grinned.

"Get married, you drip."

"Who said anything about getting married? But if we do, I want you to be my flower girl."

"And break Bliss's heart?"

Bliss! They'd been so busy gabbing they were behind schedule. There were still Bliss and Hannah. My God, mustn't forget Hannah. Not after saying she couldn't come with them because they were shopping for her gift.

"Remember Tiny Tears?" Eleanor said suddenly. One long-ago Christmas Hannah had bought one Tiny Tears for the two of them. It was the only time they had fought physically. When one of the arms came off, Hannah took the doll away until they learned to behave.

"She cried real tears. She drank from a bottle and wet her panties. Those were the days. Today, she'd menstruate and have vaginitis!"

"Jessie! Please . . ."

The Martians at the next table nearly choked.

Eleanor changed the subject. "You know what Bliss wants, Jess? A camera. She wants you to teach her how to take pictures."

A camera! Of course. Why hadn't she thought of that! "Great idea, El."

Eleanor still looked worried. "Oh, Jess. I feel so helpless at times."

The Martians had paid their bill. "Now we can talk."

Jessie knew it. Eleanor's real worry was Bliss. "She's too trusting and I'm too . . . inadequate," Eleanor began. It seemed that mother and daughter had yet to talk about sex and AIDS and condoms.

Jessie tried to reassure her sister. "Bliss knows all

about sex—and AIDS—and condoms. The kids are different today."

"I just don't know how to protect her from—you know, predators!"

"Well, she certainly knows enough not to get into a car with strangers," Jessie said.

But it wasn't strangers that worried Eleanor. "I think she has a crush on Sam's roommate. Name's Corey. He's twenty-one. Drives a pickup with a mattress in the back, for camping out he says. Plays the guitar."

"Uh-oh. A guitar? Dangerous."

"He wrote a *song* for her!"

"Irresistible! Have you asked her what she thinks of him?"

"She says he has a cute butt."

"Well, does he?"

"How would I know?" Eleanor bristled with indignation.

"You're forty years old. You're not dead."

Eleanor was close to tears. It wasn't so much the sex thing that frightened her; it was the drug thing. After Sam and Corey spent a weekend home from college, Sam's room reeked of marijuana.

"You think Bliss is experimenting?" This was serious.

"I don't *know*." Her anguish was intense. "I keep hearing about parents who think the kids are okay and suddenly they're caught dealing in the schoolyard." She dug into her capacious shoulder bag for the full-page newspaper ad listing the telltale signs of drug abuse parents should look for in their children.

"See? Bloodshot eyes can mean marijuana."

The power of the press. "It can also mean allergy. Remember? Bliss is allergic to dust."

"And a runny nose? See what it says. 'It may indicate cocaine.' "

"It may also indicate a runny rose! She's had a runny

nose since she was two, remember? Snap out of it, Eleanor. Bliss is not turning into a crackhead, okay?" So saying, she took the newspaper article and tore it into confetti strips before plopping in on top of a passing waiter's trayload of dirty dishes.

Eleanor was mollified, if not totally convinced. "Let's change the subject. How's about some dessert?" She'd paid her health dues with the four-bean salad. "Want to split the Mississippi mud pie?"

Jessie had a better idea. Her sister really needed soothing. "Let's have a glass of wine."

The chardonnay worked more quickly than Jessie dared hope. Eleanor's eyes glimmered and her body noticeably relaxed. Jessie grinned. The Cork-Sniffer. That's what the gang called Eleanor in the old days. All her sister had to do was sniff the wine cork and she was fried. One beer and she was out cold. She had only finished half the glass when Jessie took it away and finished it for her. "We've got a long afternoon ahead of us."

Eleanor gazed at her sister with a look of soul-searching introspection. "You know something?"

Jessie had seen this look on the faces of men at bars and on airplanes in that meaningful moment before they confessed their darkest yearnings. This however was not some stranger about to play Humpy Bumpy. This was her sister whose tongue had been loosened by wine as well as worry. "What?"

"You won't laugh?"

"I won't laugh. Promise."

"It's well—kind of a secret."

Once again, Jessie pressed her sister's hand. "We both know how to keep a secret, don't we, El?"

Eleanor focused her eyes on Jessie's, gauging her loyalty. "Of course, we know how to keep a secret. Luke would kill me if I ever told *that* secret. This is different. More like a decision. But forget it, it's not important."

"Of course it's important."

"I'm just a housewife. You're the *artiste*."

Jessie rolled up the sleeve of Eleanor's sweater and clasped her hands side by side over her sister's bare forearm. "Tell me this minute or I'll give you an Indian burn."

The threat reminded Eleanor of their childhood. "Forget it," she laughed. "It's really not important."

Jessie tightened her grip and began to twist her hands in opposite directions on her sister's wrist. "I'm waiting."

"Okay. But it's a really stupid thing."

"Try me."

Eleanor made a valiant attempt to gather her thoughts. "Well, you know, like everybody else I've been reading about Princess Di and Fergie and Ivana and Madonna and Liz Taylor and Demi Moore and all their terrible problems and everything and—"

"And—" Di and Fergie? What did they have to do with Eleanor's life?

"You won't laugh?"

Jessie tightened her hold on her sister's wrist.

"Okay. Okay. I know I sound like a jerk, but . . ." She took a deep breath. "I've decided to stop worrying about famous people!"

That was it? Jessie didn't know whether to laugh or cry. Her sister's sweetness and goodness floored her. In a world of deceit and shameless manipulation, her sister's innocence of heart was mind boggling. It was women like Eleanor who fell hook, line, and sinker for the hard-luck stories of the rich and famous, who worried about their love lives, their children, and the heavy burdens of their celebrity. Thank God Eleanor lived in the boonies. In Manhattan she would be a sitting duck for every scam artist and switch-and-bait game.

"You're absolutely right," Jessie said seriously. "Think of it this way. Do they give a shit about your problems?"

"Well, no. I never thought of that."

"Okay, then. You're off the hook. Let's have another cappuccino and then we're off!"

There was still the present for Hannah. "How about a jeroboam of coffee ice cream?" Eleanor suggested.

Hannah's passion for coffee ice cream triggered memories of childhood treats at Schraffts. "Ham sandwiches on toasted cheese bread with the crusts cut off! Ice cream served in metal dishes to keep it cold!" Jessie cried, then she sobered. Viktor was still on the scene the day the family had lunch at Schraffts and Jessie had used her spoon as a catapult to hit Eleanor with globs of ice cream across the marble table. When Eleanor fought back, Viktor had actually threatened to send them to Auschwitz.

That was one of the few times Hannah had asserted herself. "Remember how she told him to leave the restaurant that second and never, *ever* dare to threaten the children with a concentration camp again," Eleanor said quietly.

There was no use pretending. They had left their mother standing on the sidewalk by herself when she had expected to be with them. No matter how they rationalized it, they had ditched her. No matter how they agreed that Hannah preferred shopping alone, no matter how convincingly they might argue that they had not seen each other in weeks and had so much catching up to do—*and* Hannah's present to buy—the cold fact remained cruelly clear. They had left her alone and sad to spent the day by herself without her daughters or granddaughter to share the holiday joy.

"I've got it," Jessie said. "The thing Mom loves more than coffee ice cream?"

"Gloves!"

That was it—one or maybe even two pairs of the kind she would never buy herself, even though she could well afford it. French kid, lined with silk. Size seven and half. No buttons. No fringe. No cunning little zippers. Just the classic shorties like the ones she was wearing today that Jessie belatedly recognized as a pair she had bought her mother in Paris during a mad weekend with Jimmy Kolas.

Saks Fifth Avenue would probably be the best place to find them. Hannah would forgive them when she opened the box. She would realize they could not have bought them with her around.

Hannah was fine, they assured themselves. She'd said she was fine, hadn't she? She had her own shopping to do, didn't she?

Anyway, they would make it up to her tonight.

CHAPTER 4

December 1991

Hannah

All the way home from Macy's, Hannah fought to control herself. Was she going crazy? Her throat was so constricted she could barely whisper her address to the cab driver. Her hands trembled as she extracted a twenty-dollar bill from her wallet and scrambled out of the car without waiting for change.

Bruno, the doorman, greeted her with his usual affable smile. He did not seem to notice anything wrong. Nor did the mirror in the lobby reflect anything other than the well-dressed middle-aged woman who had left the building with her two daughters some five hours earlier.

Safe at last in the apartment, she double-bolted the door as if to shut out the memory of what had happened at Santaland. Could she have temporarily snapped out? Suffered some kind of hallucination? Thank God she could be alone to think things through. Since she alone was going to Rachel's for dinner, Jerry was out, downtown somewhere making the rounds of Christmas parties with some of his cronies. He would not be home until later.

It wasn't that she didn't love Jerry or trust him. She was happy with their marriage. And yet in a crisis, when push came to shove, she needed to be by herself. Stripping off her clothes calmed her. Running a hot bath scented with patchouli calmed her even more.

The constriction in her chest eased. She could breathe deeply again. As the tension seeped from her body she relived the events of the day that had begun with the naive expectation of taking her daughters to lunch.

Was it so unusual for a mother to want to spend time with her girls? The fact was they didn't want to spend time with her. *You understand, Mom!* Of course she understood. They didn't have to hit her over the head with a baseball bat. The two sisters wanted to be by themselves without boring old Mom spoiling everything.

So much for bonding with your children, she had thought to herself this morning as she stood alone on the sidewalk watching their taxi speed away. *You asked for it,* Jerry would say when she told him about it later tonight. He would be right, as usual. She really didn't need him to point out that, once again, she had set herself up to be rejected, with nobody to blame but herself. When was she going to learn to deal with life as it was, the reality and not the fantasy she wanted it to be?

Somehow she had become invisible to her daughters and to Rachel and even to Bliss. It wasn't that they went out of their way to ignore her. They simply didn't see her. Not one of them noticed the ten-pound weight loss she'd achieved since Thanksgiving and the resultant new wardrobe of St. John knits.

Hey—you look great! They said it to each other constantly. She said it to them at every opportunity. She had waited vainly for them to say it to her. Rachel saw only the gray hair and absence of mascara. After an initial bear hug, Bliss was always swept away by Rachel or her mother and aunt. Hannah had hoped that by insisting the girls stay with her instead of Rachel she would get to spend more quality time with her precious grandchild. But then Rachel jumped in and arranged for Bliss to spend the day with her. And Eleanor and Jessie took off alone at the first opportunity.

She felt helpless and somehow pathetic. Her crying need for their attention stuck in her craw, poisoning her otherwise healthy psyche. How she wished she'd had a sister! How she envied her daughters their closeness, their intimacy. The giggles. The whispers. The secrets they'd always shared since childhood. In times of trouble they were always there for each other. Fifteen years ago, Eleanor had even raced over to Greece despite her advanced stage of pregnancy when Jessie's Greek boyfriend walked out on her. Bliss's premature birth had further strengthened the bond between the sisters while effectively shutting Hannah out.

When Eleanor and Bliss arrived home from Greece, Hannah had gone with Rachel to meet them at the airport, only to be shunted aside by her mother and her daughter. Rachel had sprung on the infant like a pit bull baring her teeth at any attempt of Hannah's to hold her new grandchild. In the stretch limo back to Rachel's penthouse, Hannah had to force them all to make room for her.

In the ensuing fifteen years, Hannah had finally given up the attempt to find out the details of what happened on the remote Greek island. She knew there was something they weren't telling but her daughters had succeeded in making her feel nosy and intrusive. She had put on a good face, accepting crumbs instead of a piece of the pie. Other women had grandchildren they could spoil and take to museums and F.A.O. Schwarz. Rachel had pushed her aside and coopted the grandma job.

This morning Bliss arrived with her face pink with cold, carrying a basket of apples from the family orchard for Hannah and Jerry. A kiss, a hug, a handful of raisins, and she was off. "Gransy's waiting!"

A few days ago while helping deliver hot meals to shut-ins, Hannah had realized she was a shut-out. There wasn't a thing she could do about it, except pretend it didn't matter. After her daughters' taxi turned the corner, she had asked the doorman to flag another one down for her. How childish she was to have said she was taking the subway. Hoping they would worry about her safety? Fat chance of that. They were so busy laughing and talking she doubted if they'd heard a word she said.

"Where to, lady?"

She didn't know. She couldn't think. The reason she'd put on her hat and coat was that she didn't want to be left behind in the apartment while the rest of the world was part of the Christmas festivities.

"Just head downtown."

Jerry had invited her to join him on his rounds. No, she had said. *Wish I could,* she had said. Much as she would have loved to, her girls were in town and she was taking them to lunch. Jerry had kissed her goodbye and said not to be surprised if he was seduced by some sexy secretary. There was no way to reach him. Once again she'd done it to herself.

"Where downtown, lady? East Side? West Side? You think I'm a mind reader? Make up your mind!"

This she could live without. She made up her mind. "Pull over. I'm getting out."

With a spiteful show of temper, she left the taxi door open so he would have to get out and close it. No such luck. A frantic family fell gratefully on the door before it had a chance to close. Her sole hope of revenge had been that they were a gang of robbers disguised as a family and at this moment were holding a gun to the cabbie's head.

At Christmas time, Manhattan was a theme park that made others pale by comparison. Times Square

BLISS   83

looked gloriously fake with hordes of actors dressed
as tourists romping in and out of theaters and fast-
food joints, while colorful hucksters hawked designer
watches and pure silk ties at a fraction of cost. Patrol-
men in groups stood poised for the choreographer's cue
to chase perps and escort groups of uniformed school-
girls across the street.

It had felt good to walk, yet she could not totally
shake the blues. Striding east on Fiftieth Street, she
saw that the lines waiting outside Radio City Music
Hall extended as far as her eyes could see, the same as
when she was a child and Rachel had taken her and
Sam to see the Rockettes. The sense of connection
made her feel good until she saw a woman with a girl
of about seven. As the child stood motionless, the
woman undid her braids and brushed the shiny silken
hair free of snarls before rebraiding it and fastening the
ends with rubber bands and grosgrain ribbon, red on
one braid, green on the other.

Hannah had had braids at that age. *You never did my
braids, did you, Mother?* her interior voice cried. She
stopped dead in her tracks. Was she talking out loud?
What if somebody heard her? A hand touched her
shoulder. A voice behind her said, "You're blocking traffic, lady."

Ghosts of Christmas past. The year she was ten,
Billy Applebaum's mother had taken the two of them to
the Nativity. In the darkness Billy, who was twelve, had
tickled her palm and surreptitiously touched the side of
her breast closest to him where his mother wouldn't
notice. She had known she should have been angry and
pushed his hands away. She hadn't. Neither of them
ever mentioned what happened.

It was strange how the memory stirred a throbbing
response in her breasts. Was that when she began to go
nuts? A motorcycle roared to a halt in the nearby traffic

lane, the driver gunning it with furious impatience to get moving. His leather jacket and gauntlets were fringed and clinking with chains, his powerful thighs threatening to burst the seams of his jeans. Riding pillion was his woman, dressed identically, her slender body tight against his.

Hannah could feel the possession of the woman's thighs clinging to his hips and the arrogance of her contempt for the lesser mortals not lucky enough to be in her place, behind a lover like hers. It reminded her of the time after Eleanor was born when Viktor bought one of the first Harleys and had raced up and down Riverside Drive like Marlon Brando in *The Wild One*. Hannah had haughtily refused his invitation to ride until late one moonlit night when he took her up the West Side Highway as far as the George Washington Bridge and back home through quiet streets. Once home, the intensity of their lovemaking had frightened her, carrying her to a far country from which she feared she might never return. By her reckoning it was the night Jessie was conceived. Hannah often wondered if it explained the difference in temperament between Jessie and her more placid older sister.

Passing the Rockefeller Center skating rink had evoked a memory of another sort, a sweeter and sadder memory of the ice skating outfit her father had bought her a few weeks before his death. Stopping to watch the skaters, she could see it clearly in her mind's eye. The short black velvet gored skirt lined with red satin that bounced as she moved. The white angora sweater and hat embroidered with roses. The white woolen tights and lovely white double-blade skates. She remembered the hard slats of the skaters' bench and how she had extended her legs for him to tie her laces. Tight but not too tight. She recalled the cool marshmallow foam of the hot chocolate and its sweet heat racing clear through her body to her frozen toes.

This unwanted trip down Memory Lane had only made Hannah feel worse. Shopping would make her feel better. Contrary to what she'd told her daughters, she had finished her Christmas shopping early, as usual. She had solved the Rachel problem, she hoped, with an extravagance she thought her mother would enjoy—a dozen pair of real silk hose in shades ranging from palest mauve to shadowy black, imported from France in a quilted case. Rachel's legs were remarkably shapely, and not a mark on them, as if she'd never had children.

Leaving Rockefeller Plaza behind, Saks Fifth Avenue beckoned. A few weeks ago she had seen a silk dressing gown that cost more than the national debt. It wouldn't hurt to see if it had been marked down. She had nothing better to do.

But she didn't get the chance. Once inside the store, the first thing she saw were her daughters. They didn't see her. She retreated to the street, shaken to the core. They would think she'd followed them, that no matter what they did or where they went they wouldn't be able to shake her.

She walked swiftly south on Fifth Avenue, once more feeling abandoned and alone. Everyone was with someone except for her. Family groups and lovers sat with their festive shopping bags on the steps of the Forty-second Street library. The garlanded stone lions reminded her of the time her brother had brought her there to show her how to do research. "There's something I should warn you about," he had said.

"What?" It was going to be one of Sam's jokes, she'd been sure.

"Well, you're twelve years old so it's time you were warned!"

"Warned?" Warned about what?"

"You see the stone lions? The legend is when a female pats one on the nose, it'll roar if she's a virgin!"

Of course when he hoisted her up so she could pat the lion's nose, it didn't roar. "It's a joke!" he had laughed, using a stiff arm to keep her flailing arms and legs from reaching him. What would he be like if he had lived, she wondered. Still sweet and loving and funny and handsome. He would have married Kathleen whether Rachel liked it or not and they would all be together for the holidays. Let Eleanor and Jessie ditch her. Let Bliss spend the day with Rachel. She would have had Sam and Kathleen's children and grandchildren to fuss over.

The sun was bouncing off the top of the Empire State Building as she continued south on Fifth Avenue. Crowds clustered at Lord & Taylor's windows. They displayed mechanized scenes of Old New York with horse-drawn carriages and gas lamps and glamorous people frolicking with their children and pets in the snow. How she wished Bliss were with her. No point pouring salt in the wound. Bliss was with Rachel and that was that.

At the corner of Thirty-fourth Street she craned her neck in a vain attempt to see the observation roof. Her father had taken her and Sam there, informing them when they peered through the telescope, "On a clear day you can see Lisbon!" Hannah had taken his remark as fact and was upset that she couldn't see Lisbon until father and brother explained about figures of speech.

Recently, a woman had jumped from the observation roof and landed about where she was standing, Hannah remembered. How would it feel, she wondered, to sail through the air like a Big Oiseau? They'd pay attention to her then! Just for the hell of it she entered the building lobby where hundreds of visitors with cameras and children waited patiently in line. A sign proclaimed a two-hour wait. Saved by the bell. She wasn't *that* desperate. Suicide sometimes occurred to her as an option that she would most likely never use, but that was there for her if needed.

Back on Thirty-fourth Street, a magnetic force drew her west, toward Macy's, another landmark in her own personal Memory Lane. Will Lawrence had also taken her and Sam here to see Santa Claus the Christmas before he died. Just Dad and the kids. Rachel had been too busy to come. It had been warm and loving to be a child with a father like Will and a brother like Sam.

Years later, she and Viktor had brought the girls to Macy's and then to the Paramount to see *Miracle on Thirty-fourth Street* with Natalie Wood. Before Viktor had returned to the Fatherland. And Natalie had drowned in the warm Pacific sea she'd always feared.

The elevator Hannah expected to take her to the shoe department turned out to be an express to the eighth floor.

WELCOME TO SANTALAND

Lacy snowflakes danced above her head. Animated bears bobbed and beckoned her into the North Pole village of yuletide fantasy. Penguins in ski hats and red mufflers toddled in and out of igloos. Choo-choo trainloads of Santa's elves careened on railroad tracks through a cheerful woodland of fir trees and birch. Enormous wooden soldiers stood guard over giant candy canes and jelly apples.

Nestled amid the scenery was Santa's workshop, with a blanket of snow on the roof. His reindeer and sleigh were festooned with banners saying "New York or Bust." A mailbox overflowed with letters and lists for Santa from good little girls and boys.

She'd been a good little girl, hadn't she? A fat lot of

good it was doing her now. She was alone, wasn't she, in a crowd of other adults and their children. Not one of hers was in sight. Elves were capering. *Jingle Bells* and *Deck The Halls* poured over them from overhead vents, drenching them with the holiday spirit. A serpentine path snaked through Santaland like Dorothy's yellow brick road. Hannah didn't realize she was part of the surging crowd until it was too late. Once in there was no way out. Here she was a lone woman without a child. She'd look as if she were off her rocker if she tried to push her way back to the entrance. Her best bet was to keep going, give Santa a jolly peck on the cheek, ask for peace in the Middle East, and make her escape. It would make a good story to tell at tonight's dinner, assuming that she got the chance to open her mouth.

Worried that nearby families might think her odd, she tried to convey the impression that the children in her charge had strayed out of sight, glancing around with an impatient expression as if searching for mischievous little rascals. She needn't have bothered. Nobody paid her the slightest attention.

She let herself be pushed with the flow, remembering how she dolled up the girls in the sweetest little Swiss dirndl dresses with the tiny gold heart lockets Grandma Rachel had given them to come here. Back in the fifties, you dressed children up for birthday parties and seeing Santa Claus. Not like the kids today with their torn jeans and their belly buttons showing. She wished she could have been a fly on the wall when Bliss arrived at Rachel's with her midriff exposed and those horrid galoshes! Anybody else would get her head handed to her. Not Bliss. So far as Rachel was concerned, the girl could do no wrong.

Hannah felt the same way about her grandchild. Bliss was her name incarnate, a blissful child growing into a lovely, talented, and good-hearted woman. Hannah's problem was the same as when she was a child. Rachel had monopolized Sam and tried to keep him to herself. Now she was doing the same with Bliss, and Eleanor and Jessie seemed oblivious to Hannah's pain.

Thoughts of her daughters made her feel abandoned once more. Damn them, anyway. She had Jerry. She had her volunteer work. That's all she needed. If today was an example of midlife crisis, she would give it a pass. What was she doing in Santaland by herself? *Please, God, don't let anyone I know see me here!* It was an aberration, something she could not tell a living soul, not even Jerry, who loved her more than anyone in her entire life except for Sam and Sam was dead.

Tonight after dinner if anyone asked where she'd been all day, she'd look mysterious and say "Out." Not that anyone would care. She could say she'd spent the afternoon at a male whorehouse and they'd nod and say please pass the Sweet'n'Low.

"Are you alone?"

Startled from her musing, she found she had reached something called the Magic Tree. Its entrance was through an arch cut into the bark of what looked like the trunk of sequoia. A pair of elfin figures with smiles of Disney innocence held out their arms in welcome.

"Well, ye-es." Embarrassment overwhelmed her. How could she have done this to herself? She tried to make light of it. "Is it all right? I mean, should I have rented a child?"

Of course it was all right, they soothed her, drawing her gently into the inner circle of the Magic Tree. "Close your eyes. We're going to turn you around three times while you make a wish."

Make a wish? Good God, if she had any brains she'd get the hell out of there. Fast. Instead, she surrendered herself to their tender ministrations, an elderly princess in a fairy tale who finds happiness inside a magic tree.

"Have you made your wish? Have you decided what you want Santa to bring you for Christmas?"

Love! My God, had she said it out loud? The L-word, Jessie called it. The L-word trembled on her lips. It wasn't Jerry's love she wanted. She had that. She wanted the love she couldn't have. The kind of love her mother had lavished on Sam and now gave to Bliss. The kind of love her daughters felt for each other, the kind of intimacy they would not share. And woven into the same tapestry, her grandchild's love, particularly now during her adolescence, when Hannah's worldly wisdom and experience could teach Bliss so much.

Being twirled around had made her dizzy. When she opened her eyes, the elves were holding her arms to steady her. Their evident concern alarmed her. Nobody knew where she was. If she fainted, she could wind up at Bellevue in the rubber room.

"Are you okay?"

She stuttered an explanation. "You must excuse me. I was just walking through to see what it's like. You see—" Her imagination soared. "I have a grandchild visiting me . . . um, she's three years old and, and you see, she's been very sick . . . but she's better now. Only I wasn't sure she was up to it, so that's why I thought I'd walk through by myself . . ."

They were programmed to smile. In fact, it occurred to her they might be robots. Before she knew it, they had eased her out of the Magic Tree and into an alcove where Santa Claus himself waited on his gilt and red plush throne.

"This woman is alone, Santa."

By now she didn't know whether to laugh or cry. For a horrifying moment she wondered if he expected her to sit on his knee. For an even more horrifying moment, she realized she *wanted* to sit on his knee. She wanted to snuggle up and whisper in his ear and feel his arm around her and his beard tickle her cheek.

He looked at her expectantly. All she could think to do was repeat her pathetic tale about her fictitious grandchild.

"And what would you like for Christmas, little girl?" Was he a robot, too? Was he programmed to ask the same questions no matter what? Couldn't he see she was a grown woman, a woman in her sixties who'd lost her way in Santaland?

She fled without answering, eager to leave Santaland as quickly as possible and return to the real world. It was not as easy as she thought. The crowd ahead of her was backed up in a claustrophobic crush of restless parents and cranky children. The family in front of her nagged at each other in a spiralling crescendo of pique. The son, about eight, took off his coat and threw it on the floor. When his mother ordered him to pick it up and behave himself or they were going straight home, he kicked the coat under his baby sister's stroller. "I'm *hot!*"

"Dammit, Seth, pick it up!"

"*You* pick it up!"

At that his mother hauled off and slammed him across the face. "Pick up the goddamn coat!"

Hannah intervened. "How dare you strike a child!"

Mother and son turned to her in disbelief.

"What kind of a mother are you? Thank God that you have children and that they're healthy and that you can look back on this day for years to come!"

As she tried to shove her way past them, the mother recovered sufficiently to shout into Hannah's face, "Mind your own damn business. What's it to you, anyhow?"

Hannah glared at her. "I'm in mourning, that's why. For a dead child."

As the younger woman reared back in horror, Hannah had burst into uncontrollable sobs. The terrified boy clung to his mother. *Fresh air.* Hannah knew if she didn't get out of there she would collapse and be trampled to death. Using her handbag as a battering ram, she had forced her way through the crowds and made her way to the street where, providentially, a cab pulled up.

Now, soaking in the hot scented water slowly restored her. She was deeply disturbed by the episode and wondered whether she should discuss it with Jerry or figure it out by herself. One thing was certain. What she had told that young mother was true.

She was in mourning for a child.

The child she was mourning was herself.

CHAPTER 5

December 1991

Jessie

By the time Hannah dressed for dinner and walked the short distance to her mother's, the chip on her shoulder was firmly in place. She was ready for anything except for the welcome that greeted her. Jessie answered the door with a shout of excitement as if Hannah had just returned from trekking barefoot across Antarctica.

"Look who's here, everybody! You look fabulous, Mom! Doesn't she look fabulous, Eleanor?"

Eleanor agreed wholeheartedly with her sister that their mother did indeed look fabulous! That's when Bliss emerged from the library and hurtled across the foyer. "Hey, Grandma. You look, like, awesome!"

The welcoming committee then proceeded to enact the family ritual Hannah herself had invented years ago. Her daughters and grandchild, all three of them together, embraced her from all sides in a hug sandwich amid further assurances of how wonderful she was and how much they loved her.

What's the big idea, she wondered. Was she dying of cancer after all, despite the negative test results? Had Jerry walked out on her with a porn star who could beat him at chess? Here were three people who couldn't get away from her fast enough this morning. Now they were falling all over her. Something was going on.

"So tell us—" Jessie was assembling Hannah's caviar

just the way she liked it. A round of melba toast rather
than rye bread. A spoonful of the Beluga from Zabar's,
a sprinkling of chopped egg, and a squeeze of lemon.
No chopped onion, thank you. "—Tell us about your
day, Mom."

So that was it. They felt guilty and were making it up
to her. There was hope after all. "Why thank you, darling," she said as Jessie handed her the plate, a love offering and apology in one. She thought of the Magic
Tree and smiled. She'd asked for love and got it without
having to sit on Santa's knee. It wasn't that her girls
didn't love her; it was that they suddenly realized how
much they loved her and how thoughtless they'd been.

Jessie breathed a sigh of relief as she watched a look
of genuine contentment ease her mother's features.
She still felt guilty about today, but it would be all
right.

Bliss poured the champagne as Rachel had taught
her. She didn't drink it—too sour, she said—preferring
instead to dip her pinkie in her glass and anoint everyone's earlobes for good luck, as Rachel had also taught
her.

Her subjects assembled and waiting, the queen empress would soon be making her entrance. Signs of her
social triumph were artfully arranged, like a Broadway
star's dressing room on opening night. A stack of *New
York Times* tearsheets. Bouquets of flowers with their
pasteboard congratulations still attached. Faxes and
telegrams everywhere.

A muffled scampering of feet, a bustling of voices
charged with tension, and the doors from Rachel's suite
flew open. Everything but heraldic trumpets, Jessie
thought. Rachel was like the star of an old-fashioned
costume movie: Cleopatra, Theodosia, Delilah all
wrapped into one, with handmaidens swarming armed

with combs and brushes and atomizers marking her progress into the great hall.

It made no difference to Rachel that tonight's gathering was small, casual, and limited to the women in her immediate family. She would not allow herself to be seen less than perfectly groomed. Her makeup crew had arrived and prepared her. Her hair and face were a masterwork of artifice that made her look naturally lovely. Her hair seemed to have been twisted into a soft chignon by her own errant hand and fastened with a few hairpins, the calculated wisps languidly brushing her neck. Her attire consisted of hostess pajamas in a rose blush silk and matching sandals that displayed the exquisitely pedicured feet of which she was so proud.

Jessie led the round of applause. They congratulated her. They were so proud of her. She was wonderful. She deserved the award. Rachel stretched out her arms in a symbolic embrace of them all. "My girls! What a lucky woman I am. Quick someone, give me some champers before I break down and cry."

Eager to please her mother, Hannah exclaimed, "Do you know who you look like tonight? Ann Harding." When Hannah was growing up, Rachel had often said everyone told her she looked exactly like the famous blonde film star of the thirties.

"Who's Ann Harding?" Bliss asked.

Still trying to make up to Hannah, Jessie changed the subject. "Mom used to look like Dorothy Lamour. Didn't you, Mom?"

"Who's Dorothy Lamour?" Bliss looked blank.

Jessie dug into her handbag. "I've got a surprise for you." An old snapshot of Hannah had fallen out of a book in Hannah's guest room. It was taken when Hannah was thirteen or fourteen and showed Hannah dressed in a sarong with her waist-length hair loose instead of in her usual neat braids.

"It says on the back you won first prize, Mom," Jessie said proudly.

Hannah was covered with confusion. It was years since she'd seen the snapshot. "It was Sam's idea." The name slipped out before she could stop herself. It was a family rule that her dead brother's name was never uttered in front of Rachel.

Silence fell over the dining room. All eyes turned toward Rachel. Hannah, as the culprit, girded herself for her mother's wrath. For the first time in her life she felt able to cope with Rachel on the subject of Sam. Today's experience at Santaland had released her from mourning the childhood her mother had killed. Henceforth she would honor her memories of Sam and Kathleen and her father. The nagging pains of Rachel's neglect in the pit of her stomach had been exorcised, never to return, by a visit to Macy's.

She was ready to face down her enemy, but Rachel seemed impervious to the battle cry and to the rapt attention of her family. She appeared to be preoccupied with Bliss's salad, prodding the avocado slices for ripeness and cautioning her not to drown it with too much dressing.

Hannah could sense they were in for some terrible surprise. If Rachel failed to react to her mention of Sam then surely something more important was on her mind. Watching her mother fuss over Bliss she knew it must have something to do with her and that Eleanor was not going to like it.

No point speculating. When Rachel was ready to lower the boom, they'd know about it. Hannah picked up the old snapshot. "Thanks for bringing it, Jessie. Wait till I show it to Jerry. Get a load of that long black hair."

"Let me see." Rachel reached for the snapshot. She smiled winningly at Hannah. "I'd forgotten how glamorous you were." *Here it comes,* Hannah thought, but she felt secure in the knowledge that her mother's barbs would no longer sting. "Such glorious black hair, darling."

Jessie and Eleanor grinned. They knew as well as Hannah what Rachel's point was. Rachel held up the photograph for all to see. "Now tell me truthfully. Wouldn't Hannah look prettier and younger if she dyed her hair?"

Theatrical groans greeted her question. The subject embarrassed Hannah's daughters. In the past they had defended her appearance, provoking a storm of sarcasm from Rachel. Since her mother's attacks no longer signified, Hannah said simply, "You're probably right, Mom. But let's face it. Jerry likes me the way I am. If I dyed my hair I'd look too young for him."

The relieved laughter deflected the family's attention to Hannah and away from Rachel. That would never do. Rachel picked up her spoon and rapped impatiently on her crystal goblet. "Please, everyone! I have an important announcement to make." *Bingo!* Here it was. Hannah didn't care, feeling triumphant over not getting upset by Rachel's criticism.

"You're running for President, right Grandma?" Jessie cracked.

"Please, Jessie. This is serious," Rachel said sternly.

Serious thoughts sprang to all their minds. *She was seriously ill. Marcus was leaving the sanitarium and returning home to die. She was divorcing Marcus. She was selling her vast real-estate interests.*

"It's about Bliss," Rachel intoned.

If she lacked their full attention before, she had it now. "Come stand by me, Bliss."

The girl complied with an elfin grin. Rachel twirled her around. "Just look at her. Isn't she terrific? See how she's put herself together? The girl's a genius. A gift, that's what she has, and I intend to make sure she doesn't throw it away."

While Bliss stood motionless in an awkward excitement that was in itself touching, Rachel explained her plan. Bliss would complete her current year of high school at home in Riverton and then move in with Rachel. They would spend part of next summer in Europe attending the collections in Paris, Milan, and London and return to New York in time for Bliss to attend Dalton or Hewitt.

"Along the way, I will see that she meets all the right people in the fashion world. Bill Blass, Pauline Trigère, Oscar de la Renta. The works. Donna Karan started out as a pin girl at Anne Klein, didn't she? I've got the connections to see that Bliss gets her chance, too. Right, my angel? The next Donna Karan!"

Rachel hugged the girl to her. Bliss trembled with excitement, her cheeks burning as the older woman continued. "Ten years from now—and mind you, I'll be here to see it—believe me, Bliss will be the biggest name in fashion. Won't you, sweetheart? You won't let me down, will you, darling?"

Certain that everyone was as pleased with her announcement as she, Rachel raised her champagne flute in an all-inclusive toast, allowing her gaze to circle the table. She stopped with some bewilderment at Eleanor, who had risen to her feet, pushing back her chair so abruptly that it fell backward with a crash.

"How dare you!" It was not like Eleanor to raise her voice.

Rachel was genuinely caught off balance. "Why— what do you mean?"

"Bliss is *my* daughter. Mine and Luke's. How dare you make plans without discussing them with us? Without asking our permission?"

Permission? Since when did Rachel need permission? Eleanor had thrown away her own talent. Rachel was not going to allow the same thing to happen to Bliss. "I'm the head of this family. I cannot—I will not—allow Bliss to be buried alive in some jerkwater town when the whole world is open to her. I cannot—will not—allow her to fritter away her God-given talent—talent she inherits from me!—when she can make fashion history."

Eleanor refused to be silenced or mollified. When Jessie tried to calm her, she pushed her sister away. When Jessie picked up Eleanor's overturned chair, Eleanor knocked it over again. Hannah's peacemaking attempts were drowned out by the accelerating conflict between her daughter and her mother. In the midst of the uproar, Bliss stood stricken with shock, torn between Rachel's grandiose plans and her fundamental sense of belonging in rural upstate New York with her parents and brother.

Above the uproar a phone could be heard ringing, one of dozens of calls that had come in during the course of the evening. Since Rachel did not permit calls to interrupt dinner parties, Wesley took messages. This time, however, Jessie had a hunch that it was Clifford calling from London and that it was important. She rose in her place.

"Jessie! Stay where you are. You know my rules."

The swinging door opened just wide enough for a hesitant Wesley to show her face, "I'm sorry, Madam—the gentleman says it's important."

Rachel waved her away with a ferocious scowl. Jessie again rose in her place. "It's Cliff. I'm sure."

"Stay where you are, Jessie!" The authority in her grandmother's voice was not to be denied. She stayed where she was.

"And don't glare at me like a three-year-old, Jessie! I will not have guests jumping up and down like jackrabbits. If that call was for you, Wesley will take a message. Now." She returned to the matter of Bliss. "As we were saying, Eleanor—"

Eleanor's bravado had run its course. Still on her feet as a symbol of independence, her body sagged as she burst into gut-wrenching sobs. "Oh, Mom!" cried Bliss from the depths of her heart as she rushed to her mother's side.

"Get your things, Bliss. We're going home. Right this minute," Eleanor said shakily.

Sensing her mother's vulnerability, Bliss didn't refuse directly. "You know Daddy doesn't like you to drive at night!" A glance toward Jessie was a call for help.

Jessie the Smart One took charge. "Cool it, everyone. Rachel! Eleanor! For God's sake, Bliss's future doesn't have to be decided now. June is six months away." She shot a warning glance at Rachel. "Of course it's Luke's and Eleanor's decision. Rachel knows that. After all—" She found herself chuckling like some inane game-show host. "—our Rachel has just been named Woman of the Year and was no doubt carried away by enthusiasm, that's all. Right?"

Rachel did not trust herself to do anything but nod. Eleanor and Bliss resumed their seats. Rachel buzzed for the next course. Feeling the time was right, Jessie waved her hand in the air like a hyperactive kindergartner asking to leave the room. Once out of the dining room, she doubled back through the foyer and into the kitchen through the pantry. "Was that call for me, Wesley?"

Her personal radar system had been right on target. It *was* Clifford calling her from London. He *had* told Wesley it was important. One of these days she was going to wring Rachel's neck! She picked up the kitchen phone. It was after midnight in London. Clifford would be home.

"No use calling. He said to tell you he'd call back. Had to go out. Said not to worry."

Not to worry? That was a British expression that translated to mean there was plenty to worry about.

"Jessie?" Her grandmother stood at the door to the dining room. "I thought I heard you in here."

"I was getting a glass of water."

"There's water on the table," Rachel contradicted. Seeing that catching Jessie in a fib made her grandchild bristle rather than feel contrite, Rachel changed the subject.

"Did you notice the centerpiece?"

How could she not notice? Rachel's pride in receiving flowers from Brooke Astor showed how vulnerable she was. Scott Fitzgerald was right. The rich *were* different. No matter how much money and power Rachel amassed, she'd still be the sewing-machine girl from Forsyth Street. The reminder softened Jessie's heart.

"The flowers are magnificent. Brooke Astor must think the world of you, Grandma."

Rachel shrugged as if to say that was true but so what, most people thought the world of her. "I thought I'd send her a copy of your book. Signed, of course. I'll tell you what to write."

Things had calmed down in the dining room. Hannah had been silent during the chaos that greeted Rachel's plans for Bliss, thoughtfully sipping glass after glass of champagne. Now she spoke up.

"You don't have to be a fashion designer, Bliss. You can be a photographer like Jessie. Or why not a writer? Like me."

"You? A writer? Since when?" Rachel dismissed her daughter's credentials.

"Yes, Mother. You forget that I was a reporter during the war. Remember the *Red Bank Standard*? I've had articles and essays published. Bliss may have inherited my writing talent. It skips a generation, you know."

Once again Jessie tried to make up for having hurt Hannah's feelings earlier in the day. "Mom's a terrific writer. We all know that."

Rachel rolled her eyes in unfeigned exasperation and changed the subject. "So what's happening with Cliff?"

Grateful to be able to drop her defense of Hannah's talent, Jessie rapped her glass with a spoon. "Listen up. I've got great news. I wasn't going to tell you this until Cliff got here but he loves the shots I made of Bliss and Rachel and—" She paused for effect.

"And what?" Rachel demanded.

"And he definitely wants to go ahead with the sequel! Isn't that great?"

The new photo essay would focus on Bliss as a teenager in contrast to her great-grandmother Rachel, who was seventy-five years her senior. "And still looks like a teenager!" Rachel said kiddingly. The unifying element would be Rachel's fashion collection. The accumulated treasures would serve as a visual metaphor of the older woman's life and as authentic modern history for Bliss.

As Jessie grinned lovingly at her two subjects she explained Cliff's timetable. "He thought we'd do a few photo sessions now while Bliss is in town and do the rest on weekends here and in Riverton and finish up at Easter when Bliss has two weeks off from school." With any luck the book would come out in the fall of 1992 to coincide with Rachel's ninetieth birthday.

"Who's writing the text?" Hannah asked quietly.

Jessie took a deep breath. Knowing how much her mother wanted to be a part of the project, she explained as delicately as she could that there would be no writer as such. The text would come from taped comments and anecdotes from both subjects recorded during the various photo sessions.

"Someone has to carry the tape recorder and ask the questions," Hannah observed.

Jessie hugged her mother in filial relief. "You've got yourself a job, Mom."

"It's like doing a documentary, isn't it, Jessie?" Eleanor raised her champagne glass in a toast to her sister. Her elbow slipped off the table, causing the wine to cascade over her hand.

"Exactly!" Jessie agreed, removing the glass and giving her sister her own cup of coffee.

"That's what Bliss is doing, aren't you, sweetheart? She's doing a documentary, too. Tell them about your English assignment, dear."

"Oh, *Mom*! It's too dorky. I've changed my mind. No way."

The English class had been asked to pretend they were either Oprah Winfrey or Phil Donahue hosting a panel discussion on a given theme such as sibling rivalry, sexual harassment, self-esteem, the usual. To make things more interesting, Mrs. Landon had made up slips of paper on various subjects so that each student could pick one.

"What was yours?" Rachel wanted to know.

Bliss said she couldn't remember. "It's silly, anyway."

"I've got it right here, Bliss." Eleanor read from the slip of paper, " 'What is the secret you've never told another living soul?' Isn't that ingenious? Come on, sweetheart. You were all excited about using us as your panel. The women in our family. We were all going to sit around like they do on TV and you were going to tape record the whole thing."

"I can't do it."

"But why?"

"I forgot to bring my tape recorder."

"Well, I didn't forget. It's right here in my shoulder bag." Eleanor placed the recorder on the table.

Rachel loved being interviewed. There was talk that she and Brooke Astor and Pamela Harriman would be invited by Oprah to discuss power, glamour, and the responsibilities of wealth. Being interviewed by Bliss would be good practice. "Don't worry, Bliss. We'll do all the talking."

Reassured, the girl's confidence returned. The women cleared their throats and searched their archival memory banks for a secret they had never revealed to a living soul.

Because Rachel had virtually invented her life as she went along, she had never trusted anyone sufficiently to share her deepest and darkest secrets. The two Samuels figured most prominently in her memory. Samuel her first love and Samuel her firstborn child. Nor would she ever forget her first husband, Will Lawrence, and the look on his face when he told her he knew her son wasn't his. She had never told a living soul about that. Or about the defeat in his eyes when the crash wiped him out financially.

Deeper and darker was her memory of the day when she told him the very sight of him made her puke. The thing she had not told him was that she knew about his mistress, another pathetic little weasel, a librarian who shared her lunch with him on a park bench when he was supposed to be looking for work and who cut his hair and bought him his cigarettes.

That was the day she had asked him sarcastically, "What are you planning to do today?"

"What do you want me to do? Jump in front of a subway train?"

She had dug into her purse and handed him a coin. "Here's a nickel."

Hannah's secret was her brother's insurance policy. When Samuel went overseas in the final months of the war, he may have had a premonition of death. While

Rachel was the beneficiary of his regular G.I. insurance, he had bought an additional policy in his sister's name. Sam had never fully understood Rachel's antipathy toward Hannah. He loved his sister and wanted her to be looked after if anything happened to him.

Whatever his motive, Rachel was sequestered in her bedroom that morning in 1945 when the insurance company notification addressed to Hannah arrived in the mail. Rachel had literally shut Hannah out of her life. The news of Samuel's death had sent her totally out of control. Raving, screaming, tearing at her hair and rending her garments in response to some primitive compulsion, she had shaken Hannah by the shoulder with such force that Hannah had thought her neck would snap. Still ringing in her ears was her mother shrieking, "Why wasn't it you? Why didn't you die?"

Her mother hadn't known about the insurance policy. Since she refused to speak to her daughter, Hannah felt no need to tell her. In due course, the Aetna representative advised her that a check for a hundred thousand dollars drawn to the order of Hannah Lawrence was waiting for her instructions. Her mother's silence turned out to be a blessing. She could live in the same apartment without arguments. She discovered that she was efficient and clear headed when it came to money. Without seeking advice from her mother or the family lawyer, she had found her own financial adviser, a protege of Barney Baruch, who helped her invest her money wisely.

At the same time she had fallen madly in love with Viktor—love at her first sight of his drenched golden body the moonlit night he swam ashore from the Nazi submarine off the Jersey coast. Perhaps her most shameful secret was that she knew almost from the start of their affair that he was virulently anti-Semitic despite being Jewish himself. He had been the first man to trigger her sexuality, an addictive trade-off against her ethical and moral standards that humiliated her to this day.

How could she reveal the truth about Viktor's abuse, how he beat her black and blue and forced her into degrading acts of submission, all the while calling her a whore who he would have sent to the gas chamber if the Nazis had won, which they should have. How could she confess that his sadism aroused her to heights of masochistic ecstasy while he gloated at the violence of her orgasms and sneered at her self-disgust. He had made her thank him and beg for more. It had taken ten years and the birth of both her daughters before she was finally strong enough to kick her addiction to him. But even then she had lacked the nerve to throw him out. It was only when he realized she was no longer his victim that he picked up and left. But she could in all honesty comfort herself with one thing. She had never told him about her inheritance. However low she had sunk in her own self-esteem, however much in thrall she was to him sexually, her core of self-preservation had prevailed. He had for a time controlled her. Body and heart maybe. But never her money. Never her soul.

Her secret life with Viktor was much too shameful to confess. A more romantic secret, one that conformed to Bliss's format, was the truth about how she'd met Jerry. When friends and family had asked how they'd first met, she had made vague and sheepish references to some academic function or other. Jerry thought she was being silly, but he respected her feelings.

He, after all, was the one who had taken the personal ad in *New York* magazine. "And you, my darling, answered it! Where would we be if you hadn't?" Where, indeed? Thank God she had answered it and found her true soulmate. They were an old married couple now. If Bliss wanted a deep, dark secret, this was one she could deal with. It tickled her to think how Rachel would react when she described Jerry's ad. She could still remember it word for word.

INHIBITED INTELLECTUAL. RECENT WIDOWER WITH GROWN CHILDREN SEEKS EQUALLY INHIBITED WOMAN OF SIMILAR CIRCUMSTANCES. GOAL: TO READ "THIS IS MY BELOVED" TOGETHER AND LIVE HAPPILY EVER AFTER.

They had read *This Is My Beloved* together and they were as far as she could figure out living happily ever after. She wished the same happiness and contentment for her daughters. Jessie seemed happy at last with Clifford. Eleanor was the one who worried her at times. She seemed so timid around Luke, so afraid of opening her mouth. Except at dinner tonight, standing up to Rachel like that. What a shock! Rachel looked as if she'd been hit by a truck. Maybe there was more to Eleanor than they all realized. Maybe she did have a deep, dark secret too.

Eleanor was thinking along the same line. She did have a deep, dark secret. It was one she had shared with only one other person in the entire world, her sister and best friend, Jessie. It was a secret they had vowed to keep until death would part them. Declining to discuss it confirmed the fiction that it never happened.

On the other hand, she was on a high from her sudden outburst at dinner. Who'd have thunk it! The thrill of it all tempted her to throw caution to the winds, to tell the family what really happened in Greece and let the chips fall wheresoever! Not that she ever would. The truth might make her free, relieve her conscience of a fifteen-year burden. But it would destroy her daughter, wreck her marriage, and tear apart the ties that bound her to the women in her family.

No, she would think of some other dark and dirty secret for the tape recorder. Since everyone considered her a square, maybe she could shock them by admitting she went all the way with Luke before they got engaged. *Big deal.* She'd have to think of something else. Maybe Jessie could lend her one of her secrets. Her sister led a much more interesting life.

Jessie, meanwhile, was searching the archives of her colorful past for a deep, dark secret, or at least one suitable for revealing to a family audience. The problem was, except for what happened in Greece fifteen years ago, which she would *never* reveal to anyone, she had rarely bothered to hide anything. She had lived an open and flamboyant life with Jimmy Kolas, who was married when she met him and was later convicted of international currency fraud. Nothing secret about that.

Casting her mind back in time, she remembered something exactly right. The Bergdorf Goodman shoplifting caper. It was a cold February day. She was cutting through the street floor of Bergdorf's on her way to the Plaza when a handbag sale stopped her dead in her Gucci suedes. Shoulder bags. Exactly what she needed. As freezing as it was outside, the heat was suffocating on the inside. Bergdorf women had thin blood. Bulky as it was, she had taken off her coat and tried unsuccessfully to choose a shoulder bag. Bergdorf's idea of a bargain price was not hers and soon she was on her way to the Plaza.

Seated in the Palm Court, she threw back her coat and made a startling discovery. A five-hundred-dollar shoulder bag was dangling from her shoulder. In her haste to escape from the heat inside the store, she had slipped her coat back on without noticing the bag. No

alarms had gone off at the door. No heavy feet had pur-
sued her down the street. Her companions had laughed
and said she should keep the bag, but she lacked the
nerve. Not a five-hundred-dollar bag. Not when some
salesgirl would wind up being responsible. Not, as she
had reminded herself, when it was basically dishonest.
She might be guilty of many things, but stealing from
a department store was not one of them.

What made the story good for Bliss's report was what
happened the next day when she returned the shoulder
bag and tried to apologize for what had happened. The
saleswoman turned out to be French and because it
was Bergdorf's was extremely servile to her customer.
She thought Jessie was returning the bag for a refund
and would not be convinced otherwise. Finally, Jessie
gave in and graciously accepted the five hundred dollars, plus tax, in cash, and waltzed out of the store,
nodding grandly to the doorman on the Fifty-seventh
Street side. She wondered if the statute of limitations
had run out.

She also wondered why Cliff hadn't called her back.
By now it was two in the morning London time. Something must be wrong. She crossed her fingers unobtru-
sively. *Please, God, don't wreck it!* She was about to be
happy at last. She couldn't wait for him to call back.
There was a phone in the library. She slipped away
from the table.

She dialled Cliff's number. *Busy.* In the middle of
the night? She dialled again. Still busy. At least he was
home. Unless the phone had gone dead. The London
operator took an eternity to answer. She checked the
line and reported back. The line was indeed engaged.

Hannah stood in the doorway. "Forgive me, dear.
We're all waiting for you. Rachel's about to explode."

"Oh, Mom. Cliff's line is busy. It's two o'clock in the
morning. Something must be wrong! Tell Grandma—"

"Don't worry. Make your call. I'll take care of Grandma—"

The phone rang.

"Cliff? Thank God it's you. I was so worried."

Jimmy Kolas was dead. Killed in a riding accident early that morning. Clifford had quite forgotten that several years back he had agreed to be the executor of Jimmy's estate.

"His lawyer took me around to his safety deposit box this afternoon. There was an envelope addressed to me. It contained something for you."

Jimmy Kolas no longer signified. She was sorry that he was dead but wary of its effect on her happiness with Cliff. One thing she had to know. "What was it?"

"The deed to the island of Helios signed over to you."

"To me?" She was flabbergasted.

"Oh, yes. And a note that said you would know why."

CHAPTER 6

1972

Jessie

"I'm going to miss you like crazy, Jessie. Why do you have to go to London?"

"Don't move. The pose is perfect." She had positioned Eleanor amid overflowing baskets of peaches, with Jason cradled to her breast. With her hair scrubbed back in a knot and only sunglow for makeup, Eleanor's beauty was more striking than ever. Marriage was her therapy, motherhood her health club. The parade had passed her by because she had fled from it. Peace marches, abortion rights, and women's liberation had little place in her rural haven. She had chosen her life against her grandmother's arguments, but with her mother's and sister's blessings.

"American madonna and child!" Jessie enthused, her new Nikon cupped gently but firmly in her hands like a living being. The camera was *her* baby. She was taking it to London to seek her fortune. Rachel didn't approve of that either. An eighteen-year-old girl had no business running away from home. But she was not running *away,* Jessie protested, she was running *to.* Hannah understood and was perhaps a bit envious. When she was eighteen the war was on. The farthest she could run had been Red Bank, New Jersey.

"And you know what happened to her! She married that Nazi!" Rachel said, forgetting the fact that without Viktor there would have been no Jessie or Eleanor.

Jessie promised not to marry a Nazi. She would be too busy studying at the International Institute of Photojournalism and getting to know the London that had captured her imagination on that misbegotten trip with Viktor.

"One more, please." The sun setting behind the orchard enhanced the roseate glow. Jason stirred and began to howl, his tiny fists flying

"He's hungry! My little boy is hungry," Eleanor said in wonderment of the miracle she and Luke had wrought.

Jessie's eye remained glued to her viewfinder. "Well, feed him!" she laughed. "Don't let me stop you. I still have plenty of film."

Luke appeared. He too seemed suffused with contentment. Would she ever feel that way, Jessie wondered? He had filled out and his features had matured since that first meeting, yet the shyness persisted in the proud diffidence with which he watched his wife and child.

"Best to get a move on, Jessie, if you're going to make your train."

"Just one more. You stand with her with your arm around her while she feeds him."

Expose her breast for the camera? Uncertain, Eleanor turned to her husband. He nodded gravely and stood beside her as Jessie had instructed. The subject was as old as history, mother, father and infant creating a composition of sublime harmony. Deeply touched, Jessie realized that her sister really had made the right decision. Marriage and motherhood were her natural provenance. Child-bearing came easily to her. She had told Jessie that giving birth made her feel complete as a woman and worthy of Luke's love.

She had also told Jessie that the doctor had warned her against any further pregnancies, something to do with her womb. But what about Luke? Hadn't he and Eleanor planned on having a big family? Eleanor had smiled beatifically and kissed her sister. They were ecstatically happy with their son. There would be plenty of time to discuss the problem later, after Jason was weaned and walking.

Besides, doctors could be wrong, couldn't they? In the meantime, she swore Jessie to secrecy. She didn't want Hannah or, God forbid, Rachel butting in with fancy Park Avenue specialists.

"Give Mom and Jerry our best," Eleanor said as she hugged her sister good-bye. "And don't talk to any strange men on the plane." Then she kissed her husband fondly. "See what happened to me?"

There was plenty of time for that, years and years and years before Jessie would get married, if ever. Women were free to live their own lives without worrying about convention. Even her mother knew that. She and Jerry had been a couple for three years. He kept his place in the Village but spent most of his time at Hannah's. He and Hannah acted like an old married couple, yet seemed in no hurry to make it legal.

"I still don't know why you can't study photography in New York," Hannah grumbled. Since she and Jerry were driving Jessie to the airport, it was a little late to still be discussing it.

London was the place to be, she assured her mother, where photography was happening. David Bailey. Eve Arnold. Lord Snowdon.

Hannah tried to make light of it. "What is it, my breath? My deodorant? Why are both my girls running as far away as they can?"

"If you really want to know, it's because you and Romeo make too much noise at night. It's very embarrassing."

From the backseat of the car, Jerry bopped her playfully over the head. "I feel sorry for whoever falls for you."

He needn't have. Jimmy Kolas turned out to be more than a match for Jessie.

The I.I.P. held an annual exhibit of students' work at the Belgravia Galleries in Knightsbridge. Among the photographs chosen to compete for scholarship awards was Jessie's New American Family portrait of Eleanor, Luke, and baby Jason. She had taken the unexposed film pack to her first class in basic film development. The strips looked crisp and clear. She had never made her own prints before. Working in the darkroom proved how essential it was to master the techniques of shading and cropping.

A good photograph was an accident of instinct, she was told, what Cartier-Bresson called "the decisive moment." To create a great photograph, the good photographer had to have the printmaker's eye and sensibility. And persistence, Jessie realized. She knew in her gut that this photograph was definitely an accident of instinct and that she had captured her sister's family at the decisive moment. She made well over fifty prints before she got what she wanted.

It was good, she thought tearfully. But was it a one-shot miracle? Only time would tell. Meanwhile, the panel of judges consisted of Cecil Beaton, David Bailey, and Lord Snowdon. *Please God, let me win!*

When the big night came, she made her way on foot from the tiny basement flat she had rented in Lennox Gardens. It had taken hours to dress carefully enough so that she wouldn't look as if she had dressed carefully. This was one time when she secretly wished she had been the pretty one, though on balance she knew it was equally good—if not better—to be smart and ambitious.

Cutting through Belgrave Square, she stepped onto the zebra crossing. A screech of brakes brought a low-slung car to a clamorous halt inches from her. "What are you? Some flaming American?" the driver bellowed.

"No—I'm a flaming Martian! Want to make something out of it?" He looked pretty good, actually. The guys she'd met so far were hopeless.

He waved a suede-clad fist at her. "Even a Martian knows enough to look the right way when crossing the road."

"What am I, a mind reader?"

He looked her up and down with a slyly approving grin. "It's a good thing you're not. You'd slap my face."

Later that night, when her New American Family was awarded first prize and she stood flustered and joyful with the judges and the other winners, she saw him in the crowd, raising his glass and grinning the same grin. Clearly she had made a conquest. Let the games begin. He had to be somebody special. His clothes, his car, his arrogant self-confidence proved that. He didn't exactly sound English. There was something foreign in his accent. German? No, thank God. Nothing like Viktor. French, maybe? If she lived abroad long enough she would be able to tell.

"So you are an American after all." The ceremony over, he had appeared at her side.

"And who are you?"

"Dmitri Andreas Constantine Georgopoulos Kolas. Jimmy to my friends. It's fortunate I didn't run you down. May I offer my congratulations? The photograph is magnificent."

As she mingled among the guests, being introduced to magazine editors and advertising types, she was aware of him watching her. When at last the bar closed and the final stragglers were ushered out, he was gone. Of course, he would be waiting for her outside in his car. She begged off going to a pub with her classmates and spent an extended period of time retouching her eye makeup and hair before descending to the street. Make him wait.

The street was deserted. All revved up and nowhere to go. He ought to have been wildly impatient and swept her into the seat beside him, whisking her off to some private club like Les Ambassadeurs and ordering a champagne supper. Food! She was starved. To make things worse, she couldn't catch up with the gang because she'd been so full of herself she hadn't listened when they said where they were going.

It killed her to think of them wolfing down sausage rolls and ham salads and ice-cold shandys. As far as she could remember all she had back at the flat were some peanuts, a jar of mustard and some instant Nescafe. Suddenly she was homesick for New York and the availability of food twenty-four hours a day. Here there were a few nosh bars open in Soho but that was too far away.

Once back at the flat, she made herself a peanut and mustard sandwich and a large mug of instant. Rattling a tin box disclosed a forgotten chocolate biscuit. Thus comforted, she put Carole King's *Tapestry* on the record player and gazed triumphantly at her hundred-pound check. Jimmy Kolas had probably got tired of waiting for her or maybe he assumed she was busy. Now that he knew she was a student at the I.I.P. and heard her name announced, he would know how to find her. On a hunch she looked up his name in the telephone directory. Sure enough, there were two listings. Alexander Kolas Shipping Ltd., with an address in the City, and D. Kolas in Hill Street, Mayfair.

She picked up the phone and dialled a number. "Overseas operator?" It was late afternoon in New York. She needed to tell her mother about her award, proof of how well her baby girl was doing so far from home. She called Eleanor next. Remembering how deftly she had engineered her sister's courtship, she wished that Eleanor had been with her tonight to steer Jimmy Kolas. Not that Eleanor had the ability to handle a situation like that. She panicked when she had to return something to Saks Fifth Avenue, as if they were going to send her to the electric chair.

"I miss you like crazy!" she shouted over the bad connection to Riverton-on-Hudson. She insisted on hearing Eleanor's news first, before telling her own. Jason was sitting up. The apple harvest was the best in years. Luke had been asked to chair a series of seminars starting next year at Cornell. "What's with you? How are *you* feeling?" Jessie asked.

"Fine, really fine."

"I don't like the sound of that."

Only six months after Jason's birth, Eleanor had conceived again and had aborted spontaneously shortly thereafter. "Luke would kill me if he knew. I told him it was a heavy period. He made me promise to get a diaphragm as soon as the doctor says it's okay."

Eleanor closed the painful subject quickly and turned to Jessie's life. "What's happening in London? Are you famous yet? Have you fallen in love?"

Jessie told her about the photograph and her hundred-pound prize. Eleanor and Luke had never seen the actual photograph and were unaware of the poetic clarity of the infant Jason sucking greedily at his mother's breast. There was nothing to worry about. She had not identified them by name. There was talk of printing I.I.P. posters of the winning photographs. It wouldn't matter. Nobody in Britain would recognize Eleanor and her family.

As for falling in love, Jessie rattled off her conquests of "an upper-class twit" who threatened to kill himself if she didn't sleep with him but didn't, and an Irish layabout who got roaring drunk and turned up at her flat with all his worldly possessions: a pair of socks, a razor, and toothbrush in a brown paper sack.

She did not mention Jimmy Kolas. It was probably just as well. He looked like pretty fast company. He must be close to forty. He was probably married. It was just as well he hadn't waited for her. By this time she'd be in big trouble, she was sure. There were plenty of other things to think about. Several of the editors at the reception had given her their cards and invited her to come see them about possible assignments. One advertising man thought her sensitivity toward young families was just right for a new breakfast food.

A few days later, Jessie was summoned to the I.I.P. director's office. Someone had commissioned an eight-by-ten print, mounted and framed, of The New American Family. "What am I going to do?" he asked.

"An eight-by-ten print? What's the problem?"

"Not eight by ten inches. Eight by ten feet! He wants it for his library wall. Price no object. Chap's name is—Kolas. D. Kolas. Hill Street, Mayfair."

Surely now he would call her, even if it was just to show her her photograph on his library wall. Unless he was married. There was one way to find out. She dialled the Hill Street number. A plummy butler voice said, "Mr. and Mrs. Kolas have gone to Argentina. Messages will be forwarded."

CHAPTER 7

1974

Jimmy Kolas

More than a year had passed since the student exhibition. A lot of exciting things had happened. Jessie's American Family portrait had struck a responsive note with British editors. She had become a minor success, what the Brits called a flavor of the month, suddenly on all the party lists for fashion shows and film previews.

Several magazine assignments had followed, small ones to be sure: the "new Julie Christie," who looked the part but couldn't act; the first fashion collection of a Swahili exchange student; dawn at the Caledonian Market, where antiques dealers from all over the country set up their stalls and eyed each other suspiciously in their hunt for a lost Turner or a Georgian silver tea tray black with grime that would come up nice and bright with a bit of polish.

She had fallen in lust a few times—nothing serious—and was beginning to wonder even at this early stage of her life whether it was possible to combine a man with a career. So far, the men she dated seemed to be attracted by her being a photographer but raised bloody hell when an assignment got in the way of their needs. Yet they wouldn't think twice about breaking a date with her to meet their boss or go on a sudden business trip.

The end of each affair had been triggered by a conflict over her work. Ted left her a nasty note the night she unexpectedly had to cover a command performance at the Palladium. Jonathan simply disappeared and refused to return her calls after Jessie raced off to photograph twin girls swimming the English channel. William crashed his Mini-Minor against the iron fence above her basement flat in frustration at not finding her home and left it there until the police took it away.

She had not thought about Jimmy Kolas until a letter with an Argentine stamp arrived at the International Institute of Photojournalism addressed to her. Scrawled in blue ink on the flimsy blue notepaper used by the upper classes to annoy the peasants, it said, as near as she could figure out,

> Dear Martian,
> Perhaps you will recall the rather impertinent chap who nearly ran you down in Belgrave Square? I seem to have been in Argentina all this time. Much to report on the pampas and Patagonia. Did you know the latter was settled by Welshmen and the locals keep to the ancient Celtic customs? You and your camera would find much of interest.
> Perhaps you have been advised that I commissioned a blowup of your exquisite American Family photograph. My butler tells me it has arrived in Hill Street and is sitting sad and lonely in the boxroom awaiting instructions.
> I shall be returning to London in a fortnight. Would it be too much of a bore if I imposed on our brief but charming acquaintance to ask your help in hanging it properly?

He closed with the sincere hope that the letter would find her well. Since he had no idea where she lived, he asked her to ring the Hill Street house and leave her phone number. *Aha,* did that mean no wife to wonder why some strange American girl was leaving her phone number? Or, as she had learned from Jonathan and Ted, a wife might well live permanently in the country with the dogs and children, or if she were in London might blithely not give a damn who called since she had lovers of her own.

Lovers? Was she out of her gourd? The man had paid her the supreme compliment of buying her work and was now asking her to help hang it. Who was kidding whom? He didn't need her to hold the hammer and nails. He had a butler and for all she knew a special servant for hanging pictures. With an underling to hold the nails. And an underling's underling to hold the ladder.

Why was she torturing herself? Jimmy Kolas was nothing to her. In fact, the thought of him scared her a little. The rich were different, according to Scott Fitzgerald. Not that she was exactly a pauper. She might even be considered an heiress, since according to Hannah, Rachel's will divided her estate between her sister Eleanor and herself. Rachel could be called rich. But Greek shipping heirs were a different kind of rich.

For a reason she couldn't figure out, she did not phone Hill Street. *Why not?* Was she afraid of some lousy butler? *Afraid?* Eleanor would have been afraid. Not Jessie. If he wanted to find her when he got back, let him work it out. She wasn't that hard to find. All he had to do was look in the phone book. Or if that was too complicated, he could get her number from the I.I.P.

What was eating her? Why was she in such a snit? Desire and fear. She had thought of Jimmy Kolas more often than she liked to admit and had long and wildly detailed erotic dreams of him as her lover. Now that his return to London made this a possibility, the reality terrified her. He was too old, too sophisticated, too worldly for an innocent little country girl from Manhattan.

It would be better not to call. If ever she ran into him, she would pretend she never got his letter. She had more important things to think about. A month ago, the *Sunday Times* magazine had asked her to come up with an idea for an American-Visitor-in-London photo essay. Not the usual jellied eels and the Tower of London. No lunkheads in Hawaiian shirts pouring ketchup on ice cream.

"Something more representative of the American spirit, you know." She knew. They wanted something like the portrait of Eleanor, Luke, and Jason. That was special. Maybe a once-in-a-lifetime fluke. She wasn't sure she could do it again. She was about to despair when an idea came to her out of the blue as if it had been there all along.

A series on three generations of women on a shopping spree. Grandmother, mother, and daughter in London for the first time. Trying on clothes at Marks and Sparks, going upscale at Harvey Nicks and Harrods. Cruising the King's Road. Sunday morning at Petticoat Lane. Giving each other advice. Questioning each other's taste. Driving the sales people nuts. Just like her own mother and grandmother.

In fact, it was not at all like Hannah and Rachel. Jessie had never gone shopping with her grandmother and rarely with Hannah since she became old enough to travel around by herself. Not that that mattered. The *Times* loved the idea and told her to go ahead.

The photographs had turned out so well they even surprised Jessie. Maybe it wasn't a fluke. Maybe she did have an eye for the decisive moment. Her piece would be in next weekend's magazine. She had just learned they had put one of her shots on the cover. It was of all three women at Tubby Isaac's stall in Petticoat Lane, eating jellied eels.

Fingers crossed, from her lips to God's ears, if the reaction was what the *Times* expected and what she feverishly hoped, her career was established. Despite the usual Saturday-night parties and Sunday brunches, that weekend she had stayed home. Alone. In a frazzle of anxiety. She wished she did have a man in her life who really cared about her. The way Luke cared about Eleanor. And Jerry cared about her mother. And not forgetting Marcus, who had been devoted to her grandmother until he got sick. It would have been nice to wake up Sunday morning in some sweet man's arms and sprawl on the floor in the tiny drawing room drinking café au lait and eating croissants.

He would be warm and wonderful when the phone rang and be genuinely thrilled for her when a messenger arrived with flowers from the editor who couldn't wait for the florists to open on Monday and picked a bouquet from his own garden.

The next day, a photo editor at Time-Life's London bureau sent her a file photograph of Margaret Bourke-White taken in 1936. "The first great woman news photographer. A shame she didn't live to see your work! Congratulations."

When she called Hannah to tell her the news, Jerry took the phone. "Are you available for weddings?" She could hear the love in their voices. They weren't exactly sure when the wedding would be. "It's too much fun living in sin!" her mother bubbled. Could that be Hannah talking like that? Jessie wished she could be there to hug them both. After what her mother had gone through with Viktor, she deserved to be happy.

Rachel looked down her nose at Jerry. She called him a loser behind his back because he wasted his time teaching remedial reading and spelling to inner-city

kids. She called Luke's two hundred-acre fruit farm To-
bacco Road because she had never forgiven him for
wrecking Eleanor's chance to be a famous model and
movie star. Jessie wondered what her grandmother
would say if she met Jimmy Kolas—though that possibility did not seem very likely.

Her call to Eleanor began with their usual cries
of pleasure and affectionate sisterly chirps. They
missed each other like mad. They wished they could
be with each other. Eleanor was so proud of her sister.
She couldn't wait to see the magazine Jessie was sending her by airmail tomorrow.

"There's something you're not telling me, Eleanor. I
can hear it in your voice. Give," Jessie said firmly.

A brief pause followed by a barely audible whisper.
"I'm pregnant. *Shhhh.*"

Wasn't it dangerous? Did Luke know? Had she been
back to the doctor? "Please, Eleanor—" She couldn't
bear it if anything happened to her sister!

"It's suppertime here. My two guys are going to faint
if I don't feed them." She would call Jessie later in the
week.

A few days later, Jimmy Kolas's secretary rang to say
he was in New York on his way back to London. "He
hopes you might be free Wednesday week to join him
and some friends for dinner at Hill Street. Eight for
eight-thirty. Black tie for the men, so you may wish to
wear something long but informal. Shall I arrange for a
car to pick you up?"

Her nerve failed her. She could not bring herself
to ask if Mrs. Kolas would be present. On second
thought, she thanked her lucky stars she hadn't. She
had only met Jimmy Kolas once in her entire life. Why
was she complicating things? The situation was simple.
This wealthy Greek shipowner had bought her photo-

graph and was now inviting her to a dinner party. Civilized, sophisticated; from the sound of it, the evening was in her honor.

She had tried on and rejected everything in her wardrobe before blowing the entire *Sunday Times* commission on a black jersey Jean Muir that added at least five world-weary years to her appearance.

"Miss Lawrence."

The butler announced her at the library door. She felt like Eliza Doolittle on her first visit to Professor Higgins's mother. But she was not a flower girl trying to pass as a lady. She was a hot, jazzy, confident American girl who was taking London by storm, or trying to. The American Family photograph filled the space between two mahogany bookcases.

Jimmy Kolas sprang to greet her. Any sneaky thoughts she may have had about finding that the dinner part would be dinner for two, and that she would be the main course, were dispelled by the small but elegant group arranged like a society photograph. Score one for her side. The Jean Muir was exactly right. She could see the glint of label recognition in the eyes of the three other women, none of whom looked like a wife. The glint in Jimmy's eyes was something else.

"So good of you to come." He introduced her to the others. No wife. He indicated the photograph with a flourish. "It's hard to believe that such a young woman could produce such a work of art. Wouldn't you agree, Cliff, old man?"

Clifford Smith-Avery nodded thoughtfully through a cloud of cigarette smoke, prompting a laugh from Jimmy. "That's about as garrulous as he gets," he explained. Cliff published art books. "I've been telling him photography is the new form of art. Isn't that true, Jessie?"

All eyes turned to her. "As a matter of fact, it is true.

Collectors of photographs are springing up all over the place and paying top dollar. The I.I.P. is mounting an exhibition of war photographs that's going to museums around the world. Cecil Beaton, David Bailey, Richard Avedon, Milton Greene—their books have sold well for years, but now they're doing limited editions of prints. Signed by the photographer the same as if they were paintings."

Jimmy was standing close enough to her to speak low enough so that the others could not hear. "You must sign yours."

"I'd be delighted."

"Later. After the others have gone."

By the time the last cognac was poured, she had completely lost her nerve. She had eaten and drunk too much. Her head was swimming. The rich cream sauces were colliding with the vinaigrette salad dressing. There had been wine with each course, topped off with a sweet dessert wine with the chocolate mousse that tasted like cherry soda mixed with gasoline.

Jimmy's hand on her shoulder galvanized her into action. She was out of her depth. She had no business being in this kind of company. She knew if she stayed she would disgrace herself by bursting into tears or throwing up or both. She had to get out of there. The question was how to exit gracefully without making a fool of herself.

Clifford Smith-Avery was the last to make his farewells. It was now or never. "Oh, Jimmy! It is getting late, isn't it? I have an early shoot, first thing in the morning. Cliff, would you mind dropping me home?"

Jimmy Kolas accepted her departure with amused courtesy, as if to say, "Win some. Lose some." He kissed her cheek as he had the other female guests and consigned her to his friend's safekeeping. Walking them out to Clifford's car, he said to Jessie almost as an afterthought. "I thought we might lunch on Friday. The Mirabelle at one-thirty? I'll send the car."

Inadvertently, naively, she had made the right move. In the weeks that followed she began to understand the nuances of sexual negotiation and to savor, tentatively at first and then with increasing confidence and enjoyment, the strategies of courtship. Throughout a whirl of lunches, dinners, suppers, theaters, concerts, walks in the rain, and country jaunts, she learned what it was like to be romanced.

Not seduced one-two-three. Not jumping on someone's bones because she was hot to trot and the music was good and the alcohol fueled her desire and destroyed her fear. Like most young women her age, she despised the double standard. She had as much right to orgasm as any man. She understood her body, or thought she did. She sneered condescendingly at the outdated rituals of dating. Girls waiting by the phone for some clown to ask them out, pretending they weren't interested when they were. Doling out sex according to formula. Above the neck on the first date. Above the waist on the tenth date. Below the waist only if you were pinned or going steady; rubbing, touching, teasing only. No penetration.

Over their first Campari sodas that first lunch at the Mirabelle, Jimmy got straight to the point. "I feel a strange affinity for you, Jessie. Don't ask me why. Affinity is one of life's great mysteries. I feel that I can learn things from you and you can learn things from me. We can be each other's university, if you like. But the most important thing is for you to be comfortable with me, not jumpy the way you were the other night."

"Jumpy? What makes you think I was jumpy?" Jessie knew she was and was deeply embarrassed.

"What I'm trying to say is I will not make love to you until you open your arms and welcome me in." That understood, he wanted to assure her that she could relax with him whatever the circumstances. In his house, at her flat, wherever they might be alone.

"I have known many women but only recently discovered the one thing I've been missing."

"Which is?"

"You won't laugh?"

This was probably the most important turning point of her life. "I won't laugh."

"Intimacy."

In the days and nights that followed, they told each other things. He explained what it was like being an outsider in English society. He could dress like an Englishman, be educated like an Englishman, know more about English history and literature than most Englishmen, and still be treated like a foreigner.

His wealth and generosity had brought him membership to the club. Marrying an earl's daughter had strengthened his position until her flagrant affairs made him a figure of pity. During their recent visit to Argentina, she had fallen in love with a millionaire rancher and refused to return home to England.

In the steamroom of his club he overheard men he thought were his friends make cutting remarks about his being cuckold. "They called me the Greaser. The Greek."

"But that's what you are. Greek!"

"Quite right! Clever girl. It's as if the gods are telling me something. Just last week, my great-uncle Costa died and left me a private island in the Aegean. Think of it, Jessie. Sunshine. Olive trees. Lemons. Figs. Cyprus groves. Shepherds and their flocks. An ancient monastery. No cars. No electricity—"

"I'm a city girl," Jessie countered, as she tried to visualize herself in such an alien setting. Noise, traffic, chaos, rudeness, yelling. She needed them to survive.

"We could always go to a Greek restaurant in Soho," she said jokingly.

Gradually she found herself telling Jimmy things she didn't know she knew. About being an outsider, too, but not knowing what her roots were. Her grandmother Rachel had been left at an orphanage as an infant. "She never knew who her parents were. She makes up stuff. Like, I once heard her say she was born in Vienna and came through Ellis Island as a child of three. Other times she talks about being Jewish. You know, it's fashionable to be Jewish in New York. She's never been religious but she gives a lot of money to Jewish charities.

"My grandfather—I never met him—he committed suicide during the Depression. Then she married Marcus, only he had a breakdown and he's in a sanitarium."

"She sounds like a dangerous woman."

"She tries to run everyone's life, but I have to admit she's been pretty successful at her own."

Jessie had never before talked so openly about her family. Describing them all put them into perspective. Eleanor, the pretty one, rejecting Rachel's dreams of glory. Hannah allowing her mother to walk all over her but still managing the occasional act of rebellion, despite Rachel's disapproval.

One night in Hill Street after dining quietly on omelettes and salad that Jimmy himself had prepared, they were listening to Errol Garner records in the library when he pointed to the photograph looming over them. "You always refer to your sister as the pretty one. 'Eleanor the Pretty One.' "

"Well, she is the pretty one."

"And what does that make you? The plain one?"

The question was an archeologist's pick jarring loose a sharp shard of pain Jessie had never known was there. "The smart one," she corrected him. "Grandma always said I was the smart one and nobody had to worry about me. I could take care of myself." She suddenly burst into a torrent of sobs she had never before experienced.

"It's all right," he murmured, repeating his words again and again until they ran together. "It's all right to be jealous."

"I'm *not* jealous. I love my sister. She's the sweetest, most loving person in the entire world. And it's true. I *am* the smart one. I've always taken care of her until Luke came along. And I even engineered that so she'd be safe and have someone to love her. Don't tell me I'm jealous!"

"Jessie, please!"

They had been amiably stretched out on the floor. Now she turned abruptly away, rolling herself up tight in a small shell of self-protection. "Don't you have a plane to catch?" she mumbled.

It was true. He and two business partners were flying to Greece at midnight. "We're going to talk about this first."

His attempt to embrace her was met with a dead weight. "Just leave me alone," she said, and curled up even tighter.

Not to be put off, he ran gentle fingertips along the stiffened ridge of her backbone until it began to limber and relax. "You're not Eleanor. You're Jessie. Jessie's beautiful and smart and talented. Look at that portrait. Did you think I bought that so that you'd have dinner with me? Do you know how many people have tried to buy it off me? Think of how talented and lovely you are—" His hands on her shoulders, she allowed herself to be turned around to face him "—and how deeply I've fallen in love with you."

She collapsed against him. They had embraced before, but never like this, and they had kissed before with affection, but never like this. "Jimmy you've been so patient." At last she felt capable of being the lover she wanted to be. "Shall we stay where we are or do you want to carry me up the stairs to bed?"

He stood her on her feet. "I'm taking you home."

"What?"

"You picked a hell of a time to say yes. I'm due at the airport in an hour. You think I want to rush our first night of love?"

He dropped her at her door in Lennox Gardens. "Sleep well, darling. I'll be back in a few days," he said, adding as an afterthought, "And do me a favor. Wear that Mickey Mouse T-shirt to bed. That's how I want to find you when I get back."

CHAPTER 8

1974

Jimmy Kolas

He arrived without warning at Jessie's tiny basement flat. It was well after midnight and she was fast asleep in the oversized Mickey Mouse T-shirt she used as a nightgown, with a copy of *Harper's Queen* on her chest. Her first awareness of the intrusion was the sharp piquancy of the citrus fragrance he customarily wore. "Jimmy," she sighed, conjuring in her dreamlike state the man she was afraid to love. The sound of his footsteps on the worn floorboards and the weight of his body on the bed beside her and the flutter of his lips kissing her eyelids brought her to a drowsy voluptuous half-wakefulness. *Jimmy?*

It couldn't be. Jimmy was in Greece, visiting Helios, the remote Aegean island he had recently inherited from an uncle. Convinced she was dreaming, she rolled over only to find something being put in her hand.

"Darling Jessie. Wake up."

Jimmy! In the nanosecond before opening her eyes, she feverishly assessed the situation. Her first consideration was her appearance. He liked her Mickey Mouse T-shirt, yes, but she remembered thinking before she went to bed that she had dripped some tuna salad on it and it needed washing. And her hair! That needed washing, too. Pimples? What the Brits called spots? She had definitely dabbed calamine on her spots before retiring.

Dammit! How the hell had he gotten in? And why was he so sure she wasn't in bed with someone else? It wasn't as if they were engaged or anything.

"Don't turn on the light!" That final embarrassing thing was her sudden recollection of an ice cream container on her night table and her discarded pantyhose and bra on the floor.

"I want to see your face when you open your present."

Jimmy apparently thought that romantic. Jessie did not. She only liked surprises when she was prepared for them. "Please, Jimmy. Go inside. I'll be with you in half a mo'."

She wanted to pee, wash her face, do her teeth, run a brush through her hair, and jump into jeans and a turtleneck. Fortunately, she had done her toenails. The deep crimson Jimmy liked. When she was finished, she sashayed barefoot into her sitting room where Dmitri Andreas Constantine Georgopoulos Kolas, known to his friends as Jimmy, lounged against her mantlepiece languidly smoking a black Sobranie.

He grinned as she read the message scribbled on his embossed calling card. "Beware of Greeks bearing gifts!"

"Be *wary* is more like it. I'm not sure I should accept this."

"You haven't even looked at it." He opened the jewel case for her and removed the bracelet, a blood-red circlet of rubies with a golden coin as a clasp. "It's the head of Athena. My great uncle found it under a fig tree years ago when he discovered Helios." The elder Kolas had been sailing in the Aegean when a sudden storm hurled his yacht against the rocks. As if by magic, the ferocious *meltame* winds ceased and the sun shone brightly on a natural sheltered cove.

The inhabitants consisted of a few fishermen, some

shepherds and their flocks. On the island's rocky heights were the crumbling remains of a monastery. Kolas named the island Helios in honor of the sun god who led him to safe harbor, and he registered the island in his name with the government in Athens.

Except for a primitive seawall he had ordered built to protect the cove, Helios was about the way he found it, sixty years ago, one of thousands of small islands dotting the Aegean Sea and unmarked on charts. After World War II, Jimmy's uncle had installed a radio transmitter and allowed the fishermen to open a taverna at the cove. As for the monastery, he had invited an impoverished order of nuns whose home had been destroyed by the Nazi invaders to make their new home on Helios.

Jimmy had never visited the island until this recent trip to examine his inheritance upon his great uncle's death. "You would love it, Jessie."

"Sounds terrific," she said, draping herself across the sofa.

"Let me take you there."

"You forget. I'm a working stiff. I take pictures for a living."

"I'll commission you to take pictures."

"I don't take pictures of goats. I photograph people— remember?"

"I remember." He grinned irresistibly.

Being alone with him in an enclosed space still unnerved her. She snapped the jewel box closed, allowing it to slip from her hand to the floor.

"Won't you try it on?"

She wiggled her bare foot at him. "I think I'd rather wear it on my ankle. If it will fit."

"Perverse little creature!" He removed the bracelet and opened the catch. "Now give me your foot, Cinderella."

The minute he touched her foot, she knew she'd made a critical mistake. His fingers brushed her instep with lingering insistence and traced the line of her arch with tender appreciation. The ruby bracelet was, as they both knew, designed for the wrist and was much too small to go around her ankle. With a show of exasperation, he ripped the bracelet apart. The rubies scattered like cinnamon drops.

"Here's a better idea." He scooped up the rubies and inserted them one by one between her toes. "Perfect with your nail polish, darling. I'm flattered you remembered."

She thought she knew all about erogenous zones. Apart from the obvious area between her thighs and the inner circles of her ears, she'd discovered the indescribable nuances of her nipples and the corners of her mouth and the subtle volcanic eruption between her shoulder blades. But this was something new. The spaces between her toes were like the connections on an old-fashioned switchboard, sending high-voltage messages upward through her legs, fanning out to every circuit receptor in her body.

Suddenly her panic was gone, her old panic, only to be replaced by a newer, more urgent panic, a silent screaming panic that he would stop, that he would pay her back for past behavior.

"Not to worry, darling." The man was a mind reader. "And not to hurry, either. I'm here. Just for you."

She didn't and he was. In life, doors open, doors close. With Jimmy Kolas there was only one door. He opened it and invited her into a totally new world of heightened experience and closed it firmly behind them, locking out her previous life. Except for her career.

Their first night together, he showed her things she'd never heard of, and he rejoiced as much as she did in the new discoveries. At one point, he said, "Anything you want. Name it. It's yours."

What could she possibly want? An Aston-Martin? A million dollars in nickles and dimes? There really wasn't much in the way of material things. Except, maybe, her own darkroom. That was definitely too much to ask for the moment. Later, maybe. Assuming there was a later.

"What I want you can't give me," she said finally.

His face hardened. "You know I'm married."

She knew the whole story. How he and his wife had gone to Argentina on holiday and how she had run away with some polo player who owned ranches the size of Texas. What did Jessie care? Jimmy was old enough to be her father. Getting hitched was the last thing she wanted to do.

What she wanted was not his to give. It could not be negotiated. It had to be earned. Professional recognition. "You flatter yourself, my love. What I want is to be the world's most famous photographer. That's all. See what I mean?"

He chuckled indulgently, as if she had asked for another ice cream cone. "You will, my darling. Leave it to me. I have friends in high places."

Wrong! Friends in high places would resent the special friend of a rich Greek playboy. Her photographs would have to speak for themselves. "We'll discuss it another time." Meanwhile there were more pressing things to consider.

The next morning, her photo agency called with an assignment to cover an international rock concert at Hyde Park Corner. She'd been in a deep sleep. When she put down the phone, she wondered if she had dreamt the events of the previous night. Had she finally got it together with Jimmy Kolas? For one thing,

she was naked, the Mickey Mouse T-shirt nowhere to
be seen. For another, there were bite marks on her
neck and her lips were voluptuously bruised and swollen. While she was repairing the damage with makeup,
a messenger from Fortnum and Mason's arrived with a
crate of fresh figs from Smyrna. The familiar scrawl
and said simply, "The Greeks have a word for it. Expect
me at midnight!" Midnight? What if the concert went
overtime?

She had vowed love was never going to get in the
way of ambition. All through the concert she watched
the time. Unable to get as close to the stage as she
wanted, she got a better idea. She turned her back on
the performers and prowled through the crowd photographing the fans, full-face closeups of faces of all ages,
shapes, colors, and conditions of servitude to the gods
and goddesses of rock.

At concert's end she scurried to the primitive little
darkroom at back of the photo agency. What emerged
from the developer confirmed her sneaky feeling that
these were the best pictures she'd ever taken. She
would let the negatives dry overnight and print tomorrow. By a few minutes to midnight she was home and
waiting for her lover.

Night followed day in a dizzying dance. With her
senses sharpened, her inhibitions disappeared. She was
no longer hesitant about anything. The freedom she felt
with Jimmy Kolas found its counterpart in her work.
Until now she had often felt her camera to be an intruder, a foolish holdover from the childhood admoni-
tion to "respect other people's privacy."

Now she connected viscerally with her subjects.
Strangers at a concert, celebrities on the run—whoever
and wherever, when she approached with her camera,
they all responded now with forthright honesty. The
first manifestation of this was the series of faces at the

rock concert. Jessie wept as she made the prints for the small show business magazine that had commissioned her. Could this be her work or was it a fluke? Stan Evers, the foreign rights salesman for ABC Photos, rushed a set of contacts over to the London office of *Paris-Match,* who bought them at once.

The following weekend she stayed with Jimmy Kolas at his London house for the first time. Again, she girded herself against the feelings of inadequacy she was certain would come in a Mayfair mansion full of servants. But she didn't feel inadequate. Servants were not exactly top of her wish list. She preferred making her own bed and her own coffee. Scrubbing the bath-tub and vacuuming the floor were chores she paid someone to do once every two weeks.

Since servants were Jimmy's lifestyle, so be it. It was like being in a drawing-room comedy when his man-servant appeared in the bedroom and pretended not to see her while setting up the breakfast table for two. One luxury she had to admit liking was the way the grapefruit was cut into sections and served with a pointed spoon.

I could get used to this. Soaking in the hot tub, she had to admit to a delicious thrill. What would the family say if they could see her now? Rachel had not approved of her going to London in the first place. Her plan had always been for Jessie to take courses in real estate management and work for her. Rachel blamed herself for Jessie's desire to be a professional photographer. She had given her grandchild her first camera at age eight, a sorry little plastic affair that Jessie threw away "by accident."

Her mother had been more supportive, emotionally as well as financially. Hannah was getting ready to marry again, a decent guy this time. Not like Viktor the Nazi. It was still hard for Jessie to believe Viktor was

her father. She had reassured her mother that nothing
would induce her to get in touch with him again. Not
after that trip with him and Eleanor. Just because she
was in London didn't mean she would jump on a plane
to Munich.

Rachel always referred to Eleanor as "the pretty one."
Hannah always worried that Jessie's feelings would be
hurt by her grandmother's tactlessness. Jessie had always assured her mother that she loved her sister and
had to agree that Eleanor was indeed prettier and that
it didn't really bother her. But it had bothered her, and
though she loved her sister more than anyone and did
not resent her gift of nature, the comparison was still
upsetting.

When Jimmy Kolas invited her to fly off to the Greek
islands in his private plane, Jessie wondered idly if she
had embarked on this adventure to prove her attrac-
tions and her ability to snag a man like him. While it
was true that he was married, it was also true that Felicity had filed for divorce. If Jimmy asked her to marry
him, she wondered what she would do.

Meantime, the assignments were pouring in. *Paris-
Match* wanted her for a charity ball in Monaco. No
shots of Grace and Rainier and the kids, though. What
the magazine wanted were the faces of those attending
in the same way she had shot the rock concert fans.

At Hellinikon Airport, a car was waiting to drive
them to Vouliagmeni, where a seaplane waited to take
them on the final lap of their journey to Helios. On instructions from Jimmy, the pilot followed the coast to
Piraeus so she could see the bustling port before veer-
ing inland to where the Acropolis shimmered white and
mysterious in the afternoon sun and the ancient and
modern images of Athens merged in a mixture of temples, Victoriana and plate glass.

He wanted her first sight of the Parthenon to be by

daylight. Tonight, she would see it by moonlight when they returned from Helios. There being no hotel on the island, they would stay at his family's house in Glifada. Heading now for Helios, the pilot made one more detour, dipping low over the ancient Greek ampitheater at Epidaurus. Jimmy pressed the palm of her hand to his lips and held it there with his eyes closed for what seemed a long time before reluctantly releasing her.

"I feel happy when I'm with you, Jessie."

Not knowing what to say, she said nothing.

"Jessie?" He cupped her face in his hands and looked deep into her eyes.

She knew he was waiting for her response but tried to make light of it. "That's my name."

His eyes darkened. "I'm speaking to you from my heart, darling. I feel happy when I'm with you. Tell me how you feel."

She was a literal person. Men were always saying "I love you" the same way they would say they loved baseball or cheeseburgers. It was a private matter of conscience that she would never say "I love you" unless she meant it and so far she hadn't.

Was feeling happy the same as being in love, or was she splitting hairs as a defense mechanism to avoid dealing with the truth? Jimmy Kolas was saying he was happy being with her; he was not saying "I love you." Having made the distinction in her own mind, she could respond with honest and solemn conviction, "I feel happy when I'm with you, too."

What looked like hundreds of islands dotted the vast expanse of the Aegean Sea. Flying low, Jessie could see that many of them were totally barren, while a few were just big enough to accommodate a pagan shrine.

The tiny cove behind the Helios seawall was smooth as satin, the landing soft as goose down. Before she could say *ouzo* they were sipping it under a striped umbrella at the taverna with Yanni Patronis, the newly appointed island caretaker. Licorice. Licorice with a kick. It was hard to believe they had left London this morning. She had to remind herself how small Europe was and how astounding it was that so many countries crammed into so small a space maintained their own separate languages and customs.

"I brought you to Helios for a reason." He was showing her around. She was glad she had taken his advice and brought sturdy walking shoes. There was no road, only a barely discernible footpath. The ouzo had gone to her head, making her giddy and coy.

"You wanted to get me alone, right?"

He elected not to notice. "What I have to say is serious. It can change both our lives." In essence it was this: He was bored with the superficiality of his life in England. Long before he inherited Helios he had thought about what he would do with it. "There's nothing here but the old stone house, this taverna, and, of course, the monastery. Now that it's mine and I can do with it as I please, I want to create something wonderful here. Something that will reflect my heritage."

"You mean like Onassis?"

He spat with contempt. Men like Onassis were a joke, a vulgar joke. Black satin sheets? Breaking dishes in nightclubs? Inviting people of accomplishment to his private island did not mean their accomplishments would rub off on him. Marrying for prestige did not give him the prestige he craved. The Livanos heiress, the Kennedy widow were showpieces acquired for display and the envy of others.

"And Maria Callas?" Jessie asked.

She was his soulmate, the only woman he really loved and felt comfortable with. In betraying her, he betrayed himself.

Jimmy led the way up the invisible path that ended

at the highest point of Helios, the monastery, he sure-footed as a goat, she panting, with a stitch in her side and trying to hide it. No one emerged from the convent. From where they stood Jessie could see the entire island set in a sea of glass extending into infinity. In the distance were blurred intimations of other islands and what seemed like low-lying clouds. Mountains, Jimmy exclaimed. Mountains where once the ancient gods and goddesses lived and loved.

"Shall we pause a moment?" Sometimes his choice of language seemed stilted, as if English were his second language. Now that she thought about it, English *was* his second language. When he wanted to be serious, he thought in Greek and translated into awkwardly phrased English. "Do you feel happy here?"

"Yes."

"Could you spend time here with me?"

Thoughts of her assignments flashed through her mind, exciting assignments with total artistic freedom to photograph what she liked. But yes. She would make the time to spend time here with him.

"You would not rather be shopping in Athens or Paris and having your hair done?"

She couldn't help reminding him of their first night together as lovers. "All I need here is a bottle of red nail polish for my toes!"

"Ah, Jessie! You've come into my life just in time." His fortieth birthday had caused him to take stock. Like Onassis, he was a rich Greek who also broke dishes in restaurants. He too had married an heiress, the Honorable Felicity Dunham-Gray, whom he met at her coming-out dance when both were eighteen. Their children hated them. Their daughter Elizabeth lived in Sri Lanka which was about as far away from England as she could get. Their son Alexander had exchanged his privileged life in the West for a begging bowl in Tibet.

His wife and children had never visited Greece. "It was never *convenient*." In Jessie's three years in England, she had learned the nuances of British English usage as compared to American English usage. "Convenient" was a prime example of British understatement, often coupled with the word "bore." Paying debts was rarely convenient and was also considered a bore. Returning a favor? "Not very convenient, I'm afraid."

"Can't we stay here tonight?" she asked.

He stared at her with disbelief. "Do you mean that? I thought you'd prefer the house in Glifada. Dinner at the Plaka. The Acropolis by moonlight."

There was something holding her here, something that was part of her destiny. "I'd like us to spend our first night in Greece right here on your island."

As if on cue, the door to the convent opened. A wizened old woman in black addressed them in Greek. A spirited conversation with Jimmy followed. "They can give us a place to sleep in the bell tower. But not to worry. There's no bell." There was no bed either. The nuns gave them a supper of goat cheese and bread with fresh olive oil so sharp it bruised her tongue, washed down with a sweet homemade wine that felt like molten lava halfway down her gullet.

They slept in their clothes on thick multicolored mats woven by the nuns, content in each other's arms until dawn brought with it a pale pink light and the scent of the morning sea. They made love quietly before descending to the cove and the gently bobbing seaplane.

She had never felt such quiet happiness before, never such completeness in all of her twenty-one years, never such oneness with another human being. In London, what she felt for Jimmy Kolas was a wild sexual passion heightened with the excitement of being able to make him want her in turn. Being with him on Helios gave new meaning to their relationship. As the seaplane circled in farewell, she knew she would return to Helios with Jimmy and that her life would change dramatically because of it.

There would be no time for Athens, after all. They had only flown out for the weekend. Jimmy had meetings in the City. She was scheduled to go behind the scenes at the Savoy Hotel for one of those Great Hotel pieces the travel magazines love.

"So what shall we do with Helios, darling?"

We? No doubt about it. They were now a couple. Despite the fact that Jimmy was already half of another couple. When the Bentley collected them at Gatwick, Jimmy did not ask Jessie where she wanted to be dropped. "Hill Street," he instructed the driver. There was no need for discussion. Jessie would be living with him from this night forward.

"I'm keeping my flat," she informed him just before falling asleep.

"So you can take lovers?"

"Of course. You know how insatiable I am. Five, ten men a day!"

"Darling—"

"That's on a slow day, of course. Remember those stories about Catherine the Great?"

The idea both amused and aroused him. "My darling, Jessie. You can't begin to know how much you delight me."

Her reason for keeping the flat was the basic need for independence. A place for her cameras and records and books. A place to be alone when she needed to be alone. A place to be a slob and eat out of cans and let dirty laundry pile up.

And then there was her family. She hadn't run away

from home and slammed the door behind her. She had simply left home with their loving good wishes that she would find what she was seeking, supplemented by regular deposits of dollars at the Chemical Bank to smooth the way. However, the fact remained that Jimmy Kolas was twice her age and married. She couldn't just send everyone a change-of-address card without explaining why she was moving to Mayfair.

Of course, you never could tell how people might react. To Eleanor, Jessie could do no wrong. Rachel might play matriarch and insist she return home at once. Or she might send a black lace peignoir from Bergdorf's with instructions to enjoy herself, life was short.

Hannah was the one who would hit the roof if she ever found out. With one bad marriage behind her, Hannah was about to try again. Her advice to her younger daughter remained consistent. "Do as I say, not as I do."

CHAPTER 9

1975

Jerry

It was Hannah's wedding day.

Happy the bride. Sleepy the groom. Jerry lay sprawled across her bed. Correction. Their bed. Snoring gently. Mouth open. Sleep crumbs in the corners of his eyes. This man was her lover. Today her lover would disappear forever. When they got back from the ceremony, the bed would be *their* bed and the man beside her in it would be her husband.

She felt confident about this marriage. It was going to work because it was based on reality. Loving and considerate, romantic and fun, and most of all *real*, warts and all.

How naive she had been to think she could have changed Viktor's arrogant contempt for Americans, including her? How foolish she had been to forgive his assertion that the Jews of Europe brought the holocaust on themselves! It had taken several years and several love affairs for her to conclude that marriage was not for her. She did not wish to be a good listener, crying towel, sex slave, or cafeteria. She was bored stiff with pathetic tales of ex-wives, lawyers, rotten kids, digestive problems, and she was tired of whining self-pity.

She had a home. She had money. She had a family. She didn't need a breadwinner. She didn't need to get laid. What she did need was romance. Not a stud with

the I.Q. of a turtle. A man of intelligence and wit
and—God, are you listening?—a sense of the moment.

On impulse, she had answered an ad in the person-
als and that's how she met Jerry.

As if hearing his name, he stirred in his sleep. From
out of nowhere the old superstition came to mind. It
was bad luck for the groom to see the bride on their
wedding day. An old wives' tale. She didn't believe in
superstitions. Her sleep mask lay on the night table on
her side of the bed.

"What are you doing?" He laughed as she covered his
eyes with it. He gathered her into his arms and pulled
her under the covers. "Who is this lovely creature? Is
this a nubile virgin, a prenuptial gift from Hannah?" He
caressed her breasts with extravagant sighs. "No . . . no
. . . it isn't a nubile virgin! It could only be one woman
in the entire world." He pressed his masked face into
her bosom. "Darling—"

"No! Please *don't!*" She stopped him from taking off
the sleep mask.

His levity turned to concern. She did not resist when
he took away her hands and pushed up the mask.
"What is it, Hannah? Why are you crying?"

She explained about the superstition. "I feel so ridiculous, but I can't help it. I love you so much. I'm so
happy with you. I don't want anything to go wrong."

Nothing was going to go wrong, he assured her. He
put the sleep mask on. "But if you'd rather lead me
down to City Hall like this, it's okay with me. You can
even put a chain around my neck. A lamb led to
slaughter. I don't care. I love you and we're going to get
married. Besides, Kathleen flew all the way in from Se-
attle to be a witness. We can't be rude, can we?"

She took the sleep mask and tossed it over her
shoulder. "Do we have time for a quick one?"

An old joke. A private joke. A loving joke.

"If I get you back in bed, we'll never get married. What time is Kathleen getting here?"

Hannah looked at the clock. "Now! She'll be here any minute so we can have a nice visit while I get ready."

He was out of bed and standing beside her. It always amazed her to see how boyish he looked in his rumpled pajamas and overnight beard. Perhaps it was his eyes that were so bright and clear and direct. His jawline had begun to lose its definition, his neck was gnarled. The lines around his eyes and the brackets framing his mouth were etched deep. His hairline, as Rachel relentlessly noted, had receded exponentially. His body, so familiar to Hannah, had thickened and softened in their time together. So it must be the eyes, the windows of his soul that bespoke the optimism that was organic in his nature and the key to their happiness.

"I know what's really bothering you, Hannah."

She had been insisting that it didn't matter, but of course now that her wedding day was here it did matter. It mattered terribly that none of her family would be with them for the occasion. Rachel had taken Marcus to the Mayo Clinic for more tests. Eleanor had called in tears to say she'd had another miscarriage so she and Luke and Jason would not be driving down.

"Why don't Jerry and I run up and see you?" Hannah asked. Her daughter was in trouble. The wedding could wait a few days. With any other son-in-law, Hannah would have dropped everything and raced to Eleanor's side. But Luke the Great Stone Face made it clear that he did not like his in-laws or want them around. "Nothing personal," her daughter had assured her. "He's just a private person."

Eleanor might need her but didn't want her. Luke came first. Hannah would have to be satisfied with phone calls. She knew Luke was furious with Eleanor for getting pregnant again. She knew their doctor had warned them that another pregnancy could be dangerous. She knew that Eleanor had lied to her husband about taking birth control pills. Luke chose to think it was Hannah who urged his wife to ignore the doctor. The truth of course was that Eleanor loved being pregnant and desperately wanted another child.

As for Jessie, Hannah tried not to worry about her twenty-one-year-old daughter living alone in London. She had to hand it to the kid. Selling her photographs to newspapers and magazines. When the copy of *Paris-Match* arrived with Jessie's work on the cover, Hannah had been furious that Rachel had taken credit for Jessie's success. "If you remember," Rachel said smugly, "I gave her that camera for her eighth birthday!"

What about genes? What about inherited creativity? Hannah credited herself for at least some of Jessie's talent. Hadn't she worked for the Red Bank newspaper during the war and written articles over the years? And wasn't she the one who gave Jessie her first decent camera to replace the plastic cheapie Rachel had bought? Hadn't Hannah nurtured Jessie's self-confidence so that she could go off and do something so bold and exciting as become an international professional photographer?

When she and Jerry set the wedding date, Hannah had telephoned Jessie's flat and left a message on her machine. When Jessie didn't call back, Hannah concluded she was away on assignment. She called the photo agency that handled Jessie's work. They didn't know where she was. They would take a message. After several more messages left with the machine, including an offer to buy Jessie a round trip ticket to fly home, Hannah gave up.

Thank God for Kathleen. It was probably just as well that Rachel wouldn't be here. After more than forty years, her mother still thought of Kathleen as "the Irish girl" who migrated to America during the depths of the Depression and worked for them as a live-in maid. Hannah and Sam had adored her. Some five years older than Sam and seven years older than Hannah, Kathleen became the center of their world, the teller of tall tales, the teacher of jigs and songs, the maker of soda bread and real corned beef and cabbage. Their older sister; their best friend. Their source of love when Rachel was too busy to provide it.

Kathleen was Hannah's only link to her life before the war and to her brother Sam. If he had lived, he and Kathleen would have married and she'd have become her sister-in-law as well as the sister of her heart. Having her as witness at Hannah's wedding would make up for the absence of her mother and daughters.

Jerry was taking his shower when Kathleen arrived bearing a familiar shaped package. She curtsied deferentially, addressing Hannah with an *Oirish* accent. "And a top o' the mornin' to ye, Ma'am. Would ye be wantin' some fine Irish soda bread?"

On her way from the hotel, she had stopped at Zabar's for some real sweet butter to spread on the soda bread instead of Hannah's margerine, and heavy cream to pour into the strong fresh coffee instead of the skim milk in the instant decaf that had confronted her on her previous visit.

"Ahhh," they sighed in chorus, an echo of a ritual whose origins were forgotten but that reestablished their connection each time they met, like the password of a secret society.

They were deep into a discussion about whether Hannah should wear pearls when Jerry joined them in the kitchen just long enough to kiss Kathleen and announce he was going out.

"I knew it! He's running away with another woman!" Kathleen teased.

"It's okay with me; it lets me off the hook." Hannah shrugged playfully, she thought, until she saw Jerry's face. This was not a teasing matter. How could she be so stupid and insensitive! She jumped up from the kitchen table and threw her arms around his neck. "Darling, I'm sorry. It was dumb of me to say that. Forgive me. I love you. If you ran out on me, I'd die."

His body had turned as rigid as the expression on his face. He had stopped breathing and stood in the circle of her embrace, his stance cold and hard as stone. In sudden panic, Hannah clutched him convulsively to her, raising his unresponsive arms to her shoulders and murmuring, "Please, please," until she felt him relax and crush her to him.

They stood silently swaying, oblivious to Kathleen, who tried to make herself invisible by looking out the window.

"I'm sorry, Kathleen," Jerry said sheepishly.

"I'm the one who should apologize. I'd forgotten how nerve wracking a wedding day can be." Her own husband of eighteen years had got so drunk at his bachelor's party he'd been sick as a dog on their wedding day and had slept through the first two days of their honeymoon.

"He's just going to get the flowers," Hannah explained as Jerry left the apartment. "He's got terrible taste in corsages. The night he formally proposed, he brought me a spray of six orchids. So don't be surprised at what he brings back."

They had barely returned to their coffee and the matter of the pearls when the doorbell rang. "Did he forget his shoes?" Kathleen teased. Once before, Jerry had left the apartment in his bedroom slippers.

"Remember me?" For a moment the face didn't register. "Don't tell me you don't recognize me!"

"Viktor!" Flustered but too shocked to protest, Hannah opened the door. "Kathleen! Come here!" she called nervously.

"I just got in from Munich this morning," Viktor said genially, walking past Hannah into the living room. "I have an appointment just up the road. I thought you'd like to see this." The glossy magazine looked at first glance like the edition of *Paris-Match* with Jessie's photos on the cover, except that it was in German.

"Where is our lovely daughter? I want to congratulate her!" Surprised and angered though she was, Hannah maintained her composure and answered him coldly. "Jessie's not here. You could have saved yourself a trip."

She signaled the end of the visit by moving toward the door.

"But Hannah—" He made her embarrassed that she ever loved him—a slimebag with sex appeal. "You do not offer me a coffee?" The sly challenge of asking for one thing and meaning another had not lost its ability to throw her off balance.

As Hannah wavered imperceptibly, Kathleen stepped in to save the day. "You'll have to excuse us, Viktor. We're in a bit of a hurry. We're getting ready for a—"

A warning look from Hannah cut her short in midsentence.

Viktor was quick to realize Hannah was rattled. "Then it's true?"

"What's true?"

"That you're getting married today? You see, I rang Rachel's office. She was out but her secretary told me the news." So he hadn't just dropped in. He'd come to amuse himself by causing trouble. Not this time, Buster. She opened the front door. Kathleen took Viktor by the elbow and together they eased him into the hall. Good manners almost ruined the effect. Hannah could feel herself about to say, "Do give me a call the next time you're in town." Instead, she bit her tongue and said only, "Thank you for the magazine."

Kathleen and Hannah huddled beside the door, listening for Viktor's receding footsteps and the sound of the elevator door opening and closing. "Thank God he's gone," Hannah sighed in relief.

"Don't be too sure. He could still be outside." Kathleen opened the door. The hall was empty. Maybe she was right. He might decide to linger in the lobby to see where they went. She wouldn't put anything past him. He enjoyed mischief for its own sake.

"Pablo?" The doorman answered the intercom. Had a gentleman just left? Yes; did she want him to call him? No; she just wanted to be sure he had left the premises. While she had him, she reminded the doorman never to answer questions or give information to strangers. "And incidentally, why did you let him come upstairs without buzzing?" The lobby sign clearly proclaimed that all visitors must be announced.

Viktor had evidently worked his magic on Pablo. "Oh, it was okay. He said it was a surprise."

" *'You do not offer me a coffee?'* " Kathleen crooned as the two women returned to the kitchen.

Hannah tried to laugh but couldn't. Thank God Jerry was out. She was twitchy enough without having to deal with a confrontation between Viktor and Jerry. Thank God Kathleen had been here to help her throw Viktor out before he spoiled her wedding day. She couldn't have done it alone. She probably would have reverted to form and served him his coffee and hovered nervously for his nod of approval, and Jerry would have found them thus when he returned with their nuptial flowers.

Wedding day nerves. That was why tradition provided for attendants, handmaidens, loving supporters to ease the transition from bride to wife. Well, she didn't have her family but she had her friend. In fact, she was relieved her family wasn't here to steal the day's spotlight, shoving her and Jerry aside as extras in somebody else's soap opera. Her daughters would have been embarrassed. Rachel would somehow blame her for her first husband's behavior. Bless Kathleen for being in the right place at the right time. "Thank you for being my friend," she said, giving her a quick hug.

The two women resumed their places at the kitchen table, sipping the strong hot coffee laced with real cream and real sugar, no substitutes, thank you, each remembering in her own way the summer of 1944 when Kathleen and Sam got engaged behind Rachel's back and Hannah had her first glimpse of Viktor from a Jersey beach when he swam ashore from a Nazi U-Boat.

The one thing that always made them laugh was Hannah's high school graduation. "Remember how surprised my mother was to see you there?"

"To her I'll always be the Irish maid," Kathleen sighed, philosophically.

CHAPTER 10

1944

Samuel

The June 1944 graduating class of Julia Richman High School marched solemnly down the center aisle of the vast auditorium and took their places on the stage facing the family and friends in attendance. It had been two and a half years since Pearl Harbor. Uniforms of the various military services punctuated the profusion of bright summer dresses and flower-trimmed hats.

Fingers crossed, Hannah scanned row after row of eager faces until she found the one she most wanted to see. Samuel had managed to get leave after all. When he called from Fort Monmouth last night there was still some doubt, some question of Signal Corps maneuvers to test out the latest communications equipment on the Jersey shore around Long Branch. Rumors of Nazi U-Boats in Atlantic coastal waters had accelerated the vigilance of the beach patrols. As he would explain later over lunch, he had told the commanding officer that his kid sister's graduation was essential to his wartime morale.

In the dim light, she could see a female uniformed figure on one side of him and an empty seat on the other. Her mother was late, of course. "She'll be late for her own funeral!" Kathleen often said, especially when she had cooked a splendid meal only to have it dried out and leathery waiting for Rachel. *Kathleen?* Could the uniformed figure be Kathleen? When she and Sam stood up to let Rachel get by, Hannah saw that it was indeed Kathleen in her WAC uniform. From Hannah's vantage point, she could see that Kathleen and Sam were holding hands and when Rachel motioned Sam to move so that she could sit between him and Kathleen he had smilingly refused, and eased his mother into her designated place with himself between the two women.

This was to be a day of great personal satisfaction for Hannah and a few surprises for her mother. For one thing Hannah had not mentioned being the class valedictorian with the highest grade-point average on record or that she had won the Nellie Bly Journalism Award as editor-in-chief of the *Richman News*. For another, Sam had been made an instructor at Fort Monmouth and had taken an apartment off the base in Red Bank. A friend of his knew the publisher of the Red Bank newspaper and had promised to help Hannah get a summer job as a cub reporter. The plan was for Hannah to share Sam's apartment and of course to meet handsome young officers. "With me as chaperone," Sam had warned.

And who was going to chaperone Sam and Kathleen, she wondered. They had told her they were deeply in love, that the affectionate feelings of ten years in the same household had blossomed into a beautiful pairing of souls. They had taken her alone into their confidence. It was understood that Rachel was not to know, not yet. When the United States entered the war, Kathleen had given Rachel notice and taken a job in a uniform factory in Brooklyn while completing her bachelor's degree in education at Brooklyn College at night.

Rachel had been furious. "The girl's an ingrate. After all I've done for her. Giving her a home. Paying for her education. How dare she walk out on me?" It did no good to remind Rachel that the home she gave

Kathleen was part of the job and that the younger woman's education at Brooklyn College was free.

Hannah was wondering how her mother would react to Kathleen's presence beside Sam and the fact that Kathleen was joining them for lunch, when she heard herself being summoned to the dais to give her valedictory speech. The astonishment on her mother's face was a just reward for the months of grueling study. The glowing pride emanating from Sam and Kathleen added another dimension to her joy.

The theme of her speech was the responsibility of young people in wartime to do their utmost to participate in the present effort while also preparing to be useful productive citizens in the glorious era of peace that was soon to come. As she went on, her voice rose with conviction and triumph. "The war has taught us that we are not alone. That we must not lead separate, selfish lives. That we must work together for the common good. That we must help each other to reach the outer limits of our dreams."

After thanking individual teachers who had helped her and paying tribute to those who had left school to join the armed forces, she concluded, "And most of all I want to thank the four people who have been most instrumental in my development as a student and a woman. My brother Samuel, who is with us today in uniform as a second lieutenant with the Signal Corps. Kid sisters can be annoying little brats and I was like any other. But Sam always came to the rescue. Always helped me with my homework. Always wiped my tears and told me I was pretty in my braces. Always assured me I could be the best.

"Second on my list is Kathleen Fenton. She's here, too. She came all the way from Dublin Ireland during the worst of the depression to live with us. It was she who brought ethical standards to Sam and me and proved what a privilege it is for all of us to be Americans. In her short time here, she has earned her bachelor's degree at Brooklyn College and become an American citizen, and she is now a member of the Women's Army Corps."

After a pause for applause, she wound up her remarks. "And last but not least I want to thank both my parents for giving me life." A glance at Rachel revealed tears coursing down her cheeks. Feeling curiously poised and unmoved by her mother's response, she resumed, "Although my father left us when I was eight, he also left a legacy of kindness and encouragement to a little girl in need of both. And most of all, may I express my gratitude to my mother for her strength and commitment to excellence. She has taught me by her example to stand alone and meet every challenge with the best I can offer plus a little bit more. Thank you, Mother, for helping to make this the proudest day of my life."

Later, after the hugs and kisses and flowers and photographs and promises among classmates to stay in touch, Rachel followed her daughter into the cloakroom where the graduates were collecting their things. Her voice trembled with emotion. "Why didn't you tell me?"

"I tried, but you were too busy."

"Mothers and daughters are supposed to be at each other's throats, aren't they?"

"We were never at each other's throats. We were never close enough for that. The truth is, you love Samuel more than you love me—"

"Darling—"

"—and frankly, I don't blame you, Mother. I love Sam more than I love me!"

Samuel himself chose that moment to knock on the door. "Come on, you two. They won't hold the table."

"Can we try to be friends?" Rachel implored.

Seeing her mother's weakened condition, Hannah seized the moment. She announced her plans to share Sam's apartment in Red Bank and to work as a reporter on the Red Bank newspaper. "Won't it be wonderful? You can visit us on weekends."

Rachel rallied sufficiently to demand, "But what about college! You're not skipping college to work on some jerkwater paper. You've got the talent to be the next Dorothy Thompson! The next Marguerite Higgins—"

"It's just for the summer, Mother. I'll be going to Barnard in the fall." She couldn't resist adding, "We did discuss it, you know."

By the time lunch was over, Rachel had managed to turn Hannah's Day into Mother's Day. It was Rachel who wept through her daughter's speech. It was Rachel who was so overwhelmed by Hannah's tribute to her that she nearly fainted and had to hang on to Sam's hand so she wouldn't spoil everything for her daughter. It was Rachel who clutched the arms of her son and daughter while urging Kathleen to follow her example, marry and have children of her own so that she too could experience the joys of motherhood.

"You look radiant, Kathleen."

"Thank you, Ma'am!"

Rachel didn't get the reference to their former relationship. "No, I mean it. Are you in love? She looks as if she's in love, doesn't she, Sam? Make her tell us who it is!"

Sam raised his champagne glass. "It is true, Kathleen? Are you in love?" Kathleen's fair freckled coloring turned brick red.

"You're embarrassing her, Sam. She'll tell us when she's ready, won't you, Kathleen?"

Kathleen raised her champagne glass. "To love." Her

eyes lingered for a moment on Sam's and then moved to include the other two women. "To my American family!"

She would have denied it, but the champagne had gone to Rachel's head. "I'm so proud of you, Kathleen." A verbal pat on the head for the serving wench from the lady of the manor. "You've done so well, considering your background," Rachel said, conveniently forgetting her own orphaned and destitute beginnings. It was an ongoing joke among the three young people that Rachel persisted in the notion that Kathleen grew up in a shack and slept with the pigs. While surely money had been a misery in the Gardner Street district of Dublin, there had been more books than in the Riverside Drive apartment.

"Gratitude!" Rachel rambled on. "It's a rare and beautiful thing, isn't it, Sammy dear. Isn't it wonderful that our Kathleen isn't ashamed to show her gratitude to me for bringing her to America and teaching her to read and sending her to college?"

They'd all three heard this litany before. There was little use in pointing out the disparities. Rachel had sponsored Kathleen and had treated the "Irish girl" far better than the many others Kathleen shared experiences with on her days off at Holy Name Church. She'd had a room and bath of her own next to the kitchen—the maid's room they called it, but it was Buckingham Palace to Kathleen. With Rachel away all day, she'd been given the run of the house, the money to buy food, the kelvinator to store it in instead of the cold press at home that was often empty, plenty of hot water for the laundry and lovely baths with Hannah's bubbles, and two lovely children instead of the eight brothers and sisters she'd cared for at home. It didn't matter that Rachel rewrote history. Kathleen was indeed grateful. Feeling Sam's knee against hers under the table, she was grateful for more than Rachel knew. For the time being.

Throughout his mother's bravura performance, Sam had quietly eaten his shrimp cocktail and chicken divan, smiling benignly until she ran out of steam. He loved his mother dearly, however much she exasperated him. More to the point, he understood her excessive need to be the center of attention. He had shielded Hannah from the truth about their father's suicide and Rachel's desperate means of keeping the family together.

He had never discussed it with his mother. He wasn't sure if she knew that he knew how bad things were and how they would have been out on the street, living in a cardboard shack for nonpayment of rent if Rachel had not become Marcus Salinko's mistress.

He had seen other families destroyed by the Depression. He knew other children who had been sent to live with relatives or put in orphanages. Rachel had grown up in an orphanage. The way she told it, of course, an orphanage was more fun than a mansion on Fifth Avenue.

"We're all grateful to you, Mom," Sam soothed when Rachel became weepy.

Though Hannah tried valiantly to rise to the occasion, Sam was startled to see that the look on her face had the same sad defeat as the day of her tenth birthday party. She had been the heroine until Rachel barged in. Now, once again, Rachel was muscling in on her daughter's moment of glory.

Rachel's behavior was beyond his understanding. Whatever the reason, he was going to see to it that Hannah had a wonderful summer, working on the Red Bank newspaper and meeting the handsome young officers at Fort Monmouth. After all her hard work, he wanted her to have fun, a little freedom, and maybe even fall in love.

He knew from Kathleen that his sister had cried bitterly for days after that long-ago birthday party. Hannah could never understand why her mother was out of town when all the party preparations had to be made, then showed up when the party was almost over. And why she lied about the pearls.

Sam knew why. He would never tell Hannah as long as they lived. Maybe when they were in their nineties and Rachel was dead it would be okay. Rachel had not gone to Chicago on business. She had gone to be with Marcus Salinko. She had avoided accompanying him on other trips. This time he had put her on notice. He wanted her with him. If she didn't comply, she and the kids could pack their bags.

Rachel had not told Marcus about Hannah's birthday. When he found out, he was angry. How dare she make her little girl unhappy? He had sent her back to New York on the first train.

It was a birthday party Sam would never forget.

CHAPTER 11

1935

Kathleen

"Wake up, pet! It's your *birthday*, darlin'! Rise and shine, sleepyhead!"

Kathleen Fenton drew back the drapes with the expected squeaks of the metal rings grating against the metal curtain rod. Next came the window shades. With a deft yank on the pull cord, they flapped upward like thunderclaps, enough to wake the dead.

Not Hannah. Ten years old today, Hannah lay dead to the world under a mountain of covers, only her hair visible, her fifth grade reader on the floor, an empty Black Crows box beside it. Eating licorice in bed when the dentist warned her she had soft teeth and would lose every one of them before she was twenty if she weren't careful.

"Are you really asleep, pet?" Kathleen whispered. "Or are you playing me for a muggins?" Hannah did not move, but her breathing gave her away. "Enough of this foolishness!" With that, Kathleen pulled away the covers. The girl tried to prolong the game, burrowing her head into the pillow to stifle her giggles. Her heaving shoulders gave her away, but Kathleen continued the game.

"Poor little thing. Is she asleep or did she die during the night? Is this a corpse I'm seeing? Her mother, her brother will never forgive me. We'll have to cancel the birthday party. Ah, me. I'll try one more thing to see if she's alive or dead."

Hannah's toes curled in an effort to endure what was to come without moving. It was impossible. At the first tickle on her instep, she rose up shrieking with laughter and hugging Kathleen good morning.

Abruptly, Kathleen pulled away as she spotted something at the foot of the bed. "You promised not to."

"I'm sorry. I must have fallen asleep," Hannah said meekly.

"You'd be sorrier if you set the bed on fire and you were burned alive like St. Joan of Domremy." The little plastic radio had burnt through the sheet and the mattress cover and a brownish stain was spreading on the mattress itself. The radio being too hot to touch and turn off, Kathleen crept up on the electric outlet above the molding and carefully disconnected the plug.

Hannah stared at the charred result of her folly. Although last night Kathleen had brought her her Little Orphan Annie mug of steaming hot Ovaltine, she'd been unable to sleep. She was worried sick about her birthday party, worried that nobody would come and even more worried about the preparations. Rachel had said she'd take care of everything. But Rachel was in Chicago. On business.

And now today was the day. As far as Hannah could tell, nothing had been done. Weeks ago, Rachel had talked grandly about decorations and games and even a magician. Then she was called away suddenly to Chicago and had left without a backward glance, without a thought to Hannah's party.

The ten little girls would be arriving at four. Girls only. No boys. That's what Cecily Greenberg's party was like, including the magician who cut out designs from newspapers. That's what Hannah desperately wanted, and that Rachel should be like Cecily Greenberg's mother and that nothing should go wrong.

Now she'd gone and done it again, falling asleep with the radio under the covers. Rachel would kill her, make her pay for the sheet out of her allowance even if it took a hundred years.

"Please don't tell!" Hannah cried, and Kathleen held the girl to her, the needy child reminding her of her own baby sisters. Bridget and Mary Elizabeth were always in trouble and running to her.

"And why would I be doing that? Am I a squealer?"

"But the sheets! She'll see it. She'll know!" Hannah remembered the time she had measles when she was six and had wet the bed, an accident, of course, after the medicine made her too groggy to get out of bed in the middle of the night.

"Who makes the beds around here? Your mother or me? Calm yourself," Kathleen said. "Besides, your mother isn't even here."

"I know!" Hannah wailed. "And my party's ruined!"

Kathleen hesitated. "Ah, then. There was a telephone call from Chicago early this morning with a message. Your mother took the sleeper and will be home this afternoon. Isn't that wonderful news?"

"But what about the decorations and . . . the magician?"

"She said to tell you to go ahead and hire the magician."

Go ahead? How could she go ahead? Where could she find a magician? The girls were coming at four! "Oh, Kathleen! What am I going to do? Let's call it off. Let's call everybody and say I'm dead. I have infantile paralysis. They're putting me in an iron lung. Oh, Kathleen. The girls are going to make fun of me. I know it. They'll laugh at me!"

"Happy birthday, to you! Happy birthday to you!

Happy birth-day dear Hannah . . ." Sam stood in the doorway of his sister's bedroom, tall and awkward for his thirteen years, his Adam's apple prominent in the elongated column of his neck. He was dressed for his regular Saturday morning football scrimmage in Central Park and carried a heavily ribboned birthday gift.

"Hey, what's up? You sick or something? You can't be. It's your birthday! I brought you a present." Hannah had thrown herself on her bed with such despair, Sam hesitated to approach her. "What is it, Kathleen? Should we call the doctor?"

Kathleen made every loyal attempt to excuse Hannah's behavior. Times were hard. Their mother, poor thing, had no husband and had the entire burden of keeping them all together, paying the rent, buying the food and the clothes and the ice skates and the bicycles and all. She couldn't do everything, Kathleen reasoned, though she knew all three of them agreed in their hearts that it was a poor thing to forget about Hannah's birthday, magician and all.

Sam's face became so serious he looked like a schoolroom portrait of the young Abe Lincoln. Trying to keep things lighter, he teased, "That's what you get for not inviting the boys to the party! You and your girlfriends needs boys to dance with, right, Kathleen?" He whirled her around. Hannah kept her eyes clenched shut and refused to respond.

Having been banished from the apartment until after the birthday party, Sam had arranged to go downtown with some of his teammates after practice and go to the penny arcade in Times Square and maybe sneak into the Paramount through an unguarded side door.

"Wash your face, Hannah," Kathleen said.

"No!"

"How about a smile? It's your birthday? You're twenty-five years old!" Sam tried to tease it out of her.

"No."

"How about opening my present? I'll be insulted if you don't."

With sniffling reluctance, she tore off the ribbon and paper. The box gave no clue to its contents. A small tab invited her to pull it. "Something's not kosher."

"Go ahead. Open it!"

Her attempt to peer cautiously inside erupted with a shriek as the jack-in-the-box sprang into the air. "Oh, you! I hate you!" She pounded him lovingly on his chest, accelerating her attack by hurling her entire body at him with her legs around his waist, trying to slap his face and pull his ears while he pretended to fight her off. "Help me, Kathleen! She's a wildcat. She's going to kill me! Save me, Kathleen!"

There were eight hours until the guests would arrive. The football practice and penny arcade would still be there tomorrow. "When Mom's away, I'm the head of the family," Sam declared at breakfast. "We'll do what Mom does. We'll make lists."

Kathleen had already baked the layers for the birthday cake. She planned to do the icing and write "Happy Birthday, Hannah" at the last minute. What they did not have was everything else: the paper tablecloth, napkins, and hats. The frilly baskets and the candies to fill them. The paper plates and cups for the ice cream and cake and the chocolate milk and soda.

And balloons! There had to be balloons and crepe paper, too. Cecily Greenberg's mother draped the entire dining room in crepe paper. And games? Rachel had thought they could play Pin the Tail on the Donkey.

"Baby stuff!" Hannah wailed now. Cecily Greenberg played Musical Chairs, but she had a piano. Hannah didn't have a piano. They had the victrola and Dad's old Paul Whiteman records that Mom didn't like them to play. But games meant prizes. They added prizes to the list.

Hannah had been carried away with optimism but now, once again, her face fell. "I told Stephanie and Susan we were having a magician."

"We'll have something better than a magician," Sam promised.

"Better?" What could be better than a magician?

"You just leave it to me."

Kathleen followed him to the phone and beamed proudly at him while he called one of his classmates to say he wouldn't be at practice and explain about the surprise he was planning for his kid sister's birthday.

By three-thirty everything was in readiness. The dining room was a pink-and-white crepe paper palace with bunches of balloons tied to the chandelier. The birthday table was set. Each guest's name was inscribed on the individual party basket at each plate. It was Sam's idea to have a separate box of Cracker Jack for each guest, so they could all have a prize whether they won or lost the games.

Waiting in the kitchen were platters of cookies and chicken salad sandwiches. Sodas and pitchers of chocolate milk were in the Kelvinator to stay cold until served. The ice trays had been removed to accommodate Dixie Cups packed in dry ice.

The birthday cake stood in lonely splendor in the pantry, covered with enough sugar roses so that each girl would get one in her portion and no hurt feelings. Kathleen had not forgotten the look on Hannah's face after Cecily's birthday, when she insisted it didn't matter she didn't get a sugar flower.

The living room furniture had been pushed back and chairs from various other rooms arranged in the middle for Musical Chairs. Prizes including Pick-Up-Sticks,

Big Little Books, and water paints. The Paul Whiteman records were on the turntable ready to go.

"Who is this fairy princess?" Sam called. "Kathleen, what have you done with my little sister?"

With Kathleen beaming behind her and fluffing out the yellow taffeta party dress, Hannah emerged from her room to beam at her brother. Kathleen had rolled up Hannah's hair in rags to make it wavy and brushed it silky as Alice in Wonderland over her shoulders. Since Rachel wasn't there to notice, Kathleen had applied a touch of Tangee lipstick she wore on her day off, and tucked one of Rachel's white linen hankies into the girl's puffed sleeve. The white knee socks were immaculate, the black patent slippers polished to a high shine.

Hannah's poise was short lived. "What if they don't come? Are you sure they got their invitations? Nobody mentioned the party at school yesterday. What if Mom forgot to mail them?" This new possibility weighed heavily until suddenly the doorbell announced the first guests. Kathleen had changed into her good gray silk adorned with the brooch that had belonged to her grandmother. It was a traditional Claddagh brooch, two hands holding a heart, an expression of love and continuity. On impulse, she pinned it on Hannah's bodice. "Now that you're such a fine young lady," she whispered.

It was easy to see that all the guests had spent the afternoon as Hannah had, dressing and primping for the occasion. Velvet and taffeta prevailed. Some of the girls wore Mary Janes, some the flat-heeled slippers Hannah had begged for. Cecily Greenberg, of course, stole the show in a pair of her sister's silk stockings and pumps with cuban heels.

Within minutes, Kathleen and Sam were nodding happily at each other. The party was a success. The gifts were graciously accepted by the little hostess and piled in the wing chair by the window to be opened later. Most wonderful of all, it didn't take long for Hannah to recognize the excitement created by the presence of her thirteen-year-old brother. All the girls her age hated boys, of course, but she couldn't help noticing the blushing sidelong glances in his direction.

"And, now, *ladies!*" Sam twirled an imaginary mustachio. The girls giggled both from the flattery of being called ladies and from the suspense over what was going to happen next.

"Is there going to be a magician? Or a ventriloquist?" Cecily gasped.

"Something better than that," Sam boasted.

Better? He seated them on pillows on the living room floor and snapped his fingers. "Gentlemen!" he called. A small army of his friends entered the room carrying an eight-millimeter projector on a stand and a portable screen. "The drapes, if you please, Kathleen!"

With the room in darkness, he announced, "In honor of Hannah's tenth birthday, we are proud to present a special matinee showing of *Our Gang Comedies!*" Having tried to find a magician with no success, he had remembered his friend Don's father's projector and that there was a place on Columbus Avenue where you could rent cartoons and short subjects.

Kathleen and Sam supervised the proceedings like proud parents. Truth be told, Kathleen thanked Jesus in His mercy for keeping Rachel in Chicago. After the movie, Sam hit on the novel idea of having two games of Musical Chairs, one for the girls, one for the boys, with the winners of each competing for the championship. When it came down to his friend Don versus the formidable—some said pushy—Cecily Greenberg, Sam's whispered appeal to Don to let the girl win proved unnecessary. Inside Cecily's delicately embroid-

ered bodice was the heart of a warrior. When Sam
raised the needle from the record and the music
stopped abruptly, Don never had a chance to be gal-
lant. Cecily knocked him off the chair with a pendulum swing of her hip and a triumphant shout. "I won!
I won!"

Proof of the party's success was further assured
when Cecily sidled up to Hannah and whispered in her
ear, the signal to all the others that Hannah was now
the chosen best friend. "Let's do our homework together, okay?"

Finally it was time for the opening of presents, always an emotional challenge to the guests as well as
the birthday girl. Hannah had watched others in this
situation, including Rachel, and tried to emulate their
delighted smiles and happy cries. She exclaimed, "Just
what I wanted!" and "I love it to pieces!" while remembering to thank the giver by name as her mother had
taught her.

In the midst of this happiness, it occurred to Hannah that Rachel had not yet arrived. The afternoon was
speeding by. Sam and Kathleen had tried to prolong the
games so that Rachel could be there for the gift ceremony and for the refreshments and birthday cake to
follow.

"Go ahead, pet. Your mother will understand,"
Kathleen encouraged.

The gifts were more wonderful than she ever
dreamed possible. A manicure set. A pencil box with
her initials. Monopoly. The latest Nancy Drew mystery.
A Chinese jewelry box with its own key. A fountain pen
that looked familiar until she remembered Enid Co-
hen's brother got three of them for his Bar Mitzvah.

In a separate pile were the family gifts. From Sam,
roller skates to replace the ones she'd left in the playground and was afraid to tell Rachel. From Kathleen, a

white angora sweater she had knitted herself. The last gift, in the biggest and heaviest package of all, had to be from her mother. She had seen Sam bring it in from Rachel's bedroom.

"What is it?" Hannah asked excitedly. Her mother should be here to watch her open it. Other mothers were always there and always hugged their daughters and maybe even cried a little.

"Open it and see!" Sam encouraged.

The guests leaned forward expectantly. *Please God let it be something wonderful! Not pajamas or underwear like Rachel had given her for Christmas.* Her heart pounded. Her hands shook. With everyone watching her, she wanted to drop everything and run. It was the same panicky feeling she'd had in school when she was called up before the assembly to accept the award for the best fifth-grade essay. She wanted to be the center of attention. She envied the girls who were. But when it was her turn, like at this moment, with all eyes on her and Sam and Kathleen grinning in the background, she wanted to die.

Inside the elaborate wrapping was a white box. Inside that? With some help from Sam, she got it out. What was it?

"A little suitcase!" a voice cried out.

"A trunk doll! With clothes!" sighed another.

It was heavy. There was a key.

"Open it!"

"Let's see!"

A typewriter. A grown-up typewriter. Not like the toy typewriter her father had bought her when she was six and taught her to tap out her name, address and the words "I love you." A real typewriter with separate keys in its own carrying case. A piece of Rachel's stationery was in the roller. "Happy Birthday to the next Dorothy Thompson. With all my love to my talented and beautiful daughter." It was signed *Mommy*. In Sam's hand-writing, though Hannah could see he had tried to dis-guise it.

Rachel chose that exact moment to appear in a cloud of Chanel Number 5. Slender and taut as a greyhound, wearing a glen plaid coat with a white fox collar and a brown slouch hat pulled low over one eye, she burst into the room with arms outstretched.

"Happy birthday, darling!"

Hannah's moment of stardom came to an abrupt end. The spotlight instantly shifted to the gorgeous creature making her way through the guests as if she didn't see them and had eyes only for her daughter. She enveloped the girl in an unaccustomed embrace before turning her attention to those watching. "Forgive me, everyone. The train was late from Chicago. I was so afraid I would miss the party entirely!" Another shift, in emotions now, as a wave of sympathy assured her that all the guests shared her anxiety and were as relieved as she was that Rachel had arrived in the nick of time.

"Darling!" She addressed her daughter. "How pretty you look! But what have you done to your hair?"

Kathleen was quick to sense danger. "Isn't she a pic-ture? Just like Alice in Wonderland, she is."

Rachel next set her sights on the boys who were horsing around at the far side of the living room. "Boys? Oh my, when the cat's away, the mice will play! I thought this was going to be a hen party, Hannah." Hannah knew her mother was being unfair. Rachel was supposed to have been here. Hannah often did sneaky things, but this wasn't one of them. How could she be accused of inviting boys behind Rachel's back when Rachel had left the entire thing in her hands?

Now Sam stepped in to smooth the troubled waters. "It was my idea, Mom. We couldn't get a magician so Don brought over his projector and we rented some

Our Gang shorts and the rest of the gang helped put up the decorations and blow up the balloons."

"Clever boy. Thank you, darling." She seemed about to embrace him but sensed that it would embarrass him in front of his friends. To Hannah she said, "I hope you thanked your brother."

"Refreshments, everyone!" Kathleen sang out, throwing open the dining room doors. To accommodate the boys, she had put the extra leaves in the table and quickly made more sandwiches. Chaos reigned as paper hats were donned, whistles blown, snappers snapped. A knocked-over cup of chocolate milk. A flurry of preadolescent tossing of jelly beans between the girls and the boys. The disappearance of all the sandwiches and cookies. And it was time for the birthday cake.

At a signal from Kathleen, Sam led the singing of *Happy Birthday*. The young Irishwoman, radiant from the excitement of the afternoon, entered the dining room, bearing the cake before her on a silver tray as if it were the crown of the ancient Celtic kings.

"That'll do, Kathleen." Rachel relieved her of her burden and with elaborate ceremony placed the tray before her daughter. The eleven candles burned brightly. "Are you sure you can blow them out by yourself? Don't forget to make a wish."

"I'm not a baby!" Hannah snapped. While the other girls giggled in sympathy, she blew out all the candles with one breath. Another lusty chorus of *Happy Birthday* followed. Hannah shut her eyes tight in a silent wish and a beaming Kathleen assured the girls that each would get a sugar rose.

Rachel meanwhile had changed out of her travel clothes into a black crepe Nettie Rosenstein cut on the bias and adorned with a single strand of pearls. It was calculated to impress the other mothers when they arrived to take their daughters home.

"Say cheese!" Sam's friend Don raised his Baby Brownie camera for a shot of Rachel. "Now, Hannah. Stand next to your mother. And no silly faces. You'll break the camera!"

Rachel fussed maternally with her daughter's appearance, puffing up the already-puffed sleeves, smoothing her hand over the bodice. "What's this?" She touched the Claddagh brooch as if it were a bug.

"It's Kathleen's. It belonged to her grandmother."

With a deft movement, Rachel unpinned it and dropped it on the table like a discarded walnut shell. "A lady wears only one piece of jewelry at a time." Smiling benevolently, she raised her perfect manicured hands behind her neck and unhooked her pearls. "For my sweet little Hannah." She fastened them around her daughter's neck. "Your father's last gift to me before he died."

It was a lie. Hannah had been with Rachel when she bought them in that little shop on Columbus Avenue.

She stood stiffly beside her mother, confused and furious, and was incredulous to find herself being hugged. Could her birthday wish be coming true, her wish that her mother loved her even if she did forget the party and lie about the pearls? She knew that Rachel loved Sam best and that was okay. All Hannah wanted was for her mother to love her, too.

Her joy was short lived. With her mother's arms around her and her mother's pearls on her neck, she could see their reflection in the mirrored wall behind the credenza. Rachel was holding her close but her eyes were focused on her son. As Hannah watched, her mother wrinkled her nose at Sam and sent him a silent kiss, shifting her glance downward on Hannah as if in sufferance.

Hannah worshipped her brother. If not for him and Kathleen her party would have been ruined. Her whole life would have been ruined. The girls would have made fun of her. Cecily Greenberg wouldn't have wanted to do homework with her.

Yet, seeing Sam's grin and feeling Rachel's embrace slacken, she wished with every threatening teardrop that her brother was dead.

Years later, when she remembered Kathleen's grim expression as she searched through the crumpled party debris for her grandmother's brooch, Kathleen's warning about wishes came back to her: "Be careful what you wish for. You might just get it."

1944

Viktor

Life is bare.
Since I lost my underwear. Stormy weather—

Sam's voice soared with happiness over the din of the shower. It was Saturday. It was summer. It had been a month of lonely weekends since he and Kathleen had seen each other at Hannah's graduation. Now it was just a matter of hours before Kathleen arrived on the afternoon train with a weekend pass. Hannah, too, was buoyant with anticipation.

With meat rationing ended, Hannah had cooked a small roast beef in the ancient oven so that they could have a cold supper if they decided not to go out. Or sandwiches if they decided to have a picnic. Or . . . she stopped herself from making further mental plans for them. Sam and Kathleen were in love and didn't need any help from her, except to be merciful by pulling a disappearing act tonight so the lovebirds could be alone in the tiny apartment. She and the other cub reporter, Nell Bentley, were going on a double date with two second lieutenants. Nell was a local girl and had invited Hannah to spend the night at her family's home in Long Branch.

It was hard to believe she'd been away from New York for just four weeks. It felt like months. Years. Her new life as an adult was more exciting than she'd ever dreamed. She was her own person, responsible for the little things like food and laundry and making things comfortable for Sam and herself, and more importantly, for the big things. Although Sam's friend had arranged for the interview at the newspaper, Hannah had handled herself with confident maturity—at least she thought that was the impression she made.

Her credentials: Class valedictorian. Winner of the Nellie Bly Journalism Award. A pile of clippings from the school newspaper and magazine. Fortunately, she did not confide her desire to be another Marguerite Higgins sending dispatches from dangerous war zones or that she was inspired by Rosalind Russell as Hildy Johnson in *His Girl Friday*. It didn't matter a bit when Marcus said the original Hildy Johnson in the original play was a man. She would be Hildy Johnson anyway, trading wisecracks and kisses with an editor like Cary Grant, covering murders and exposing corruption in high places.

The Red Bank Weekly Times fell short of her expectations. The editor, Slim Collins was not Cary Grant. Advertising and circulation rather than political exposés, were his primary concerns. Her assignments so far had been covering Ladies Sodality meetings, church suppers, and scrap drives for the war effort. "Get lots of names, the more the better, and be sure you spell them right," her boss advised. People liked to see their names in the paper. That's why they subscribed and took ads.

Yesterday she had been sent to interview a Gold Star mother who had a fifteen-foot sunflower in her backyard. Hannah had taken a picture of the woman beside the plant to illustrate its size. The towering stalk gave her the willies, as if she'd been shrunk by a mad scientist. Since the woman had little to say, she decided to "interview" the sunflower about how it felt to be so tall and have people stare and make remarks.

"You are not Dorothy Parker. You are a cub reporter on a small-town newspaper!" The editor shouted when he read her copy. If S. J. Perelman had written it, they'd have put it on the front page! But Hannah was not S. J. Perelman. The photograph ran with a caption, without a story. Her name did not appear as the photographer, the cut line a succinct, anonymous, *Staff Photo*.

There'd been a bad moment at the end of the day when Slim Collins called her into his office. "Don't look so worried. I'm not going to fire you. I just want you to know you're a very good writer for someone your age but you've got this romantic notion of what a newspaper is all about. I know you want to expose scandals. I've heard you talk about the Nazis spies coming ashore from U-Boats. I know you're bored with the engagement parties and sewing bees."

It was all she could do to stay calm and try to look like Lauren Bacall standing up to Humphrey Bogart. "So . . . ?"

So he had a real assignment for her. He wanted her to interview Army wives who had followed their husbands to Fort Monmouth and found places to live, however primitive, in order to be with their men for as long as possible until they were shipped overseas. "I want heartwarming anecdotes of young love, devotion, fear, and heartbreak on the eve of separation." He paused for effect. "Perhaps forever. Think you can do that?"

Her youthful inexperience broke through. "Where will I find them?"

He tipped back in his swivel chair and put his feet on his desk. "You're a reporter. Find them. Where would you be if you were an Army wife?"

Sure enough, they were exactly where Hannah's common sense told her they would be. The volunteers serving sandwiches and doughnuts at the army canteen were all wives filling in time. She had talked to them last night. They were thrilled with the idea of being interviewed.

Instead of setting up separate interviews, Hannah invited them all to a picnic the following Monday and asked them to share their stories, their hopes and dreams. She had told them to dress their prettiest. She would take their photograph as a group, a wide photograph of beautiful young women united in friendship and love for their husbands and country. It would be difficult to crop a wide picture. If she were lucky, Slim might run it on the front page with her story and her by-line.

Then she would be in a better position to propose doing a piece on the U-Boat patrol. The Jersey beaches were restricted, cordoned off with barbed wire and patrolled by troops with highly trained attack dogs. There were constant rumors of German submarines surfacing offshore on moonless nights, of Nazi spies dressed in American uniforms speaking perfect English paddling ashore in rubber boats. One story had Hitler and Goering disguised as Red Cross nurses, Der Fuhrer having sacrificed his mustache in the deceit.

This was the kind of story Hildy Johnson would go after. Handsome young soldiers and vicious dogs guarding our precious coastline against Nazi saboteurs. Danger lurking beneath the depths of the North Atlantic. What a story. Human interest. National security. The good guys against the bad guys. She had talked to Sam about getting permission to go out on patrol. He'd told her to forget it. It didn't hurt to ask. And ask. And *ask.* One of these days he would give in and try to pull some strings. Then, if, as Kathleen often said, God was in His heaven, the night she went on patrol would be the night a U-Boat did appear and a boatload of saboteurs paddled directly to where she was standing on the beach.

Sam had shaved and dressed in a freshly pressed uniform, his shoes shined, his buttons gleaming. He was eagerly gulping down the breakfast Hannah had prepared when their landlady rapped on the door with a message. Because of wartime restrictions, there was no telephone in the apartment. "A lady just called. Asked me to give you a message." She handed it to him. Sam's face went suddenly white with anger or fear, Hannah couldn't be sure.

It was Rachel. Earlier in the week she had written to say she and Marcus were going to Boston for the weekend. Apparently the trip was cancelled. Her message said she would be on the one o'clock train from Pennsylvania Station, and to meet her at Red Bank.

"That's the train Kathleen will be on, Hannah," Sam said numbly. "Hannah, what the hell am I going to do?"

Everyone always said Hannah had a great imagination. Now was her chance to prove it. On Saturdays, the one o'clock train was always jam packed with visitors to Fort Monmouth, standing room only most times. If they were lucky, Kathleen and Rachel would not see each other in the crowd. If they were luckier still, there would be sufficient time for Hannah to board the train at Matawan, the station stop about twenty minutes north of Red Bank. If luck—and true love—guided her, she would find Kathleen and stay hidden with her until Rachel got off at Red Bank, where Sam would be waiting to escort her to the Molly Pitcher Hotel. Three minutes later, the train would stop at Little Silver, the station closest to Fort Monmouth. From there the two women could make their way to the apartment.

"You really think you can do it?" Sam pleaded.

Hildy Johnson was Hannah's model. Hildy Johnson wouldn't let Rachel spoil the weekend for Kathleen and Sam. It was probably their last weekend together for some time. The scuttlebutt was that she was being transferred with the WACs on special duty to Fort Bragg, and then to the Pacific.

"Leave it to me, Lieutenant!" Sam had always come to her aid. She would never as long as she lived forget her tenth birthday party. Now it was her turn. "When we get to the apartment, I'll call you at the hotel," she said confidently.

"And then what?" His misery broke her heart.

But Hannah's mind was in high gear and the next part of the scenario was falling into place. "Just leave it to me. If I can get Kathleen off the train without being seen, I know what to do."

He smiled wanly. "Ike should have known about you. You could have helped plan D-Day. Or maybe infiltrated enemy lines. What a great spy you'd have made."

He was right. She could see that she had a talent for deception. The challenge energized her body and honed her brain. Not normally athletic or graceful, she felt as lean and intuitive as a cat. A northbound train deposited her at the Matawan station with just enough time to cross over to the southbound track and board the one o'clock train. She had changed into a nondescript brown dress. With her hair tucked into an unbecoming brown turban and her face downcast, she felt invisible.

Luck was with her. She saw Kathleen standing at the end of the rear car smoking a cigarette.

"Don't say a word. Where's the toilet?" Hannah hissed.

Kathleen jumped and let out a squeak just as the conductor's voice called out, "Middle-town! Next stop, Middle-town. Followed by Red Bank! Middle-town. Next stop!"

"Quick. Lock the door," Hannah said as she shoved Kathleen inside. The compartment was too small for both of them. Hannah got on top of the toilet seat as the train caromed around a bend. The two women clung together.

Kathleen recovered herself and could not help laughing. "What's going on? A scavenger hunt?"

"It's Rachel. She's on the train. She decided to come down for the weekend!"

A majestic knock on the door was followed by Rachel's unmistakable voice. "Excuse me!" A more demanding rap this time. "Excuse *me*! Kindly open the door."

Hannah disguised her voice. "Go away!"

Pressure was exerted on the door handle. Kathleen gasped. "She's strong as an ox. Another minute and she'll have it open."

"I'm sorry!" Hannah moaned through the door. "I'm sick . . . find another toilet."

That ended the discussion. The conductor bellowed "Red Bank! Red Bank! Watch your step." Through the isinglass window, Kathleen could just make out the figure of Sam welcoming his mother.

Fortunately there was a taxi at Little Silver. In a very few minutes they were at the apartment. By now, Kathleen was fighting back tears. "Why did she have to spoil it? Our last weekend together. We might not see each other for months. Years. *Forever*." She gathered her things together. "When's the next train to New York? If I see her, I'll punch her right in the snoot!"

"Wait here while I call the hotel," Hannah said calmly.

Kathleen lurched toward the door. "I'm leaving!"

"*Wait here*, Kathleen." The quiet command stopped her dead in her tracks.

"Just for a minute, then. But I won't see her. I wouldn't be able to stand a weekend of pretending I'd come just for a friendly visit with the two of you."

"Trust me."

As she expected, Hannah found her mother and brother in Rachel's room. "Mom? I'm so glad I got you. Put Sam on quick! He just got a message from his commanding officer."

"Hannah?" Sam was wary.

"Don't say a word. Kathleen is at the apartment. I just told Mom your commanding officer called. You're to report for duty immediately."

"Oh, my God! Captain Nathan really called?"

Love muddled even the best minds. "No, Sam. Listen to me. I only said Captain Nathan called. Kathleen is waiting for you. Tell Mom I'll be right over to see her, okay? Tell her I can only stay a minute because I've got a date, remember? On second thought, I'll tell her myself!"

Arriving at the hotel, Hannah was not the least bit surprised to find that her mother had managed to twist the circumstances to her own advantage. She had discovered there was a train back to New York in less than an hour. When Hannah found her at the front desk, she was explaining about her son. "You saw him when I checked in. The handsome lieutenant? Well, he's been called away on a secret mission. I can't tell you where, of course, but I'll need to cancel my room."

"Hannah, darling." Hannah noted that Rachel did not draw the desk clerk's attention to the fact that this was her other child, her son's sister, in point of fact her daughter. "Sam was a dear to send you over. You shouldn't have bothered, darling. This nice man has arranged for a train ticket back to town." She allowed Hannah to kiss her and then held her by the shoulders for inspection. "I'm not sure I like your hair that way."

"I like it."

"I know but—" A flicker of concern. "Oh, dear. Oh, Hannah, I'm sorry. I should have thought . . ."

"Thought what?"

"You poor child. You came to spend the evening with your mother. And here I am leaving you flat. You must be lonely here. Forgive me, darling. Do you have food at the apartment? I hate to think of you having dinner alone—"

"Mother, dear. There are seventy-five thousand men at Fort Monmouth. I'm going on a date with one of them tonight. I just wanted to see you and say hello."

"You see?" Rachel beamed at the desk clerk. "Aren't I lucky to have two such devoted children?" She kissed Hannah's cheek. "Run along, darling. You'll need time to get fixed up for your date, won't you? And please," she stage-whispered, "do something with your hair."

Not even her mother could upset Hannah today. She'd done it! She saved the day for Sam and Kathleen. She'd stood her ground with Rachel, proving to herself that she had really and truly left home. In the fall when she returned to New York to start college she would move back into the Riverside Drive apartment, no longer a child but an independent woman.

The weekend was back on track. She did not change her hairstyle. Sam had told her she looked like Lauren Bacall. When Nell and the two lieutenants showed up with a jeep, a guitar, and a picnic supper, Hannah was wearing a houndstooth check suit like the one Bacall wore in *To Have and Have Not*. She had not met her date before this evening, but after they'd driven around and had their picnic and drank some wine, she necked with him enthusiastically and found it just as hard to stop as he did, though she knew she wasn't supposed to admit it.

By the time she returned to the apartment Sunday night, Kathleen had left. Sam lay on his bed in a euphoric reverie, drawing voluptuously on a cigarette and making concentric smoke rings. "I'm in love with her, Hannah, and she's in love with me, too. Can you beat it? We've decided to get married the minute the war's over."

Hannah was filled with joy. She loved Sam and she loved Kathleen, and now they would be together forever!

"We talked and talked about everything for the entire weekend." Sam went on. "How we felt about the world, what we would do when the war was over and got married and had kids of our own."

He sat up and faced Hannah with the most serious expression she had ever seen. "We thank you for the weekend, Hannah. We wouldn't have had it without you. How can I repay you? Name it. My Heinz pickle pin from the World's Fair? My autographed copy of *Dawn Ginsbergh's Revenge*? My cigar band collection? Name it."

"You mean it?"

"Anything."

A week later on a balmy moonlit night, Hannah got her wish. When the midnight patrol slipped onto the sandy beach, she was with them, dressed in black from head to toe to prevent detection from a German periscope, an Army canteen of strong coffee laced with brandy around her neck to prevent night chills. Sam had got her the necessary permission provided she signed a promise never to write, broadcast, or otherwise

reveal in any way anything she saw, heard, or partici-
pated in during the exercise, at least until the war with
Germany was over, and then only with permission.

A few hours later she got more than she bargained
for, more than she ever imagined. They were trudging
along an open stretch of beach. The Atlantic Ocean
stretched far and wide like a black mirror reflecting the
overhead light bulb that was the moon. On the eastern
horizon where the sea indiscernibly met the sky, several
darker smudges moved across the line of vision like
ducks in a shooting gallery. A convoy, she was told, supply ships enroute to French and Italian ports to support
the allied invasions.

Was it her imagination or did she see something
closer to shore? What looked to her like the head of a
sea monster broke the surface of the water. A periscope. The whispered word was passed along. The gray
body of the submarine rose like the back of a hippopot-
amus. The hatch opened. A figure emerged, followed
by another that tried to pull the first back inside. In the
ensuing struggle, guttural shouts could be heard. The
sound traveled clearly across the water. It looked like
the second figure had succeeded in pulling the first
back into the submarine. The hatch closed. The hippo-
potamus began to sink.

Just as the hatch was about to disappear, it flew
open. A figure vaulted out as if shot from a cannon and
began to swim furiously toward shore. *"Schiessen!
Schiessen!"* The submarine surfaced far enough for a
sailor to man the machine gun on its deck. The rat-a-
tat-tat reminded Hannah of jackhammers repairing city
streets. The bullets roiled the water. She couldn't tell if
the swimmer had been hit.

"Searchlights! Now!" The order came from the sergeant in charge of the beach patrol. It was like the time
Sam took her to a night baseball game at Yankee Sta-

dium. A battery of onshore lights danced across the water like sunshine breaking through clouds. The machine gunner scrambled back into the open hatch. The submarine submerged. The searchlights swept back and forth across the water while soldiers on shore trained their binoculars on the illuminated area, but there was no sign of the swimmer.

"Nothing, Sergeant! Not a goddamn thing!"

"The bastards! Like shooting fish in a barrel!"

Hannah felt sick to her stomach. Some war correspondent! She breathed as deeply as she could. This was no time to throw up and disgrace herself. She had never in her life seen gunfire. She had never seen a man killed. The bastards! Nazi bastards! No American would shoot a defenseless man in cold blood!

The thought of the dead body sinking in the sea and being eaten by fish sent a new wave of nausea through her chest. Whoever he was, he was a human being. The bastards!

"One more sweep, Corporal. Just to be sure." In any case, the body would wash ashore with the next tide. With any luck there would be identification. According to intelligence reports, both the U-Boats 1226 and 1229 had been spotted in North American coastal waters. The sergeant had radioed a submarine alert to Fort Monmouth where it would be relayed to the Navy and Air Force.

"That's it, sergeant. If he was alive we'd have seen him."

"Wait!" The loudness of her own voice startled Hannah. "I just saw a splash!"

There it was again. A splash and then another splash. "The son of a bitch must have been swimming under water," the corporal breathed in awed disbelief.

On command, two members of the patrol stripped down to swimming trunks and raced into the ocean. In a few minutes their raised arms signaled they had reached the swimmer. The searchlights moved with them until the shallow water allowed them to stand upright. The man shrugged his rescuers aside and walked arrogantly ashore.

"Who is in command?" he asked in nearly perfect English.

"Sergeant Carter, United State Signal Corps."

"Thank you, Sergeant. I am Colonel Viktor Von Sternberg. I wish to be interned."

Realizing that she should not have been on patrol in the first place and that she might get Sam in trouble if word reached headquarters that she was a witness to what happened, Hannah had kept discreetly in the background during the actual rescue. She could hear what was going on but could not see over the heads of the soldiers blocking her view.

"Would someone be kind enough to offer me a cigarette!" It was clear from his arrogant tone of voice that Colonel Von Sternberg was used to giving orders and used to being obeyed. There was an uncomfortable shuffling among the patrol. Then the sergeant spoke up. "My men are prohibited from carrying cigarettes or matches on beach patrol."

Hannah could not help herself. "Have one of mine." The ranks of soldiers parted to let her through. There in the moonlight, standing languidly and gracefully at ease, was a naked, god-like creature risen wet and glistening from the sea. In all of her eighteen years she had never seen an entirely naked man.

"A woman?" he observed, accepting one of her cigarettes. He gazed speculatively around the circle of men.

"I happen to be a journalist," Hannah snapped.

"Light, please!" he demanded.

Stepping close to him to light his cigarette, she could smell the salt on his skin and feel the stiletto probe of

his eyes. Her senses in turmoil, she tried unsuccessfully to shake the matchstick free of flame.

"Allow me." He crushed the head of the match between his thumb and index finger.

Stepping back in confusion, her glance fell on his
sole adornment, a chain around his neck.

"Your eyes do not deceive you. It is a Star of David.
I am a Jew."

CHAPTER 13

1945

Samuel

"Happy New Year, Mom." It was six o'clock New Year's morning. Hannah had taken off her shoes and crept into the apartment in stockinged feet, not wanting to waken her mother and most certainly not expecting to find her in her negligee, smoking a cigarette.

"Tramp! Staying out all night! Where the hell were you?" Rachel leapt off the couch to block Hannah's escape route.

"Cecily Greenberg's. I told you."

"Liar! Tramp!" Rachel slapped her daughter across the face. "You think I liked calling the Greenbergs? You think I liked being made a fool of, not knowing where my own daughter was, thinking my daughter was at a New Year's Eve party? How do you think I felt when they said you weren't there?"

How did *Rachel* feel? How did it look for *Rachel* not to know where she'd been all night? Hannah knew she should be used to it by now. "Why did you call, Mom? Is something wrong?"

"If you must know, some people are more considerate than others. It was Marcus. He was worried about you coming home alone in the middle of the night with all those drunks on the street. We were going to pick you up. You can imagine what Marcus must think. My own daughter. Staying out all night with some bum. Did he at least bring you home? Let me look at you."

Hannah stood stoically for her mother's appraisal. Well, let her cut out her tongue, gouge out her eyes, pull out her nails, burn the soles of her feet with hot pokers. She would never confess that she had spent New Year's Eve with Viktor at the detention center on Governor's Island. It was a minimum-security facility, more like a college dormitory than a prison. They had bribed the duty officer with a Christmas "gift" and seen the new year in from his room. The torch on the Statue of Liberty was lit for the first time since 1940. The ships in the harbor, from the largest to the smallest— tankers, cargo boats, ferries—were ablaze with light and tooting their horns. Fireboats at the Battery piers sprayed water in rainbow arches. Viktor's radio, the one Hannah had bought him, carried the music and sounds of Times Square celebrating what everyone knew would soon be a new year of peace.

"How dare you come home like this!" Rachel wrenched Hannah's sweater as if she could remove it without pulling it over her daughter's head. "It's inside out! Don't kid me. I can see what you were doing! Bite marks on your neck. Who were you with?"

"Count Dracula!"

Rachel shoved her roughly away. "You think you're so smart. Valedictorian! You think this man's going to respect you? You think any man wants to marry damaged goods?"

There was no point arguing, no point telling her that Viktor and she planned to marry once the war was over. Good reporter that she was, she had found out that as a German POW he would be repatriated, but as a Jew seeking asylum he might be allowed to stay. Especially if he had a sponsor. Because of censorship, Hannah had not been permitted to report the story of his escape from the U-Boat. However, at any future hearing she would be an eyewitness to his actions.

There was also no point reminding her mother that Marcus Salinko respected her and endlessly proposed to her, despite the fact that Rachel was damaged goods. Another example of do as I say not do as I do. Frankly, Hannah couldn't understand why Rachel didn't marry Marcus. They were together all the time. He'd taken her into his real estate company and taught her the business. When the war was over, there would be a massive upsurge in the construction of apartment houses and office buildings.

At Christmas, Marcus had been more lavish than ever with his gifts. A sheared beaver coat for Hannah. Matched luggage for Sam. And for Rachel? Flowers, caviar, champagne and, almost as an afterthought, a coy little package containing a red velvet case that in turn contained a gold key engraved PH-I. As a surprise for Rachel, he had refurbished the top three floors of the apartment house on Riverside Drive, as a triplex penthouse with wraparound terraces.

"Well?" Rachel was glaring at her.

"Well, what?"

"Is that all you have to tell me?"

"I'm tired."

"I'll bet you are. If you're pregnant, don't come crying to me."

"What time is Sam coming?" She felt a twinge of sympathy for her mother. Sam had stayed on duty at Fort Monmouth to allow a married officer to spend New Year's Eve with his family. He didn't mind. Kathleen was in San Francisco. Rachel still didn't know about his engagement to the woman his mother persisted in calling the Irish maid. What's more, Sam had got himself reassigned to the European theater. The newsreels of American troops liberating Paris had reinforced his longing to get into the real war before it was too late.

Hannah had promised her brother she'd be there when he broke the news. It thrilled her that they were confidantes. He knew about Viktor. She knew about Kathleen. Rachel would blow her top when she learned he was going overseas. Hannah was worried too, but she didn't admit it to Sam. Anything could happen to anyone. A person could be killed by a trolley car crossing Broadway.

"Good night, Mom. I've got studying to do. Let me know when Sam gets here."

Her mother's voice followed her down the hall to her bedroom. "Get some sleep. You look like hell. I don't want my son to see you looking like a tramp!" Her *son*, as usual. Never *your* brother! Ironically, Hannah's English literature assignment over the Christmas vacation was *Sons and Lovers*. At first reading she had thought there was a parallel between Paul Morel's mother and Rachel's devotion to Sam. She decided there wasn't. Paul Morel was unable to love Miriam or Clara or any woman other than his mother. But Sam was fully and passionately able to love Kathleen. Yes, it was definitely Rachel's problem, not Sam's.

She wondered whether such devotion existed between mother and daughter. So far, she had not found it in novels she'd read or movies she'd seen, except for maybe *Stella Dallas*, where Barbara Stanwyck sacrificed everything for her daughter's happiness. Hannah had sat through that movie dry-eyed with annoyance while Cecily Greenberg sobbed uncontrollably and nearly choked to death on her bubble gum.

Hannah couldn't explain exactly why she found Stella pathetic rather than noble. Stella was a fool for giving up her husband and child without at least getting a substantial settlement. Why wasn't Stella living it up somewhere like Rio instead of standing in the rain while her simpering ingrate daughter married some wealthy weakling?

Alone in her bedroom, Hannah stripped off her clothes and crept naked into her bed. The crisp sheets cooled and soothed. Last night had been a turning point in her young life. By giving herself totally and completely to Viktor she was now a woman in every sense of the word. If that made her a tramp, so be it. Somewhere in the world there was a mother who would listen to her daughter's first adventures in love and answer her daughter's questions from the storehouse of her own experiences.

If only she could explain this to Rachel. If only she could slip into her own negligée—a castoff from her mother, come to think of it—and stretch out on Rachel's chaise longue with her own cigarettes and talk woman-to-woman about love.

The next best thing would be a letter. Not typed. Beautifully written in ink. Thoughtful and touching in the English literary tradition, like Lord Chesterfield or Mary Wortley Montagu or Virginia Wolfe. Propped up on pillows, with more pillows across her knees as a desk for her loose-leaf notebook, she uncapped her father's Waterman pen and began.

Dear Mom. Too informal.

Dear Mother. She paused. The date was important. *January 1, 1945.* Should she add *The day I lost my virginity*—? It had happened after midnight, hadn't it? Too coy, she decided. Do not confuse coyness with erudition, Professor Menten had warned. She tore up the sheet of paper and began again.

New Year's Day, 1945

Dear Mother,

Since we can't seem to speak without fighting, I thought I would write you a letter. I'm the writer in the family. You've said so yourself, even though you never read anything I write, not even my article about the Army wives that the *New York Times* picked up from the Red Bank paper.

Before anything else, I think you should know I'm wearing your old silk negligée with the flamingoes, the one with the Milgrim's label that Daddy gave you when I was born, the one you told Kathleen to cut up and use for rags. I've had it hidden away in a drawer all this time. Don't laugh. I've been afraid to wear it. I never even tried it on until a few minutes ago. Unfolding it and opening it has released your old perfume—Shalimar, I think—the one you used to wear.

The silk fabric touching my bare skin once touched your bare skin. The perfume was your perfume. Wearing something of yours makes me feel closer to you. I've always wanted to be close to you. I thought things would change after graduation but they haven't.

I've been wanting to have a conversation with you for weeks, ever since I got back from Red Bank. Don't laugh, Mom. I'm in love. I lied to you about Cecily's party because I was going to see Viktor and I didn't want an argument. Well, we're engaged, Mom. Unofficially, anyway. I was going to tell you about it today, ask your advice, stuff like that. I didn't expect to find you up and frankly I didn't appreciate being called a tramp for going to bed with the man I love. That would make you a tramp, too, wouldn't it, Mom?

Hannah paused with satisfaction. That would really make her blow her stack! She went on to write about meeting Viktor.

The July night on the Jersey shore sprang vividly to life as she described the circumstances of his escape. How Sam had arranged for her to accompany the submarine patrol and how the U-Boat surfaced and a man dove into the water and made it to shore through a hail of machine gun bullets.

He rose from the sea like a god of myth. My heart stopped at the sight. He was magnificently formed, tall and tan all over, I blush to say. He was naked, Mom. I'd never seen a naked man. I've never been so stirred up by the sight of any man.

It felt good to be writing about it. She could never have said these things to Rachel in person. How she trembled when she lit the cigarette. How she thought she would die if he touched her. How she felt his eyes reaching into her very soul when he confirmed that what she saw around his neck was a Star of David and that he was a Jew.

She knew what Rachel would say. "A Jew on a U-Boat? Weren't all the Jews in concentration camps?" That was what Hannah herself wanted to ask that night as well as what was he doing on the submarine and why had he jumped into the ocean?

She never got the chance. The officer in charge had shunted her roughly aside while his men covered their prisoner with a blanket. "Not a word about this. To anyone," he had warned. "I can lose my bars. You can be arrested under the official secrets act. Understand?"

Everyone was nervous and upset. You could taste the tension. Everyone but Viktor. He was totally relaxed like a king or a prince, treating his captors like his personal retinue. As they led him from the beach, he took a final drag from the cigarette and flipped it away. "I shall be wanting cigarettes. Camels. And shaving soap. You'll see to it?"

She'd seen to it. Lieutenant Myers couldn't tell her where he was being held but did allow her to send packages through him while Army Intelligence investigated his story. By Viktor's account, his family had been wealthy landowners for many generations. Members of the same Jewish community as the Rothschilds, the family had begun to build its fortune as moneylenders. Unlike the Rothschilds Viktor's family decided to assimilate by way of advantageous marriages to non-Jews, and went so far as to add an aristocratic "Von" to the name Sternberg. During the rise of the Third Reich they regarded themselves as Germans, not Jews.

Apparently Viktor had designed some advanced underwater tracking devices that made the U-Boats superior to American submarines. The Fuhrer himself decorated him and everything was fine until a couple of his colleagues got jealous and schemed to discredit him. One of them discovered his Jewish ancestry and waited until they were in American waters to accuse him of plotting to run the submarine aground and turn all their secret equipment over to the Americans.

That night, they confronted him, and to show their contempt hung a star of David around his neck. There's no brig on a submarine. All they could think to do was strip him naked, the way it was done at Auschwitz. When Viktor heard the order to up periscope, he waited for the sound of the hatch being opened and made a dash for it.

By September he had been moved to Governor's Island instead of a German POW camp. By October, Lieutenant Myers gave in to Hannah's pleas and permitted weekly visits with an intelligence officer present.

Viktor was the most fascinating, the most intelligent, the most philosophical man she had ever met. He spoke five languages. He had read everything. He knew everything. They had real conversations, deep discussions about the meaning of life. And then . . .

Could she really tell her mother about last night? The soft silk of Rachel's old negligée soothed the bites and scratches on her back and thighs and buttocks. The sweet soreness of her nipples. The place between her legs she had never touched from nameless fear. Her breasts swelled. Her thighs parted. For the first time she knew the meaning of the word voluptuous. Hannah rallied her courage and went on with the letter.

I want you to know about last night, Mother. Lieutenant Myer gave me a special pass to visit Viktor. There was just a skeleton crew on duty. They knew me. I've always brought them CARE packages. So when I asked if Viktor and I could celebrate the New Year alone in his room, they laughed and locked us in together.

We were alone. The door was locked. And you know what, Mom? I couldn't move. Your sophisticated daughter stood there like a statue. I didn't know what to do or what he was going to do. Would he throw me on the bed and rip my clothes off? For a moment, I was terrified. I wanted to run. I thought he would laugh, but he didn't.

Hannah closed her eyes and gave herself to the memory of what happened next. On all of her previous visits, she and Viktor had sat opposite each other at a table under close supervision, unable to touch except for a peremptory handshake. "We shall proceed slowly," he said. The little radio she had given him was tuned to Guy Lombardo at the Waldorf-Astoria. The cold supper she had brought was set out on top of his dresser. The bottle of Leibfraumilch she had bought because it was German lay in the tiny sink with cold water cascading over it.

From the Waldorf-Astoria Hotel, Guy Lombardo's orchestra was playing "Long Ago and Far Away." Viktor bowed formally before taking Hannah into his arms. She had heard about melting in a man's arms and dismissed the idea as hyperbole. Always an awkward dancer, fearful of stepping on her partner's feet, she suddenly found herself fitting into his body and following his lead as gracefully and lyrically as Rita Hayworth.

She had slipped into an erotic haze of taste and touch and scent and the sound of her lover's voice when a louder more urgent sound of rapping on her door and her name being called brought her sharply alert. Her bedside clock said ten o'clock. She'd fallen deeply asleep, the letter to her mother on her knee.

"Hannah?" There was something wrong. Rachel never knocked timidly on her door. Rachel never knocked at all. She always burst in with no regard for her daughter's privacy. "May I come in?"

"Of course. Come on in!"

Only one thing could upset Rachel like this. Her face was pinched. Her nose was red from crying. "Oh, Hannah. What am I going to do?"

"Sam? Is he hurt?" Not dead, please not dead.

"He just called. He's leaving for Paris. Today. It's dangerous. He'll be killed!"

"Paris is liberated! The German occupation is over. He'll be fine. You know how much he wanted to go overseas."

"I know. I know. He said to wish you a happy new year. He said he hoped you had a good New Year's Eve. I told him you did. Oh, Hannah darling, I'm so sorry for what I said. Please forgive me. I've got a lot on my mind. Marcus has given me an ultimatum."

"Uh-oh. Does that mean we're not moving?" There went the penthouse with the wraparound terrace.

"We're moving, all right. Marcus is too much of a

gentleman to go back on his word. It's just . . ." She hesitated in an unusual show of reticence. "I'm so glad we can talk woman-to-woman now. As you know, he's been asking me to marry him for years. Only this time he's put me on notice. He wants to settle down. He wants an orderly life with a wife—"

"—and children?"

"Of course I look young enough to be your sister, everyone says so, but no more children, thank you. After all, I'm almost forty years old."

Forty-three, Mom, but who's counting? "Did he give you a deadline?"

"June. The man's a romantic. He said he's always wanted a June wedding." Her delighted laughter made her seem younger than forty-three, younger than forty. "There's plenty of time. I'll be like Scarlett O'Hara. I'll think about it tomorrow."

Hannah's notebook chose that moment to slide off the bed. Before she could retrieve it, Rachel picked it up. "So what's this?" Rachel held it tantalizingly out of Hannah's reach. "One of your little articles for the school paper? Let me see what my brilliant daughter has to say."

"It's personal, Mom! Give it to me." Hannah leapt out of bed.

"Personal? This I've got to see." Playful now, Rachel turned her back, the notebook clutched to her chest.

"Mother!" Hannah spun her around and tried to retrieve her property.

"Tug-of-war!" Rachel was exhilarated, clinging fiercely to the notebook. "What's in it you don't want me to see?"

"It's a letter to Sam! You've always taught me it's wrong to read other people's mail!"

Rachel's mood changed abruptly. "Of course! I wouldn't dream of reading your private correspondence." She slung the notebook on her daughter's bed. "No point mailing it to Red Bank, though. He said he'll send his APO address as soon as he knows it."

"Speaking of Sam." It was her mother's favorite topic. "We're doing family trees for a genealogy seminar. Who married who and stuff like that, and how names are passed down from generation to generation. Like me, for instance. You and Daddy named me Hannah for his mother and his grandmother. But there wasn't a Samuel in Daddy's family, and you being an orphan and all—so how come you picked the name Samuel?"

Rachel was obviously taken aback. "It's such a long time ago. I really can't remember." From her troubled expression, Hannah could tell that she remembered perfectly.

CHAPTER 14

1918–1920

Will Lawrence

Private Samuel Harrington's son was born on a raw April morning in 1918. Private Harrington was unaware of this milestone in his personal history. He was in France with the Fighting Sixty-Ninth, serving to make the world safe for democracy. Rachel Forsyth, the boy's mother, had tried but failed to reach him both before and since the blessed event.

On the October night in 1917 when the troopship *America* weighed anchor in the Brooklyn dockyards, Rachel had stood in the drenching rain hoping against hope that her note had been delivered and that Samuel would find a way to send back word that he loved her and they would marry as soon as he won the war.

There was no word that night nor any of the nights that followed. "I don't understand!" she wailed to Becky. "We were going to be married. We had our picture taken. See?"

Becky had seen the photograph a million times. Rachel in her walking suit. Sam in his uniform. The laveliere he had given her and the gardenias she wore that were now brown and pressed in the only book Rachel owned, a Webster's dictionary. Even more innocent than they looked in the photograph, the young couple had been carried away by their night of love. Delirious with sexual fulfillment, ecstatic in their new-found happiness, they agreed that fate had brought them together. What did it matter that they had met only the previous day? Clearly they were destined for each other. They mustn't allow the war to separate them. They would marry at once.

At City Hall, the marriage registrar crushed their romantic dream. They needed birth certificates for one thing, or other proof of citizenship. Parent permissions, for another. The law was odd in this respect. Women over eighteen did not need permission, while men had to have their parents' consent until they reached twenty-one. They could meet none of the requirements. So Samuel went to Europe leaving Rachel with only a promise and the photograph.

She had planned to wait until after he returned to tell him she was pregnant.

"You never told him?" Becky cried.

"I couldn't. He was going overseas. I didn't want him to worry. I didn't want him to think about anything but not getting killed. He'll write to me. I know it."

Private Harrington did not write.

"Maybe he hurt his arm," Rachel rationalized.

"Maybe he's found some Red Cross volunteer." Becky was realistic. She wanted Rachel to forget about him. She also wanted Rachel to have an abortion. "A young girl like you has to be smart. The only one in this world to take care of you is you."

Rachel listened, watched for Samuel's name on the casualty lists, bought herself a ten-cent wedding ring for her visits to the clinic, and gave birth in Becky's bedroom with only Becky in attendance.

"Baby Sam," Rachel declared immediately, enchanted by the red-faced little bundle Becky handed her.

"Isn't he beautiful? The image of his father." She refused to consider giving the boy up for adoption. Nothing could shake her conviction that his father would return from the war and they would all three live happily ever after.

The orphanage was the ideal place to keep her baby without raising eyebrows. She could care for him when she came home from the job as an alterations girl at Bergdorf and Goodman that Hattie Manheim had arranged. Baby Sam was six months old when the armistice was signed and a few weeks older when the final list of New York-area casualties was printed in its entirety. Private Samuel Harrington was not among them.

Every night, Rachel held her baby son close and sang him to sleep. She couldn't get enough of him. *Bye, baby bunting. Daddy's gone a-hunting.* Hunting the Hun. She pointed the child's chubby finger at the precious photograph. "That's your Daddy! I want you to recognize him. When he comes for us, you'll make him so proud!"

All was well until the morning she awoke to find little Sam hot with fever, his tongue dry and protruding. He could not cry. He could only look at her with pleading eyes. Spanish influenza had invaded the orphanage during the night. During the many weeks of the epidemic, Rachel and Becky had rubbed camphor oil into all the children's chests and prayed the angel of death would pass them over.

By nightfall, three of them were dead, baby Sam among them. The next morning when the casket man arrived, a folded newspaper protruded from his back pocket. He put it on the kitchen table while he and his assistant did their work. On the front page was a photograph of Samuel Harrington. Rachel stared at it in disbelief. Had she gone crazy? Was she seeing things?

RETURNING HERO TO WED ARMY NURSE.

They had met at a field hospital in France. He was so badly wounded he hadn't been expected to live. She had nursed him back to health. The bride-to-be said they would get married in their uniforms in tribute to those who had perished, and promised they would have lots and lots of children.

"Come," Becky urged Rachel after the funeral. "We'll go home. We'll have a cup of tea. We'll talk."

"No. I'm going to work." Funeral or no funeral, Bergdorf and Goodman might decide she wasn't reliable and hire another alterations lady.

"Tomorrow. You'll go tomorrow."

"I need the money!" Rachel cried, nearing hysteria. The little casket. The little burial plot.

"You look sick, Rachel. You haven't eaten or slept."

"Working will take my mind off things."

She walked rapidly away. Toward the Brooklyn Bridge. The thought of jumping into cold water refreshed her. It comforted her to know that she was dressed in her best. She wondered if Sam Harrington would read about her death and recognize her name. She hoped they would run the picture of her in her walking suit.

She had made it in order to find love and she had found love with Sam Harrington. It was her wedding suit for the wedding that never was. She had worn it this morning in grief for their infant son. Now it would be her own winding sheet. She could not go on. Everything she thought was right had turned out wrong. She had stuck her finger in the eye of God by trying to better herself and the angry God of the heavens was taking his revenge. Still, she didn't understand why God would punish her and not somebody evil like Mo Schweitzer. She would take that riddle unanswered with her to the bottom of the East River.

She had gone as far as the Bowery when an overwhelming weakness forced her to stop. With the roar of the elevated trains overhead and the clatter of trolley

cars and horse-drawn wagons around her, she felt battered by the noise. *God, help me!* she cried silently. But
when she looked up, she saw moving toward her
through the chaos the unmistakable figure of Mo
Schweitzer. Maybe God was being playful today. At
that moment, an uptown trolley car stopped beside her
just as the man she most hated and feared spotted her
and shrieked her name.

She leapt onto the car and despite Mo Schweitzer's
furious pounding on the door, the conductor clanged
the bell as the signal for the motorman to proceed.
"Are you all right, Miss?"

Rachel sank gratefully into the rattan seat. "Thank
you. That man—that man was making indecent suggestions."

"A crying shame," he sympathized. "Glad to be of
service."

It was a long ride uptown. She would shut her eyes
and rest. The image of both Samuels, her first and only
love in his uniform, and their son in his tiny casket,
swam behind her closed eyelids.

"Are you all right, Miss?" The conductor was clearly
alarmed. She had slumped down in her seat, then slid
to the floor with her head resting on the rattan.

Sweat was seeping through her hair. Sweatshop Rachel. That's all she was. No better than the thousands
of girls who squandered their youth and beauty and
passion on sewing machines. At least Bergdorf and
Goodman was better than the Triangle Shirtwaist fire
where all those girls died. She would not be locked in
a room with oily rags and no escape.

"I'm all right," she finally managed. They had
reached her stop. Food was what she needed. There
was always a pushcart near Bergdorf's that sold frank-
furters and lemonade. She'd feel better when she ate
something. Alighting from the trolley car, she missed

her footing and fell against an Essex Runabout driven by one William J. Lawrence, which fortunately was stuck in traffic.

A small crowd materalized, hungry for tragedy, asking each other excitedly what had happened, hoping for the worst so they could feel the emotional release of sympathy. "Is she dead?"

Will Lawrence sprang from the driver's seat and knelt at Rachel's side. "She's breathing!" he announced. Rachel's eyelids fluttered. She tried to stand up. "I—I'm sorry," she apologized. As she tried to brush herself off, she swayed against him. "I've got to go. Over there."

He smiled sadly. "Bergdorf and Goodman? I should have known. That's my wife's favorite shop. My late wife, I should say—the flu—"

"You don't understand. I don't shop there. I work there. I have to earn the money for my baby's funeral. He died from the flu, too. Now do you understand? I've *got* to get to work."

Her knees buckled as she walked away. Had he not caught her, she'd have slid to the ground once more. "Young woman, I'm driving you home," he said firmly.

Burning with fever and shivering with the shakes, she could no longer resist the inevitable. Instead of the clean cold death of the East River, she realized she was going to suffer the agonizing death that killed her son. And this Good Samaritan's wife. "Forsyth Street," she told him, providing explicit directions when he admitted he'd never heard of it. *You're getting more than you bargained for, Mister,* she thought as she lost consciousness.

When she came around a few minutes later, Rachel's first thought was that traveling by automobile was a definite improvement over the trolley car. Sick as she was, she luxuriated against the smooth leather seats, stealing glimpses of her rescuer. The hands on the steering wheel were large and broad, the nails clipped short and amazingly clean. The shirt cuff nearest to her was monogrammed WJL. She wondered idly what the initials stood for as she drifted off again.

The area south of Houston Street offered striking contrast to the area around Bergdorf and Goodman. Pushcarts clogged the streets surrounded by women with baskets and black oilcloth bags, hectoring the peddlers about the disgracefully poor quality of the produce, the clothing, the household items on sale. Shrieking children. Horse-drawn carts trying to make their way through the chaos. Pieceworkers carrying bundles on their heads to their cramped rooms where family members waited. The raucous sounds of the Lower East Side brought Rachel back to her senses.

As the Essex inched slowly down Forsyth Street, children jumped on the running boards and stuck out their tongues. *Nyaah, nyaah, nya-naa-naaah!* Tony the hurdy-gurdy man tipped his hat at Rachel in recognition and sent over the tiny monkey on his shoulder with his tin cup. "A penny, *Señor?*" However embarrassed she felt about her neighborhood, she was glad to be in a fancy automobile with a man stylish enough to reach into his pocket for a nickle!

Her pleasure was short lived. As they pulled up in front of the orphanage, the door flew open. Mo Schweitzer skittered backward onto the sidewalk. Becky towered above him in the doorway still in her good black bombazine dress that she had worn for the funeral. She waved her heavy iron frying pan menacingly. "Stay away from here. I'll call the cops!" she bellowed. Rachel jumped out of the car to go to Becky's aid.

"You'll call the cops? That's a laugh," Mo mocked.

"*I'll* call the cops." Suddenly seeing Rachel, he shouted exultantly. "I'll call the cops right now! Thief! Thief!" He addressed the gathering crowd. "I knew she stole from me but I couldn't prove it. Here's proof, she's wearing it!" In a rage, he tore at Rachel's arm as if to rip the sleeve off. "Proof! Proof!"

Will Lawrence moved swiftly but calmly. "Take your hands off this lady." He motioned Becky to put down the frying pan.

"Some lady you got there. A thief. A sneaking thief."

"Come now, man. Control yourself."

"The goods. She stole my goods. A length of gaberdine. See? She's wearing it. The best quality. Cost me a fortune!"

"Exactly how much of a fortune?"

Mo Schweitzer licked his lips. He hadn't counted on this. He affected the look of thoughtful calculation Rachel had seen when he bargained for trimmings and thread. "I'd say twenty or thirty dollars!"

Woozy as she was, Rachel managed to sneer, "*Seven* dollars! I saw the invoice."

"Ten dollars should do it, I think," Will said and handed Mo the money.

All would have been settled if Rachel had not roused herself sufficiently to spit in Mo Schweitzer's face and shout an insult in street Yiddish. The ten dollars in his hand could not make up for this assault on his manhood. With the crowd around them eagerly waiting to see what would happen next, he threw the ten dollars at her.

"No bribes. Not Mo Schweitzer. She stole from me. She goes to the hoosegow! With the bedbugs and the rats!" He turned and pushed his way through the sniggering onlookers. "I'll be back. With a policeman!" He turned and shook his fist at Will Lawrence. "You, too! Bribery. I'll swear to it."

Becky hurried to Rachel's side. "He means it, Rachel, honey." She touched the younger woman's face. "God in heaven, you're burning up!"

Rachel turned toward the steps of the orphanage. "I don't care. Let them send me to jail."

Will Lawrence gently took Rachel's arm and introduced himself to Becky. "I think I'd better get her away from here."

Tears filled Becky's eyes. "She's been through a lot."

"But tell me, that is if you don't mind. What is all this about stealing?"

Becky looked to Rachel for permission.

"Please—what's past is past!"

Becky liked the look of this Will Lawrence, a solid (not to mention rich) citizen, maybe someone who would take Rachel away from all this. She ignored Rachel's protest and described the abomination Schweitzer had tried to force on her and the clever way she had locked him in his office with his pants down. As for the length of gaberdine, "She saw it. She took it. The man deserved worse."

"Quite a girl," Will said with genuine admiration. Rachel's breathing had worsened. "Quite a sick girl. I'd better get her away from here."

"No." She tried feebly to prevent him from steering her back into his car. "Why bother? My life is over. Leave me here, please."

For a while, they rode in silence. "May I ask your name?" Will said finally.

"Rachel," she replied. "Yours?" He told her.

"Where are we going?"

"Riverside Drive. The apartment house where I live."

Her moan of resignation struck his funny bone. "Don't worry. I'm not like that man downtown. I'm not going to force myself on you. There's a doctor's office in the building. He couldn't save my wife, but maybe he can help you."

The apartment house was one of several built on the west side of Manhattan by the Salinko Brothers just before America entered the Great War. Designed to meet the needs of a burgeoning middle class, the apartments were modest in comparison to the luxurious proportions and amenities of Park and Fifth Avenues. Will and Laura Lawrence's accommodations consisted of a living room, dining room, kitchen, pantry, and three bedrooms—a master bedroom with its own bathroom, two smaller bedrooms with a connecting bathroom for the children they had planned to have, and a small powder room off the foyer for the guests and parties they had also planned. Adjacent to the pantry was a narrow room with a half-bathroom—a sink, toilet, and shower stall, no tub—for the live-in help they would eventually need for their growing family.

Dr. Aaron Levy was not in. He had not come home from Mt. Sinai Hospital for over a week. Ruth Levy brought him changes of underwear and socks. He slept wherever he could. Every bed was filled with flu patients. Folding cots lined the hospital hallways.

By now Rachel was too weak to walk. "Can you help her, Mrs. Levy?" Will asked as he carried her into the elevator, ignoring the huffy look given him by the elevator man. Will needed no reminding that his wife had only been dead a few weeks. Laura had come from a wealthier family than his and had tried to educate him about "the help." *What we do is none of their business,* she had told him again and again. *They are paid to do their job and otherwise be invisible. We never, ever explain our behavior. Get drunk. Come home late. Quarrel in the elevator. Kiss in the elevator. No explanations required.*

Of the two smaller bedrooms, one had become the

library, the other a guest room where Will deposited Rachel on the bed. Together he and Ruth Levy removed her outer garments. "What a lovely girl, Mr. Lawrence. Who is she?"

"I don't really know."

"You don't know?"

"Too complicated to explain. Want me to leave the room?" The doctor's wife was untying the ribbon on Rachel's camisole and unhooking her petticoat. Both garments were soaked with perspiration. Mrs. Levy glared at Will impatiently. This was no time for respecting the girl's modesty. Rachel didn't know he was there anyway.

"Is there anything of Mrs. Lawrence's? A nightgown of some kind? That is, if you don't mind."

Laura would want to help, he was sure. He returned with a white silk nightgown and exquisite Japanese kimono. "It was all I could find," he said in response to another impatient glare. Mrs. Levy left Will with Rachel and rummaged through the late Mrs. Lawrence's bureau drawers and returned with a cotton batiste nightgown, pale pink and embroidered with blue flowers. "Help me get her into this. She won't bite."

She gave him the instructions she had heard her husband give flu victims these many horrible weeks. Camphor oil on her chest to help her breathe. "Don't worry about the nightgown. It will wash." Enough covers so she wouldn't catch a chill. Witch hazel or toilet water on a cloth. "On her forehead and neck and do her arms, especially inside her wrists to try to reduce the fever. And as much water as she'll drink. If she can't drink, keep moistening her lips."

She gathered up Rachel's clothes. "What a beautifully made suit. I wonder who her dressmaker is!"

"If she doesn't die, I'll ask her," Will said grimly.

"That was totally uncalled for. I was merely making an observation."

He apologized. "Maybe it would be better to move her to the hospital."

Will Lawrence never listened! She remembered his wife complaining about it. "There's no room at the hospital, Will. If you don't want her to die here, do what I said. And pray."

He did what Ruth Levy said and more. Sponging the girl's body, easing spoonfuls of water and the broth Ruth brought between the parched lips. His sense of mission replaced any further embarrassment. He changed the soiled sheets and washed her clean. Late that first night, she sat bolt upright screaming that her baby wasn't dead. "He's alive! He's calling me. Mommy! Mommy! Oh God, he's alive!"

Her screams woke Will in the master bedroom. He hurried to the guest room just in time to keep her from climbing out the window. She fought him off. "It's okay, Becky," she panted. "It's faster. I always go through the window." She thought she was home on Forsyth Street. "Don't stop me. It's Sammy. He's alive!" Her momentary rush of strength collapsed like a leaky balloon. She allowed herself to be taken back to bed. "Who are you?" she asked Will, sinking back into unconsciousness before he could answer.

He slept on the floor beside her for the rest of the night and moved in a folding bed the following day. He called his office and canceled his appointments. Not that he needed to be there. With the war's end, orders for cheap women's dresses were pouring in. He and his partner made them cheaper and better and faster than any factory he knew.

After a week, the fever refused to come down. Dr. Levy paid a house call but could add little to his wife's advice except to prop Rachel up on pillows to try to keep her lungs from filling with fluid. "If it turns into pneumonia, she's finished," he said flatly. She needed nourishment, too. Will Lawrence had to get her to take more than broth. Some egg custard. A boiled potato mashed with a little milk and butter.

She was skin and bones. It horrified Will to see how quickly she had deteriorated. Just since they met, she had changed from a lovely full-figured young woman into the nearest thing to a cadaver. He could count her ribs. Her pretty face was like a skull, her parchment skin drawn taut across her cheekbones, her glossy hair now stringy and dull.

On the seventh night, he lay in the darkness, his bed abutting hers, his head as close as possible to hers in order to hear her breathing. The witch hazel and toilet water were on the night table. He had schooled himself to wake up every few hours to sponge her skin and spoon feed her broth.

In a half-sleep he suddenly felt light piercing his closed eyelids. It must be dawn, he decided. He had forgotten to close the blinds. He opened his eyes to find the lamp on and a hand on his shoulder. "I'm thirsty," Rachel announced in a firm if raspy voice.

He took her hand and pressed it to his lips. It was cool. "Thank God," he whispered.

At first she was too weak to do anything more than open her mouth like a baby bird and allow Will Lawrence to feed her and explain where she was and how sick she'd been. Soon she was sitting up and voraciously consuming every morsel of food on the trays Will and Ruth Levy set before her. Walking came next. Her body had begun to fill out but her legs were still like sticks. Supported by her two friends, she made her way to the bathroom for the first time since her arrival. "A bathtub!" She thought of Hattie Manheim's bathroom. It was more luxurious than this. *But who's complaining?* She was feeling more like her old self.

Ruth Levy was almost as excited as she. They threw

Will out of the bathroom. "Women only!" Ruth laughed. She poured Laura Lawrence's bath salts into the hot water and helped Rachel in. She scrubbed the younger woman's back and washed her hair under the faucet. She wrapped her in a terrycloth bath sheet and towel-dried her hair.

In the days that followed, Ruth described in detail how Will had brought Rachel home half-conscious and nearly dead with fever. And how he nursed her night and day, refusing to let her die. "He *forced* you to stay alive," Ruth asserted.

"He saved my life in more ways than one," Rachel replied softly. She felt she could confide in Ruth. The whole story poured out. How she'd been abandoned on the orphanage steps, how Becky was her only family, how she'd fallen in love with a soldier who was shipped overseas before they could marry and how he was killed before their son was born, and finally how she supported them both as an alterations girl at Bergdorf and Goodman until her baby boy caught the Spanish flu and died.

At last, Dr. Levy gave his permission for Rachel to go out. "Just a short stroll in Riverside Park." Will had gone downtown to his showroom and would join Ruth and Rachel later at the Soldiers and Sailors Monument. Rachel was wearing her gaberdine suit and for a reason. "I'll be leaving as soon as Will gets home," she explained.

"You can't do that!" Ruth pretended to misunderstand. "Will asked me to take you shopping. Get you a new wardrobe after all you've been through. I thought we'd go to Lord & Taylor. Tomorrow."

"I can't just stay here, Ruth. I'm back on my feet. Will's done more for me than anyone in my entire life except for maybe Becky. I've got to go back to work. I can't go on accepting his charity."

"It's not charity, Rachel. Will Lawrence is in love with you. He wants to marry you, dear."

"Marry me?" For once, Rachel was speechless.

"It won't be like your soldier, of course. Nothing is ever like your first love. In fact, Dr. Levy was my first love and believe me, after a few years, first love is no longer what it was. Your first love died before you could find that out. Don't pass up this chance, Rachel. I watched Will take care of you night and day. He'll be good to you. He'll take care of you. He'll give you a home and children and security. You'll never have to worry about anything ever again."

Rachel soon discovered she was not as well as she thought. She tired easily. Dr. Levy gave her an iron tonic and prescribed daily doses of cod liver oil and orange juice. When, as Ruth Levy predicted, Will asked her to marry him, she asked if they could wait until she fully recovered her health so as to fulfill her role as wife and mother of their children.

"Does that mean 'Yes'?"

She didn't love him the way she had loved Sam Harrington. On the other hand, loving Sam Harrington had nearly destroyed her life. Will Lawrence had saved her life. To walk out on him would be cruel and ungrateful. It would also leave her without a home or a way to earn her living. She could not return to Forsyth Street because of Mo Schweitzer; Becky said he still skulked around threatening to have her arrested if she ever showed her face. Nor could she go back to Bergdorf and Goodman even if they wanted her. She was still not strong enough for a day's work.

She took the hands that had washed her and soothed her and raised them to her lips. "Yes, Will. If you will give me a little more time."

They celebrated her decision with the Levys at a chop suey joint off Columbus Circle. For propriety's sake, now that she was up and about and highly visible to the building staff and other neighbors, Rachel moved into the Levy's apartment. Because Ruth had admired her suit, Rachel offered to make some clothes for her as a way of thanking her for her friendship. Soon the Levys were forced to have their meals in the kitchen. The dining room had been transformed into a workroom strewn with patterns and pins and snippets of fabric and trimmings. When a neighbor saw Ruth's new outfit, she wanted one, too. Friends, sisters, mothers, aunts, neighbors, and strangers flocked to the Levy apartment demanding to be next. Ruth became the buffer, arranging appointments and setting prices, all the while protecting Rachel's health by permitting her to work only a limited schedule.

On November eleventh, there was something more to celebrate. The war was finally over. Peace and prosperity lay ahead. Will Lawrence often looked at Rachel longingly, but he never pressed her to set their wedding date. Nor did he press his attentions on her in any way. His patience was finally rewarded the following Valentine's Day during the worst of a February blizzard. He woke up to find his bedroom windows thick with frost and a warm, silken body snuggling beside him. "Mr. Lawrence, will you be my valentine?" Rachel purred.

They chose the first day of spring for their wedding. On March 21, 1919, Rachel Forsyth and William J. Lawrence exchanged vows in the presence of Dr. and Mrs. Aaron Levy and Miss Becky Lodz. Except for Becky, Rachel put her previous life behind her. The war was over. The entire country was starting anew and so was she, beginning with the Riverside Drive apartment.

"It's your home now, my love. Do whatever you like. Whatever will make you happy," Will said indulgently.

"Marriage agrees with you," Becky observed. It was true in a way. She had never felt better nor looked more beautiful. Yet as the weeks turned to months, the rapture of choosing furniture and carpets, china and silver and glassware and linens, the latest model victrola, the leather-bound Shakespeare and Dickens— none of it was enough to counterbalance the lack of rapture in the arms of her husband.

He tried so desperately hard to please her that Rachel pretended he had, which only made matters worse. He was not crude. He was not brutal. For that she was grateful. She was not foolish enough to have expected the overwhelming passion of that long-ago time with Sam Harrington. But she had hoped for more than the timid rabbit who was so frightened of doing something wrong that he could do nothing right.

From listening to Ruth and the other women, Rachel realized a husband was the chief inconvenience of marriage. Using the common sense she was born with, she soon established a sexual routine that satisfied her husband with minimum discomfort for herself.

She consoled herself with her status, her possessions, and a growing confidence in her abilities as a seamstress and designer. She believed in simple lines. After seeing a teagown she'd made, one of Ruth's Park Avenue friends ordered it in six colors.

Will showed her work to his partners. They were impressed. "How would you like to set up shop with us?" he asked his wife, beaming with pride.

"Oh, darling, how wonderful! But let me think about it. I want to finish the apartment first, and I already have more orders than I can handle."

What could he be thinking? Didn't they spend enough time together at night? What Rachel had in mind was to find a small loft in Little Italy. Not a sweatshop like Mo Schweitzer's. A bright, clean workroom. She remembered the Italian immigrant girls learning English at the settlement house. Embroidery and beading were skills they brought from the old country.

She would start with her teagown design and offer it in a variety of fabrics and colors embellished with individual embroidery or beading. If a woman found a style that suited her, she would order it again and again.

Figuring things out took time. More than a year had passed since her wedding. A real estate ad in the *Herald* seemed to be exactly what she wanted: 500 square feet, light, airy, low rent. The address was an old factory building on Greene Street a block west of Washington Square.

"Stop at the arch!" The taxi dropped her at the north side of the square. As she started across the grass, she realized she had dressed with special care today, more care than was necessary to impress a potential landlord with her ability to pay. She had not been anywhere near Washington Square since the time Sam Harrington brought her home to the family mansion. Was that where he and his army nurse wife were living?

Not that it mattered after all this time. She had her own husband and her own home. As she watched a band of children play tag at the fountain, she thought of her baby boy. He'd be walking by now. The image of his father.

Turning reluctantly from the children to continue on her way, she was not totally surprised to see the actual image of his father striding toward her. "Samuel Harrington, I presume?" Seeing that he did not recognize her, she smiled and extended a richly gloved hand. "I believe we met during the war. My name is Rachel."

"Rachel! My God! I can't believe it. How beautiful you look."

"Mr. Harrington, sir?" A nursemaid in a gray-caped uniform pushing an English perambulator halted beside him.

"Oh, yes, Miss Oliver. I was about to look for you when I met an old friend. I'll join you in a moment."

"Was that your child?" Rachel asked.

"Yes."

"The son you always wanted?"

"A daughter, I'm afraid. Mary Frances. I'm praying for a son next time. And you? Is that a wedding band I see?"

She had sometimes wondered what she would do if ever they should meet. Now she knew the answer. Her physical desire for him was the same as before but she herself was different. She was no longer the pathetic waif crying her eyes out on the rainswept Brooklyn pier. She had weathered betrayal and grief and survived the epidemic when thousands had died. That she owed her life to Will Lawrence was a debt she acknowledged in her heart and intended to repay to the best of her ability. He was an exemplary husband in every aspect but one. *You can't have it all*, Rachel heard often enough.

But why not? Why couldn't she have everything?

She knew at that moment that Sam Harrington and she would arrange to meet.

She knew what would happen when they did.

She also knew she would go on meeting him until she got what she wanted.

CHAPTER 15

1920–1925

Samuel Lawrence

"Please, Rachel. We must talk!" Sam Harrington's plea was in urgent contrast to his air of casual delight in suddenly running into a former acquaintance.

"We are talking."

He glanced nervously across the square to his daughter's nursemaid. "I mean—dammit—I must see you!"

"My, my," she trilled, indicating to all who might be witnessing the charming reunion that he was a very funny fellow, indeed.

"Just name it. The time, the place. Whenever—wherever you say. Uptown, downtown, wherever you say. Luchow's. Voisin. Henri's? Lunch. Tea. Please say you will."

With calculated reluctance, she suggested tea. "Next Thursday. At the Brevoort." She allowed him to smile with happy anticipation before adding, "I can't promise, of course. I may be able to come and then again I may not."

His stricken expression nourished her through the days and nights before their rendezvous. Having dinner with the Levys Wednesday night, Aaron remarked, "Look at her, Will. Your wife is positively radiant tonight. What's going on, Rachel? Is there a little stranger coming to Riverside Drive?"

Ruth slapped her husband's hand. "Stop that. You're making her blush!"

"Is that it, dear?" Will Lawrence made no secret of wanting a family, although he had assured Rachel again and again that he wanted her to be certain she had fully recovered from her illness and was strong enough to bear a child. Up until now he had been wary of imposing himself upon her physically. Not wishing to hurt her, he courteously waited for signs of encouragement. "Is it, sweetheart?" Sweat beads pulsed on his forehead.

As usual when Will got on her nerves, Rachel reminded herself that he had saved her life. She had made a bargain and intended to keep it. Marriage, she had discovered, was a safe haven for a woman of ambition. Never having had a father to protect her, she was still learning the advantages of having a husband. Today, for instance, she had negotiated the rental of the loft she wanted for her new enterprise. The landlord's agent had agreed to all her demands. The floor scraped and varnished. Fresh white paint on the walls. A cracked window replaced.

"You drive a good bargain, Madam," he complimented her. Of course he would expect her husband to sign the lease.

She squeezed her husband's hand. "Not yet, Will." With their best friends watching, she threw her husband a crumb. "But we'll go right on trying, won't we? If at first you don't succeed—" She spider-walked her fingers up her husband's arm to the ticklish spot on his neck "—try, try *again!*"

That night in bed after her husband had fallen asleep, she figured out to the last detail exactly what she was going to wear for her rendezvous with Sam Harrington.

She still had the walking suit she was wearing the day they met at the Liberty Bond Rally. That would give him a shock. She could wear the lavelier he'd given her and buy a gardenia on her way to the

Brevoort. The idea appealed to her sense of the dramatic, but on second thought she decided against it. The suit was part of her history. Having nothing from her past, not even a pair of ivory combs like the ones Becky's mother left her, she considered the suit an heirloom from her own past. It had been caked with dirt from her fall off the trolley car when Will brought her home. Ruth had brushed and sponged it clean. Together they had packed it in layers of tissue paper and stored it in the foyer closet.

No. She wanted Sam to know how far she had come from that poor girl whose love he had thrown away so heartlessly. She would wear something new of her own design, one of the samples in soft lavender and rose pink that Will had shown his partners. She had no intention of letting them produce cheap copies to sell off pushcarts and in dry-goods stores. She and Becky knew dozens of sewing machine girls who she would pay well for piecework, not like Mo Schweitzer, the thought of whom still made her tremble.

Her shuddering woke her husband. "Dearest!" he reached for her. It seemed a good time to say, "Will, my darling. I forgot to mention, I have an appointment for tea tomorrow. With a fabric importer. So I may be a bit late for dinner."

It wasn't nice but it made her feel good. For nearly half an hour Rachel positioned herself behind a potted palm where Sam Harrington couldn't see her but where she could watch him fidgeting and fretting at a table for two. She noted the spray of gardenias and his growing agitation until finally, after several cups of tea and a tray of little cakes, he called for his bill.

"Mr. Harrington?" Rachel could feel the murmurs of approval for her appearance as she moved gracefully through the Café du Thé. Cutting the fabric on the bias caused the dress to cling to her body's contours. The result, as she had intended, was ladylike sophistication, seductive without being vulgar.

Before he could speak, she pressed a kid-gloved finger to his lips. "Sssh. I know I'm late. I was so afraid you wouldn't wait. Do you forgive me? Now tell me everything." She slid into the chair next to him.

"I thought you weren't coming."

"But here I am."

"I waited and waited . . ."

Poor man. How did it feel to wait and wait? To wonder why you've been abandoned without explanation. To ask yourself what you have done to deserve this. Or was it all a mistake? Are you waiting in the wrong place? Or perhaps there was a message you never received.

Poor man, so agitated and hurt at being kept waiting an hour in this luxurious cafe with music and cups of tea and cakes. Had he any idea what it had been like to wait for days and weeks and months for word from the man she had expected to marry and who was the father of their son?

"Silly man. So little faith. I said I'd be here and here I am. *I* keep my promises." The intended irony failed to register. He snapped his fingers for the waiter.

"China or India?"

Not exactly Becky's samovar. "China."

"Sugar?" he offered after pouring her tea.

The silver sugar bowl was divided in half—fine white granules on one side, small perfect white cubes like dice on the other, with their own silver prongs. "Thank you, no," Rachel declined. It seemed to her more aristocratic to eschew sugar.

"Scones. Banbury cakes. Strawberry tarts?"

"Just tea, thank you." She had too much at stake to

be distracted with food. Her mission was not suste-
nance but retaliation.

"These are for you, Rachel." The spray of gardenias
covered nearly half the table. Six of them at least. Who
did he think she was, Mrs. Astor's pet horse?

"I'll wear them on my purse," she said nonchalantly.

His eyes seemed to devour her. His voice shook. "I
remembered how much you liked gardenias."

Sentimental baloney. She refused to give him the satisfaction. "Did I?"

Bullseye. "Of course, you did! Don't you remember—"

She cut him short. "Enough about gardenias. Tell me
everything, Sam. France. Father Duffy. The Fighting
Sixty-ninth. You were one of the heroes, weren't you?
Where did you get wounded?"

In a wan attempt at congeniality, he made a joke,
"On my arm."

"Which arm?" she demanded, unamused. "Is that
why they gave you a medal?"

She was sorry she'd come. She hated the way she
was behaving. She stood up abruptly. "Forgive me. I
must go. Please help me on with my coat." It was then
that she realized he could not help her because he
could only use his right arm. The other hung limply by
his side.

She fell back heavily onto her seat. It was horrible
but she would not allow it to obscure the central question. Why should she care if he had lost the use of his
arm? Others had lost far more. She saw them on the
street with tin cups. Blind. Legs blown away. The logic
of her anger kept her from confusing the issue. He had
left her in the lurch. He had never tried to reach her,
either before or after he was wounded. He didn't know
he had had a son. She hadn't yet decided whether or
not to tell him.

"We can't talk here, Rachel. People are watching us as it is."

It was true, but where did he suggest they go, the old family mansion off Washington Square? Surely his wife would notice. Perhaps she would offer Rachel another cup of tea and then retire tactfully from the drawing room while they continued their tête-à-tête.

"It's getting late, Sam. My husband will be expecting me." She stood up.

He smiled wryly. "You know that's not so. You know you made an excuse to meet with me and be with me." With his good hand, he arranged her coat on her shoulders as best he could, using the opportunity to press his lips to her ear. "Why did you waste our precious time together by being late?"

Like many men of wealth, Samuel's father, Seamus Daniel Harrington had kept a set of private rooms in a house on Charles Street where he could entertain political cronies and women of generous nature without fear of spilling whiskey or dropping cigar ash on Sophie Harrington's furnishings. Before he died, he gave the keys to his son with the proviso that he be discreet in his pleasures and never embarrass his family.

Rachel's excuse to herself for going with him was unfinished business. She was not ready to let him off the hook without paying for what he'd done to her.

The door squeaked on its hinges. Dust sheets covered the furniture. A musty aroma rose from the carpet. Sam Harrington turned on the table lamps and opened some windows.

"Sam!" What was she doing in this place?

"Yes, Rachel!" His exasperation matched hers.

"Is this where you take all your lady friends?"

"Help me with this." He needed her to fold back the sheet on a horsehair sofa. "A place to sit."

"It's caked with dust."

"That should answer your question. My father died two years ago. I have not been here since."

"No mistress?"

"It was a mistake to come here. I didn't figure on two years of dust." As if on cue, a pair of mice scampered across the room. With peels of laughter, Rachel jumped on the sofa. Not to be outdone, Sam jumped up beside her and shrieked in mock terror.

"You're the man. You're supposed to protect me!"

"Have you ever had a mouse run up your pants leg?"

They collapsed in a heap like tired children, their merriment gradually becoming a sweet exchange of affectionate pinches and pecks. "Have you ever been tickled to death?" Rachel asked. Taking advantage of his useless arm, she held him down and rediscovered the remembered sensitive places on his body. "Give up?" she challenged. "Give up?"

They rolled off the sofa in another cloud of dust and exhilaration. They both knew it was in fact getting late. They also knew that the dust and mice would be cleared away by this time tomorrow and that this would be their secret meeting place. With this established, Rachel suddenly realized she was no longer interested in knowing why he had never written from France. Danger did inexplicable things to men. After he was wounded, Letitia had nursed him back to life as Will had done for her.

Returning to Riverside Drive alone, Rachel felt serene in the knowledge that she and Samuel Harrington would soon be lovers again. Her anger had become resolve. She made three promises to herself. She would never tell him about his child. She would see that their affair continued until he gave her another child to replace the one they lost. She would then disappear from his life as he had disappeared from hers, without informing him that she was pregnant and planned never to see him again.

Her orphan cunning served her well in the months that followed. She could lose herself in his arms without losing control of her emotions as she'd formerly done. Nor did she take the chance of jeopardizing her marriage. An afternoon with Sam was always scrupulously followed by a night of love with her often incredulous husband. She learned by experience what the courtesans of history have always known. Having a satisfactory lover in one man is the key to enthralling another.

While she felt fundamentally aloof from both men, there was neither contempt nor condescension for their innocence. She felt somehow protective of their fragility, and she threw herself into her roles as mistress and wife with genuine passion and affection.

After six months, her pregnancy was confirmed by Dr. Levy. Without a word of apology or explanation, she disappeared from Sam's life. In a city the size of New York, there was little chance he would find her. Smitten as he was, he had not complained about her refusal to reveal her husband's name or where they lived. From their first chance meeting in Washington Square when they had arranged to meet at the Brevoort, all of their clandestine arrangements had been made in person. No phone calls. No letters. No go-betweens.

"For your sake as well as mine," she had insisted. "It works both ways, you see. You may be sure I will never send you scented love notes or show up on your doorstep with a baby in my arms." Mollified by her logic, he couldn't believe his good fortune. The callow girl from the slums had turned into a real humdinger. Unlike his wife, she knew how to make a man happy.

The afternoon she left him waiting in vain held little interest for her. She didn't relish his misery. A few hours' suffering was hardly worth thinking about. As for the flowers he ritually brought, he could take them home and surprise his wife. He had served his purpose and paid his debt. Much as she had enjoyed him, she didn't expect to miss their times together. She would be too busy having their baby.

Her baby, that is. The father a mere accessory before the fact. Although she purposely encouraged Will to make love to her following each of her encounters with Sam Harrington, her husband's performance was more often than not pathetic. Rachel had every reason to credit Sam for her condition. The proof would be in the baby's features which was hardly a problem since she was the only one who knew of Sam Harrington's existence.

Will Lawrence was so ecstatic about becoming a father, he stopped his daily complaints about prohibition and women getting the vote. He readily agreed to banishment from the marriage bed and spent the remainder of Rachel's confinement in the small bedroom where he had nursed Rachel through the flu. Soon it would their child's nursery.

With little fuss and almost no bother, the baby boy was born at home in the middle of the night, tap dancing and telling jokes, according to Rachel. Dr. Levy agreed there was no point going to the hospital. Mother and son were doing extremely well. When an hour later the father was permitted to enter, Rachel was sitting up in their double bed, her hair down and brushed to a glow with a white satin ribbon that made her look sixteen. Their son was at her breast.

"I'm calling my son **Samuel**," she informed him politely.

"But, you said we'd wait 'til the baby was born."

"I have waited 'til the baby was born. It's a boy and his name is Samuel!"

Will Lawrence knew that tone of voice all too well. It did not encourage discussion. He reminded himself that Rachel had just given birth. The Levys had warned him that women sometimes behave strangely after childbirth. "Sometimes the pain is so terrible, they hate their husbands. It's natural. It goes away," Ruth had said.

"Whatever you say, dear. Samuel it is. Little Sammy. May I hold him?"

She didn't bother to hide her exasperation. "Can't you see he's nursing? What's wrong with you?"

He hovered like a gawky seabird at the foot of the bed, fearful of upsetting her further. "Rachel," he whispered. The baby's mouth was suckling but his eyes were closed.

"What?"

"I—I just want to thank you for making me the happiest man in the entire world."

She softened. "I'm sorry, Will. Come and kiss me. You can hold him in the morning." Ruth Levy tiptoed in with the basket she had adorned with white ribbon. "Ruth's going to stay with me to make sure I don't fall asleep and smother him by accident. Go on, now, Will."

He felt left out and pushed out. The maternal instinct was how Ruth Levy explained it to him the next morning. "It happens to a lot of new mothers. It's very primitive. You can see it at the zoo. The mother tiger protecting her cubs and threatening the father if he comes too close. Give her a few days, Will."

A few days, a few weeks only made things worse. Banished from the master bedroom, he was met with frosty silence when he dressed in the morning and used the bathroom. One night when he came home from the showroom, he found his clothes in the smaller of the two bedrooms where he had been sleeping and his toilet articles in the bathroom connecting to Sam's room. Will looked around in dismay. The shelves and cabinets overflowed with baby things. A collapsible rubber bathtub stood in the porcelain tub. How was he supposed to bathe?

"Use the shower in the maid's room." Rachel knew he preferred a tub bath.

"Why don't I just move into the maid's room?"

"You can't. Becky is coming to live with us. She's the only one I'll trust with Sam."

"The only one?" Wasn't he the father?

"Except Ruth, of course. But I can't expect her to be at my beck and call."

That ended the discussion. He could not bring himself to confide in the Levys. It made him look like a fool. Keeping in mind Ruth's earlier assurances that Rachel was suffering from postpartum anxiety, he did his best to adapt to what he hoped was a temporary situation. He put away his clothes and used the maid's bathroom. He consoled himself that at least he knew Becky and felt sure she understood the nature of his exile for the baby's sake. He also felt sure things would get better in time.

They did not. Other fathers were allowed to feed their babies, change their diapers, bathe them, take them for walks in their English perambulators, play with them on the floor or on the bed. But Rachel made every excuse to prevent it. Will's hands weren't clean enough. Will looked as if he were getting a cold. Will's voice was too loud; it would scare the baby. Will was too clumsy; he might drop the baby.

Only when Rachel was out and Becky was in charge was Will Lawrence permitted to hold his son. Becky, ever loyal to the young woman she had raised since finding her abandoned on the doorstep, was mystified by Rachel's behavior. The poor man had changed drastically since Sam's birth. Never a sport or a jokester, he had become a gray ghost, lumbering silently to his little room, his shoulders slumped, his face haggard, dark circles under his eyes. After noticing his rundown shoes and soiled shirt cuffs, Becky surreptitiously saw to his personal laundry, pressed his suits, and polished his shoes. He didn't seem to notice.

Raising a child was considerably more costly than he expected. Rachel bought enough clothing for a dozen children and ordered the newest and most expensive high chair, playpen, and swing available. He paid the bills without complaint.

"I'm saving you a fortune, you know!" Rachel remarked.

How was that?

"I'm giving up the loft. Going out of business. No more rent. No more payroll. I can't be two places at once, you know!" She bristled defensively as if Will had been the one demanding she start a business. The truth was she didn't want to risk running into Sam Harrington accidentally as she had the day she was crossing Washington Square to see the premises. On a recent morning she had glimpsed him in the distance striding right toward her.

"That's very generous of you, Rachel. Thank you."

She dismissed his thanks with what had become her preferred way of communicating with her husband, an exasperated nod. "There's something else."

Hope sprang eternal. "What is it, dear?"

"Ruth Levy's been telling me you have dinner with them three or four nights a week."

"Ruth's a wonderful cook."

"Well, it's very embarrassing for me to have my husband begging for food at the back door like some tramp. They'll think I never feed you."

"You don't."

"How dare you say that? There's always plenty of food in this house."

"Baby food. Strained carrots. Mashed bananas. Whatever happened to pot roast and potatoes?"

"If you want that, you can eat out. But I will not have you mooching off our friends."

He was a fly caught in a spider's web he had helped to weave in the mistaken belief that it would be a safe and friendly place. He continued to dine a few nights a week with the Levys with the unspoken agreement that nothing would be said to Rachel. So as not to abuse their hospitality, he brought gifts of imported caviar and paté, and the occasional bottle of genuine Scotch whiskey from his bootlegger.

More and more often he would sleep in the Levys' guest room and bathe in their extra bathroom without fear of being in the way. Other nights, he returned to his own apartment very late and very drunk. Becky could tell when he was home and would bring him breakfast and strong coffee on a tray.

As Sam's first birthday approached, Rachel intercepted Will long enough to inform him that there would be a birthday party. "I expect you to attend." A faint smile, a small peck on his cheek, and he was back on his hind legs, his tail wagging, his paws in the air, panting with delight at her merest show of affection. Could this be the first step in a reconciliation?

The birthday party was a wonderland of ribbon streamers and balloons. With the exception of the Levys and Becky, the tiny guests and their parents and nursemaids were people he'd never met. Little Sam in his white sailor suit sat in a high chair festooned with cutouts of teddy bears.

Will had dressed carefully and arrived early with his gift for his son, the smallest-size tricycle from F.A.O. Schwarz. Just as the guests began to arrive, Rachel emerged from her boudoir to greet them. She favored Will with a radiant smile and linked arms with him, as if by habit. "This is my husband." she introduced him with a charming show of affection.

Ruth had been right to urge patience, Will realized. Rachel was her old self. Beautiful as ever, maybe more beautiful. Dazzling their guests. Flattering him with passing remarks about her handsome husband.

When it came time to blow out the two candles on the birthday cake, she stationed him on one side of the birthday boy, herself on the other. "One—two—three!" Mother and father helped blow them out.

"Did you make a wish, Sam?" she teased the little boy, who was intent on throwing candy on the floor.

"I did, Rachel," Will said quietly. The hoped-for reassurance was not there. Rachel's attention was elsewhere.

"Rascal!" she chided her son, gently taking away the candy. "It's time to cut the birthday cake!"

Suddenly, the child looked up at Will Lawrence. "Da-da! Daa-da!" Banging a spoon in rhythm, he repeated "Da-da! Da-da! Da-da!" to the mounting amusement of the older guests. He sure knew who his daddy was! Will's enormous smile could not contain his joy.

"I know what you've been doing, you sneaky bastard!" Rachel shrieked at him after the guests had left and Becky was getting Sam ready for bed.

What could she mean? What could he have done? Had Ruth let it slip about his visits? She couldn't be talking about Ninette, could she? The model they had hired for the showroom? As a courtesy, he had taken her out to lunch the day she started work. Just lunch. Only that once. Nothing more. Maybe one of Rachel's new friends had seen them. What else could make her so mad?

"What? Tell me what."

"Sam calling you Daddy, that's what."

What was wrong with that? Will stared blankly at his wife.

"You've been sneaking in here behind my back, that's what's wrong. Teaching him to say 'Daddy'! Trying to win him away from me. Get out of here. Don't let me catch you around my son again."

The Levys were surprised to see him when he rang their doorbell. They had been the last to leave the birthday party. Rachel's behavior seemed a sure sign of a reconciliation.

"But all babies say 'Da-Da'," Ruth exclaimed. "They call the dog 'Da-Da' and anyway, what's wrong with calling you Da-Da?" Ruth had run out of excuses for Rachel. She and her husband had spent many an evening discussing Rachel. They always came back to the death of her first child just a few days before Will met her and brought her home. She'd lost one child and was terrified of losing this one.

"He's my son, too!" Will cried bitterly. "How much can a man take?"

The next day he moved into a furnished room near his showroom. Most nights he drank himself to sleep. He continued to meet his obligations, of course. The rent. Rachel's housekeeping allowance. Becky's wages. He sent regular gifts for Sam but had no idea if Rachel opened them.

Months passed in a haze of hard work by day and alcohol by night. Several times on a sunny morning, he stationed himself in Riverside Park across the street from the apartment house in the hope that Becky would be taking Sam for a walk.

"Be careful," Becky warned the first time. "She watches from the window. Go around to the playground. I'll meet you there."

"What have I done? Why is she treating me like this?"

Becky had no explanation. "She has started sewing again. Mrs. Levy and her friends come every afternoon for fittings. You have to admit it, she has a way with the needle. And don't think she doesn't charge them a pretty penny!"

His last vestige of manhood was now in jeopardy. Whatever Rachel might feel for him personally, he was still the family breadwinner. It was a matter of personal pride that he took care of his wife and family. If the time came that she no longer needed or wanted his support, he would be totally stripped of his dignity.

That time came a year and a half later with a lawyer's letter advising him of his wife's decision to file for divorce. Before consulting his own lawyer, he decided to see her face to face and force her to tell him why she had turned against him, to explain what he had done to deserve this. Needing to fortify his resolve, he drank steadily in a speakeasy before making his unsteady way to Riverside Drive.

It was much later than he thought, after midnight when he entered the familiar building. The night doorman recognized him and allowed him to enter without buzzing the apartment. His door key worked. Rachel was so sure of her powers of intimidation she had not bothered to change the locks. The interior of the apartment was dark. He didn't need lights. "Becky," he whispered at the maid's room door. Getting no answer, he slowly turned the knob. Becky's things; no Becky.

He tiptoed to Sam's room, half-expecting Rachel to spring at him with a rolling pin from behind the door. Sam was no longer a baby. He was now a little boy of two and a half. In the dim nightlight, Will could see the sturdy little boy clad in blue Dr. Denton pajamas, damp ringlets framing his face.

Through the connecting door he half-expected to find Becky or Rachel herself curled up on the guest room bed. His eyes having adjusted to the darkness, he could discern bolts of fabric strewn around, a sewing machine, and a dressmaker's dummy.

Becky must be out. That meant Rachel would be alone and asleep. He would catch her by surprise and insist that they talk. The possibility of finding her in bed with a lover was quickly dismissed. Both Becky and the Levys had assured him there was no other man in her life. He took off his shoes and opened her door without a sound.

Old habits prevailed. She lay gracefully on her back on her chosen side of the bed, a faithful wife expecting her husband to join her. Her satin gown had twisted in her sleep, exposing one long, slender leg. The sight of her loveliness brought him to tears of loss and despair. She sighed deeply and turned on her side, her outstretched arm seeming to reach for him as in earlier times.

Rachel. He swayed woozily above her, the tears coursing down his cheeks. *I love you, Rachel. I did everything I could to make you happy.* There was still some whiskey in his pocket flask. He gulped it down and took off his jacket. *Rachel.* Her arm fell back; a clear invitation. He sipped into bed beside her but not touching her. An errant strand of her hair brushed his cheek. The fragrance of her skin further intoxicated his senses. He caught the unmistakable scent of the tooth powder they both used.

Just for a minute. He would only stay a minute and then he would go. He was crazy to have come. Stupid to have thought he could get her to discuss things this late at night. A sweet lassitude crept through his body. His eyes closed. He was home where he belonged in his own bed with the wife he adored.

Rachel. He brushed his hand across her breast, lightly like a feather duster. *Oh, Rachel.* Her breast swelled and rose to fit his hand, the nipple hard. He remembered all that she had taught him. How she liked her nipples to be pinched, gently at first and then harder. How she liked her breasts to be caressed with fluttery fingertips along the side and upward into her armpit.

Her breathing became heavier, her back arched, her head thrown back with a moan as she seized his hand and thrust it down the length of her body to the wetness between her thighs. Her moans quickened in rhythmic counterpoint to the thrashing of her hips. From the spiralling frenzy of sound a single word became clear.

"Sam! Oh, Sam!" *Sam* repeated like a drumbeat with accelerating intensity. *Samsamsamsamsamsam*—SAM! A final lingering shriek and she gathered him to her.

"Rachel—"

Her eyes opened and widened in horror. "Oh, my *God!*" she recoiled from Will Lawrence in disgust.

"Please, Rachel," he begged. "I love you. I just made you happy, didn't I? Admit it. I made you happy, didn't I?"

"You revolt me. I'll have you arrested for rape."

"I'm your husband. Your lover. A good lover. I just proved it."

Her scent filled his nostrils. After all the months of rejection and celibacy, after what had just transpired in their marriage bed, he was physically aroused as never before. "You're my wife and you're going to act like a wife for a change!"

She rolled herself up in a protective ball. "I'll scream the place down!"

"No, you won't. You'll wake up Sam."

Sam! So that's what she had cried out. Their son's

name. He had heard of degenerate acts performed by men with little girls. The thought of Rachel in such a situation with their son brought out a savagery he never knew he possessed.

"So that's it, you pervert!" he cried. "I'll have you arrested for molesting our son!" The satin gown fell to pieces in his flailing hands. Her nails found targets on his face and chest. Her knees attacked his thighs and groin. But he was too much for her, too angry and too strong.

"You're insane," she hissed. "I'll have you committed. How dare you say such revolting things." The accusation was so appalling it diminished her ability to fight back. She no longer resisted. He was right about one thing. Little Sam was getting big enough to climb out of his crib. She didn't want her screams to wake him and bring him running to her side.

With Will Lawrence forcing himself on her, she felt oddly detached. His sexual exertions were pathetic as ever. What offended her more was the desperation in his eyes and the stale alcoholic stench of his breath. She couldn't bear the thought of telling him she had changed her mind about divorcing him.

Ruth Levy had told her the Christchurch School was the best private school for boys in the city. Most students were enrolled at birth. Sam was going on three. Smart, affectionate, sociable, he would surely be an asset to any school. During her preliminary interview with the headmaster last week, Rachel was given the criteria for future acceptance. Along with suitable income and family stability was the restriction on children of divorce. "A disruptive influence, Mrs. Lawrence. I'm sure you understand. We want students with both parents in the home."

She had understood well enough to reconsider her

plans for divorce and to work out an arrangement for her husband's return.

At last he rolled off the bed and stared down at her sheepishly. "I'm sorry."

"It's all right." It wasn't, but why bother discussing it?

"I didn't mean what I said about Sam."

"Don't think about it." She was not about to tell him about Sam Harrington.

"Do you forgive me?"

She said yes, knowing full well she never would.

Three months later, when Dr. Levy confirmed that she was again pregnant, Will Lawrence asked for the hundredth time "Do you forgive me?"

"It's important for Sam to have a playmate, isn't it?" she replied coldly.

Pregnancy might be an ordeal for other women. Not Rachel. Why all the fuss? Having a baby was a cinch. She was a modern woman. She was too busy for morning sickness and swollen ankles and endless hours of labor. She had proved this with Sam, hadn't she? Gaining less than twenty pounds. Never sick for a minute. Dancing to the victrola the very night he decided to be born, popping out like a cork from a bottle of champagne.

Dame Nature must have been listening. She evened the score over the next six months with nausea, bleeding, palpitations, and outbreaks of pimples on Rachel's otherwise satin skin. Her crowning glory looked and felt as if she had rubbed it with glue. Her face was pinched and haggard in stark contrast to her ballooning body. She ate nothing but gained weight anyway. Dr. Levy ordered her to bed.

She was wrong to have allowed Will Lawrence back into her home. She would never forgive him. Nor would she forgive the unborn child who was causing her so much pain and suffering.

Perhaps sensing her mother's displeasure, the baby girl clung ferociously to her warm, safe place in Rachel's womb, refusing through twenty-four hours of labor to enter a hostile world.

"It's a girl!" Dr. Levy wept with relief.

Rachel did not shed a tear.

"She's beautiful, Rachel. Just like you," Will said shyly.

Rachel turned her head without a word.

"She's totally worn out. I'll give her something to ease the pain. She'll be a different person when she wakes up and sees her daughter."

Several hours later, Rachel awoke in her private hospital room to find her husband waiting patiently with a bouquet of roses. Seeing her stir, he pushed the button to summon the nurse.

"Here she is, Mrs. Lawrence. Eight pounds, seven ounces. Everything's there. Ten fingers. Ten toes—"

"Take her away!"

"But, Rachel—" Will sprang to his feet.

"It's all right," the nurse soothed. "She's been through a lot. It's a common reaction. Would you like to hold your little girl?" She placed the small pink bundle in his arms. "Don't drop her. I'll be right back."

As physically painful as it was, Rachel managed to turn her back on her husband and child. Baffled as always by his wife, Will Lawrence tried to make conversation. "Have you thought of a name?"

"She's your daughter. You decide. I don't care what you call her."

Dr. Levy had urged him to be patient; she'd soon be herself.

"My mother's name was Hannah. What do you think of that?"

"Fine. Hannah it is."

The new father was jubilant. "See? She's smiling. She likes it."

"It's gas."

"She likes her name, don't you, little Hannah?" He held the baby upright, grinning into her face.

"Be careful, you'll scare her."

"You hold her, Rachel." Before she could refuse, he placed the pink bundle into her hands. "Come on, now, Rachel, don't be a sourpuss. Say hello to Hannah."

The man was beyond exasperation. He had no idea how much he irritated her. "Hello, Hannah," she addressed the tiny face that was still brick red from the delivery. The eyes that stared unblinkingly at her were her own eyes, the same shape and, unless it was her imagination, the same unflinching stubbornness.

"She says, 'I want my Daddy!' "

"She does?" Will Lawrence beamed with paternal pride as Rachel transferred the infant to him. That settled that. She wished Sam could be there. This was the first time she'd ever been separated from her son. The hospital forbade visits for children under ten.

"Say bye-bye to Mommy!" Will raised Hannah's tiny hand and waved it in Rachel's direction. "That's a good girl. Isn't she wonderful?"

Daddy's girl. Watching him kiss his daughter before surrendering her to the nurse, Rachel felt the familiar twinge of envy for something she'd never known. She often wondered what it would have been like to have a father, someone strong to hoist her on his shoulders for parades, someone who would have read her Peter Rabbit and put mercurochrome on her skinned knees.

Everyone always said men doted on their daughters. Will Lawrence might not have much, but she could see he would devote all of it to Hannah.

CHAPTER 16

1932

Will Lawrence

It was well after three o'clock. All the other children and the teachers had left the school. The custodian had locked the door. Hannah waited impatiently for her father, hopping from one foot to the other, her braids dancing behind her. She was seven years old, tall for her age, and had been allowed to walk home from school by herself until a few weeks ago.

The streets were getting too dangerous. Beggars sleeping in doorways. Men selling pencils and apples. Kidnappers everywhere since the Lindbergh baby, according to Rachel. "From now on, your father will call for you and walk you home." It would give him something to do and get him out of the house, her mother added under her breath but loud enough for Will Lawrence to hear.

The Crash had taken his business and his dignity. Rachel blamed him more than the Wall Street debacle. Other small companies had survived because they weren't acting like bigshots, overextending their credit, using what little cash they had to buy stocks on margin. Hannah could hear the nightly arguments. From a Kid Detective Comic she had learned how to place an empty drinking glass against a wall in order to snoop on private conversations.

"We're flat broke. We haven't got a pot to pee in. And what are you doing about it? Nothing but sitting around and reading the papers like some gigolo. Well, let me tell you one thing, you're not good enough to be a gigolo!" Rachel screamed. Next came the sound of a newspaper being torn to shreds. "You think Walter Lippmann is going to tell you how to get a job?"

Will's voice had faintly rejoined, "I was reading the want ads, Rachel."

"Too bad you cashed in your life insurance. You *could* jump out the window!" The slam of the bathroom door had ended the battle. This morning, Hannah heard her father go out early for the *Times*. He had it under his arm when he walked her to school. "See you later, kitten. Wish me luck." He was answering an ad for a salesman.

That was it, she decided. He was late because he got the job and had no way of letting her know. She would get home as fast as possible. The kids would all be in the playground by now after their milk and cookies. She wanted to change out of her middy blouse and pleated skirt and the brown shoes that were too small for her and were crushing her toes. She knew better than to complain, of course. Rachel was wearing her last pair of silk hose. "See how important it is to have a skill? Then you never have to depend on anyone!" She showed Hannah the needle and thread that were so thin as to seem invisible, and how she mended the runs in her stockings so they could not be seen.

For more than a week, her mother was gone when Will brought Hannah home from school. Rachel would return in the early evening saying only that she was exhausted. One night, Hannah noticed she was wearing a kind of bracelet with a kind of pin cushion attached to it.

"What's that, Mom?"

Rachel had snatched it away. "My advice to you is mind your own business. And marry a rich man!"

Today the apartment was silent when Hannah got home. She missed Becky even after three years since her death. Sam was at band practice. Sounds from the kitchen stopped her dead in her tracks. Burglars? There were so many stories of people coming home unexpectedly and getting beaten up or killed. Should she run and get the elevator man? Drawn as a moth to flame, she tiptoed to the kitchen door.

Will Lawrence sat slumped and muttering at the kitchen table, an empty liquor bottle on its side. He tried to pull himself together. "Hannah, dear! What time is it? I'm sorry. Please don't tell your mother." He pretended to tremble with fear. "She'll boil me in oil."

He staggered to his feet, knocking over his chair. Hannah made a joke of setting it right while he poured her a glass of milk. "I don't see any cookies."

It was then that she noticed the open oven door. "Daddy," she admonished. "Were you going to bake some cookies? You know you can't cook!"

"I—I was only trying to see how the stove works."

She picked up the folded newspaper from the table. Of the job possibilities he had circled, the one for salesmen was crossed off. "It was a fake," he explained. "They're not hiring salesmen. They want you to buy merchandise from them and sell it on your own, door to door. Shoelaces. Garters. Socks. Like a peddler with a pack on your back. But never mind. Come sit on Daddy's knee. How was school?"

"Tell you later." She had to get her roller skates. The kids were at the playground. She didn't like Daddy like this. When she was ready to leave, he was waiting for her at the door, his hair slicked. He was wearing a freshly pressed suit and the blue silk tie Rachel had bought him during happier times.

"I've got one more appointment. How do I look, kitten?"

With a burst of maternal care, Hannah assessed his appearance seriously before patting his hair, straightening his tie and brushing imaginary lint off his shoulders. "You look like—a movie star!"

He smiled sadly down at her. "What a nice child you are. Maybe too nice for your own good."

Outside on the sidewalk, he held her to him for an urgent moment before sending her on her way with a pat on her behind. "Be a good girl! Promise?"

Something in his voice made her turn and run back for another hug. "I promise."

"And don't be mad at your mother. She's doing her best."

Rachel had warned her not to roller skate. Tightening them with her skate key had loosened the soles of her shoes. It cost money to have them repaired. She slung the skates over her shoulder, planning to put them on when she got to the playground. Luck was on her side. The kids were playing blind man's bluff. She left her skates on a bench and joined in. Sam's outgrown oxfords were now hers. With her toes stretched out, she flew like the wind.

When it was time to leave, the skates were gone. Rachel would kill her. Skates cost money. Her heart pounding, she canvassed the entire playground several times, certain of the bench where she had left them but haunted by the possibility of being wrong, of having left them somewhere else.

Darkness was beginning to fall. The western sky across the Hudson River and above the Jersey palisades was a blaze of purple, red, and orange sunset. She suddenly realized she was alone with the fear of her mother's anger compounded by the fears of kidnapping and murder pounded into her with every account Rachel read aloud from the newspaper.

She was running as fast as her exhausted legs would

carry her up the deserted path to the park entrance when she heard the familiar sound of roller-skating. Two boys about the same age as Sam blocked her path. In the fading light she could see that each of them was wearing one roller skate. Her skates.

"Hey, give those back. They're my skates!"

"Oh, yeah? What're you going to do about it."

She used Rachel's voice. "Those are my skates. Give them to me this instant!"

One of the boys rubbed his crotch. "I'll give you something better."

The other boy snickered. "We'll give them back if you let us feel you up!"

This was more than she bargained for. "You shut your trap. I'll tell my brother on you!" Iron railings alongside the path prevented her from cutting across the grass and escaping that way. Her only option was to push past them in a mad rush with her elbows flying.

"Is that nice? We just want to be friends!" Struggling, biting, screaming, she was forced to the ground with the assailants grabbing at her. Then she heard her name.

"Hannah—Han-nah!" Sam was running toward them. Tall for his age, he looked older than his ten years. The two boys jumped up and disappeared into the underbrush.

"Sam—" She tried to tell him what happened. He was not listening. When they reached the street, she could see he was ashen and shaking. "I'm sorry I'm late—I—those boys—they stole my skates—"

But he wasn't listening. "Thank God I found you. Hannah! Hurry!" They ran so fast, she felt as if a knife were stabbing her chest. As they reached the apartment house entrance, Rachel emerged between two uniformed policemen. At the sight of her daughter, Rachel sprang at her with a howl of fury, grabbing her by her braids and slamming her back against the brick wall. Before the girl could recover, her mother repeated the attack with a strike across her face that sent her sprawling.

"Mom, please!" Sam helped his sister up. "It's bad enough."

Hannah was too frightened to cry. "What's wrong? Where's Daddy?" she whimpered.

Rachel seemed about to strike Hannah again. "You stupid little bitch! Why didn't you stop him?"

Sam shielded Hannah. "Please, Mom. It's not her fault." The tears streamed down his face.

"Whose fault is it? Mine? Couldn't she see he was going to do something drastic? My smart daughter. All those A's in arithmetic. Geography. History. A genius. A scholar. High marks but no common sense." Rachel's rage was dissolving in tears.

"Go on upstairs, Hannah. I can't stand the sight of you." The storm seemed to have run its course but not quite. Rachel seized her daughter's arm and almost pulled it from its socket as she sent the weeping girl flying into the lobby.

Sam ran after his sister and gathered her into his arms. "Daddy's dead, Hannah. It's not your fault. He fell off the subway platform. We've got to go and identify the body. The Levys are meeting us."

"Why can't I go, too? He's my father."

They both knew why.

"Go upstairs, Han. Don't pay any attention to her. She didn't mean what she said. Dad's dead." Tears choked his voice. "Mom's upset. Understand?"

She understood plenty. She understood that her mother hated her and that the father she loved and who loved her was dead. From now on the only one she had left in the entire world was Sam.

PART TWO

CHAPTER 17

1945

Viktor

As the war in Europe ended, the domestic conflict between mother and daughter settled down into an uneasy truce based on a mutual agreement to stay out of each other's hair. They lived under the same roof but rarely met. Hannah's classes at Barnard began at eight, which meant leaving the apartment at seven to take the Broadway trolley, or earlier still if she decided to walk the two miles to Morningside Heights. Her extracurricular activities included the campus paper and the American History Club. Her nights were spent sequestered in her room with the radio on while she did her assignments and wrote her daily letter to Viktor.

Every few days she wrote to Sam describing her efforts to find a Jewish refugee agency to help Viktor win the right to asylum as an escapee from Nazi terror, instead of the saboteur the United States Army accused him of being. With nowhere else to go, she called Marcus Salinko at his office when she knew Rachel would be at the hairdresser's.

"I'm sorry to bother you."

"Rachel isn't here."

"I know. I need—well, I need some advice."

He laughed indulgently. "And you don't want your mother to know, right?"

Within weeks of Will Lawrence's death, Rachel's fortunes had taken an abrupt change for the better. Barely able to put food on the table, months behind in the rent for the apartment, she had taken herself to see Marcus Salinko, who owned her building and several more. "I don't want charity. I want a job." As he was to tell her many times, hiring her was the smartest thing he ever did.

If any of the staff deluded themselves that Rachel was Salinko's mistress and would soon be bored with working, they were quickly set straight. Having no duties except to look around and make herself useful, Rachel set to work with a vengeance to root out waste and step up efficiency. At first she tackled the offices, starting with the supply room. It was a hopeless jumble of paper, envelopes, pads, typewriter ribbons, paper clips, and dust-coated stacks of real-estate contracts and leases. At her imperious command, the entire staff, including Marcus, came in on a Sunday to take everything out, wash the shelves and floor, and replace everything in orderly fashion under her direction.

The office manager had reluctantly sacrificed his Sunday golf to participate in the cleanup. This earned him no mercy. "I wonder, Mr. Meadow, why you keep ordering new supplies when we have plenty of everything right here," Rachel demanded.

Mr. Meadow took his lumps. He could not afford to resign. Jobs were hard to find.

The next day, when regular work resumed, the staff found the door to the supply room locked. Rachel had the key. Henceforth every dispersal of supplies was to go through her. A used typewriter ribbon had to be turned in for a new one. Carbon paper had to be worn thin before it could be discarded. Pencils were to be sharpened to stubs before they could be exchanged for new ones. This was the Depression, after all.

From this beginning, she moved from strength to strength, over the years learning every aspect of residential real estate in New York City. Wartime restrictions had put a halt to construction but that didn't stop Rachel from making elaborate plans for what everyone in the industry knew would be a postwar building boom. She and Marcus walked through neighborhoods of old-law buildings that she knew could be bought and replaced with modern structures. The area around Columbus Circle was one. The Lower East Side was another. The tenements on Second and Third Avenues were ripe for her vision. There were rumors aplenty that the elevated railroads would come down after the war, turning the dark saloon-lined streets into wide boulevards. "Like the Champs Elysees!" she enthused.

"You've never seen the Champs Elysees!" Marcus had chided, delighted with her energy and still-stunning beauty.

"You'll have to take me there after the war, won't you, Marcus?"

"If you'll marry me."

He had proposed before. Her answer had always been, "How can I marry you? You're already married."

Rose Salinko had assumed her husband's infatuation would eventually run its course. She had refused to discuss a divorce until a few months ago. She had met someone she wanted to marry. A jubilant Marcus Salinko told Rachel the good news. His wife would be leaving for Reno in a month or so. "Six weeks' residence and I'm a free man!"

"Congratulations," Rachel said dryly.

"But I don't want to be a free man. I want to be your slave for the rest of our lives!" Marcus had shouted dramatically and fell to his knee in the middle of a crowded Fifth Avenue sidewalk to propose.

Rachel wanted things to stay as they were. She liked her life as it was. She was fond of Marcus and felt comfortable with their intimate times together but she preferred living separately. She was excited about the big development plans they had for the future. When Sam came home from the war, her life would be complete. She and Marcus had been together for more than ten years. They were a good team. Why couldn't he leave well enough alone?

And if he wouldn't, what then?

If she had to, she would go out on her own. She knew her way around. She could get backing from the banks. Or join forces with one of the other property giants: Tisch, Durst, Helmsley, Chanin. There were no other women in the industry. With her experience and her ideas, she could name her price!

In any case, she would make no decision until Sam was safely home. She wanted everything in the Riverside Drive apartment to be exactly as he left it. Hannah had wanted to use her brother's room; Rachel put a stop to that. She had to admit she did not understand her daughter. Staying out all night like a tramp. Going to Greenwich Village at night, to see some folksinger, of all things. The next thing Rachel knew, Hannah was trying to play the guitar! Rachel could hear the sounds coming from Hannah's room, the phonograph records of some man moaning and groaning while Hannah tried to play and sing along. Whatever happened to Bing Crosby and Frank Sinatra?

Now her darling daughter had come up with something else. She had left a note saying Kathleen Fenton was coming to New York and Hannah had invited her to stay. She had had the nerve to ask if Kathleen could sleep in Sam's room!

Rachel could not understand why Hannah insisted on being friends with their Irish maid. Not that she didn't admire Kathleen for bettering herself, working in a war plant and then joining the WACs. She was still puzzled by Kathleen's appearance at Hannah's graduation, but then Hannah was always concerned with the underdog.

A few days before Kathleen's arrival in New York, Sam managed to get a phone call through. Rachel waved Hannah away. "Please, darling. I'm talking to my son. Wait your turn." Before Hannah's turn came, the connection was abruptly disconnected. "He sends you his love. He said he had a letter from that nice Kathleen and that she was coming to New York on leave and that I should be nice to her. Why wouldn't I be nice to her when both my children are so crazy about her? You must invite her to stay with us, Hannah. We'll give her Sam's room." Hannah was dumbfounded by her mother's breezy about-face.

It was a warm April afternoon when Kathleen arrived. "How did he sound?" she begged Hannah as soon as they were alone.

"I don't know. Rachel wouldn't give me the phone 'til it was too late," Hannah said.

In Sam's last V-mail to Hannah from France, he wrote almost exclusively about Kathleen and how they were thinking of moving to Oregon or Colorado after they got married, somewhere with lots of space where Kathleen could have her vegetable garden and they could raise a family.

He hoped Rachel wouldn't be upset. "Maybe if I'm out of the way, she'll marry Marcus," he'd written.

They sat in Sam's room and turned on his radio. The war could be over at any moment. The Battle of the Bulge had scared everyone, but it was over. The Germans' last-ditch attack on Bastogne had killed and wounded thousands of America troops, a disaster made all the more tragic with the victory so inevitable and so close.

The capture of Cologne, the crossing of the Rhine at Remagen, and the news bulletins were coming thick and fast. Any minute. Any minute it would be over and the troops would be coming home!

"We interrupt this program to bring you a news bulletin from Washington, D.C."

The two young women hugged each other. "It's over. The war is over!"

"President Roosevelt is dead. At three thirty-five this afternoon, the president suffered a massive cerebral hemorrhage at the Little White House in Warm Springs, Georgia. Vice President Harry S. Truman has been summoned to the White House to be sworn in as the thirty-second president of the United States. Mrs. Eleanor Roosevelt is on her way to Warm Springs to accompany her husband's body back to Washington for the state funeral."

Hannah and Kathleen stared at the radio in shock, their joy instantly turned to sorrow.

By the time Hannah could get permission for another visit with Viktor, a month had gone by. The war in Europe was over. Mussolini and his mistress had been executed and strung up in a public square in Milan. Hitler and his mistress had married before committing suicide in a bunker in Berlin.

"Isn't it a shame FDR didn't live to see the victory?" Hannah asked conversationally.

Viktor was in one of his angry moods. Not that she blamed him. It had been ten months since he walked ashore like a bronzed sea god. His solitary incarceration was getting more and more intolerable.

"He was a hypocrite!"

"How dare you say such a thing?"

"You think he loved the Jews? You think he didn't know about the camps? You think he wasn't told about the refugee ships that were turned away from American ports or about the offers to sell Jewish prisoners for money?"

Hannah had come to report on the latest legal developments in Vickor's case, not to argue. "Well, anyway, Mussolini and Hitler are dead, too," she said.

"Low-class scum. Ignorant men with no education. No sense of the finer things. No taste in clothes. Look at those uniforms. No taste in women. Look at that Clara Petacci! Look at that Eva Braun!" He pounded the table in anger and frustration before regaining control of his emotions. "Darling, I'm sorry if I upset you." He gathered her hands in his and kissed each finger in turn, his shoulders shaking with sobs.

"My poor darling." She buried her face in his hair. "I'm doing my best. The lawyer says the liberation of the camps will help. Those pictures. My God! He says being a Jew is the best thing you've got going for you."

Marcus Salinko had agreed to be a sponsor for Viktor. He and Hannah agreed to keep this a secret from her mother. Rachel knew nothing of their meetings or of Salinko's help. Her mind was entirely obsessed with her son's return from the war.

Sam would be coming home as soon as he could arrange it, and Hannah and Kathleen were prepared. The plan was this. Sam would spend a week of celebrating with Rachel, letting her get used to the idea that he was back in one piece, and then he would tell her he and Kathleen were getting married.

In mid-July, a telegram was delivered to the Riverside Drive apartment. Rachel crushed it unopened in her palm, her eyes clamped closed, her body swaying as if she would faint. "You open it!" she told her daughter. When Hannah reached for it, her mother slapped her hand away. "He's my son! If—if anything happened—I'm the one—not you—"

The envelope slipped from her hand and sailed across the floor just as Marcus arrived to drive Rachel downtown. "The door was open," he explained. He picked up the envelope. "What's this?"

"Can't you see it's a telegram!" Rachel turned her back. "I don't want to know what it says."

"Let me, Mom. He's my brother." Hannah was calm; she couldn't believe it was bad news.

Rachel whirled around and knocked the telegram out of Hannah's hands. "You read it, Marcus."

It seemed like hours until he got the envelope open. The paper stuck to his sweating fingers. The folded message clung stubbornly to its secret. "It's okay! He's coming home! On the *Queen Elizabeth.*"

"Thank God!" Rachel threw herself at Marcus in a wild embrace, dancing the two of them around and around in exultation. Hannah's attempt to join them was shrugged off, leaving her to stand rejected and alone in her joy and relief. *Thank God*! she silently echoed her mother's cry. She knew she should be used to Rachel's attitude by now. She should ignore it and think only of having her brother back and telling him about Viktor.

First and foremost she had to leave a message for Kathleen. Not wishing to be overheard, she used the telephone on Rachel's night table. While waiting for the switchboard operator at Fort Hamilton to transfer her to the message clerk, she berated herself for being angry at her mother. She knew how terrified Rachel was of anything happening to Sam. She promised herself to be more understanding, until she noticed something in Rachel's bedside waste basket. It was the copy of the campus paper that featured one of Hannah's articles. She had left it, with a little note, for her mother. The note was still attached, the newspaper folded. On top of it were a clutter of peach pits and cottonballs stained with Rachel's nail polish.

July thirtieth marked a record statistic in the return of American troops from Europe. On that one day, 31,445 personnel arrived in New York harbor on seven ships. Among them was the *Queen Elizabeth*, originally built as a floating palace to join her sister ship the *Queen Mary*, on the luxurious North Atlantic run, but converted into a troop ship when Britain entered the war in 1939.

As the entire harbor erupted with welcoming whistles and geysers of water from the harbor patrol boats, the huge but graceful ship still painted in camouflage gray was eased into its North River berth by tugboats that looked like bathtub toys in comparison. Crushed in the waiting, screaming crowd, Rachel, Marcus, and Hannah held red balloons in hopes of attracting Sam's attention. Kathleen had agreed with Hannah that it would be more tactful in the circumstance for her to wait in her room at the Astor Hotel until Hannah could tell Sam where she was.

The ship itself was 1,031 feet long, like a ten-storey building on its side. Thousands of men lined the upper deck, cheering and holding up handmade signs. Faces filled every porthole. From one, an extremely thin soldier had managed to work his upper body through the opening. He waved his arms as if conducting the Army band welcoming them from the pier.

"Sam! We're here! *Here!*" The fact that her voice could not possibly be heard above the uproar, Rachel nonetheless kept on shouting and jumping up and down. Several times she thought she saw him. "Look, Marcus. There he is! Why doesn't he see us!" She collapsed momentarily against his shoulder, whimpering, "I want my boy. I want my son."

The huge liner finally in place, the band playing *East Side, West Side*, confetti falling like multicolored snow, the conquering heroes roared down the gangways like a championship football team entering the home stadium. Tens and then hundreds poured onto American soil. The lucky ones were instantly swallowed up by loved ones. The less lucky whose families and friends lived too far away to make the expensive journey to New York, hugged and kissed anyone who was willing.

"Lieutenant Lawrence! Lieutenant Sam Lawrence? Do you know him? I'm his mother. Have you seen him?" There was no holding Rachel back. "Please. Do you know Lt. Lawrence? Sam? Everyone calls him Sam!" the soldiers were polite but in a hurry. *No, Ma'am. Sorry, Ma'am. He'll be along. Don't worry.*

She was worried. All three were getting more and more panicky as the great ship emptied. Could he have missed the ship? Or been given different travel orders? Had he sent a message they never got?

"Let me try to find the officer in charge," Marcus said.

"It's about time you did something instead of standing there like a jackass!" Rachel shrieked.

"You and Hannah wait here," Marcus replied calmly.

The pier by now was virtually deserted. The Army band was packing up its instruments. Confetti and paper streamers lay limp on the concrete amid chewing gum and candy wrappers and empty soda bottles, crumpled signs, and spent balloons.

"Look down there! Maybe they know!" Rachel began to run down the length of the pier to an opening on the side of the ship where a small group of men in fatigues were offloading boxes. Hannah was wearing her new high-heeled pumps for the occasion. In trying to keep up with her mother, she failed to notice a small iron bollard until it was too late. Her heel caught in the metal ring and sent her crashing to the ground on her hands and knees. The heel had snapped like a string bean. Shards of concrete stabbed her arms and legs like hundreds of daggers.

"Are you okay?" Marcus had seen the two women running and was hard on their trail when he saw Hannah fall.

"Did you find anything out?"

"Everyone's gone. There must be a message at home."

"We'd better get Mom."

"What's she doing down there? That's the cargo door!"

A piercing scream shattered the relative quiet of the pier. "No—nooo-nooooo-NOOOOOOOOOOOOO!"

They found her face down on an oblong wooden crate, pounding it with her fists. Stencilled on the side of the crate was the name 2ND LT. SAMUEL LAWRENCE.

The dropping of the atomic bomb on Hiroshima and the Japanese surrender aboard the battleship *Missouri* had only a marginal impact on the Riverside Drive apartment. The shock of Sam's death was all consuming, the scene on the Cunard pier etched permanently in their minds. It had taken all of Marcus Salinko's considerable strength to pry Rachel off the wooden crate that contained her son's coffin. The fingernails she had manicured so exquisitely for the occasion were ripped raw and bleeding from clawing at the unfinished wood. She could not stop screaming. Frustrated in her attempt to penetrate the crate, she hurled her entire body against it, pummeling it with her fists, cursing incoherently in her frenzy. When Marcus tried to calm her, she turned her rage on him, punching and kicking him away until at last she gave up and collapsed against him.

Taking charge, he sent Rachel home with Hannah and requested the officer on duty to keep the crate in the cargo depot until arrangements could be made. As to the question of how Sam had died, it turned out to have been a freak accident that could have happened to anyone. Four nights before, Sam had awakened in his bunk and apparently decided to get some fresh air. There had been squalls; the sky was heavily overcast. When his body was found the next morning, the theory was that he was climbing the outside steps to the promenade deck when the ship lurched. He must have lost his footing on the slippery metal and broken his neck in the fall.

Rachel sat upright in her bedroom for three whole days, smoking cigarettes and refusing to eat or sleep. Hannah and the Levys were banished. Only Marcus was allowed in. She had not washed her face or combed her hair or changed her clothes. The new summer silk shirtwaist dress she had bought for Sam's homecoming was snagged and coated with shavings from the rough exterior of the wooden crate.

She listened to the explanation of the accident with so little reaction, Marcus was not sure she had absorbed what he said.

"No burial!" were her first words since he found her screaming on the Cunard pier. "No worms having a picnic on my son!" Cremation, she decided, followed by a simple ceremony. "Nondenominational. I don't know whether or not I'm a Jew. Will Lawrence didn't believe in religion. I used to think I believed in God. I thought God liked me. He didn't have to love me. I just thought he liked me enough not to hurt me. But not any more!" she cried. "I don't believe in anything. I don't even believe in myself."

The crematorium offered mourners the use of a small and tasteful retiring room. When the enamelled box of ashes was presented to her, Rachel jumped back with alarm. "Take them away. I don't want them. Please—"

Hannah stepped forward. "I'll take them. I'll scatter them on the grass near the Soldiers and Sailors monument. Sam loved Riverside Drive."

Rachel seized the box and thrust it at her daughter. "Why isn't it you?"

There was a collective gasp as everyone in the room turned to Hannah.

"She doesn't mean it, Hannah!" Marcus said. "She's heartbroken, you know."

I'm heartbroken, too. Rachel's possessiveness of Sam in life became fiercer yet in death. If only she and her mother could mourn together, share memories of him the way other people did at funerals and wakes. That was the ceremonial purpose. Tears and laughter to ease the grief. At least she had Kathleen.

At first she didn't recognize her without her uniform. Kathleen was waiting for her at the Soldiers and Sailors Monument dressed in an apple-green organza print that complimented the thicket of silken red hair that hung loose over her shoulders instead of pulled tight in the severe bun required by WAC regulations. A wide leghorn straw hat danced behind her shoulders, held in place with a green velvet ribbon tied under her chin.

Both young women had had the same idea to honor Sam by dressing gaily. At Rachel's insistence, Hannah had worn one of her mother's old black dresses for the cremation. The heavy black wool and black felt hat were suffocatingly hot for August. Sam would probably get a kick out of his mother's relentless tricks. She knew he would definitely applaud her decision to change into the houndstooth check he said made her look like Lauren Bacall.

Kathleen had a different suggestion from the Soldiers and Sailors Monument. Farther south on River-side Drive was a huge stone eagle standing guard on a retaining wall that was waist high on the drive itself but dropped precipitously on the park side some thirty to forty feet.

"Don't laugh, Hannah. The last time Sam and I were in New York we bought a bag of cherries. We leaned over the wall to see how far we could spit the pips!"

Passersby might have thought the two women were throwing breadcrumbs to the pigeons. Each took a turn scattering a handful of ashes. Kathleen recited from John Donne.

Death be not proud, though some have called thee
mighty and dreadful, for thou art not so,
For those whom thou think'st thou dost overthrow,
die not, poor death, nor yet canst thou kill me.

Hannah had recently discovered Conrad Aiken's *Bread and Music*, a poem she was sure Sam would have loved.

Music I heard with you was more than music,
And bread I broke with you was more than bread.
Now that I am without you, all is desolate;
All that was once so beautiful is dead.

There was more, but she was unable to continue.

"Ashes to ashes. Dust to dust." Kathleen's lilting voice intoned. "In pure and certain hope of the resurrection unto eternal life. Amen."

A Good Humor ice cream wagon stopped beside them affording a perfect conclusion to the ceremonial. Hannah was too close to tears to tell Kathleen what was in her heart. She thought the chocolate pop would help, but it only reminded her of the countless times

Sam spent his meager allowance on Good Humors for her, and now it only made things worse. She would write to Kathleen. Fate may have prevented them from being sisters-in-law, but they would be sisters under the skin forever, amen.

"I almost forgot something, Hannah." Kathleen removed a thick white envelope from her handbag. "It's from Sam. He sent it to me because he knows—knew, dear God—he knew Rachel opened your mail."

It was an insurance policy for a hundred thousand dollars naming Hannah as beneficiary. The note with it was frighteningly prescient. "For God's sake, don't let Mom know I've done this. And if anything should happen to me, don't let Mom know you're an heiress. If I'm stupid enough not to be around, remember you're one smart cookie. Whatever happens, remember I love you and believe in your ability to make a rewarding life for yourself."

The postscript said, "Stop eating those Black Crows and Tootsie Rolls. Kathleen and I don't want a butterball for a flower girl."

"But what about you, Kathleen? You were going to be his wife."

"Thinkin' of others as usual, aren't you, now? Well, not to worry. He bought the same policy for me. And you're not going to tell Rachel and let her take it away from you! You're going to take charge of your life. The money's yours. You can throw it away on high living or you can do something practical. It's up to you."

Visions of sugarplum dreams danced through her head—clothes, furs, a red convertible—and were all quickly pushed aside. She had better things to do with the money. One was to buy property. From listening to Rachel and Marcus discuss the coming postwar real-estate boom, she knew it would be possible to find a small but sound building, add some cosmetic touches like a decent lobby and new awning then sell it at a profit and use that capital to buy something better, and so on.

The second thing was to secure Viktor's release. With her new found wealth she could hire the best legal minds in the city and nominate herself as his sponsor. What she would need over the next several months was patience. Until the insurance claim was paid, she would endure Rachel's tantrums and sarcasm by continually reminding herself of their cause. Her mother had lost her beloved son. Hannah would stay out of Rachel's hair, would refuse to be drawn into a shouting match or worse. She would mourn her brother in her own way, alone and in company with Kathleen before she left New York to take a civilian job in San Francisco.

Marcus was letting himself out of the apartment when she returned home that afternoon. "Dr. Levy was here. He gave her a shot. She went out like a light."

"Fine."

He followed her back into the apartment. "Hannah?"

"That's my name."

"Listen to me."

"I know what you're going to say, Marcus. She didn't mean what she said, okay? Let's forget it, okay?"

He followed her into the kitchen. "I know how you feel."

"Dammit, you don't know how I feel. He was my brother. My friend. My *best* friend. Don't tell me you know how I feel."

"Then you must know how your mother is suffering."

It came to Hannah with something like a shameless thrill to realize she had no sympathy for Rachel's suffering because it excluded her. Why should she give a damn about her mother? Thanks to Sam, she was an heiress now. Not a major heiress, but an heiress nevertheless. What's more she was smarter than most. She would make her money work for her and make Sam proud. And marry Viktor and have children she would love to pieces.

CHAPTER 18

1951

Eleanor

When Kathleen cancelled plans to fly in from San Francisco for Hannah and Viktor's wedding because of little Bryan's measles, Hannah had promised to write her friend a long, detailed letter. A whole month had gone by, and Hannah was ashamed to say she had failed to keep her promise. This morning, however, she had awakened early full of pep and resolved to remedy the situation. Creeping barefoot out of the bedroom, she left her husband asleep tangled in the silk sheets he preferred, his silk pajamas, one of her many wedding gifts to him, flung on the floor on his side of the bed.

Married a whole month, she marveled. She could hardly believe it had finally happened. After more than five years of agonizing red tape, military tribunals, petitions to the Justice Department, hearings before the Immigration and Naturalization authorities, and plaintive appeals to Jewish refugee organizations, Hannah's persistence had prevailed.

The process had been painfully slow, but finally Viktor was cleared of the charge of being a Nazi spy; a lengthy investigation had failed to find his name on lists of German war criminals, and his defection from the submarine was supported by Army witnesses on the beach as well as by a civilian journalist, Hannah Lawrence.

Six weeks ago, he had at last been granted resident alien status, thus clearing the way for him to marry an American citizen without fear of being accused of collusion.

Settling down at the kitchen table, her body ached for him with a craving that was as strong today as that first sight of him striding naked through the surf to the Jersey shore. She had attributed the frenzy of their early lovemaking to uncertainty and the whims of the guards on Governor's Island, where he had remained under house arrest until she had finally achieved his release. Never knowing when or if they would be alone together only added fuel to their desire when the bribe was tactfully accepted and the door locked.

After his release, she had assumed sleeping together every night would soon become routine. If anything, she found herself in an advanced stage of sexual addiction. She could not get enough of him. She was voracious and never completely satisfied. Regardless of the variety and intensity of her orgasms, she wanted more.

Did this mean she was a nymphomaniac, that creature of legend men joked about? Or could it have something to do with the little green tablets Viktor had given her to make her sexually strong and fertile? Whatever the cause, she was looking a gift horse in the mouth. For the time being she should remind herself that she was on her honeymoon. Her only concern should be shopping for a large supply of cheaper nightgowns. While Viktor enjoyed approaching their bed brushed, combed, and drenched in Guerlain Imperiale and making a ceremony of stripping off his pajamas for her delectation, he insisted she keep her nightgown on.

"You must not give yourself to me, Hannah. You must make me take you."

Among the casualties were Kathleen's trousseau gift of three satin gowns that she herself had embroidered with dainty pink rosettes. Viktor had torn them off her body with a surgeon's precision. The sound and feel of ripped fabric frightened and exalted her.

"My savage!" he shouted. "Who would think it to look at you? Our secret, my darling."

She brought her Olivetti portable to the kitchen table, where the typing could not be heard from the bedroom. For a moment she was tempted to go back to bed, slide between the sheets beside him, wake him slowly and voluptuously in the ways he had shown her. Not today, however. *You must be brave, Schatzi.* Today he was to start his new job with the Adler Society, the organization formed to help German Jewish refugees rebuild their lives. He needed his sleep.

It was the Adlers as much as the lawyers who had worked tirelessly for Viktor's vindication. Now he would be a spokesman for their fund-raising efforts. As a member of the executive committee confided to Hannah, "The American people are getting tired of the pathetic victims of the Holocaust. Viktor is ideal for projecting the new image of the postwar Jew. Strong, handsome, charming, cultured.

"There are plenty of other organizations for building settlements in Israel. Our interest is cultural. Libraries. Schools. Museums. Archeology. All dedicated to educating and encouraging a future generation of worldly, sophisticated Jewish leaders who photograph well and speak several languages."

It all sounded highfalutin to Hannah but she couldn't worry her head about it. The important thing, the miraculous thing, was Viktor was free. They were married. He had a job. She was happier and more fulfilled as a woman than she had ever been in her entire life, and if her hunch was right they would have their first child at the beginning of next year.

There was so much to tell Kathleen. How to begin?

Dearest Kathleen,

You haven't seen our apartment but I know you'll like it. Remember, now. You're staying with us your next trip East, and that includes that handsome husband of yours! My instinct was right. Marcus always said I have a good head for business. I was able to buy the building for a song. You remember: rundown street, rundown facade. Bathrooms that came over with the Mayflower.

Well, it turns out a major developer is putting together a parcel that includes my building and has offered me three times what I paid for it! I'm still determined to keep my private affairs private. I don't want my mother to know what I'm doing. If I go to Marcus for advice you can bet he'll go running to her like a bunny rabbit!

They're finally getting hitched by the way. Not that she told *me*. She told *Viktor*! It's really a shame you weren't here for my wedding. It's hard to describe how she tried to make herself the center of attention.

I knew I shouldn't have invited her. I should have sent her a postcard afterward. We waited and waited for her. The judge was blowing his top. Viktor looked as if he was going to run for the hills. But I've got to say this for my husband—did you catch that?—*husband*—he charmed her socks off. She was simpering and blushing and stammering. I'm sure she's wondering how I managed to hook someone like Viktor.

She flirted with him, Kathleen. It was a scream. She said she was sure I wouldn't mind if she and Viktor had a tête-à-tête lunch. Marcus looked as if he wanted to kill Viktor. And me! Well, at least he got her to marry him finally. And you know what the killer is? She called me. My own mother called me to say she thought it best not to have me and Viktor at her wedding! No reason given. Only that she knew I'd understand!

Understand what, I ask you? The only one who understood her was Sam, and I wonder if even he really did. I think of him every day, Kathleen. I still wish my mother could bring herself to talk to me about him. It's a closed door. After all this time, I suppose I could get even with her by telling her about the insurance policy. But like I say, the less I have to do with her, the better.

By the way—and don't start knitting yet—I think there may be a little stranger on the way! I'm a week overdue and my breasts are tender but of course that could be from the married life! I'll let you know as soon as I'm sure. And I'm not telling my mother about that, either. Hey, maybe the reason she doesn't want me at her wedding is she thinks it'll make her look old. Think how she'll feel about being a grandmother!

That's about all for now. Oh, yes, one more thing. You know how I was trying to be writer? And my clips from the *Red* and my *Bank Weekly Times* college paper didn't impress anyone at the *Times* or the *Trib?* Well, it's not much but I just sold a piece to *Glamour.* I'm so excited! I haven't told Viktor. I'll wait till it comes out and then just casually have it lying around! Isn't that great? Oh, Kathleen, how I wish you were here. Letters are okay, but nothing beats sitting around the kitchen table, does it?

I hope little Bryan is fine by now. Give him a hug and a kiss for me and tell him to expect a big surprise from Auntie Hannah on his birthday!

All my love. And just in time, too. I've just been kissed on the back of the neck!

As ever, Hannah.

"Why do you make a carbon copy?" Viktor wanted to know.

"Just a habit I guess."

"You make copies of all your letters?"

"It's a habit, Viktor."

"My letters? The letters you've written to me?"

Pretty steamy, now that she thought of them. "Yes, I've got them somewhere."

"For posterity?"

What did he mean? She had cleared the typewriter and paper from the table and was setting it for breakfast. "Toast, darling?" Some mornings he just had coffee, very strong with heavy cream and a single cube of sugar.

"You're changing the subject. I asked if you were saving your letters for posterity. You know. Like other famous authors bequeathing their papers to a university or library."

What in the world was he talking about? Making the *cafe filtre* was still a challenge. She had to concentrate on getting it right.

"You are a famous author, aren't you?" he persisted. "Your mother showed me your cuttings. Very impressive. I'm very impressed with my talented wife."

Years later she would remember this moment as the beginning of the end of her marriage. He had never been sarcastic before. It was a side of his character that would become increasingly evident. Seeing her expression, he had laughed and taken her in his arms. "I was just teasing. Don't be so serious. It was just a silly little joke."

A cruel joke, making fun of her failure as a writer. How many times had she shown him the rejection slips she had received from the *New Yorker* and the *Saturday Review*? His sympathy had led her to unburden her secret hopes and dreams of someday writing a great and classic novel.

Hopes and dreams were fragile and helpless, an easy mark for bullies. The incident was surely trivial, at worst a heavy-handed attempt at humor. Yet her emotional radar picked up the danger signal. She had been attacked at her most vulnerable part. She had withstood the attack without any visible scar, though internally she was wounded.

Can't you take a joke? was the bully's national anthem. Ironically, it was the subject of her forthcoming article in *Glamour*. No, she had written, she could not take a joke. She refused to accept insults and humiliation as humor. Sarcasm, she said, had no place in the postwar world. She ended it with a highly passionate plea for nations as well as men and women to stop being nasty to each other and start being nice.

"Naive perhaps, but heartfelt and extremely well presented," the editor wrote in accepting her submission.

Equally naive and certainly heartfelt had been her unquestioning certainty that Viktor's love for her was as generous and protective as hers for him. Teasing was meant to be gentle and give pleasure, not pain. There could be no mistaking Viktor's little joke. He had tried to make her unhappy for no reason at all.

"The coffee is superb!" He knew he had stepped over the line, but not how far.

"Are you sure that's enough?" A loving wife was solicitous.

"I'll be late if I don't hurry. You don't want me to be sacked my first day."

That night she had dinner ready and waiting and the dining room table set with silver, crystal, china, and candles. Viktor arrived on time with flowers, champagne, and caviar. He had somehow sensed that something serious had occurred and he must do his utmost to make amends. No reference was made to the morning incident. Her husband regaled her with a lively report of his first day's experiences in an American office. The shocking informality of being called by his first name by everyone, including the office boy. The key to the men's room in the public corridor. The water cooler with the paper cups shaped like little envelopes so that they could not be set down but had to be used and thrown away.

Flattery and attention got Hannah where she always wanted to be. In bed with her husband, the dinner forgotten, the champagne bucket and crystal flutes carried with them to wash down the little green pill. Later, all passions spent, he bathed her as if she were a child, going so far as to test the water with his elbow. "Tonight I shall be your nursemaid," he whispered huskily. He washed her hair with the spray attachment and wrapped her head in a towel turban.

Her breasts bobbed on the surface of the water. He aimed the spray at first one and then the other. "Like spring rain." Her nipples hardened. He leant over and kissed them gently. "Your nursemaid wants only to please." The sexual ambiguity of the nursemaid kissing and fondling her breasts frightened her. He had once talked about the delights of watching two women make love. Her appalled reaction had silenced him and the subject had never come up again.

What had been discussed was the feminine aspects of the most masculine of men and the masculine aspects of the most feminine of women. Thinking of this concept helped her to understand Rachel's pendulum swings of behavior and her own weaknesses and strengths as well.

"Now close your eyes like a good little girl. I'll be right back." Sweet lassitude. Indescribable contentment. *If I die now, I'll know I have lived.* She could hear him return and put something heavy on top of the hamper. Keeping her eyes tightly closed, she tried to identify the sounds. The record player, of course! The turntable squeaked as the first record dropped. The needle arm fell, hesitated and found its groove. *Chopin!*

Viktor returned to his task. Like a rag doll, she submitted herself to his ministrations. Using the big natural sponge she had bought for him at Caswell-Massey he bathed every inch of her, standing her up at the last in order to do her back and legs. "See how lovely you are?" He turned her toward the full-length mirror behind the bathroom door.

He dried her with slow, scrupulous care, as if she were a fragile piece of sculpture. The black terrycloth robe she had bought for him at Bernini because it looked like European aristocracy, hung from its special hook. Slipping into it, he held it open, his arms outstretched. "Come to me, my darling."

She stepped out of the tub and into his embrace. He wrapped the voluminous robe around them both, holding her nakedness against his in a cocoon of comfort and safety, her face nestled on nature's special niche between the neck and shoulder.

"Sleepy?"

She was beyond speech and could only sigh and cling to his neck as he picked her up and carried her to the rocking chair in the bedroom. The last thing she could remember before drifting into oblivion was Viktor holding her in his lap with the warm, thick terrycloth covering them both while he softly sang a German lullaby.

Two weeks later, Dr. Levy confirmed her suspicions. She was pregnant. He had brought Hannah into the world and remembered Rachel's suffering through the long labor and difficult delivery. He wanted Hannah to be healthy, strong, and flexible.

He outlined a program of diet, vitamins, exercise, and rest. "By the way, are you taking any medication?" he asked.

No, she knocked wood, she was healthy as a horse. "Except for—"

Dr. Levy was instantly alert. "Except for what?" These days people were gobbling up over-the-counter remedies like they were candy. "Except for what? Aspirin? Bicarbonate of Soda? I need to know. Anything can affect the development of the fetus."

She mentioned the little green pills Viktor gave her. "What for?"

He was a doctor. Why did she think he'd be shocked? Or judgmental? "For our love life."

"Do you know what's in them?"

Viktor was her husband. She trusted him. "I—I didn't ask."

Dr. Levy tried to conceal his exasperation. "Taking pills without knowing what they are? I'm surprised at you, Hannah. Be so kind as to ask him what they are."

"I—can't. I'm sorry, Aaron. I just can't."

"All right, then. Bring one to me, and stop using them immediately. We mustn't jeopardize the baby. I'll send it to my lab and find out what it is."

Cantharides was the medical term for Spanish Fly. "The man is crazy!" Dr. Levy cried. "He could have killed you." Tersely and with mounting fury he explained that cantharides was a crude aphrodisiac used for centuries by ranchers to increase their herds of cattle and flocks of sheep. "People think it's made of crushed flies. It isn't. It's made of beetles—*cantharis vesicatoria*. All the fellows at medical school thought they'd sneak some into their girl friends' drinks and get lucky!" He managed a laugh that was more of a cough. "Our old professor must have been through it a hundred times. He warned us in vivid terms that cantharides was dangerous as hell! It can tear your insides to shreds and destroy your urinary tract."

In examining her, he had thought the swelling and irritation was due to what doctors call the honeymoon disease or the excessive lovemaking of newlyweds. "Your husband should be horsewhipped! I'll tell him so myself," Dr. Levy fumed.

"Please, no! Let me handle it." Hannah couldn't believe Viktor would risk hurting her. She had to believe he only wanted her to experience the heights of passion.

"You will not take another green pill?"

"I will not take another green pill. I'll tell him I'm pregnant and you advised me not to take any pills without clearing it with you first."

Aaron Levy took off his glasses and toyed with items on his desk while trying to figure out how to say what was in his heart. "Marriage should be based on trust. You can no longer trust this man. He's got a twisted idea of sexual satisfaction."

She rushed to her husband's defense. "He's a wonderful lover and now he's given me a baby." She patted her belly with joyful anticipation. She hoped it would be a girl so that she could give her the love and attention Rachel had never given her.

She assured the doctor that she would be fine. It wasn't cowardice that prevented her from confronting Viktor. It was a primordial desire to cloak herself in serenity while her baby grew.

Viktor took the news of her pregnancy as an inconvenience. "You shan't be ill every morning, I hope." Rachel took the more practical view. "When are you due? Marcus and I are planning a trip to Europe at the end of the year so I may not be here to hold your hand."

Someone once said to be careful what you wish for; you may just get it. Hannah had built an edifice for

Viktor and herself and discovered its foundations were in quicksand. Being with him still stirred paroxysms of desire. He needn't have given her the cantharadies. He was aphrodysiac enough. The problem was becoming one of searing ambivalence between her body and her mind, her flesh craving him, her brain reminding her of his perfidy.

The placenta growing around her baby had its counterpart in the invisible wall of protection she erected around herself. She knew from her college psychology course that first-time fathers often felt threatened by their wife's pregnancy, felt excluded and competitive. As the professor explained, society insists new fathers be thrilled, but in point of fact they feel angry and deprived. The class giggled with embarrassment when he concluded, "They can't admit it of course, but they're furious at being displaced at the mother's breast!"

Dr. Levy had assured her that making love would not harm the baby. Viktor accepted Hannah's explanation for curtailing the little green pills with a sarcastic shrug. How could they hurt the baby? Taking them had helped create the baby, he insisted.

Viktor's mood turned angrier and more sarcastic in direct ratio to Hannah's growing girth. He criticized her appearance, her greasy hair, her decision to stop wearing makeup because her skin was too oily to hold it. Her blithe refusal to argue with him turned his wrath to other targets. Their apartment, for one. A West Side slum. The important people, the people he worked with, lived on the East Side. Park Avenue. Fifth Avenue. With maids and cooks. Not the ignorant cleaning woman who could not iron his shirts properly!

She refused to let him get to her. She declined to remind him of the time and money she had spent on his release. She chose to ignore his failure to contribute a nickel of his salary toward the upkeep of their home.

She insisted on maintaining a civilized dialogue with this stranger who looked like the man she had once worshipped and adored. How were things at the office? She relied on the safe questions when silence grew onerous. She listened attentively to his recitations of success. Often his business meetings over cocktails would culminate with a phone call explaining they were going on to dinner at the Colony or the St. Regis. Gradually he stopped bothering to phone and simply came home after she had gone to sleep.

She allowed nothing he did to upset her. She kept enough food handy for an instant dinner in case he did show up. His favorites: German sausages and baby lambchops that could be grilled to perfection in minutes. Jars of fruit compote and sliced cucumbers with dill. The new instant rice. Liqueur-filled chocolates and petits fours. Heavy *schlag* for his coffee. Never, by word or nuance of expression, did she question his behavior. It was simply easier this way.

One night as she was clearing the table, the phone rang. Lately there had been several disconnects when she answered, and once a woman with what she thought might be a German accent said she had the wrong number. If there were a new woman in his life, and she didn't especially care if there was, she preferred to let Viktor take the calls and be done with it.

"Kathleen?" Viktor offered the phone to his wife. "It's for you!"

"Talk to her for a minute while I stack the dishes," Hannah said.

When she was ready to talk, Viktor covered the mouthpiece of the phone with his hand. His eyes were blazing. "Why didn't you tell me?"

"Tell you what?"

"About your article in the magazine. She said wasn't it thrilling about your article in *Glamour!*"

"So what did you say?"

"What did you expect me to say! That I didn't know my own wife's article was in a national magazine? Of course, I said it was great. Where is it?"

"In the bedroom."

Talking to Kathleen made Hannah feel like she had won the Pulitzer Prize for literature. "You've the gift of language, my girl. Are you sure there wasn't an Irish bard in Rachel's background? Erudition skips a generation, you know." They had often speculated on who Rachel's people may have been.

"Well, I hope it won't skip another generation. My baby is going to come out reciting—" She searched her mind for a suitable writer. "—Dorothy Parker!"

Kathleen had something more important than the article to discuss. She was coming to New York to be with Hannah during her delivery. Little Bryan's measles had kept her from the wedding. He had since had mumps and chickenpox. There being no other common childhood diseases, she felt certain nothing would interfere this time.

"I need you, Kathleen," Hannah whispered as Viktor returned from the bedroom.

"I know," her friend whispered back, intuitively understanding.

Viktor fanned himself with the magazine, his brow furrowed. "I suppose I must show this to my colleagues at the agency. They often ask after you." Her pregnancy had been his excuse for not including her in the agency's various social activities.

"That would be nice," Hannah said noncommittally. Having a wife who was a published author was certainly a feather in his cap.

"Of course . . ." he hesitated.

"Of course . . . ?"

"Of course, *Glamour* is not a journal for the intelligentsia. It's a fashion magazine. Women buy it to look at the clothes. Nobody reads the articles."

Hannah was fine until the final few weeks of her pregnancy, when fear and panic set it. Rachel visited her bearing a gift of damson plum preserves. She seated herself comfortably while Hannah shuffled around the kitchen making tea and toasting pound cake. To entertain her daughter and take her mind off her condition, Rachel recounted in horrifying detail the prolonged agony of Hannah's own birth.

"Be a good girl," was Rachel's parting advice. She and Marcus were leaving for Europe as scheduled. "We'll call you from Paris to see how you made out."

Ruth Levy and Kathleen were with her when the labor pains began in earnest. When Ruth called Viktor's office to say they were on their way to Mt. Sinai Hospital, she was told he had gone to Connecticut for a conference.

The three women held hands and wept when the nurse brought the infant. "All babies are beautiful, but let me tell you something. In all my thirty-four years on the maternity ward I've never seen such beautiful features, such a perfectly shaped head, such eyelashes. She's only a couple of hours old, but I can see she's got double eyelashes like Elizabeth Taylor. Thank God it's a girl. It would be wasted on a boy. She's going to be a heartbreaker, this one!" Having settled the infant at Hannah's breast, she gently patted the new mother's cheek and beamed at her.

There was still no sign of Viktor. By now his office was closed. They had no idea if he had got the message. Calls to the apartment went unanswered. When Dr. Levy came in to check on mother and daughter, he joined the three women in quiet celebration of the miracle of birth. Viktor was not mentioned.

"Have you thought of a name?" Kathleen ventured.

Rachel had scribbled some suggestions. Viktor had offered several names for a boy. If it were a girl, he would leave it to her.

A heroine's name was what she wanted. A name associated with a genuine heroine like Clara Barton or Florence Nightingale or Amelia Earhart or Marguerite Higgins. Dorothy Parker? Brilliant and witty but her own worst enemy. Clare Booth Luce? Brilliant, too, but she had ridden to fame on her husband's coattails.

She wanted her daughter to be independent, to take charge of her own destiny so far as God and fate would allow. A fearless, caring woman who would speak her mind and contribute to humanity. Her glance fell on the morning paper that the volunteers distributed to each room. There on the front page was a picture of Eleanor Roosevelt, a delegate to the United Nations being honored for helping draft the U.N. Declaration of Human Rights. By any criteria, it was not unkind to say she had never been pretty. Now at sixty-eight, she had attained a radiance that transcended mere physicality.

There was no question that Hannah's baby girl would be a creature of dazzling beauty, a source of enormous pride to Rachel, a trophy for Viktor to display as proof of his aristocratic bloodlines. Hannah could only imagine the uproar if she explained her hope of inculcating her daughter with Mrs. Roosevelt's high principles and dedication to the greater good. To name her daughter for Eleanor Roosevelt would only invite laughter and scorn. It would be her secret.

"I've always liked the name Eleanor." There being neither grandmother nor father present to demur or offer a counter suggestion, Dr. Levy inscribed the name on the birth certificate.

As visiting hours ended, the pounding of masculine heels in the corridor announced Viktor's arrival. He fell to his knees at Hannah's bedside and pressed his lips to her hand. "Forgive me, darling. Tell me you forgive me for not being here."

All visitors were asked to leave except for the fathers, who could remain overnight if they chose. Hannah closed her eyes in contentment of a job well done. Viktor remained where he was, murmuring words she could neither hear nor understand until his daughter was brought in for her next feeding.

"I've named her Eleanor," Hannah informed him without apology or explanation. If she expected an argument, she was wrong. He held his daughter between his palms, raising her to eye level, tears coursing down his cheeks.

"Eleanor, *liebchen. Ich bin dein papa,* Eleanor." He placed her in Hannah's arms. "It's a beautiful name, Eleanor."

"Then I gather you approve of your daughter?"

"She's beautiful, sweet. Just like her mother."

When the baby was once again taken back to the nursery, Viktor lay down beside Hannah.

"*Please,* Viktor—" She shrank from him.

"Don't be alarmed. And please don't turn away from me, Hannah. It breaks my heart. All I want to do is hold you close until you fall asleep."

She slept deeply and peacefully until baby Eleanor was returned for her midnight feeding. Viktor had left a note in her hand saying he loved her and would be back in the morning. She could taste his salt tears and smell his Guerlain Imperiale.

Despite everything, or perhaps because of everything that had passed between them, she wanted him more than ever.

CHAPTER 19

1953

Rachel

Rachel looked up in surprise when the housekeeper ushered Viktor into the den she used as an office when she worked from home. Marcus had left for an early meeting. She was expecting Hannah and the baby later in the morning.

She strained to look past Viktor for her first glimpse of Eleanor. "What's got into Hannah? She knows I make phone calls first thing in the morning. I wasn't expecting her until later." Half-jokingly she added, "And I wasn't expecting you at all."

He stood awkwardly at her desk like a schoolboy called to the principal's office. "Hannah doesn't know I'm here. I had to see you, Rachel. I'm desperate."

Again? It was an old story by now. A running tab at the 21 Club that Viktor hadn't a hope in hell of paying out of his salary. Bridge club losses. Rachel agreed with him that a gentleman of his aristocratic background should keep up with the new friends he was making through the refugee committee. As he said, they were stepping-stones to a more lucrative career. But Rachel was baffled by the very idea of not being able to live within one's means.

She often wondered how he and Hannah managed. The rent for their apartment in that broken-down building couldn't be that much. She never asked, of course. Marcus and she had showered little Eleanor with gifts of nursery furniture and an endless array of clothes and toys from Best & Company's Lilliputian Bazaar. On the child's first birthday, Marcus created a trust fund for her education and an income for when she turned thirty.

Rachel took out her checkbook. Whatever he cost, Viktor was a good investment in the future. She liked being surrounded with beautiful things. By any standard, Viktor was beautiful. Between her own looks and his was where Hannah's baby got her perfect little features and bone structure. Rachel appreciated Viktor's appearance as she would a work of art. His thick wavy hair sculpted to perfection, a hint of gray beginning to show at the temples, his custom-made suits and shirts from Knize. All in all, if he weren't her son-in-law, she could have gone for him herself. If only Marcus would allow her to take charge of his appearance! He chose his suits off the rack. The shirts and ties she bought him languished in his closet. "Don't try to teach an old dog new tricks," he'd say sheepishly when Rachel complained.

"How much, my darling?" She smiled reassuringly at Viktor. This was between the two them. What would she have him do, go to loan sharks and get his knees broken? "Don't be shy. I can afford it. I want you and Hannah to be happy."

"*Gott in himmel!* It's not money."

She had seen his histrionics before and admired his performance. But this was no performance. This man was genuinely trembling with emotion while trying desperately to maintain his dignity.

"What is it? Is it Eleanor? Is the baby sick?"

He visibly steeled himself. "Hannah wants a divorce."

How could Hannah do this to her? What kind of future would her grandchild have growing up in a broken home? Hannah was one cold potato. Rachel had gone out of her way to be friends with her daughter, to keep her mouth shut and not criticize even when she knew Hannah was wrong. How dare she ruin everything? Today was supposed to be a really happy time, a family time—baby, mother, and grandmother.

Most of the renovations on the Riverside Drive apartment were complete. The triplex penthouse was a castle in the air high above the Hudson River, a monument to Rachel's tastes and wishes. The Taj Mahal was built for a dead woman, Marcus said. Their new home atop Riverside Drive was a gift of love for the living, breathing queen of his heart. She had looked forward to showing her daughter around, especially the cedar-lined closets that held her growing collection of clothes dating back to before Hannah was born. Before Sam was born, for that matter, a subject she still couldn't discuss without crying.

Then, she had planned lunch on the glassed-in terrace, where Eleanor could play with her toys while the two women gossiped companionably the way socialites did in the pages of *Town & Country.*

"I thought you had the perfect marriage," she responded at last.

"I thought so, too. I love her, Rachel. I adore her, worship her with all my heart. She's my life. She *saved* my life. I thought the baby would make things better! But—" His voice dropped to an agonized whisper. "She has banished me from our bed. I know what happens to some women after childbirth, but—think what it's like for me—being in the same house with her. She takes Eleanor into bed with her in the morning and I have to watch from the doorway!"

There must be more to it than that, Rachel thought shrewdly. "Be honest with me, Viktor. Hannah's an old-fashioned girl. Did you give her any reason—?"

"Never! I swear to you."

"Were you—good to her? You know what I mean."

His peacock vanity reasserted itself. "I think I can say without fear of contradiction that I am a skilled and generous lover, not like the American men who brag about their conquests. In this regard, the European way is best. I had a mistress when I was fourteen. She taught me how to arouse a woman and satisfy a woman and teach a woman how to satisfy me."

Lucky Hannah, never letting on behind that prune face of hers. Nevertheless, something must have gone wrong. "What about money? If she throws you out, how is she going to pay the rent? She can't be making that much from her writing."

"What rent?" He was puzzled.

What rent did he think? "For your apartment!"

He shook his head in bewilderment. "But there is no rent. She owns the building. Didn't you know?"

How could Hannah own the building? It was impossible. Unless there were things about her own daughter she didn't know. Admittedly, the period after Sam's death was a mess. She knew how much she'd hurt Hannah's feelings, but Marcus said Hannah understood and forgave, and when she and Viktor got married, and Rachel and Marcus tied the knot as well, they were one big happy family.

Had Marcus secretly helped Hannah, she wondered? It was the only possible explanation. When Hannah showed up, she'd better have a damned good story.

"It's getting late, Viktor. You'd better run along. I'll get to the bottom of this. Drop by for a cocktail on your way home so I can tell you what happened. Now, be a good boy. Hannah loves you, no matter what she says now. Just give me a chance to talk some sense into her."

She rose to embrace him, deliciously aware of how

slim and young she looked in her new Dior suit, with her hair pulled back in the new George Washington style with a black velvet bow at the nape of her neck. She allowed herself to melt in his arms just long enough to feel his response. Her daughter must really be out of her mind. How could she throw a man like this out?

She would soon find out. More to the point, she would learn about this apartment house business. She had always thought Hannah was a sneak. This proved it. The question was where did she get the money? The Irish maid? Another sneak. An ingrate. Making a play for Sam after all Rachel had done for her; bringing her over from Ireland, giving her a wonderful home, and that's how the little bitch paid her back. Rachel had been far too trusting. People took advantage of her kindness all the time. She had no idea what that Kathleen what's-her-name was up to until she went through Sam's things and found the snapshots of the two of them. In a rowboat and feeding the squirrels in Central Park. Having a picnic somewhere in the country with Hannah and some other soldier in uniform.

Just then Hannah arrived with Eleanor.

"Nana! Nana!" The excited little girl broke free from her mother's grasp and ran to her grandmother. "Cookie! Cookie!"

Rachel swept her into the air, failing to notice the furious expression on Hannah's face.

"What was Viktor doing here, Mother!"

"Not in front of the child. Come on, Eleanor, Nana has a surprise."

Hannah followed close behind, stepping on the backs of Rachel's shoes in her haste and anger. "No cookies. She does not eat between meals!"

"Raisins?"

"Mother, I asked you a question."

"And I have a question for you, my girl." They sat on canvas terrace chairs facing each other as Eleanor played on the floor between them. "Where did you get the money to buy an apartment house? Here I've been so worried about how you and Viktor have been managing your bills."

"Since when have you worried about me, Mother?"

"Don't change the subject. Answer the question. How did you manage to buy an apartment house? Was it Marcus? Did Marcus give you the money?"

"Marcus?" The thought of his doing anything behind Rachel's back sent Hannah into gales of laughter.

"Well then, who?"

"None of your business. And neither is my husband or my marriage or my divorce. That's why he came, wasn't it? The divorce?"

"First things first. You can tell me or you can put me to the trouble of finding out."

After eight years it would be a relief to tell her and get it over with. This would be one time when Rachel couldn't refuse to talk about Sam.

"Well, Hannah, I'm waiting."

"You really want to know."

"Quit stalling."

"You don't think I have a right to privacy?"

"You're making me very angry."

Tough! "You'll be angrier when I tell you." As the truth formed on her lips, a pang of sympathy for her mother throbbed and passed. "O.K., Mom. Don't faint. The money came from—you might as well know—it came from Sam!"

"Sam?" The answer was so remote from Rachel's expectation, she was genuinely bewildered. "Sam who?"

Her mother's response exasperated Hannah almost beyond endurance. She had to use considerable self-control to keep from shaking Rachel until her teeth rattled. Instead, in a quiet, conversational voice, she explained. "You know—Sam! My brother! Remember?" Without warning, the pent-up years of Hannah's grief exploded in sobs. Her pain communicated itself to Eleanor, who broke into matching sobs and climbed into her lap. "Mommy! Mommy!"

Hannah had heard about color draining from someone's face. She had never really seen it until now. Rachel's skin had turned to parchment. For once, she could barely speak. "What are you talking about? How could he buy you a building. He's dead—my son is *dead!*" The facade of sleek sophistication fell away to reveal the ravages of grief. As if acknowledging her cruelty to her daughter, she sat with her arms limp on the arms of her chair. "I'm sorry, Hannah. So sorry. Sorry."

Having her baby's plump little arms around her neck, the sweet little body warm against her breasts, Hannah found a resource of poise and clarity with which to at last tell her mother about Sam's insurance. "You shut me out, Mother. You wouldn't speak to me. I was as shocked as you when I found out. I wanted to tell you, but you couldn't stand the sight of me."

Rachel's voice seemed to emanate from a deep cave of memory. "You don't have to be tactful. I remember exactly what I said. Oh, Hannah, please forgive me. I *am sorry!* Can you ever forgive me?" She gazed upward. "Can Sam forgive me?"

The sight of her mother piously looking heavenward broke the spell. Hannah burst into peals of uncontrollable laughter. "Oh, Mother—asking Sam to forgive you?"

The laughter was contagious. Rachel's sobs changed into hiccup spasms that struck little Eleanor as hilarious, and soon the three generations were clutching each other and gasping for breath.

Asked how she knew enough about real estate to

make deals on her own, Hannah explained that she'd always been a little pitcher with big ears. She had learned a lot from listening to Rachel and Marcus. As in many of life's challenges she had relied on common sense. However, now that the secret of her real estate holdings was out, she wanted to turn the management of the building and its eventual sale over to Salinko Realtors. She also had some interesting marketing ideas, but they could wait.

The subject exhausted for the time being, they ate their tuna salad sandwiches and drank their iced coffee and took turns feeding Eleanor her mashed potatoes, carrots and apple sauce.

"Now, what about Viktor? The man was literally on his knees, Hannah, begging me. Pleading with me—"

"He's damned good at that, isn't he, Mom?"

"He seemed very sincere to me."

"He invented sincere. He can ask you to pick out the tie he should wear and make you believe he could not have done it without you."

Rachel regarded her daughter thoughtfully. "There's something more, isn't there? Something you're not telling me?"

"Don't be redic."

"There is. I can tell by your eyes." She replenished their iced coffee from the sweating silver pitcher and made a Joan Crawford production out of graciously offering Hannah the silver platter of exquisitely arranged fresh fruit. Her daughter declined in petulant silence.

Rachel studied the grapes as if they were sculpture and chose one, holding it up to examine it for a blemish and consuming it in two precise bites. "I guess I can't blame you for keeping it to yourself. We haven't exactly been close, have we?"

"Not exactly."

Rachel's words tumbled one atop the other in a rush

of memory. "I was so proud of you the day you gradu-
ated from high school, and I remember how we vowed
to be friends. But then when Sam passed away—"

"Died, Mom. Sam didn't pass away. He *died*. And
you said—" her voice shattered as she fought to control
it. "—And you said, 'Why wasn't it you!' I've forgiven
you but I'll never forget what you said."

Tears filled Rachel's eyes. She sighed as if her heart
would break. "You think I've forgotten? You think I
don't think about it every day of my life, wishing I
could take it back? Wanting to be friends with you, really friends who love each other a lot and help each
other when they're in a jam? I want us to be friends,
Hannah."

"You said that once before."

"I want to be friends now. I want us to be a family.
Marcus and me and you and Eleanor and Viktor. Don't
you see, we're all we have. We need each other. You
need Viktor. Be honest. You still love him, don't you?"

"Depends what you mean by love."

"Okay. Okay. So I didn't go to college. I don't know
what I *mean* by love. Let me put it another way. Do you
still want him?"

"If you must know, I'm thinking of seeing a psychia-
trist."

Rachel shook her head in exasperation. "I'm talking
about bed. Sex."

"You want the truth?"

Rachel glanced at her granddaughter who was trying
to feed a carrot stick to her Raggedy Ann. "Please, not
in front of the child."

Despite herself, Hannah laughed. "All I can say is
the clichés apply. Sirens go off. The earth moves.
Sometimes when we make love—correction—when we
used to make love before Eleanor was born, I used to
feel like the ballerina in *The Red Shoes*. That once we

started, I was unable to stop. That I felt driven—compelled—to go on and on and on until I died! Do you know what I mean?"

"I had a love like that—once."

"You mean Daddy?"

Daddy? Rachel had to stop and think before she realized who her daughter meant. "No, darling. I'm sorry to say it was someone else. My first love. He was killed in the first war."

"Oh, Mom—"

"Will Lawrence saved my life but he couldn't save his own. I'll never forgive him for throwing it away."

"That's not fair."

"Life isn't fair. Your father left me with two children and a pile of debts as high as the Empire State Building. We'd have been out on the street if it hadn't been for Marcus!"

"You hate him that much?"

"Oh, Hannah. I don't sit in judgment on him. And neither should you. Think of all that Viktor's been through. A Jew in Nazi Germany. Jumping off that U-Boat knowing he could be shot! Use your noodle. Add up the credits and see how they balance against the debits. Let's start in the bedroom—"

"For God's sake, Mom—"

"Is he good to you in bed?"

Hannah flared out at her mother. "Okay, you want to know what he did? He gave me aphrodisiacs before Eleanor was born. Dangerous aphrodisiacs. They could have killed me—and the baby, Dr. Levy said!"

"He's an old woman, that one. I've heard him talk. He thinks women's bodies are made for two things, having babies and giving pleasure to men. Nothing about pleasure for us! Think of it this way. Maybe Viktor was reckless but answer me this, wasn't his motive to give you pleasure?"

Hannah had to admit this was so. She also had to admit that Viktor was a wonderful, devoted father. He read to Eleanor every night. He taught her little songs. The times she had a cold, he rubbed her little chest with Vicks and fed her broth through a glass straw.

"Give him another chance, Hannah."

Hannah shook her head vehemently. There was something else, but she didn't want to talk about it.

Rachel took her daughter's hand. "I'm worried about you. You look exhausted from all this."

"I haven't been sleeping. I've felt so alone in all this."

"I wish you'd come to me. I know, I know, you don't have to remind me. I've been a terrible mother. But I want to be your friend, darling. Please confide in me from now on."

Hannah sipped the last of her iced coffee and with the grinning defiance of a child crunched the ice cubes between her teeth. Both remembered Rachel's warning that eating ice cubes would ruin her teeth.

"Still no cavities, Mom!" Hannah rose to go. "I'd better get Eleanor home. It's time for her nap."

The child had not waited. She was curled up with her Raggedy Ann fast asleep on the floor. "What a picture she makes," Rachel sighed. Mother and grandmother looked in awe at the wonder of God and nature. "Don't wake her, Hannah. Let me have her for the afternoon."

"I couldn't. She looks like a little angel now but when she wakes up—you've heard of the terrible twos?"

"I remember you at that age."

"You do?" Hannah was clearly astonished. Her childhood memories were of Will and Sam, nothing of her mother.

Rachel was hurt. "Of course I do! You were adorable. I remember making your little frocks and taking you out for walks with Sam and everyone saying what lovely children I had. You don't remember?"

Hannah embraced her mother. "Of course I do, Mom," she lied. This new side of Rachel was too precious to let slip away.

"That settles it, then. Here's your hat. What's your hurry? I'll just call the office and let Marcus know I'm playing hooky. I'm taking the afternoon off to stay home with my beautiful grandchild. As for you, do yourself a favor. Go home. Have a bubble bath. Take a nap. Read a magazine. Do something with your hair!"

Hannah hesitated, tempted by the offer, not even bothered by the age-old feud over her hair.

"Keep your eye on her while I call the office."

Alone in the bedroom, Rachel made two calls. One to her office and the other to Viktor.

"Now get your behind out of here," she commanded her daughter.

Hannah hesitated once more. "Mom—"

"Out—get out of here this second."

"I just want to say how sorry I am—about Sam, I mean—"

Rachel held her daughter close. "And I'm sorry for what I said. Sam did what he had to do, what he wanted to do. I lost my son but I'm glad I still have my daughter. Now run along before I wreck my eye makeup. You don't think these lashes are real, do you?"

When Hannah got home, Viktor was waiting for her. Not the smug and confident Viktor with flowers and champagne, but a solemn, earnest Viktor with tears of pleading in his eyes.

CHAPTER 20

1956

Jessie

The world was made for love but not for Hannah. While Grace Kelly married Prince Rainier, Margaret Truman married Clifton Daniel, Barbara Hutton married Baron Von Cramm, Gregory Peck married Veronique Passani, and Frank Sinatra put his imprimatur on "Love and Marriage," Hannah devoted much of the year to getting divorced. Among the complications were Viktor's abrupt disappearance upon being served with divorce papers and the subsequent discovery that he had absconded with several hundred thousand dollars' worth of Salinko Realtors assets.

Rachel's stage-managed reconciliation had worked long enough for Hannah to become pregnant again. In honor of Jessie's birth, Marcus had at Rachel's prompting taken Viktor into the business. "A gift from heaven!" Rachel had declared. Viktor's charm and command of several languages made him ideal for convincing European companies to set up their American headquarters in Salinko buildings.

"It's all my fault!" Rachel berated herself now. "I should have let you go ahead with the divorce."

"Why didn't you, Mother?"

"I thought you loved him. All I wanted was your happiness."

Oh, sure, Mom, thinking only of me. Not how nice it was to have a handsome, sophisticated son-in-law flattering the life out of her and giving a little class to Salinko Realtors. Getting to hobnob with French and Italian industrialists, Danes and Swedes in their first postwar economic expansion. Being introduced with continental flair as his oh-so-young mother-in-law and Boss Lady, a slangy affectation the foreigners seemed to appreciate.

To give Rachel her due, Hannah was the first to admit at least to herself that her mother's intervention with her husband was the start of more than a year of connubial happiness. Perhaps his fear of being thrown out into the cruel world had caused him to behave. The regression to his old ways began with the birth of Jessie. Viktor had wanted a boy. He tried to sound humorous when he railed, "I'm surrounded by women. My wife, my mother-in-law, little Eleanor. It's enough. This time, I must have a son!" Adding to the injustice was the new baby's failure to repeat her older sister's beauty.

"Are you sure this is our daughter? Could she have been switched at birth? She looks nothing like our Eleanor!"

Sarcasm had a strange effect on Hannah. It made her sad rather than angry. While she knew she possessed the necessary vocabulary and invective to skin him alive, she was reluctant to cross the line. She knew things about him that he had probably forgotten she knew. Things she had chosen to forget once she had taken him back and they had resumed their marriage. Things she had been on the verge of telling Rachel that afternoon when her mother urged her to reconsider a divorce.

She knew he was a liar, a Nazi spy, and an anti-Semite. She had found this out in a very direct way. He had told her. At first she hadn't been certain of what he was saying. In the early months of their marriage, his habit was to keep a carafe of cognac at his side of the bed. The intensity of their lovemaking left her limp and clinging to him in a haze of erotic suspension while he sipped and spoke softly. His voice was what soothed her. She paid no attention to his words until the night his tone of voice turned belligerent.

He seemed unaware that she was there. He was like the crazies on the street or in the subway, proclaiming their rage at the stupidities of fate. "Fools and idiots. All of them!" She stirred. "Hannah?" She pretended to be asleep. "Ah, *Schatzi!*" He kissed her hair and pulled her closer. His voice grew more lachrymose as she heard the sound of the carafe being raised to his lips and the sips grew longer. She forced herself to breathe with a steady rhythm while trying to clear the erotic cobwebs from her mind. His harrangue became a mixture of German and English but gradually the truth emerged.

From what she pieced together, Hitler had been the biggest fool of all. The Jews of Germany would have supported his policies if he hadn't been stupid enough to turn on them. Especially the rich Jews like Viktor's family, the Jews who had assimilated, the Jews who felt superior to the riff-raff and peasants.

"The master race? The Jews *are* the master race! Together, *mein fuhrer*. Together, we could have ruled the world!"

He was contemptuous of the Jews who failed to see what would happen to them, who allowed themselves to be rounded up and marched into the crematoria. "Singing 'Hatikvah'. Martyrs for what? 'Hatikvah!'" His voice cracked as he sang with derision.

" '*Ha-a-tik-vah, shee-not-al-pa-yeem . . .*' "

"Fools and idiots" was the pervasive theme. The officials who never noticed his forged papers. The naval headquarters in Bremerhaven where he offered his plan to spy for the Fatherland. He had told them his English was perfect, which was true, and that he had lived in

New York as a youth and knew the mid-Atlantic coastline like the palm of his hand, which was a lie. He
knew of U-boats landing saboteurs on the American
shores, all of whom were caught.

"I will be too smart for that. I will allow myself to be
captured and taken to American Intelligence and offer
to work for them." A good plan. A perfect plan. Germany would win and he would be one of the leaders of
the German occupation. Stationed in New York!

His plan had come apart swiftly minutes before he
was to have been sent ashore in a rubber dinghy. It was
hot on the submarine. He was drowsing in his hammock
in his underpants waiting until the last possible moment
to put on the dungarees and sweatshirt of his disguise
when he suddenly found himself hurled to the deck.

"Juden!" A young sailor who fancied Viktor had seized
the opportunity to whisper words of farewell. An unin-
vited caress and all was revealed by his circumcision.
Stripped and surrounded by a furious crew, Viktor felt
the vessel surface, saw the hatch open, and made his
mad dash for freedom.

Hannah lay still as Viktor rambled on. "And when
you gave me that cigarette, I knew God was good. God?
Of course I believe in God, after what He did for me."
As they watched from shore, an American patrol boat
hit the submarine. There had been no survivors except
Viktor. None to tell the tale.

"I was wrong," Rachel had said when the embezzlement was discovered. "I should have let you divorce
him when you wanted to."

You don't know the half of it, Mom! The embezzlement was bad enough. Hannah would keep the rest of
Viktor's story a secret until the day she died. To expose
him further would jeopardize Salinko Realtors for hiring him and would cast a shadow on her two little girls.

The detective Marcus hired had found him living at the Waldorf-Astoria. Under his own name. His arrogant explanation? "I have left my wife. Don't tell me that's a crime in America."

Marcus and Rachel met with him privately. Salinko Realtors was about to merge with a major development company and would soon be going public. They could not allow a hint of scandal or impropriety to rock the boat. The deal they worked out was this. Viktor could keep the funds he had transferred to a numbered account in Switzerland. Salinko would pay him an annual retainer for "services rendered." Viktor would not contest the divorce nor would he in any way attempt to see or communicate with Hannah or the girls.

At their final conference when the agreement was signed, Rachel told Marcus to wait for her in the car. She wanted a moment alone with her soon-to-be ex-son-in-law. "What will you do now?"

"I shall return to Europe, where I belong."

"I don't understand you, Viktor. You could have had everything right here."

He clicked his heels and bowed, raising her hand to his lips. "I know."

The son of a bitch! Her cheeks flushed, she made a hasty departure. She and Marcus were late for his doctor's appointment. A neurologist, this time. So far nobody could find the cause of his headaches and listlessness. He was still a young man with everything to live for. Money, success, respect from the community for his philanthropy, a beautiful home, a gorgeous wife! So why couldn't he sleep and what made him burst into tears and cling to her when she found him out on the terrace threatening to jump?

On the brighter side, Hannah seemed genuinely relieved to be rid of Viktor. She sold another article and was working on a novel, her ambition rekindled. A chance meeting in Central Park had led to some photographic modeling for Eleanor. Hannah's childhood friend Cecily Greenberg was now married to a hotshot advertising executive.

Little Eleanor was exactly what he wanted for a new cereal campaign. "She's glorious. Do you have an agent?"

"She's not even four years old!"

"Shirley Temple was two."

Both became aware of little Jessie tugging at Cecily's coat. "I'm two!"

Cecily swooped her up with delight. "Two! Too much is what you are. This one's got enough personality for both of them." Eleanor, however, was the one the camera loved. Everyone at the agency agreed this angelic child with the thick lashes that cast a velvet softness on her cheeks was a natural.

"Too bad the other one's so ordinary looking," the photographer commented, living up to his reputation for regarding models as meat.

"How dare you hurt my baby's feelings!" Hannah hissed.

If Jessie heard his remarks, it didn't seem to bother her. She worshipped her older sister and seemed to be the one Eleanor looked to for encouragement between takes. For Hannah, her daughters were a constant source of wonder. No matter what Viktor had done, she was still grateful to him for her girls. Being scrupulously fair, if she hadn't taken him back there would be no Jessie.

"It may be my imagination," she confided in Ruth Levy. "But I was watching the girls play checkers and I swear to God, Jessie was letting Eleanor win! I guess we won't ever need to worry about her."

As her mother's oldest friend, Ruth was like a member of the family. "The one we do need to worry about is Marcus."

CHAPTER 21

1968

Eleanor

The courtesies observed, the neurologist gave Rachel the summary of the many weeks of the most recent series of tests and evaluations. Marcus was still in superb physical condition, amazingly fit for a man his age. That being the case, why couldn't he sleep or eat? What made him fly off the handle and accuse people he trusted of stupidity and disloyalty. And what about the memory loss and the crying fits? For over a decade they had tried every known medication and therapy. Nothing seemed to help.

Could it be some weird allergy? A brain tumor? It broke Rachel's heart to see him deteriorate before her very eyes. As for these bigshot doctors, all they could do was order tests and more tests. She had called Dr. Levy in Boca Raton, where he and Ruth had retired. The symptoms sounded like depression to him.

"Depression?" What did Marcus have to be depressed about? The man had everything a person could wish for. Success. Respect. A well-run home. A wife who loved him and catered to his needs. Two granddaughters who adored him and filled the shelves of his office with ashtrays and drawings they had made as children and framed photographs documenting their development into young womanhood.

Could Viktor's betrayal have caused such havoc? Marcus had taken to heart his role as Hannah's stepfather and had gotten a kick out of taking his "son-in-law" into the business. So Viktor had turned out to be an ingrate—worse than an ingrate, a double-crossing thief who should have been sent up the river to make mailbags for the rest of his life. But that had been years ago. They'd absorbed the loss. Hannah was happier without him and Eleanor and Jessie were doing fine, so good riddance to bad rubbish.

"Depression?" she repeated. "Like a bad case of the *blues*?"

"It's more serious than that, I fear," said Dr. Levy. "Your husband, as far as we can determine, is suffering from an organic affective syndrome, commonly known as manic depression."

Was it catching, she wondered, like herpes or syphillis? She was ashamed to ask. It would sound as if all she thought about was herself. Well, she had to think of herself, didn't she? Who else was in charge of Salinko Realtors? Who else had moved into her husband's big corner office and taken over the day-to-day operations, ignoring the raised eyebrows and petty resistance to her decisions.

The staff might not think so, but Rachel knew more about real estate than all of them put together. They might sneer at her behind her back and dismiss her as the boss's wife in her furs and pearls and perfect grooming. But they had another think coming. Almost forty years as Marcus's mistress and then his wife had given her a superb education in New York City real estate and construction. Added to that foundation was a God-given talent for absorbing the essence of increasingly complex regulations afflicting the industry.

For some time now she had been quietly buying up tenements and lofts on the Lower East Side and in Little Italy. The possibilities of gentrification and upscale development were as plain as the nose on her face.

Salinko was small potatoes compared to the Helmsleys and Dursts and Tisch boys uptown. The abandoned factories and light-industry lofts downtown were solidly built, the floors strong enough to hold the heavy machinery that had long since been dismantled. The tenements had to be gutted and rebuilt from the inside out or bulldozed and replaced with modern apartments. The point was, they could be had for a song. Under the Salinko umbrella, Rachel had created several collateral companies in order to buy property without attracting attention.

She wondered what Becky Lodz or that bastard Mo Schweitzer would say to the old Lower East Side being changed into the ritzy East Village and the area around Little Italy becoming Soho. Such a brilliant idea, she wished she'd thought of it herself. Taking a cue from the Bohemian section of London while attributing the designation simply to South of Houston Street!

Money was no object, she told the team of doctors. "I want you to make him well."

They reviewed the possibilities of the new antidepressant drugs combined with psychotherapy. "Daily medication. There's something new called Lithium that has shown some amazing results. And of course the one-on-one sessions with the therapist, possibly under hypnosis."

Her poor darling! Rachel had clung tenaciously to the conviction that there was nothing seriously wrong. What he needed was an extended vacation. Deep-sea fishing. Golf at St. Andrews. They had talked about Scotland, but something always came up.

Was it too late? Would the Connecticut sanitarium make matters worse, convince him he really was off his rocker? Rachel's style as always was to stay calm in all circumstances, but she could not stop the trembling of her hands.

The doctors viewed her with compassion. One of them spoke frankly. "Your husband's chief worry is disappointing you. His chief motivation for recovery is to be with you. I assure you the therapist I have in mind is the best in the field."

Marcus slept in the chauffeur-driven car all the way to Connecticut, or perhaps pretended to sleep to avoid conversation. He held tightly to Rachel's hand, tightening his grip when she shifted position and tried to relax in the roomy backseat.

Hilldale was just as described, a rambling Victorian mansion set in ten acres of gardens and lawns with a swimming pool, tennis courts, and a track for running or cycling. The scene she dreaded did not materialize. The director of the sanitarium came out to the car to greet them. Hannah had been advised to say good-bye there rather than accompany Marcus inside. Her husband kissed her good-bye and disappeared inside the house without turning back. For some reason, it reminded her of the day long ago when she and Sam had driven Hannah to sleep-away camp. Other youngsters were crying and clinging to their parents. Not Hannah. With the box of peanut brittle and Indian nuts Sam had bought her under her arm she had marched away from Marcus's car without a wave or a kiss good-bye. At the camp reunion, the counselor had told Rachel that Hannah was the only camper she'd ever had who was never homesick.

Returning home from Connecticut, content for the time being that Marcus was in good hands, she turned her thoughts to the evening ahead. Eleanor was one of the contestants in the Beautiful Newcomers contest sponsored by *Seventeen* magazine and the Ford Model Agency, all proceeds going to underprivileged children. Not that she was prejudiced or anything, but there was no doubt in Rachel's mind that Eleanor would win the title.

At sixteen, the girl's loveliness had the authenticity of a perfect flowering peach. Her contours and coloring a fusion of nature at its most generous and inspired. Her shyness in direct proportion to her appearance, she had been quite upset when Jessie the camera bug sent her picture to Eileen Ford. Her career as a baby model had begun by accident. She romped happily with toilet paper, ate cereal with her hands, and jumped gleefully in a playpen until she grew old enough to be aware of the cameras and the towering creatures giving her orders.

There were no tantrums. Eleanor was not temperamental enough to have tantrums. She simply melted into a puddle of shyness, trying to please but utterly unable to relax. Hannah had frankly been relieved. She didn't much like being a stage mother dragging the child to auditions and look-sees. The other children revolted her with their belligerent charm; the mothers were worse. Rachel, on the other hand, had been profoundly disappointed. Eleanor could be another Shirley Temple, another Elizabeth Taylor, another Natalie Wood, she insisted.

"No, Mom. She doesn't want to be an actress! She's afraid of her own shadow." Not like Jessie. Jessie wasn't afraid of anything.

"It's too bad she isn't as pretty as Eleanor," Rachel often said, until Hannah told her mother to shut up.

"Well, it's true, isn't it? Jessie knows it's true, don't you darling. It doesn't bother you a bit, does it? She'll be fine. She's got her head screwed on. She's smart as hell. She won't need a husband to take care of her. She'll take care of herself, and from the looks of things, she'll take care of Eleanor, too."

Rachel's prediction turned out to be true. As the sisters grew older, Jessie was the protector. When the high school drama department cast Eleanor as Madge, the small-town beauty in William Inge's *Picnic,* Jessie brazenly demanded the role of Millie, the plainer younger sister. Eleanor's performance was inaudible and stiff as a board. But without her sister out there too, Eleanor would never have been able to leave the wings. It didn't matter to the audience. She lit up the stage with a radiant sweetness that brought them to their feet cheering.

The trouble was that praise and adulation panicked her. Every time she had to appear in a play, she was sick to her stomach and thoroughly miserable. Rachel's pride in her granddaughter's success was overwhelming. The girl dared not disappoint her beaming appreciative grandmother, nor could she bring herself to tell Hannah how she really felt.

When Eileen Ford herself called to say how impressed she was by Jessie's photographs of Eleanor, Rachel happened to be there and instantly launched the girl's career as a Ford model.

She had accompanied Eleanor to Mrs. Ford's office and announced herself satisfied with the other woman's integrity and purpose. Eleanor's shyness could be turned to her advantage, Rachel said. It was touching and made people feel protective, a quality that would set her apart from the others.

All this had happened several weeks earlier. In the meantime, Eleanor had learned to walk, apply her own makeup, and change clothes in seconds without messing her hair. Tonight in the grand ballroom of the Waldorf-Astoria, she would be appearing on stage before a large audience for the very first time.

Rachel got home from the sanitarium with just enough time to change and call Hannah. "I'm leaving in five minutes. Be downstairs." The traffic was always bad at this time of night.

"We're not going," Hannah said flatly.

"What do you mean, you're not going? You're going to let Eleanor march down the runway and not find us there?"

"Eleanor's in her room."

"Hold everything. I'll be right there."

No match for her grandmother, Eleanor sat silently in the limousine clutching Jessie's hand. The general air of excitement in the dressing area seemed to restore her confidence somewhat. "Don't worry. I'll be fine," she said softly.

She was more than fine. As each fashion category was presented, Eleanor was the standout. Sportswear. Back-to-School. First Job. First Date. Holiday Sparkle. Ski 'n' Sea. Whatever she wore, whatever the context, the ballroom buzzed each time she appeared.

At last came the moment for which everyone had been waiting. With the contestants gathered on stage in nervous anxiety, the editor of *Seventeen* announced the winner. "The Most Beautiful Newcomer for 1968 is— Eleanor Lawrence of New York City!"

As was customary at events of this kind, good sportsmanship compelled the losers to shower the winner with hugs and kisses of congratulations while propelling her into position to accept her great honor.

Eleanor stood stricken and trembling, her face like marble, drained of color, looking, as her mother later said, like Joan of Arc about to be burned at the stake.

As the applause mounted and voices called out for her to step forward, she cringed visibly and looked around frantically for a way to escape. One of the organizers hurried to her side and gallantly took her arm, winking merrily at the audience by way of explaining the young woman's emotional state.

Suddenly, Eleanor pulled free and began running first one way and then another like a trapped animal. Tears poured down her face. "I'm sorry. I'm really sorry," she kept repeating.

Hannah leapt to her feet and pushed her way to the stage. Eleanor saw her and in her haste to reach her tripped and fell. Everyone was extremely understanding. Glasses of water, cold compresses hastily assembled from icecubes and napkins, smelling salts and good wishes followed them until they reached the safety of Rachel's car. "Forgive me," Eleanor sobbed.

Hannah caressed her daughter's hair. "It's you who have to forgive me. I should never have let this happen." Her face saddened as she sought Rachel's eyes in the darkness. "A mother's job is to protect her children."

The next morning, Eleanor was still asleep, Jessie had left for school, and Hannah had made a pot of strong coffee and was about to open the newspaper when the telephone rang.

"Is that Hannah? I'd know that voice anywhere."

"Viktor?" She'd know his voice anywhere, too. It still had the uncanny power to make her hot. Thanks but no thanks.

"What do you want?"

He was in New York on one of his frequent business trips from Munich. "I know I agreed to stay out of your life, you and the girls. But I just read about what happened to Eleanor—"

In the newspaper? In a minute she'd have seen it herself. One of the photographers covering last night's event had taken a series of shots documenting Eleanor's triumph and fall.

"Page thirty-six."

"Oh, my God!" Her daughter's stricken face would

haunt her forever. How could she have allowed this to happen to her child?

"Is she all right?"

"She's sleeping."

"Is there anything I can do?"

Only retroactively, she thought bitterly. If he had been the man she had thought he was, she would not have had to raise her daughters alone. There would have been a husband, not to mention a lover and a father, sharing their lives.

"She'll be fine, Viktor."

"I see she's not using my surname."

He knew as well as she did that was part of the divorce agreement. She had gone back to being Hannah Lawrence and had legally changed the girls' name as well.

"She's still my daughter—our daughter—and so is Jessie. Our Jessie. Hannah, please! Listen to me. I have something very important to ask you." She knew what was coming. He wanted to see his daughters. "I'm as much a part of them as you are."

His logic was patently false, yet she wavered. Much had happened since the divorce. As Kathleen would say, he had picked up his socks and become a solid citizen and a successful exporter of German cameras and binoculars. To his credit he had written Marcus some years back to stop paying his monthly alimony, as he called it, and to put that money into trust funds for the girls.

"Please Hannah. I beg you."

The mind can play naughty tricks. For no reason she could fathom, she thought of a book Sam had shown her when she was little and had sworn her to secrecy about. It was a fat little book of photographs of a man and woman embracing. When you held it in a certain position and flipped the pages, the photographs moved.

Flipping the pages of her life with Viktor was a testament to selective memory. Tenderness cast its rosy glow on common sense.

"How about coming to dinner. Tonight."

The fact that she would not only see Viktor, but that Rachel would have a conniption when she found out, revived Hannah's spirits considerably.

CHAPTER 22

1968

Viktor

Hannah had drawn the blinds in Eleanor's room to prevent the morning light from waking her. *My sweet little girl.* Modeling be damned. She was not going to expose her daughter to that kind of pressure ever again. Rachel be damned, too. Carrying on like a fishwife in the car taking them all home. *Eleanor did not throw up on your precious upholstery on purpose, Mom!*

Last night anyone could have seen Eleanor was terrified. Other girls her age were thrilled to be fawned over and complimented on their looks. Eleanor hated it. She cringed if someone on the street said she looked familiar and was she on television. Boys filled her with trepidation. When they spoke to her, she froze, not knowing what to say and envying the other girls their easy jokiness. Once in the school lavatory, she overheard two girls she had thought were her friends agreeing that she was stuck up and full of herself and that they hated her guts.

"Frightened?" Rachel had scoffed. "What's to be frightened of? Fame? Fortune? Meeting interesting people? Any girl would give her eyeteeth for such an opportunity. You would, wouldn't you, Jessie?"

Jessie, the smart one, at fourteen-going-on-thirty, was too smart to be drawn in by her grandmother's divide-and-conquer style. "What are eyeteeth? Teeth that have eyes or eyes that have teeth?"

Hannah could have kissed her but was too busy holding Eleanor's head down and massaging her back.

"Mom!" It was noon when she checked her daughter's room for the zillionth time. It must have been after two in the morning before Eleanor had finally fallen asleep. The long rest had done her good. As she sat up in bed with her long hair tousled and her skin glowing, she reached up for Hannah with baby arms. "Mommy! What time is it? I'll be late for school."

"Simmer down. I called to say you were sick."

"But I have a perfect attendance record!" Each year students with perfect attendance received a plaque.

"You were sick. You couldn't help that, could you?"

Over weak tea and dry toast, Eleanor lapsed into tears. "I'm so ashamed. Is Grandma still mad at me?"

Mad? No, darling daughter, *mad* could not begin to describe the fury of Rachel's anger once she got Hannah on the phone. A starving pitbull would have quaked with fear at her outrage. Confronting Rachel, members of street gangs would have thrown down their guns and turned their turf into vegetable gardens. So far as Rachel was concerned, Eleanor ruined the pageant and destroyed her big chance on purpose, and brought shame on the family, and on Rachel in particular, who had planned to name the new playground she and Marcus had funded Eleanor's Secret Garden.

The whole disgraceful episode was, as usual, Hannah's fault. She didn't know how to raise children, or, while Rachel was at it, she didn't know how to do a long list of other things.

"Mad at you? Honey, how can anyone be mad at you? Grandma was a little disappointed, that's all. She was thinking how much you'd enjoy posing for pictures."

"Where's Jessie?"

"In school."

"Oh, Mom. I wish Jessie were the pretty one. I hate

being the pretty one. Jessie would be so much better at it. She loves having an audience. She told me I was going to win and she was going to take pictures of me and sell them to all the magazines. Is she mad at me?"

"Of course not. Everybody loves you. In fact, Eileen Ford herself called to see how you're feeling. She said it happens to everybody. Everybody gets stage fright. She wants you to rest and have some fun for a few months and then come back to try again. She said you've got a unique quality and a major career waiting for you."

"Oh, Mom. I can't." Eleanor collapsed in tears. "I can't do it. I feel sick when they start touching me and saying those things." One photographer had whispered in her ear things that brought the scarlet flush to her cheekbones that he wanted. "Please don't make me!"

If Hannah had told her daughter once, she had told her a million times. Nowhere was it written that she had to do anything she didn't want to do. Her daughter was obviously intimidated by the new rules of sexual liberation. The girls at Eleanor's school were sporting diaphragms and taking the Pill. The magazines were full of articles on a woman's right to have many sexual partners and enjoy many ways to experience orgasm.

This was all well and good for women, Hannah agreed, perhaps even for women as young as her daughter, but clearly not for Eleanor herself. A few weeks ago, she had gone out on a first date with a pre-med school student name Ace. He was not dressed in a jacket and tie as Hannah expected. Kids these days dressed like bums. He had seemed nice enough, although he did snap his fingers at Eleanor to signal it was time to leave.

A half hour later she had returned in tears. In the elevator going down Ace had rubbed himself against her and forced her hand into his pants. She knew right then she should have told him to go fly a kite and returned to the apartment. "But once we hit the lobby, he was so polite! I thought maybe I was wrong. You know, exaggerating?" Eleanor explained, mortified.

His friend Wade, and girlfriend, Jeannie were necking in the front seat of the car. Ace pushed Eleanor into the backseat and offered her a beer. Wade drove to a secluded spot in Riverside Park. He and Jeannie got out and spread a blanket on the grass, leaving the car to the other couple.

Hannah felt guilty about not providing her daughter with contraception. So many of the other mothers were doing it. Were proud of doing it, in fact. There was still time, Hannah thought. Eleanor did not seem ready for sex. "Tell me exactly what he did," Hannah urged gently. If there were even a chance of pregnancy, she wanted to know and be prepared to arrange an abortion. In Sweden if need be, where it was legal.

Ace had managed to push up her skirt and pull down her panties. "He kept saying, 'Trust me. I'm a doctor. You'll like it. I know what I'm doing. I'm a doctor.' "

If it weren't so wrong it would have been laughable, this horny schmuck trying to force himself on her daughter in the backseat of a car. Eleanor had struggled free and made it home on foot in tears.

Now, after last night's disaster, Hannah had considered hiding the newspaper article from her daughter, an act of futility since everyone would have seen it. She took the positive approach. "Guess who called out of the blue? Your father."

"My father?" Eleanor was four at the time of the divorce. For a short while she had asked about him and gradually lost interest. Hannah had simply stated that Daddy had left for good. Jessie at two was more interested in her toys. The subject never came up.

"You remember. Viktor? Very handsome? Very charming? He saw your picture in the paper and called to ask to see you and Jessie, so I invited him to dinner."

Eleanor surprised her by finding the situation romantic. "He never married again, did he?"

"I wouldn't know." She didn't think so.

"That means he's still madly in love with you. And you never married again, so that means you're still in love with him! You'll fall in love all over again and get married and we'll be a real family!"

Without their mother's knowledge, Eleanor and Jessie had often discussed Viktor. Jessie was the little pitcher with the big ears who pieced together bits of overheard conversations between Hannah and Kathleen and had pumped Ruth Levy for details. Between them they had created a debonair European, equal parts Louis Jourdan and Omar Sharif, an old-fashioned type like Charles Boyer. They had fantasized about him living in a castle with hundreds of servants and horses and dogs, and one day sending for them and giving a great ball in order to introduce them to men as handsome, rich and charming as he.

When Jessie got home from school, she was as excited at the news as her sister. Together, mother and daughters prepared the meal. The German potroast the way Hannah remembered Viktor liked it. The potato pancakes and red cabbage. The cucumber salad. The prune compote.

By the time her ex-husband arrived, Hannah was having second thoughts. She had no doubts that she herself was free of any lingering vulnerability to his charms. What's more, there was a new man in her life, the first she just might possibly take seriously since her divorce. She had been seeing him casually for several weeks and was beginning to feel there might be something more.

What worried her was a mother-hen instinct to protect her young. Her vigilance melted as Viktor walked through the door bearing flowers, champagne, chocolates, and a selection of the cameras and binoculars his company exported to America. He was, if possible, more devastatingly handsome than ever. Lean and graceful with a year-round tan earned on the slopes and tennis courts rather than under a sun lamp, the few signs of aging enhanced his appearance, with a shock of gray at the temples, laugh lines adding humor to his eyes, and the deep brackets etched alongside his mouth making his lips more seductive than ever.

Hannah savored the shameful pride of having fallen hook, line, and sinker for a card-carrying rat. Her daughters were having the time of their lives. Eleanor had come out of her funk and was describing the previous night's disaster as if it had happened to somebody else. Hannah had never seen her daughter so animated. Jessie was ecstatic over her new camera. She ran to her room and brought out for Viktor's inspection her collection of cameras, including the plastic one Rachel had given her as a child, along with a portfolio of the photographs she had taken.

"Such beauty. Such talent. You've done well, Hannah. I salute you for giving me such exquisite and brilliant daughters," Viktor said gallantly.

A tiny warning signal. She had given him no such thing. They were *her* daughters, not his. Tonight she could be generous. The girls were having a wonderful time. Afterward she would explain to them that this was a one-time-only event. She would tell them about Jerry and explain that it would not be such a hot idea to have her first husband on the scene while she was testing a new and possibly permanent relationship.

She certainly had to hand it to Viktor. He literally had them eating out of his hand. Dipping chunks of bread into Hannah's richly seasoned gravy and popping the succulent morsels into their eager mouths like chicks in a nest. Cracking the Brazil nuts and picking out the meaty tidbits with a surgeon's precision. Plucking grapes and tossing them in a perfect arc for each to catch.

At the height of the merriment, Rachel called to see how Eleanor was feeling. Jessie answered the phone and with no thought of the consequence told her grandmother that Viktor was there.

"She hung up, Mom," Jessie said, stunned.

"I'm not surprised." She was even less surprised when the doorbell rang a few minutes later. Not that Rachel stormed in like a lunatic. Elegant and smiling with just the suggestion of a pout, she reproached her daughter. "Why didn't you let me know Viktor was coming?"

Viktor sprang to the rescue. "It's my fault. I wanted so much to see my little girls—my big girls—and when Hannah agreed, I begged her not to tell you. I was afraid you'd forbid it."

He had appealed to her vanity and power. "Forbid my grandchildren from seeing their father? How could you think such a thing! What's past is past. Let bygones be bygones."

He had poured her a glass of champagne and brought a chair to the table to seat her close beside him. "Then you're just in time to hear a suggestion I was about to make. But first we must all make a wish for happiness." Up to the same old tricks, Hannah realized. And it was beginning to wear thin. Dinner was over. A few more minutes and Hannah could say it was getting late, thank Viktor for his gifts, and send him out of their lives.

Eleanor remembered the champagne ceremony and demanded to be first. Viktor dipped his pinky finger into the bubbles and dabbed her earlobes, front and back. "Close your eyes and make a wish." Her eyes closed, her face raised to him like an angel at prayer, Eleanor's beauty cast a hush over the assemblage. Her

resemblance to her father, while not immediately no-
ticeable, was nevertheless apparent in the sculpted
jawline and cheekbones. To have sired a child like this,
he couldn't be all bad, could he?

When Rachel's turn came, the act of closing her eyes
robbed her of her ability to dazzle and coerce. Without
those piercing eyes that cut right through to the gizzard, her face was a tapestry of accumulated tension
and grief, reminding Hannah that Marcus had entered
the sanitarium only yesterday and that the Salinko
board was trying to throw Rachel out.

Jessie interrupted her wish making several times. "I
changed my mind! I changed my mind!" she cried before finally clenching her eyelids shut for what seemed
like hours. "Okay! Now, Mom."

Hannah dutifully complied, enjoying her ex-husband's
performance and enjoying even more his implied suggestion that her wish was for a reconciliation. Not in a million years. Her wish was for her affair with Jerry to grow
stronger and more mutually loving and develop into
something solid and permanent.

"And now for my wish." Viktor closed his eyes and
anointed his own earlobes. "I shall not keep my wish a
secret. Eleanor? Jessie? Hannah? Dearest Rachel, who
can't possibly be old enough to have such grown-up
grandchildren!"

Yes? Yes? Hannah held her breath with the others.
What in the world was he up to?

"I would like the honor of taking my daughters on
holiday in Germany. Their Easter break is in a few
weeks. I'll be back in New York to escort them myself.
It's part of their heritage, you know. My family goes
back hundreds of years before the Hitler regime and
now I am helping to build a new economy and a new
society."

Before Hannah could object, Rachel beat her to it.

"No! No! *No!*" She slammed her champagne glass on the table so hard it shattered. "I absolutely forbid it!"

Once more her mother was riding roughshod over her. It didn't seem to matter that she was forty-three years old, had turned Sam's legacy into a considerable fortune, and had raised two healthy, functioning daughters who were not on drugs or running to Haight-Ashbury to be flower children. "I believe the decision is up to me, Mom," Hannah said. Rachel hated to be called Mom. "The girls are under age. I am their mother and legal guardian, if you remember."

"Do I remember? You ask me if I remember what this—this Nazi—did?"

Hannah stood her ground. "Whatever Viktor did, he was not a Nazi and you know it."

"All I know is I will not permit this to happen."

She reminded herself that her mother was overwrought. Marcus was refusing medication. The vultures were circling his company. Rachel was alone in her triplex penthouse. Compassion stopped short of caving Hannah in. She could not have her mother dictating her life.

"I'm sorry, Mother. I respect your opinion, but this is my decision. I'm their mother and I think it will be a great chance for them to get to know their father and see something of Europe. What's more, I think it's wonderful of Viktor to invite them and I for one thank him for his generosity."

She also silently thanked him for the opportunity to be free during the spring break. She would now have the time and the privacy to audition Jerry on her home turf and see if he was right for a permanent role in her personal soap opera.

CHAPTER 23

1968

Luke

Hannah expressed her doubts to Kathleen. "I picked the wrong time to assert myself," she admitted. Rachel was right. Viktor should not be allowed to take the girls abroad. But it was too late. She couldn't back down now.

Kathleen suggested sending them to stay with her in California. They'd never met her family. Kathleen would see they had a good time.

It was too late for that, too. Jessie had told the entire school and everyone in Riverside Park, including the squirrels, that she and her sister were going to Europe. They'd had their passport pictures taken. Eleanor couldn't even take a bad passport picture. At the library, Jessie got a booklet on how to pack light and a German phrase book from Berlitz.

"Leave it to Jessie. Rarin' to go as usual," Kathleen commented.

"I know, Kathleen. I never worry about Jessie. You could drop her down in the middle of Africa, she'd wind up making friends and taking everybody's picture. It's Eleanor who worries me."

On returning to school after the *Seventeen* fiasco, Eleanor was met with hostility from schoolmates and even some teachers. Her first day back, Hannah got home in the late afternoon and found her daughter sobbing her heart out. "What's wrong? I thought you had your Drama Club today." Hannah encouraged both girls in their extracurricular activities. Jessie was currently on a student tour of Time-Life's photo labs as a member of the New York Junior Photographers.

"They're all mad at me, Mom. They said I screwed up. Miss Merrivale made me stand up in English Lit and apologize to the class for letting them down. She made me look around the classroom. She said everyone was trying to achieve the American dream and I was a traitor to the American dream because God gave me the opportunity to achieve the American dream and I failed."

"You have not let anyone down. If anyone's upset it's Eileen Ford, and you know as well as I do she said you have the looks to be a famous model, but not the drive. They can't send you to the electric chair for that!"

"Grandma wants to send me to the electric chair!"

Hannah laughed it off. "Your grandma just got a little excited the other night. She loves you, Eleanor, and she thought you'd enjoy being a famous model."

"She keeps telling me I'm the pretty one!" she moaned. "I don't want to be the pretty one. I hate it when people stare at me like I'm some kind of a freak, like they hate me or something."

Hannah explained as best she could about envy and how the girls in school were really angry because she was turning her back on what they would have given anything to have.

Eleanor's chin dropped to her chest. "There's something else, Mom. I can't talk about it."

Pregnant? Oh, God, it couldn't be. Unlike Rachel, who had ignored the subject of sex and let Hannah find out about it by herself, she had scrupulously and thoughtfully prepared her daughters for menstruation, explaining how their bodies worked and how at some future time when they were ready for a sexual relationship there were various forms of contraception available. She had impressed on them how lucky they were to be virtually the first generation in the history of the world to have the Pill and the diaphragm.

Jessie had learned to use tampons and made them all laugh by announcing she expected to have a thousand lovers by the time she was twenty. In contrast, Eleanor solemnly accepted the demands of feminine hygiene and listened to Hannah's warnings about teenage boys' raging hormones.

"You know you can talk about anything to me, Eleanor. And I mean anything."

It all poured out. The girls were all making fun of her. They all had diaphragms or their moms put them on the Pill. "They call me the virgin, Mom! Jeannie shouted at me in the gym, 'How's the class virgin!' Somebody cut out my picture and pasted it on the Virgin Mary. 'The Immaculate Deception,' it said."

What's more, several of the senior girls had formed the ATW Club. To be a member you had to swear you went All The Way with boys. "I don't want to go all the way, Mom! I'm never going to go all the way!"

Yes, she would, Hannah assured her. When she fell in love with someone who fell in love with her. Then they could go all the way together, and she would enjoy it.

"Not me. I don't care what they say. I'll never, ever do that."

Hannah was surprised her daughter felt that way. With the sexual revolution running rampant, Eleanor's virginity might qualify for the Guinness Book of Records. But Hannah was relieved that for the moment her daughter was not sexually active. She felt like going to the school and giving Miss Merrivale and those stupid girls a piece of her mind. It made her glad Eleanor and Jessie were going abroad. Eleanor needed to see there was more to the world than her school and a bunch of spoiled brats she had thought were her friends.

Her doubts about Viktor subsided. He returned to New York exactly when he said he would, in plenty of time to come to dinner and make sure the girls' passports and visas were in order. Jessie nearly gave her a heart attack when she postured before her father like a Gestapo officer in a movie and snarled, "Here ahr ze papers!"

Viktor roared with laughter and cautioned her not to do that when they passed through German customs. His reaction was further reassurance that everything was going to be fine and she could stop feeling guilty about sending the girls away so that she could be alone with Jerry. Yet just to be sure, she got five hundred dollars in travelers checks and on impulse gave them privately to Jessie. If anything went wrong, she knew she could count on Jessie to—as Rachel would say—use her noodle.

"I have a surprise for you," Viktor said enroute to Kennedy Airport. Hannah had come along to see them off. What now? The old mistrust flared. They were in her mother's limo. She could always tell the chauffeur to turn around and head back to Manhattan.

Viktor smiled knowingly at her. Could he have read her mind? "It's all right, Hannah. I have a meeting in London tomorrow, so we're spending a day there before going on to Munich. The girls can take one of those tours—Buckingham Palace, the Tower of London, and all that—while I take care of business."

Eleanor remained silent. Jessie squealed with excitement. "Wait till I tell Miss Morrow!" Her history teacher was a devout Anglophile who doted on the more bloodthirsty aspects of the Tudor period. "Will we get to see where they chopped off Anne Boleyn's head?"

* * *

Jessie was not disappointed. Their one day in London turned out to be wet and clammy, the Thames eerie with fog. The excursion boat from Westminster Pier had moved slowly down river amid foghorns and the looming hulls of other craft. A squeamish Eleanor clung to her younger sister's arm when they reached the Traitor's Gate and the guide informed them that this was where the young Princess Elizabeth, later Queen Elizabeth I, was imprisoned by her half-sister Queen Mary and how she had sat on the cold wet steps and refused to be taken into the Tower where her mother Anne Boleyn was beheaded. "Oh, *Jessie* . . ."

"It's okay, Eleanor! Honest. It happened over four hundred years ago," Jessie comforted.

Eleanor perked up considerably on the Mall, when their taxi was stopped along with the rest of the traffic to clear a path for an enormous Rolls Royce to pass through the Buckingham Palace gates. "It's the queen!" Jessie's camera was at the ready.

"I got her close up. Inches away. Looking right at me and waving!" Jessie could not contain herself as she described the incident to Viktor and the associate who had joined them for dinner at Claridge's. Over Eleanor's faint objections that it might not be correct, Jessie still wore her camera around her neck. Professional photographers never went anywhere without a camera. You never knew who or what you might see.

Proving her point, Elizabeth Taylor and Richard Burton were escorted with obsequious ceremony to a nearby table. "See what I mean?" Jessie half-rose in her seat, camera poised.

"No, darling." Viktor stopped her. "Not at Claridge's!"

Not to be thwarted, Jessie told Viktor to move his head slightly to one side. "Talk to Eleanor like you don't see what I'm doing." From her seated position, she casually raised her camera and snapped her picture over Viktor's shoulder. As she lowered the camera in triumph, Richard Burton waved, threw her kiss, and gestured that was enough, no more.

I love it here. I'm an Anglophile, too, Jessie thought. Other girls at school talked about living in Paris. Or joining the Peace Corps and going to Africa. After less than one day she was certain. London was the place for her. Everything enthralled her, especially the way they talked. Viktor's friend Guy kept calling her a poppet and Eleanor a glorious creature.

After dinner Guy took Eleanor's arm and said he was taking them all to Annabel's for a spin around the floor and a spot of bubbly. Eleanor appealed to Viktor. "I'm tired. Couldn't we do it another time?"

"We're only in London one night," he reminded her.

"Viktor!" Men called out his name in greeting. One shimmery woman managed to brush by their table and kiss his ear before looking around to see who was with him.

"My daughters," he explained.

"Of course. You old liar."

"May I present Eleanor and Jessie."

"Shall we dance, my dear?" Without waiting for a reply, Guy whisked Eleanor onto the dance floor.

The woman was reluctant to leave. "What a charming frock," she told Jessie. "Absolute heaven." Peering closer she asked, "How old are you, my dear?"

"Fifteen." Everyone said she looked older than her age.

"Really, Viktor, I know you like them young but—"

Viktor patted the woman intimately on the behind. "On your way, angel. Ronnie will be wondering where you are. And none of your gossip mongering, if you don't mind. They really are my daughters. My ex-wife has let me have them for a holiday."

This was something new for Jessie. Did that woman think she and Eleanor were Viktor's girlfriends? He was old enough to be their father, wasn't he? Of course he was old enough to be their father; he *was* their father. The champagne was the problem. The champagne had gone to her head.

Eleanor returned to the table, frazzled and breathless. She fumbled for her seat and sat shaking with her hands covering her face. Guy appeared a moment later and nonchalantly took his place. "Jet lag, I fear," he shrugged.

"A ripe peach, but not yet ready to be plucked," Viktor observed.

"*Dommage, mon vieux.* Perhaps another time?"

Jessie watched in fascination as the two men embraced European style. Guy then kissed Jessie's hand in farewell and gazed deep into her eyes. "This is the one to watch, Viktor. This one has the fire and the spirit to meet life head-on. Give her a few years. You'll see."

Back at the hotel, Eleanor went right to sleep. It wasn't until they were airborne the next morning and seated together beyond earshot of Viktor that Jessie demanded to know what had happened at Annabel's.

"He kept rubbing himself against me and saying stuff."

"You sure? He had such good manners."

"Oh, Jessie. I don't know what to do. Why do men act that way? It's so disgusting."

"What's so disgusting? What did he say?" This promised to be good.

There were dark circles under Eleanor's eyes. "I kept dreaming about what he said. It *was* disgusting. I can't repeat it. I really can't. I'm never going to let another man near me. Ever. Never."

"I know." Jessie could not stand to see her sister so upset. "You can become a nun!"

Eleanor managed a smile. It was one of the many running jokes between them. "You're absolutely right, Sister Jessie. 'Get into the habit with me!' "

A gleeful Jessie responded, " 'I'm telling my beads but I'm not telling you!' "

Eleanor could not keep it up. "Seriously, Jess. Do you think Viktor knows what a creep his friend is?"

"Of course not. He was trying to give us a good time."

Her sister's question disturbed her. She'd heard about pimps. Not the street hustlers in the mink coats and shades she'd read about in *New York* magazine. They had stables of runaway girls in hot pants hanging around outside the big hotels. There were the other pimps, the high-class pimps who provided wealthy men with beautiful young girls in magnificent penthouses and hotel suites.

She thought of the woman's cynical disbelief when Viktor said they were his daughters and Guy's expression when he said *"Dommage!"* A shame. Jessie's first-year French was enough for her to understand that. Maybe their grandmother was right in not wanting them to go with Viktor. She determined to be on the alert for any possible trouble.

Their arrival at the Bayerischerhof Hotel in Munich did little to assuage her growing uneasiness. As at Annabel's in London, men who knew Viktor materialized out of thin air, jumping up from comfortable chairs to greet him, stepping out of elevators as they were getting in, all with the same conspiratorial look when he introduced his beautiful daughters.

This was where he lived, he explained, in a permanent suite of rooms, luxurious yet practical for the bachelor entrepreneur who traveled much of the time. His suite was always ready and waiting for his return, fragrant with furniture polish and fresh flowers. The hotel staff catered meticulously to his needs. The laundress knew exactly how he liked his shirts. Suits were examined for loose buttons before being sponged and pressed. He seemed to live like a feudal prince in a palace full of servants.

There was much for them to see in such a short visit. Viktor decided to give them the postcard tour of museums and cathedrals and historic sites. There would be time enough as they got to know each other better to confront the Hitler years and the destruction the new Germany was determined to rebuild.

Jessie's image of her father as pimp dissipated. Viktor became the caring and concerned father showing his children the city of his birth. *Munchen* was the capital of Bavaria, dating back to the twelfth century. He showed them the Holbeins and Breughels and Rembrandts at the Alte Pinakothek museum, climbed them to the top of the Peterkirche tower to see the wonders of the distant Alps and drove them to the outskirts of the city to Nymphenburg Palace where Mad King Ludwig had kept his mistresses, including the infamous Lola Montez.

"Is that how we got the word nymphomaniac?" Jessie asked with a seriousness so intense that Eleanor laughed and danced her little sister around in a delighted circle.

Viktor joined the laughter and smiled paternally at Eleanor. "I'm so happy you're feeling better. It's good to see you laugh. This afternoon we go shopping for Rosenthal china. I think your grandmother will like me better if I send you home with some of those little blue animals . . . and tonight?"

"Tonight?" The two sisters were wide eyed with anticipation.

"Tonight we go to the artists' quarter for sausages, schnitzels, and yodeling! That's how the people in small villages communicated over long distances before the days of the telegraph and telephone."

Yodeling was easy, he told them. Driving back to the hotel, he showed them how. By the time they reached the Bayerischerhof, all three were yodeling in ear-splitting disharmony. Eleanor's eyes were shining when she and Jessie retired to their room to rest and change for the evening.

"It's nice having a father, isn't it?"

Very nice. Exhilarated by their newfound intimacy with their newfound father, they bathed and changed and wrote picture postcards home. Tonight was going to be wonderful. Tomorrow they were going to Garmisch-Partenkirchen, where they could rent skis and ice skates even this late in the season. If there were time, they could take a cable car up to the top of the Zugspitze, ten thousand feet high and perfect for yodeling.

When the phone rang, Jessie pounced on it. *"Guten abend, mein Herr!"* She handed the phone to Eleanor. "He wants you."

After speaking briefly into the phone, Eleanor hung up. "He wants to have a little talk with me. Alone. About Mom or something. He said you should wait here and we'll pick you up in a little while."

Not fair, Jessie sulked when her sister had gone. On second thought, maybe he'd bought her a present or something and wanted Eleanor to check it out.

Curiosity killed the cat, as Hannah always chided her when she found Jessie snooping through her things or listening through walls with an inverted water glass. But there were no two ways about it. She had to know what was going on. Viktor's suite was at the far end of a deserted corridor. What if the hotel gestapo stopped her and asked her where she was going? To her father's apartment, of course. Why was she so twitchy? There was something ominous about Viktor's door. She had brought a water glass with her.

Was it her imagination? Could it be she was hearing the sounds of a physical struggle and her sister's voice begging someone to stop it and leave her alone? She tried the doorknob. Locked, of course. At that moment, like the cavalry in a Western, a waiter came down the corridor pushing a dining cart.

"*Bitte?*" Bitter was right. She mimed the arrogance with which she had seen Viktor give orders. She had forgotten her key and motioned for him to open the door. "*Schnell!*" Hurry.

Her ears had not deceived her. Her sister was indeed being pinned down on Viktor's capacious sofa, but her attacker was not Viktor. Unperturbed by the intrusion, the man adjusted his trousers, slicked back his hair in the rococo mirror above Viktor's desk, and bowed to both young women before making his escape.

Eleanor's hair was a mess. The belt to her dress was torn. One of her heels had broken. He'd said his name was Dieter and that he was Viktor's best friend and that Viktor had been called away suddenly and asked Dieter to entertain her!

Jessie had been right all along. Their father was a dirty, rotten, lousy pimp. Was this how grown-up men acted? Marcus wasn't like that. She didn't think her mother's new boyfriend was like that.

"What are we going to do?" Eleanor turned to her younger sister.

"We're going home." If her guess was right, Viktor was out drinking somewhere. He would not be back for a while. "I know he bought round-trip tickets. Where do you think he put them?" They found the tickets in his briefcase. His passport, too. Perfect. If she took that, he wouldn't be able to follow them.

While Eleanor packed, Jessie called Lufthansa and

got two seats on the late flight to New York. There would be an additional charge for changing their reservations. That's where Hannah's mad money came in. They smiled their way across the hotel lobby, praying they wouldn't run into Viktor. They left behind the lederhosen he had bought them but decided to take the Rosenthal china for Rachel.

Before boarding the plane, Jessie threw Viktor's passport into a trash bin. Too late to check their baggage through; they were carrying it on board when a young American in blue jeans and windbreaker picked up the heaviest ones and stowed them in the rack above their seats.

As fate would have it, his seat was in their row with Eleanor between him and Jessie. Was he really American or did he only look American? It was hard to tell; he hadn't said a word. When Jessie thanked him, he merely nodded, his face a study in shyness. Just like Eleanor. Once again, Jessie's romantic imagination ran wild. She had read about couples meeting millions of miles from home and discovering they actually lived around the corner from each other. She had to restore her sister's faith in men. Otherwise, Eleanor might really join a convent. This guy looked about twenty-two, and he seemed intelligent. Jessie imagined he was well read and the son of a millionaire, which would explain the good manners.

Why didn't Eleanor say something! She was sitting next to him. She could comment on the weather or ask him to adjust her reading light. Being two seats away, Jessie couldn't really lean past her sister, could she?

In the cool darkness, all three had drifted to sleep when supper was served. Jessie caught a glimpse of the young man stealing a glance at her sister and swallowing hard, as if he were about to speak but changed his mind.

"Chocolate cake!" Jessie exclaimed. "Don't you love it?" She directed her question to the stranger.

"Well—yes. As a matter of fact, I do." It was not a New York accent. Still . . .

"It's Eleanor's favorite. In fact, she makes the best chocolate layer cake you've ever had."

Eleanor blushed uncomfortably. The morsel of cake on her fork fell into her lap.

"Here, let me." Jessie pretended to read while their fellow passenger raised Eleanor's tray so she could find the lost piece of cake.

From their painful spurts of conversation punctuated by even more painful lapses into silence, Jessie learned that his name was Luke Calloway. He was an agricultural student. His family had orchards in Columbia County in upstate New York, near Albany, he explained.

Walking through Kennedy Airport toward Immigration and Customs, Jessie took the bull by the horns. She had not seen nor heard him ask Eleanor for her phone number. Eleanor would die before she gave it to anybody. "Can we give you a lift into Manhattan, Luke?"

"Thanks a lot, but I'm catching a plane to Albany."

Jessie found a piece of paper and scribbled Eleanor's name and their phone number on it. "Well, listen. Our grandmother has a couple of fruit trees on her terrace. Maybe the next time you're in town you'd like to see them. Okay?"

He tucked the piece of paper in his coin pocket. *Oh, no!* Jessie knew exactly what was going to happen. He'd forget the piece of paper. His mother would throw his jeans into the wash and that would be that. Love's labor lost. Swift as a Dickens pickpocket, she retrieved the piece of paper. "Put it in your passport so you won't lose it."

"I won't lose it!" His smile transformed his features. A broad smile revealed perfect white teeth. He saluted both girls, lingering that little significant bit longer on Eleanor.

"You really embarrass me, Jessie," Eleanor said once they were settled in the taxi. "I don't know how you do it. I'd never have had the guts to give him my number."

And he'd never have had the guts to ask. "You think I want an old maid for a sister?"

"Or a nun?" Eleanor shrieked. They hugged each other and laughed their relief at being back in New York.

Before reaching home, there was one important subject to discuss. They agreed to say nothing about Viktor's treachery. It would make their mother feel guilty and give their grandmother an excuse to take revenge. They would just say they were homesick and decided to come home.

"It's our secret." Jessie linked her pinkie finger with her sister's. "Let's say it together."

"Our secret. To keep forever," they intoned solemnly.

Just as they reached the apartment, Eleanor said, "There's one more thing."

"What, for God's sake?"

"Don't say anything about Luke, okay?"

"I'll bet you a million dollars he calls you the minute he gets home."

Eleanor hugged her sister. "You really think he will?"

Jessie puffed an imaginary cigar. "I guarantee it."

CHAPTER 24

1975

Eleanor

One more baby, that's all Eleanor wanted. Why was it asking so much? Less than a year ago when she thought she had conceived, the only person she told was Jessie. She had planned to wait until she was a few months along before confronting Luke with a *fait accompli*. The miscarriage had not stopped her. It had merely delayed her purpose. In fact, she couldn't even be positive she really had been pregnant. Her cycles had been erratic since Jason's birth and the two subsequent miscarriages.

Miscarriage was the right word. Miscarriage of justice. But this time she was not only sure she was pregnant, she also felt in her bones that she would carry to term. *Just one more baby, please God.* She would be grateful and satisfied and be the world's best mother and wife for as long as she lived.

Luke need never know about the pinholes in her diaphragm. Everyone knew there was no hundred-percent contraceptive method except abstinence. The Pill had caused unpleasant side effects. The coil caused cramps, and after only a few years on the market had become the subject of what the medical profession called "concern." When she and Luke asked the gynecologist whether he let his wife use the Dalkon Shield, and he paused before weaseling out of it, Luke agreed the diaphragm was the way to go.

As she lolled in bed with the patchwork quilt Luke's grandmother had made pulled up to her chest and Jessie's letter waiting to be reread for the umpteenth time, Eleanor listened to the familiar sound of the bathroom shower and lazily pictured her husband's hard, tanned body. Not an ounce of fat on him, she reminded herself with the smug knowledge of his physical beauty that she alone enjoyed. Luke was not one for bikini bathing suits or tight jeans. Often when tourists stopped at their farm to buy apples or peaches, women would try to prolong the transaction by asking Luke a million questions. He always answered politely and seemed impervious to their come-ons.

When one particular brunette bit into a peach and licked the juice voluptuously, he didn't seem to notice. When she asked if he had a mailing list and gave him her card, he handed it to Eleanor and said cordially, "My wife takes care of that sort of thing."

In a few minutes the running water would cease. The shower curtains would part with the screech of the plastic clips on the metal rod. He would step out on the fluffy white bathmat and slip into the fluffy white terry robe she had washed in the machine and hung in the sweet country air. He would towel-dry his hair and brush his teeth with long and lingering gargles before finally, his ablutions accomplished, the bathroom door would open.

Whether they made love or not, he always held her close while they fell asleep. When they did make love, she could tell that he was delicately, tenderly, yet deliberately checking her out to be sure the diaphragm was in. He was doing it because he loved her and was determined to prevent a pregnancy that could harm or even kill her. She knew that he wanted more children as much as she did.

She was lucky to have a husband like Luke. Marrying him and leaving the New York rat race were the smartest decisions she had ever made. She was more than happy. She was content. She prayed for the same kind of fulfillment for her mother and sister. Hannah seemed happier than Eleanor had ever seen her. She and Jerry were so comfortable together, like a couple married for years instead of being newlyweds.

Rachel, of course, made her disapproval of Hannah's second husband abundantly clear. He was not rich or famous or even very handsome—he was practically bald, for God's sake!

"You can't win with Rachel," Hannah had sighed a few weeks ago when Jerry drove them upstate for a visit. "She actually told him to get a toupee!"

She remembered how Jerry sat at the kitchen table pulling pennies out of Jason's ears and trading bites of one of Eleanor's homemade doughnuts with the little boy. "Forget it, sweetheart," Jerry said. "Eleanor, tell your mother to forget it." On impulse, he put one of Eleanor's potholders on his head. "She wants a toupée? I'll give her a toupée!"

No question about it, her mother was happy.

So that left Jessie. The shower was still on. She could hear muffled singing. *High above Cayuga's waters.* Once a Cornell man, always a Cornell man. Moving to the middle of the old-fashioned double bed, she spread-eagled her arms and legs so that when the bathroom door opened she could pretend to be asleep and that there was no room for him until he gently eased her to one side and she pretended to wake up and throw her arms around him.

Her sister's letter sounded happy—ecstatic, in fact. Jimmy Kolas was the most extraordinary person—not just man—*person* she'd ever known. He was friend, adviser, and teacher as well as lover. He was exciting and fun, too. She had known him for months before she slept with him and was glad she had. Okay, so he was married. But only technically.

Don't tell Mom, Jessie begged Eleanor, but she was virtually living with him, although she was keeping her basement flat in Lennox Gardens. "And best for last—" Jessie always loved saving best for last. At the very end of her letter was the news that she was going to Helios with Jimmy for an extended stay—five or six months, maybe.

As Eleanor knew, Jessie had spent a rapturous weekend in Greece some time earlier and fallen in love with the remote island Jimmy had inherited. "I never thought a city kid like me would go bananas over a place with no cars, no TV, no stores or movies or supermarkets!" It was an island paradise and Jimmy's plan was to turn it into a luxury anchorage for the international yachting set. No tour boats from Piraeus. No souvenir shops with Jackie Onassis postcards. A strictly high-class operation.

Jimmy's plan was to develop Helios as an exclusive private club. Taking his cue from the way many exclusive London clubs operated, members would pay an exorbitant annual fee, fifty thousand pounds or so, and pay additionally for services provided. A refueling station and repair dock. A fresh-water swimming pool. Tennis courts and exercise gym. A restaurant, bar, and discotheque with state-of-the art temperature control for foodstuffs and other perishables. A scattering of individual fishermen's "huts" that looked primitive from the outside and featured every luxury and convenience for those wishing to abandon ship while the crew washed the decks, polished the brass, and repainted what the sea had eaten away.

Later, perhaps, on the far side of the island out of sight of the yachts, he might develop a getaway spa for the merely rich, top executives who had not yet reached yacht status but who had disposable income or preferably unlimited travel expense accounts.

"And then there's *my* idea for an artist's colony on the highest point of the island," Jessie went on excitedly. "There's a crumbling old monastery. The views are cosmic—oh, Eleanor! Jimmy and I are going to do such wonderful things together. And I know what you're going to say. 'What about your career? What about photography?' "

Having kept Eleanor current on all her assignments and sent her tearsheets of her published work, she explained how important it was to take some time to recharge her batteries. For several months there had been a Jessie Lawrence photo essay everywhere you looked.

Her new agent agreed. "You're making it look too easy. Stay out of sight for a while. Have them begging for more."

Just to make sure she wasn't out of mind as well as out of sight, she accepted a *Harper's Queen* commission to photograph Helios in detail for a series of pictures. They could stand on their own as lyrical mood pieces and eventually become the "before" in a "before-and-after" report of Jimmy's development of the island.

As for the future, Jimmy had asked her to marry him and Jessie said yes, but again, Eleanor was not to say a word to anyone. His divorce still hadn't come through but there was no hurry. It was just a matter of time. Hannah had taken years to marry Jerry, after all. Just recently, Jimmy had brought Jessie matching rings he had commissioned from Zolotas—platinum, with an acanthus motif and the Greek word for love, *eros,* inscribed in cyrillic letters.

"There's no post office and only one telephone on the entire island," Jessie marveled. "Can you imagine me with no TV and no phone?" She would call Eleanor from Athens. If there were an emergency and Eleanor had to reach her, she gave her the Athens cable address for the Kolas Shipping Company headquarters.

"Repeat! Not a word to Mom or Rachel! Wish me luck, Sis. I'm sure I'm doing the right thing."

"Tired?" She had been engrossed she had not heard Luke enter the bedroom. He stood over her, smiling. It was too late for their ritual of her pretending to be asleep. She opened her arms to him.

"Not too tired."

Happiness engulfed her. She wished the same for her beloved sister.

CHAPTER 25

1975

Jessie

The two sisters seemed to be on a parallel course. Eleanor was pregnant. Now all the relevant signs indicated that so too was Jessie. Eleanor had not told Luke. She confided in no one but her sister. Jessie had not told Jimmy, and there the parallel ceased at least for the time being. Jessie had confided in no one, Eleanor included, for one simple reason. If it turned out she was pregnant she might decide against having it. Bearing in mind Eleanor's desperate longing for another child, she could never in a million years admit to having an abortion.

There was still time to figure things out. Her period was often irregular. Being a month late could easily be attributed to the frenzy and stress of leaving London for a possible four- to six-month stay on Helios. Two of her four cameras needed repair. She had to find airtight containers to protect the hundreds of film packs she had bought. Then there were the clothes, toiletries, laundry soap, shampoo, water softener and paper goods by the carton, tissues, toilet paper, and tampons, assuming she would need them. She could not expect to get even basic products on Helios until Jimmy's plans came to fruition.

The possibility of motherhood both thrilled and terrified her. There was no question about her relationship with Jimmy Kolas. They had pledged themselves to each other and their future life together. His wife's lawyer had confirmed her agreement to the divorce. From being something of a dissolute playboy, Jimmy was applying himself fully to the Helios Development Project.

Jessie could hardly believe her eyes when the seaplane touched down at the island. In the months since her earlier visit, Kolas Shipping had sent out a fleet of cargo barges carrying an electric generator and the equipment and supplies for building a temporary dock, installing a shortwave radio and telephone connection to Athens and creating living quarters for Jimmy and her by gutting three stone huts that had been abandoned by fishermen and assembling them into a single edifice.

It looked like an igloo, Jessie thought at first glance of the gleaming white exterior. She laughed delightedly at herself. No igloo would last more than ten minutes in the Aegean heat. The structure was more like the photographs she had seen of Mykonos. As Jimmy explained, the thick stone walls kept the interior cool. Ancient Greek air conditioning, he called it.

In Athens they had chosen marble tiles for the floors and terraces and miles of colorful fabric for wall hangings, curtains, and bedspreads. It would all be arriving by sea in a few days, along with the thick white *flokati* rugs to be scattered throughout once the floor tiles were installed.

Workmen from the mainland slept in hammocks aboard the Kolas company barges. They set up a field kitchen on the beach with a charcoal spit for lamb and the local red mullet they caught from the tiny *benzines*, the oil-powered boats they had brought along for the purpose.

The furnishing of their own house would be the prototype of the architectural style for Club Helios. Because metal rusted in the sea air, wooden frames were assembled for bedsteads and couches were fitted with heavy woven ropes instead of springs for supporting mattresses and pillows. They had bought some local pottery at the Plaka just to have something to eat off and decided it was perfect for their restaurant.

"You've got the artistic eye, my darling," Jimmy smiled at her.

They were sipping *ouzo*, stretched out on the coolness of the marble tiles. The clouded licorice packed a subtle wallop that brought out the kitten in Jessie. She hurled a pillow at his head, which brought out the tiger in him. A tussle, a struggle, a moan of submission as he pinned her to floor.

"Christ! What brought that on?"

"My artistic eye. Is that the reason you brought me here? My artistic *eye*? What about the rest of me? My incredible thighs, for instance." He had once said her thighs were so hard and strong they could crack walnuts.

"Jessie, what is it? What's bothering you?"

She couldn't tell him. For all their intimacy, she couldn't come right out and say she was pregnant or thought she was pregnant.

She took the easy way out. "It's the *ouzo*, love. I'd better stick to apple juice." If in fact she was pregnant—and she was beginning to believe it was so—she'd best get off the booze anyway.

Days followed nights with dizzying speed. One morning a team of government inspectors flew out from Athens in the Kolas company seaplane, at Jimmy's invitation. Official papers had to be filed, licenses approved for building a marina and installing inter-island communications. After the initial courtesies, it became clear that Jessie's presence was not wanted. "I'm sorry, pet. I explained that you are an American and American women participate in business arrangements. But it simply isn't done here. I'm afraid you'll have to make yourself scarce while we men—" He pounded his chest Tarzan style to make a joke of it "—we men get things in order."

Oddly enough, in all the weeks since their return to Helios, she had not visited the monastery. They had discussed it. Several times they had planned to take a picnic on the long climb up. But something had always come up. A leaking barge. A problem with the tiles. A problem with the fresh-water well. A problem with the generator. Men's problems, weren't they? Then let the men take care of them. She would take her cameras and explore the upper reaches of the island for the photo essay she had promised to deliver.

It felt good to have a camera in her hands. Walking alone up the barely discernible path, she became aware of movement and of being watched. A child stepped out into the path and grinned. A woman leading a donkey came up swiftly behind him and scooped him up on her hip. "Yassu!" Jessie called out tentatively. "Kahlee mehrah!" Hopefully, she was saying "Hello, good morning."

That established, they fell back on sign language. The woman beckoned Jessie to follow her through some underbrush, on the other side of which was a cluster of stone huts around a crumbling fountain. Jessie raised her camera in a gesture of asking permission. The woman nodded. The seemingly deserted buildings came to life. Through open doors, Jessie could see women working at looms. Beside and behind the huts were vegetable gardens, and here and there fragrant fruit trees. Luke and Eleanor should be here to see this, Jessie thought. She could only imagine what these island inhabitants would think if they saw the vastness of Luke's orchards in bloom.

The weaving fascinated her the most. Why had she

and Jimmy brought fabric from Athens when there were artisans right here? By signs and smiles, she was able to photograph the tethered goats and the step-by-step method by which the women pulled the hair into skeins, dyed it with natural fruit stains, and wove it into magical patterns.

When she indicated her wish to continue on her journey upward to the monastery, two men materialized holding what looked like bagpipes. The women pointed to the goats and made squeezing gestures. Goat bladders! Their cheeks bulging the men piped her up the path followed by the women and children in a bizarre but cheerful parade.

One of the nuns Jessie remembered from her earlier visit emerged from a back room, her hands covered with blood. A young girl of ten or twelve was trying to pour water over her hands in order to wash them. The nun recognized Jessie and rocked her arms as if cradling a baby. A piercing cry confirmed the fact that she had just brought a newborn infant into the world.

"Kala! Kala!" was all Jessie could remember. "Good! Good!" She gaily distributed the hard candy she had brought for them in her knapsack and again asked for permission to photograph.

The midwife chattered excitedly to the others until they all turned beaming faces toward Jessie. The midwife pressed her hands to her own belly with a complicit smile while the others clapped their hands in agreement. "Kala!"

Just from looking at Jessie, the women knew that she was with child. "Good!"

CHAPTER 26

1975

Eleanor

How to say it?

Please pass the salt and oh, by the way, I'm pregnant.

How could she casually lead up to revealing what she'd known for several weeks?

I've been meaning to tell you something but it sort of slipped my mind.

She could delay no longer. This morning in bed Luke had kissed her belly. "Better go easy on those chocolate-chip cookies!"

Brewing the morning coffee, washing the berries for the cereal, fixing Jason's lunch in time for the school bus to pick him up, Eleanor knew she had no choice but to come right out with it.

"I'm pregnant." She said it softly, her back toward the kitchen table. The radio was on. Luke was riffling through the morning paper. Jason was testing his developing reading skills with the back of the cereal box.

She drank deeply from her coffee mug and faced them, standing at her place at the table. "I'm pregnant!"

Luke looked up uncomprehendingly. What had she said?

Tears of defiance sprang to Eleanor's eyes. "I'm pregnant! I'm sorry. I know what the doctor said. I know it's dangerous but I can't help it!" The long-suppressed words poured out. She wanted their family to be complete. She wanted Jason to have a baby brother or sister. Her school yearbook had said six children. She would have loved having six children, but she wasn't greedy. Two would be enough. "That's all I want. Just one more child. Try to understand."

Luke was so upset that when he stood up, his cereal bowl went crashing to the floor. "I don't believe this. Are you out of your mind?" He circled the table and took her roughly by the wrists. "Do you want to die? Can't you think of anyone but yourself? Haven't those miscarriages taught you anything?" Her usually laconic husband bellowed into her face. "What about Jason? Do you want him to be an orphan? I thought we agreed that Jason was enough for us to raise. And thank God for the opportunity!"

Her attempt to speak was trampled over. "See what you made me do?" He took aim at the cereal bowl on the floor and kicked it against the stove, smashing it to smithereens before storming out the back door.

Jason had slipped down from his chair and was cringing under the table. "Please, Jason." Eleanor drew him out and tried to gather him in her arms. His little face contorted, he hit her with his fists and struggled to be free. She held on tight. "Listen to me, sweetheart. Don't you want a baby brother or sister? Think what fun it will be. You'll be the big boy. The big brother."

"You'll die! You'll leave me all alone like Frankie's mother!" Frankie was Jason's best friend. His mother, not yet thirty, had died of cancer.

"I am not going to die. I promise." She cajoled him into letting her hold him and dry his tears. She covered his face with tiny kisses. Nibbles, she called them. "Do you think I would ever leave you? I love you and Daddy too much for that."

Luke stood in the doorway. If he heard her declaration of love, he did not acknowledge it. He snatched his son from Eleanor's arms. "I'll take Jason to school."

"But the bus? The bus will be here any minute."

He was shaking with emotion. "Can't you understand English? Tell them we left. Tell them anything you want. You're good at lying. I want to be with my son."

Jessie! Eleanor desperately needed to talk to her sister. Getting a phone call through to Helios was like trying to reach the moon. The overseas operator got through to Athens easily enough, but making the connection to Helios could take hours or days. Jessie had said if ever there were an emergency to call the Kolas office in Athens and leave a message. Fortunately, the person she got spoke English.

Alone in the house, she cleaned up the mess on the kitchen floor and tried to continue with her usual household routine. Unable to concentrate, she threw Jason's cereal bowl into the garbage can by mistake. Retrieving it she knocked some of the garbage onto the floor.

She had to talk to someone. She was falling apart.

"Why didn't you tell me?" Hannah exploded.

"Because you'd haul me off to some Park Avenue doctor!" Eleanor yelled back. And force her to have an abortion. A "therapeutic" abortion was how her own doctor described it the last time she conceived. Her miscarriage had ended any further discussion.

Her mother sighed. "I'm sorry, darling. I'm not upset *with* you. I'm upset *for* you. This is serious stuff. How far along are you?"

"Almost five months."

"And Luke didn't notice?"

At least she could laugh at Hannah's astonishment. "I've been very careful with my diet. I'm just starting to show. He thought I was eating too many chocolate-chip cookies."

"You really want this baby, don't you?"

"Oh, Mommy, I wish you could talk to Luke. I know

you think he doesn't like you. He's just shy. Really he is. He does like you a lot. He told me."

It was a situation Eleanor had tried and failed to resolve. Luke *was* shy. The few times Hannah and Jerry paid a visit, Luke always managed to be occupied elsewhere by a fence that needed mending or a stand of fruit trees that required his immediate attention.

On Eleanor's rare trips to the city, Luke invariably found reasons not to accompany her. She persisted in taking Jason to see his grandmother. Children needed grandparents. Hannah liked her grandmother role. Not like her own mother, who made Jessie and Eleanor call her Gransy or, preferably, Rachel. After Jason suffered a series of winter colds, Eleanor had given in to Hannah's insistence on a New York pediatrician. The day before the tonsillectomy, Hannah took the boy to F.A.O. Schwarz and bought him a teddy bear almost as big as he. When they brought him home after the operation, she sat up with him feeding him ice cream while sending Eleanor to the movies with Jerry.

"Let's put this into perspective, Eleanor. Luke isn't angry. He's frightened. Scared stiff. So am I."

"There's nothing to be scared of. I'm having a baby. Women have babies every day!"

"Come on, now. You know you're at risk. Don't try to kid anybody. Tell me how you feel."

"I feel great. Wonderful. Better than when I had Jason."

"And you're certain you want to go through with it?"

"I'm certain. I know it's going to be fine." What's more, she was equally certain she would have a little girl. "It'll be perfect. A big brother and a baby sister, just like you and Sam, right?" When her daughters were small, Hannah had often talked about the brother who died in the war and how wonderful it was for a little girl to have an older brother while she was growing up.

Eleanor and Jessie had never known their uncle, of course. He had died in 1945 long before they were born. Hannah had sometimes jokingly apologized to them for not giving them a brother. "You gals don't know what you're missing," she'd say.

Eleanor had thought she had found a brother in Luke. A brother, a husband, a father, a lover, a friend, an amalgam of everything a man could be. But this morning's tantrum had deeply shaken her.

In the next several days, instead of continuing the argument, Luke clammed up. He did not look at her. He did not speak to her. His attempted conversations with Jason were painfully forced and ultimately lapsed into silence. "I think you'll be more comfortable," was all he said before deserting their bed for the narrow couch in the den.

Life was so mysterious. Here was the man she loved. Sometimes she felt she understood him completely. Other times like now, he was a total stranger. He frightened her. Following the miscarriages and the doctor's warning, she had accepted the situation and raised the question of adoption. But Luke was furious and appalled. He wouldn't hear of it. He forbade her to even mention the subject again.

Eleanor knew that whether biological or adopted, children were the luck of the draw. There were no guarantees. By the grace of God, Jason was a wonderful little boy, sturdy, bright, and affectionate. The baby in her womb—Luke's baby—might be as blessed or, God help them, flawed in some way. She was willing to take that chance.

Three days later, Jessie finally called from Helios.

"Luke won't speak to me, Jess. He looks right through me, like I'm invisible. I can't take it."

"Maybe I should call him," Jessie offered.

It was no secret between the sisters that Luke did not approve of Jessie's lifestyle. Eleanor laughed mirthlessly. "I don't think it would help. He thinks you're a bad influence as it is."

The ingrate. Had he forgotten who made the match the day they returned from Munich? "If I hadn't been so pushy and given him your number, he'd have vanished into thin air and married some farmer's daughter. Maybe Mom can talk to him."

Eleanor explained that Hannah was against the pregnancy, too.

Jessie's naturally high spirits bubbled to the surface. "Why don't you come here! Jimmy's dying to meet you. The house is comfortable and we even have a resident midwife in the convent." Even as she said it, Jessie knew it would be too dangerous.

"Oh, Jessie . . . I really do miss you a lot. Anyway, enough about me. What about you and the Gorgeous Greek? Do I hear wedding bells?"

"Any day. We have matching rings. All we're waiting for is the final divorce decree. So you have to come over before you get too close to term. We'll get hitched in Athens and you can be my matron of honor."

"Sounds wonderful. But seriously—"

"Seriously, go easy on Luke. The guy is crazy about you. He must be worried sick and doesn't know how else to express it."

"Thank you, Mrs. Freud. I'm feeling much better."

"But seriously, seriously—we've just had a new phone system installed. It'll be easier to get through from now on. Promise me you'll call?"

"I promise."

Jessie's voice became confidential. "As a matter of

fact, there's something I want to tell you—" Sounds of voices in the background interrupted "—but it'll keep for another time. Jimmy just brought some of the work-men home for an *ouzo*. Bye! Big kiss!"

1975

Felicity

"Follow your bliss." The words of Joseph Campbell echoed in her heart as Jessie made her way down the path from the convent, rapturous yet taking scrupulous care not fall. She had made the rugged climb many times since the day the nun noticed her pregnancy. Clifford Smith-Avery in his usual clench-jawed, mumbling way, had brought Campbell's work to her attention months ago.

Since that first disastrous dinner party in Hill Street when she asked him to see her home, he had become a peripheral part of her life. Jimmy's best friend, he often joined them for a meal or a film. Being in publishing, his name was on many cultural invitation lists. Occasionally he would ring to see if she were free for a look-see at a new exhibit at the Tate or a champagne reception for an author.

Whereas Jimmy expressed considerable pride in her accomplishments and bought up dozens of the magazines where her work appeared, Clifford was more intent on discussing her photographs individually as well as in context of a theme. What interested him, he said, was the craft behind the art, the technical aspects of printing and cropping and the choices of paper that could make such a profound difference.

A respected editor at a publishing leviathon, he confessed to her that he felt battered and lost in the commercial jungle. What he really wanted was to start his own imprint. In five years he would come into a family inheritance.

"By then I think you will be a fine photographer, an artist, and I shall publish your first retrospective," he told Jessie confidently.

"Me an artist? I'm just a photojournalist. I intend to marry Jimmy, have a couple of kids, and help him make Helios into an Aegean paradise. Of course I'll continue to take pictures. As long as anybody gives me an assignment."

"Save your negatives."

"I save them!"

"I mean in temperature-controlled files. Not in those Charles Jourdan shoeboxes!"

"So okay, I like shoes."

Cliff had seen her and Jimmy off at Gatwick. "Remember, sweetie, follow your bliss and don't be afraid. Doors you never knew were there will open and welcome you in."

If she had had any doubts about committing herself to Jimmy Kolas, they were by now gone. All the jagged pieces were falling into picture-perfect place. All the basics were ready—bottled gas, generated electricity, fresh water. An agora paced out at the dock. Their own white stone house a prototype for those to come. The ramshackle taverna painted a glistening white with blue shutters and the deep-freeze hooked up and ready.

Best of all, the baby. The divorce wouldn't be final in time for a nine-month legitimacy, but what did she care? Women were having babies out of wedlock all over the place. There was no longer any such thing as an illegitimate child. How could a child, any child, be illegitimate? From what she'd heard, the word illegitimate was no longer permitted on birth certificates. Just the parents' names.

Dmitri Andreas Constantine Georgopoulos Kolas, father; Jessie Kathleen Lawrence, mother. Nearing their house, she could see the seaplane bobbing in the water off shore. The house was deserted. Jimmy must be down at the taverna. She had decided to tell him about the baby, but she did not want to do it in public. She would wait until they were alone, later, in bed.

She washed and changed. Did her nails, fingers and toes. Removed the exposed film rolls from her cameras and stashed them in the metal containers that would protect them until they could be developed.

She refused to be annoyed. It wasn't like Jimmy to forget she was alive. She knew he was still negotiating some of the permits and licences, so maybe that's what kept him. The men would obviously be having dinner. She could understand not being asked to join them. What she could not understand was not hearing a word from Jimmy. The taverna was a five-minute walk. He could have excused himself and come back to tell her what was going on. At the very least he could have sent Yanni or one of the other workmen with a note.

To pass the time she made herself a light meal and settled down with Joseph Campbell. Apparently she was more exhausted than she thought. She awoke in darkness to find herself in bed beside her soundly sleeping lover. She ran her fingers lightly over his face, longing to kiss him but afraid to wake him. Poor baby, he'd been working so hard.

"Darling?" she whispered, thinking she felt him stir. "Are you faking?" She could understand it if he were only pretending to be asleep. "Okay. I forgive you. See you in the morning, and sleep well."

When she awoke, he was sitting in a chair several feet from the bed. She knew something was wrong before he spoke. He was wearing a suit and tie, the suit and tie he had worn on their journey from London. His briefcase and overnight bag were at his feet.

"I'm sorry, darling. The licenses are a royal cock-up. They didn't bring the right forms. The government seals are out of date. The inspectors insist I didn't register my intentions properly. So it looks like I have to go to Athens to straighten things out."

"Why didn't you wake me? Give me five minutes. I'll be ready in a flash!"

His face was her answer.

"I'm sorry, but it isn't possible. The sea plane's full. As it is, we'll have to hold our breath."

She could not let it go. "Then send the plane back for me. It's only a couple of hours away. We can stay at the Grande Bretagne and have dinner at that place in the Plaka where you can throw dishes—"

His face was drawn, his tan tinged gray. "I'll be busy. There'll be nothing for you do."

She could feel the rising hysteria in her voice. "There'll be plenty for me to do. I'll take pictures." She told him about the women she had found weaving cloth in the area surrounding the convent. "They lent me some samples. I bet I can show them to somebody in Athens. Make a deal for them. Shoulder bags! Cushions—"

"Jessie!"

Discussion over. He would be gone two days, three days at most. Why didn't she go on taking her pictures? He placed a large pile of *drachma* on the table. If she thought it worthwhile, she was to buy the weavers' output. She was a clever girl. He would be back before she knew it. Was there anything more?

"Yes, there is." Was it better to say she was pregnant or that he was going to be a father? The same thing but from a separate perspective. She remembered the many times Rachel had called her the smart one. Before she left for London, her grandmother had cupped her face in her soft jewelled hands. "In any negotiation with a man, deal from strength but always make him think his interests are more important than yours.

"Better yet," her grandma added with the hint of a Mona Lisa smile. "Change the subject. Don't let him know what you're thinking."

"Well?" He was itching to go. This was no time to ask for wool to knit booties.

"Film." That was it. She had enough to photograph all four thousand Greek islands. Better safe than sorry. She knew she would be sorry if she told him the truth now. "I'm afraid I'll run out."

The foolishness of her request moved him to embrace her. He knew she couldn't possibly need more film. "It's just for a few days, I promise. I'll be back before you know it."

Nearly a week elapsed before she saw the seaplane circle and land. Something was terribly wrong. He looked haggard and unkempt. His hair in need of a trim. His suit crumpled, a stain on his tie. "Jessie!" he swept her up in his arms and buried his face in his favorite spot where neck and shoulder met. "Darling! I've missed you so much. Forgive me for leaving you. Forgive me."

When reunions are sweet, separations are forgotten. After making love they lay quietly in each other's arms. Was everything all right? she asked. Had he gotten the authorities to cooperate?

All was well, he assured her. "Now tell me what you did while I was away. Have a mad affair with Tasso Capedis?" Tasso was the oldest man on Helios. He had been a sponge diver in his youth. He had got the bends and now could scarcely move.

Not funny, in fact not at all like Jimmy to make fun of someone's physical infirmity. Everyone reacted differently to stress. She knew Jimmy must have hated kowtowing to bureaucrats and letting government pipsqueaks jerk him around.

Calling on her journalistic skills, she sought to enthrall him with her adventures. She told him everything. About the convent where she gave half the drachmas he had left her to the midwife nun. She had used the rest of the money to buy up every last piece of weaving and to convey as best she could that there was more money where that came from.

She told him about photographing Yanni and the other workmen stripped to the waist in the broiling sun. About finding the first ripe figs and photographing them close up so that when she opened them their shape and coloration transcended any recognizable form of fruit, seeming, in her view finder, to be a powerful expression of sensuality.

In short she told him every last detail about everything except that she was with child and increasingly with doubts about revealing it. But her doubts seemed silly when after a few days all was back to normal. The building continued apace. Whatever was troubling Jimmy vanished. His boyish exuberance returned. He stripped to the waist and worked side by side with the men. Greek music emanated from an Athens station on the powerful shortwave radio he had brought back with him. Hearing his voice and watching him snap his fingers and throw back his head in spontaneous exultation when one task was completed and another about to begin, she knew what farm women of past centuries must have felt when they heard their men singing in the fields.

A week after his return it was as if he had never left, the passion and intimacy between them never more intense. The changes in her body were beginning to show. She could no longer delay. She had no doubt he would be as happy as she. Her plan was to spend the afternoon at the convent photographing the nuns doing the weekly wash and then visit her weavers. She had made some sketches of table mats and runners for them to follow as to size and dimension.

Anna, she had learned, was the midwife's name. Now Anna pressed her hands to Jessie's belly and again pronounced it *kala!* Jessie translated. "Good!" Anna and other other nuns repeated in chorus, "Good!"

She saw nothing amiss when she got back to the house and found it deserted. She thought nothing amiss even as the sun began to set, assuming Jimmy was with the workmen, probably standing them to an ouzo or retsina after a long day in the hot sun.

Jimmy didn't encourage her to go to the taverna. It was a male tradition. She hated to seem like one of those shrewish women who dragged their men out of the bar, but she was feeling antsy. She wanted to see Jimmy.

Was something wrong? Had he been hurt? "Yanni!"

A slight movement behind an inner door alerted her senses. Robbers? Kidnappers? Helios was a remote island. Maybe word had spread about the building supplies. Anything could happen. A figure of a man shuffled into view.

"Yanni! You scared the daylights out of me!" Not that he could speak English. "Jimmy. Where is Kyrios Jimmy?"

He handed her a note and darted into the night.

My dearest Jessie,

By the time you get this, I will be in Athens with my wife. My family was so against the divorce they sent emissaries to Argentina to bring Felicity back. I saw her in Athens last week. I'm sorry, Jessie.

The problem with the licenses and permits was a

trick to get me to Athens. One cannot imagine my horror when I reached our offices to find my wife waiting for me. You may not find this amusing, Jessie, but if there's one thing I admire about you it's your American sense of humor. My wife actually said, "I want you to know I forgive you." After how she humiliated me!

I told her, I told them all in no uncertain terms that the marriage was over. If she wouldn't divorce me I would divorce her on grounds of desertion, adultery, and you name it. That's when I returned to you, my dearest. To you and Helios and our wonderful project.

I know I must have acted strangely. I was trying to work up the nerve to tell you we couldn't marry just yet and that I hoped you would trust me and stay with me. We were so happy together, I felt certain we could work things out. You looked so lovely this morning, so sassy with your cameras around your neck, like a little girl taking snaps on holiday until the snaps turn out to be art of the highest order. How much you have grown since the "American Family"!

I had planned to tell you everything tonight. But then shortly after I watched you disappear up the path, the phone rang. My wife has attempted suicide. The plane arrived a short time later. I've kept it waiting while I write this farewell.

He and his wife would return to London as soon as she was fit enough to travel. He would leave instructions for the Athens office to provide Jessie with money and any assistance she might require.

He knew that this turn of events would come as a shock and would naturally be an embarrassment to her when the story got around in London. He also knew she had not finished her magazine assignment.

Please stay on Helios as long as you like. Take your magnificent photographs. Use it as a base to tour the Greek islands. Invite anyone you like to stay. Your sister perhaps? I know how much you miss her. Have Athens make the arrangements.

In closing, Jessie, I remember how you once told me your philosophy of life could be summed up in three words. "Follow your bliss," you said. I know that without you there can be no bliss for me. I pray you have the courage to follow yours.

Jimmy

1976

Eleanor

Eleanor had felt something must be wrong when she stopped hearing from Jessie. The postcards and phone calls from Helios had ceased abruptly several weeks ago, a fact she had only gradually realized because of the problems in her own life.

The entire world had turned against her. Luke had shown no mercy in his refusal to speak to her directly. He used poor little Jason as the go-between. "Tell your mother I'll be late tonight and to leave me something cold to eat."

"She's sitting right here. Tell her yourself!" Defiance was not in the boy's nature. Always he was a good-hearted little guy. The tension between his parents was affecting him badly. The other night he had wet his bed. Eleanor had assured him everyone had accidents and promised not to tell his father.

"Don't take it out on the boy," she begged her husband. "What I'm doing isn't his fault. It's my fault and I accept the consequences."

She had hoped her mother would be more support- ive. Somehow in her unhappiness she wanted Hannah to come to the rescue. She wasn't being fair, of course. Hannah had volunteered to drive up and stay with her. Luke wouldn't stand for that. He didn't like mothers-in- law, period. His father had died young; his mother lived with her second husband far to the north near Buffalo.

It wasn't just prejudice against Hannah; he didn't encourage his own mother to visit, either.

She couldn't confide in Rachel. Having chosen marriage and motherhood over fame and fortune, she couldn't bear to have Rachel say I told you so! Not that her grandmother would say it in so many words. Rachel would probably send an ambulance for her and arrange a police escort to speed her to the hospital for tests and God knows what.

Rachel and Hannah were always so sure of their opinions. Why was she so confused? She had boxed herself into a corner. She had nowhere to turn. By now more than six months into the pregnancy she could tell something was very wrong. There was pain and bleeding and most frightening of all the kicking and movement had stopped. *Please, God. Let my baby be okay!*

Her sole inner resource was stubbornness. She had come this far and would not give up. Her baby was not dead. It was sleeping and garnering its strength for the big day. If she gave in and went to the doctor she knew beyond doubt her dream would turn into a nightmare.

Still her symptoms were beginning to worry her. She had heard of women going nuts from hormonal imbalance. Maybe she *was* nuts, soothing her hands round and round in a circular motion on her belly as if it were the baby's back, crooning the lullabies she had sung to Jason.

Jessie was the one she needed. She and Jimmy were probably cruising through the Greek islands on a yacht, nowhere near a post office. Or traveling on the mainland as they had planned. That's why when she tried the Helios number a few weeks back there had been no answer. A check with the overseas operator had confirmed the circuit was in working order. *Please God, let her be there,* she prayed as she dialled the number again. She desperately needed her sister. "Hello?"

"Eleanor!" Jessie sounded as if she were in the next room. But Jessie didn't sound like herself. There was no verve, none of the usual exuberance that always made Eleanor feel she was the one person in the entire world Jessie wanted to hear from. Now Jessie sounded—she couldn't put her finger on it. Timid? Nervous? Never. Not Jessie.

"You sound funny. Are you okay?"

"Have you been calling me?"

"A couple of times. I assumed you and Jimmy were away somewhere."

A pause and then Jessie's voice disintegrated into a whisper. "I've been here. I just didn't answer the phone. I've made a terrible mistake, Eleanor." Her voice rose to its highest register in a series of keening moans that frightened the daylights out of Eleanor. "He walked out on me, the bastard. His wife came back from Argentina and the son of bitch said 'Sorry about that' and took off like he had a firecracker up his ass!"

Jessie's choice of words snapped the tension and made both of them laugh. It was a phrase Jessie had brought home from kindergarten. The more it shocked people, the more she used it, until Hannah finally advanced on her with a bar of soap and the threat of washing her mouth out. While she never again said it in front of the grownups, it was one of the secret passwords in the sisters' private club.

"So why are you still there?"

Another pause, one so prolonged Eleanor thought she had lost the connection. "Jessie? Are you there? Jessie!"

"It's okay. I'm here. I had to stay on. For one thing, I have an assignment from *Harpers Queen* to photograph the island. Undiscovered paradise and that kind of thing. And also, to tell you the truth, I like it here. Jimmy invited me to stay as long as I like—"

"That was generous of him."

Jessie had to laugh at her sister's sarcasm. Eleanor didn't even know she was being sarcastic. Hearing her voice bristle, Jessie wanted to hug her. This was some tough kid since she got married.

Gaiety faded as she continued her explanation. "I needed time to think things out, decide what to do next."

"Come home. We miss you. We'll burn that stinker in effigy."

"No. I've got to go back to London. I've got a career going there. Editors snapping up my work. But it's going to be hard on me—humiliating to go back alone and have everybody know he's back with his wife."

"Who cares?"

A mini-pause this time. "I'm afraid I do."

"Oh, Jessie. I'm sorry."

"Hell, so am I. But enough of me. What's with you?"

"You think you've got troubles—" Eleanor started off spunkily enough, but quickly broke down "—Luke still refuses to speak to me about the baby."

"You can't be serious."

"Worse than serious. It's over three months since I told him. He sleeps on the couch. He talks to me— what little he has to say to me—through Jason and now Jason's so upset that he's started wetting his bed again."

"I can't believe it."

"Believe it."

"And he's let you go through the pregnancy without a hug or a kiss or rubbing your feet like he did with Jason? I was so jealous of the way he rubbed your feet. But you must be miserable!"

"I'm—not so hot. I'm scared, Jessie. I'm sitting here scared silly that the baby's dead." Sobs choked her. "And next week Luke's going to Cornell to give a seminar on running a family orchard successfully. He's taking Jason with him and after that they're going camping for a week. I'm going to be all *alone*! For two whole weeks!"

The phone connection was beginning to crackle.

"Eleanor!" Jessie shouted. "Should I call Mom?"

"No! Please—I started this. I'll handle it myself. Promise me on your word of honor? You won't call anybody?"

Jessie promised as the line went dead.

A week later Eleanor woke up feeling so sick she couldn't raise her head. The sound of Luke's pickup pulling up to the back door reminded her that he and Jason were leaving that morning for Ithaca and the Cornell seminar.

"Jason! Get the lead out!"

She could hear Jason in the hallway. He turned the knob of her door and pushed it open a few inches. He said in a stage whisper, "Mommy? I hope you feel better."

Her husband and son had been gone less than an hour when she erupted with pains so violent that she lost consciousness. It was afternoon when she came to in a fetid swamp of bloody excretion. Between her legs lay the most pathetic sight she had ever seen, an unformed baby strangled by its umbilicus. For the poor little creature, her womb had become a tomb. It was a girl, just as Eleanor had known.

She had brought this disaster on herself. Luke might forgive her but she would never forgive herself. In a way she was glad Luke wasn't there. His presence would only have made things worse. Her sewing basket was beside the bed. She found the scissors and cut the cord and gently wrapped her unborn daughter in a pillow case. Her bed linens in the washing machine, she eased herself into a lukewarm bath and visualized with abiding grief the unhappiness that lay ahead. Her home and marriage destroyed, her son condemned to the trauma of divorce. Her mother and grandmother pitying her being the lamebrain they always thought she was. Only Jessie would understand, but what could Jessie do, deserted and miserable on that Greek island? The two of them were quite a pair. Jessie too smart for her own good, Eleanor too dumb.

Weak from her ordeal but clean and fragrant in a fresh nightgown, she could no longer put off what must be done. She had to call the doctor and tell him what happened. She had to find out the proper way to honor the tiny white bundle on her chintz-covered stool. Would there be a death certificate for the baby? Should there be a burial? A cremation?

She was about to dial the phone when it rang. *Luke?* Was her husband concerned about her, after all? She would tell him what happened and he would cancel out of the seminar and rush home.

"Oh, darling! Something terrible has happened."

"Eleanor?" It was Jessie. "I was worried when I didn't hear from you. What's going on? What terrible thing happened?"

Jessie listened to every detail and then asked, "You're sure nobody knows?"

"I told you, I'm alone in the house. Luke took Jason with him to the seminar and then they're going camping. They won't be back for two weeks."

"Listen to me, Eleanor. Sometimes God works in mysterious ways. I've just had an idea—a crazy idea. Don't say a word. Just hear me out.

"The other day a baby girl was born at the convent. They wouldn't say who the mother is—one of the nuns, for all I know. They asked me if I wanted to adopt her. I didn't know what to say so I said I'd think about it."

It was providence. The plan crystallized as Jessie got

more and more excited. "It can work, I tell you. No-body knows you lost the baby, right? Okay then, you get on a plane and fly here. I'll arrange for the adoption."

"But Luke put his foot down. He won't stand for an adoption."

"Eleanor—"

"What?"

"You're not listening! Luke won't know it's adopted. You'll tell him it's yours. That I begged you to come to Greece because Jimmy dumped me and I was having a nervous breakdown. So you came—you were still preg-nant, remember—and you went into labor and had the baby on Helios. A couple of weeks later you go back to the states with your new baby girl. Get it?"

Eleanor was overwhelmed. "It's crazy!"

"Crazy enough to work. Think about it. I'll call you back in an hour. Meantime, answer me this: Do you want another baby?"

Eleanor's head was spinning. What to do? Stay home and face the music? Fly to Greece and take a chance?

She closed her eyes and tossed a coin. *Heads I stay; tails I go!* Why was it that she couldn't take charge of her own destiny? The coin rolled under the bed.

Luke! That was it. Luke could make the decision for her. By now it was dinner time. He and Jason would be back at their Ithaca motel. This was when a husband who was out of town would call home, especially if his wife were alone and pregnant.

If he called before Jessie got back to her, she would confess everything and beg his forgiveness. If he didn't, she would go to Greece.

By the time her sister called back, not one but two hours had passed, plenty of time for Luke to pick up the phone. She had known in her heart he wouldn't call and had spent the time making lists of the things she must take care of before leaving. An efficient homemaker made lists. As for the tiny bundle of what was never meant to be, her precious baby girl, she decided on a private and solemn burial under the oldest apple tree in the orchard. She would be preacher and chief mourner and would in years to come sit in its summer shade in remembrance.

Jessie had clearly bounced back from Jimmy's desertion and her energy and optimism were contagious. Whatever happened, she would not be sitting around crying and brooding for two weeks. As Jessie pointed out, there was no downside to her trip. If Jessie's plan worked, Eleanor would return home in triumph with her newborn babe in her arms. But even if the plot failed, Jessie could send back the sad news that Eleanor had suddenly gone into labor and that the baby had been stillborn.

Now that she would be seeing Jessie in just a few days, Eleanor realized how desperately she missed and needed her sister.

CHAPTER 29

1976

Jessie

The idea had hit Jessie like a bolt of lightning, a dazzling, brilliant solution to the dilemma she had been trying to resolve throughout the final weeks of her pregnancy. There had been times immediately after Jimmy Kolas left her when she thought of following him back to London and making a scene on his doorstep. Or, alternately, slinking back to London to have an abortion at some private clinic in Wimpole Street and no one the wiser.

She had delayed and delayed until it was too late for the latter. Nor could she really see herself in Hill Street with a big belly. There were professional as well as personal considerations. She could jeopardize her growing reputation as a photographer with a sleazy scandal. Having an affair with a glamorous Greek was chic; having his baby when he went back to his wife was not.

Harpers Queen had cabled to congratulate her on her photographs. They planned to do a separate Helios portfolio in a travel issue and urged her to come back as soon as possible to plan her next assignment.

She had had to take special pains to prevent Jimmy's workmen from noticing her condition. It turned out to be easier than she supposed. They lived on the barge, worked all day, and drank *ouzo* most of the night in the taverna. They rarely if ever looked in the direction of

Kyria Jessie, and when they did what they saw was a woman in a flowing tent of a dress taking pictures.

Most of her life centered on the convent. Anna the midwife saw to her diet, preparing luscious rice puddings made from goat's milk and fish stew made from the local fish they called *bourbounia*. There were herbal concoctions as well, weird-tasting powders ground with mortar and pestle that she drank as in a dream without question.

She had followed her bliss and given birth a few days before amid the tender ministrations of Anna and the other nuns. The convent was on the highest point of the island. Through the open doors, she could feel and smell the fragrant breeze and as she obeyed Anna's urgings she could catch glimpses of cerulean sea and matching sky.

With the baby's first cry, she felt like an ancient goddess surrounded by her handmaidens. With the infant at her breast she knew she could rule the world. *Bliss.* She had followed hers. That's what she would name the baby girl. The question of what to do with her remained up in the air.

Before the birth she had thought she would go to Athens, to the American Embassy perhaps, to find out how to place the child for adoption. Holding her baby changed everything. She had heard of socialites who could not risk scandal. Their solution was to go away on an extended trip during pregnancy and later "adopt" their own babies.

Perhaps she could do that, become one of the new breed of liberated women who chose to raise a child without the boredom of marriage. Eleanor's call had triggered a hazy possibility. With baby Bliss snoozing in the tiny woven hammock made by one of the island women, Jessie refined the details of her plan.

Much of it depended on the inability of Anna and

the nuns to understand English. Since Jimmy's departure, she realized they had no idea who he was. When she mentioned his name, they had shrugged uncomprehendingly. When Anna produced a crumpled certificate for Jessie to fill in, she knew it must be a birth certificate. With Eleanor enroute to Athens, she had scrawled Eleanor's and Luke's names in the spaces that seemed right and held her breath while Anna, too, scribbled her name in the remaining space presumably meant for the doctor or midwife.

A ceremonial sip of a warm honey drink was followed by warmer embraces and best wishes that transcended the language barrier. In a gesture of gratitude, Jessie gave them an envelope containing a thousand dollars worth of Jimmy's *drachmas*. There was wry satisfaction in being the lady bountiful with Jimmy's money.

By now, if her watch were right, Eleanor's flight had landed and been met, as per her instructions to the Kolas office, by a limousine that would drive her to the seaplane marina in Glyffada. In a short while her sister would step ashore. Jessie had to be letter-perfect with her story.

This was the delicate part. She had to carry it off without a hint of deceit. No one must ever know that Bliss was her child. She and Eleanor shared many a secret, the darkest one being their father's obscene behavior. But this was one secret she had to keep solely and forever to herself. Eleanor would never knowingly agree to raise Jessie's child. She wouldn't understand it, and her own maternal instincts were so strong she would be appalled by Jessie's willingness to give a baby up. It was a low price to pay for her sister's and her child's happiness. Instead of arranging to "adopt" Bliss and taking her back to London as a single mother with all the problems that would entail, she could be Aunt

Jessie, the lovable, eccentric *Tante* Jessie who sent expensive birthday presents and who in future years would perhaps be a glamorous heroine to her own little girl.

Determined to take no further chances, Jessie was ready and waiting when the seaplane landed and Yanni brought Eleanor ashore in his *benzine*.

"Here she is!" Jessie cried. She thrust the infant into Eleanor's startled embrace. "Everything's set. We're going straight back to Athens. I've got so much to tell you. Isn't she beautiful? Her name is Bliss, if it's okay with you. We'll talk about it on the way."

Her sister was all but speechless. She was obviously exhausted from her ordeal and from the long journey. "I—I thought you were going to show me the island— the convent—what's going on?"

Jessie thought fast. "It's the—water. Something happened to the fresh-water well. It's polluted. It could hurt the baby. We'll be more comfortable at the Grande Bretagne. You can rest and get to know your daughter."

As if on cue, the baby nuzzled against Eleanor's breast, sending a pang of deprivation through Jessie, dampening her blouse with milk. That was another reason to get Eleanor on her way back to New York as quickly as possible.

"I can't believe I'm doing this." If Eleanor said it once, she said it a hundred times.

"You're doing it," Jessie insisted.

"Tell me again what I'm supposed to say."

"Keep it simple. Don't volunteer details that can trip you up. You were alone in the house when I called. Luke and Jason were away. Jimmy Kolas had dumped me. I sounded desperate. Suicidal. I didn't realize how advanced your pregnancy was. I begged you to come and be with me.

"You weren't on Helios more than five minutes when

the pains started and you gave birth. The long trip probably triggered it. Thank God, the baby is fine. Your visit probably saved me from having a breakdown. Thanks to you, I've snapped out of my depression. You can even say the birth of Bliss made me realize there's more to life than some son-of-a-bitch Greek bastard."

"Pull-ease, Jessie, your language. Not in front of the baby!"

"You're absolutely right." She patted the infant's cheek. "Sorry, kid." Her Bogart delivery sent the sisters into peals of laughter.

"And if they ask why you didn't fly home with me?"

"Between you and me?"

"My lips are sealed."

"Say I'm embarrassed and humiliated. I really don't want to face Mom or Grandma. Can you imagine what Rachel will say? I made my own bed—" Her sense of humor had really returned. "—And now it's up to me to get myself out of it."

Besides, Jessie had loved living in London and would be returning there immediately. Her career was thriving. Too much was going on for her split with Jimmy Kolas to be anything more than a passing bit of gossip. She had more important things on her mind, like becoming the world's top photojournalist, *tra-la*!

Her final instruction to Eleanor was to keep the birth certificate in her bag but separate from her passport. "Only produce it if American immigration asks you why the baby isn't on your passport. You will giggle and blush and explain the baby was born earlier than you expected. And dig out the birth certificate. Okay?"

Eleanor's face contorted with tears at the departure gate. "Oh, Jessie. It's like—like—" With Bliss in danger of being squashed between them, the sisters embraced.

"I'll be in London tomorrow night!" Jessie called after them. "I'll ring you from the flat."

It felt good to be speaking Brit again. She had fallen easily back into *ringing* instead of calling and having a flat instead of an apartment. It would be great getting back. Another day on Helios was all she needed to pack her things and leave the house neat and clean as Hannah had always taught her.

The pilot of the seaplane knew she didn't speak Greek but that didn't stop him from chattering on and on with elaborate gestures and smiles. She thought he was making some kind of polite conversation until they arrived at Helios and she opened the door of her house.

Jimmy Kolas was waiting for her. "Forgive me, Jessie," he said with a grin that could always melt her heart. "I've been a swine but I know now that we belong together. Please, darling, let me make it up to you if it takes a thousand years. I've come on bended knee to beg you to take me back."

CHAPTER 30

1986

Clifford

"A letter from the colonies, darling!" Jimmy Kolas sailed the envelope across the breakfast table to where Jessie sipped her decaf, no milk, no sugar, to offset the caloric impact of her favored morning meal of peanut butter, orange marmalade, and mashed banana on toast. Even after ten years of living together, it was an American barbarity that defied Jimmy's understanding.

"It's a birthday invitation, darling. Bliss is going to be ten years old." Ten years? It was hard to believe. "And listen to this! 'Dear Aunt Jessie. Mom says you should drop everything except your camera and come to my party. And bring Jimmy, too. Love, Bliss. Also Mom, Dad, and Jason. P.S. Your room is ready!' "

She sailed the invitation back to him. "Look at that penmanship. Have you ever seen such beautiful hand-writing?"

"Shall we go? It might be rather fun to meet your sister and this remarkable child. What do you say?"

Time had eased Jessie's anxiety in the years since Jimmy gave her the shock of her life by showing up unannounced on Helios. Another bit of grace-of-God timing. A few days earlier and he would have found her with an infant in her arms. It wouldn't have taken a genius to find out that the baby was his. It was strange how things had worked out.

Her first thought on seeing him that day was to get

him away from Helios as quickly as possible. All that
had to happen was for Anna to take a morning stroll
from the convent and pour out her congratulations to
Jimmy in Greek. All she could think of to do was to
throw her arms around him, tell him how miserable she
had been, and insist they leave for London at once.
She could no longer bear the sight of the island that
had caused her so much heartbreak.

Her plan had been to make him feel that he was forgiven. Once back in London, she would dump him the
way he had dumped her. Sweet revenge. Give him a
taste of his own medicine. But that wasn't how things
worked out. There was no doubt about it, Jimmy Kolas
possessed the magic for her, an indefinable chemistry
that drew her to him. After a few days in Athens and
a week in Paris, she had to concede they were indeed
still made for each other. And it seemed his wife really
had put him through hell.

Her need to recover physically from giving birth gave
her a psychological advantage she would not otherwise
have had. By necessity, she kept him at arm's length
and in sexual suspense while she "decided" whether to
forgive him and take him back.

"You're enjoying making me suffer," he said when she
once more declined his invitation to stay the night at
Hill Street and insisted he drop her at Lennox Gardens
without inviting him in.

"A little bit. You see, I thought I had lost you forever.
Now I have to get used to the idea of having you
again."

When at last she was ready to resume their relationship, they picked up where they had left off. Divorce
was no longer discussed. His wife had returned to her
Argentine lover. After a few months, Jessie gave up her
flat and officially moved into Hill Street. The critical
success of her Helios photographs had firmly estab-

lished her career. She could virtually name her own assignments. She and Jimmy became one of the sought-
after couples at cultural events and country weekends.

As self-protection, she had made excuses to avoid
seeing Bliss. It was better this way, better to protect
herself from emotional backlash. It helped being an
ocean away. She sent so many gifts of clothing and
books and toys, Eleanor had to write and beg her to
stop. She kept Jessie up to date with regular batches of
snapshots. "I wish I were as good a photographer as
you!" So did Jessie. And one of these days she would
have to stop being a jerk and spend some time with
Bliss. And, incidentally, take some decent pictures.

Her opportunity came sooner than expected. Jimmy
was on a trip to Hong Kong and points east on the Pacific rim and she was spending a quiet evening at home
with Clifford when the doorbell rang. She had just
beaten him to the ground at Scrabble and was making
him feel better by getting him to discuss his new publishing venture. Getting Clifford to talk about anything
was like pulling teeth. Jimmy often joked that he knew
Cliff ten years before he heard his voice.

"A gentleman from Interpol," the butler announced.

Interpol? It had to be some kind of joke. Jimmy pretending to burst in on her having a tête-à-tête with his
best friend? It was no joke. The visitor showed his
identification and asked most politely where he might
find Mr. Kolas.

Events accelerated with breathtaking speed. Jimmy
was escorted home from Hong Kong and charged with
fraud and participation in an international conspiracy
involving a stock swindle and currency embezzlement.
Inland Revenue moved quickly to impound the Hill
Street house and freeze Jimmy's bank accounts, including one in both their names containing most of Jessie's

earnings and assets. Her jewelry and Land Rover were technically owned by him and were therefore forfeit.

Through Cliff's old-boy connections, Jessie was able to salvage her personal belongings, including her cameras and files of negatives. It was to her benefit that she and Jimmy were not married, Cliff said. The law in its wisdom dismissed her as a mere mistress, and as such a victim rather than a spousal participant in his schemes.

Shaken to the core and having no place to live, she accepted Cliff's offer of the tiny carriage house in the mews behind his house in Hampstead. "No strings attached."

When the Fleet Street terriers tracked her down, Clifford invited them in for a sherry. While Jessie hid quietly behind closed shutters in the former servants' quarters above the garage, Cliff convinced his guests that he had no idea where she was and that she must have gone home to America.

That night, they talked seriously about her future. His idea was to publish a book of her work.

"I'm too young for that. I haven't developed enough to merit a book. I'll look like a conceited jerk."

"You are an artist," he said. "Don't underestimate my opinion, Jessie. I am fascinated by the merciless American naiveté of your photographs. Others, I am sure, will agree."

She was incredulous. She considered herself a photojournalist, one step up from the paparazzi hiding in bushes, but an artist? "You really mean it?" she asked a dozen times.

"I do. Most sincerely."

"You're not pulling my leg?"

He turned red. "A very beautiful leg, if I may so say, but no—I mean what I say."

An awkward silence followed. He rose as if suddenly

remembering an appointment elsewhere. "Excuse me." She watched him straighten some pictures on the wall that didn't need straightening.

"Clifford?"

His back was to her. "Yes."

Their friendship dated back to that first night at Jimmy's dinner party in Hill Street. Since returning from Helios and moving in with Jimmy, Cliff had become part of the furniture, a constant in her personal scenery. "Are you by any chance in love with me?"

His shoulders stiffened. He lit a cigarette and inhaled deeply, allowing the smoke to billow and dissipate slowly before he turned around. "Silly girl. Of course, I'm in love with you. A man would be a fool not to be in love with you."

She touched his arm tentatively. "Why haven't you told me?"

"You were living with Jimmy. My role is a cliché of drawing-room comedies. Family friend. Always there when required."

It was true, of course. She and Jimmy had slept together, traveled together, entertained together, but had never really been together the way she and Clifford were. She and Jimmy never talked. Yet neither did they manage to share companionable silence. Jimmy looked at her photographs but never saw them. He was proud of her work but had no appreciation for what it was.

"I'm living here now," she said.

He gazed at her wistfully. "No strings."

So he'd said. *Merciless American naiveté?* She riffled through the desk drawer until she found what was appropriate to the occasion. "Come here. I have something to show you."

She held up the ball of string for his inspection and slowly wrapped it several times around the two of them, binding them together.

The next day the press was back in force. Jimmy Kolas had been spirited out of prison in the middle of the night by persons unknown.

"Bloody fools!" Cliff thundered at them. "Do you think he'd be stupid enough to come here? He's thousands of miles away by now, the idiot."

Hearing the fuss but not realizing the cause, Jessie emerged from the carriage house to see what was going on.

"It's Jessie!" The piranhas swarmed. Had she heard from him? Did she know where he was? Had she helped him escape? Would she follow him to the ends of the earth?

She retreated inside and locked the door. The telephone rang. Clifford. "Draw the curtains and don't make a move. These people are shameless but they're not stupid enough to break down the door. That's a criminal offense."

They talked for a long time. Only a few yards separated them. "You're sure there isn't a tunnel connecting the house to the garage?" she asked. It would have been nicer being trapped together.

Cliff explained to her that the paparazzi were relentless and would not go away. The queen's prosecutor was in an embarrassing position and might try to save his own skin by charging Jessie with aiding and abetting. Even with no proof, her testimony would divert attention from weak prison security.

"You must leave the country at once," he decided.

His plan was inspired. During the night, the press left a skeleton force of piranhas to keep watch while the rest slept. In a stakeout like this, they cooperated with each other with a rare camaraderie of all for one. Cliff waited until the darkest hour before dawn. In a way he could feel sorry for the louts standing around in

the damp deluding themselves that they were journalists.

When he opened his front door, they sprang to life
and rushed forward. His face wreathed in a cheshire
cat smile, he wheeled a tea trolley out to the front
steps. "Tea and sandwiches, everyone?" Poor things, so
young and gormless.

"Mighty nice of you," they said.

"Sorry if we kept you up," they apologized.

"Just doing your job," he agreed, chatting them up
while Jessie slipped through the back gardens of adjoining houses to a waiting minicab around the corner. A
few hours later Cliff waved companionably as he drove
off to collect her from the Bloomsbury hotel his family
had used for donkey's years.

On the chance she might be recognized at Gatwick
or Heathrow, they drove instead to Manchester for her
flight to New York, and from there to Albany, where
Eleanor would meet her. Over the phone they impressed upon her sister the need for secrecy. Once
Fleet Street realized she had slipped through their
tobacco-stained fingers, they would reckon she'd gone
home to America and would have their New York
bloodhounds on the case. For the time being it would
be better all round to keep Hannah and Rachel ignorant of her whereabouts.

A chapter in her life had ended; another was about
to begin. As the plane roared into the western sky, Jessie Lawrence realized with a rush of tender expectation
that she would soon be in Riverton with her sister. And
with Bliss.

CHAPTER 31

1987

Bliss

"Tell it again, Aunt Jessie. Tell about how I was born in Greece."

Bliss never tired of the familiar tale. Luke stayed silent and aloof. Jason was by this time going on fifteen and was permanently exasperated about life in general and his sister's birth in particular. "Not again! How many times do we have to hear it?" He mimicked Bliss's voice. "'Did you know I was born in Greece?' Everybody in Columbia County knows you were born in Greece so why don't you cool it, okay?"

"Oh, Ja-*son!*" She hugged her brother with exuberance and planted a kiss on his ear. "I love you!" He pretended to fend her off but Jessie could see he was putty in her hands.

Eleanor took a sip of coffee. "Isn't she something?" The children had gone to school, Luke was examining some new saplings. The sisters were alone. "I think of you and of Bliss and thank you every day of my life. And the crazy thing is, everyone says she looks just like me. Can you believe it?"

"They always say people who live together begin to look alike. Something to do with facial expression. You know how babies imitate adults."

"You'll get a kick out of this. Rachel insists Bliss is the spitting image of *her*! Isn't that a howl?"

"We all know she takes credit for *everything*!"

"That's right, Jessie, and don't you forget it!" She wagged her finger menacingly. "If Grandma hadn't given you that crummy plastic camera, you wouldn't be the world's greatest photographer today."

"Ah, Eleanor. I've missed you so much . . . but how is Luke?"

"Same as usual. Doesn't say much." Since Bliss came into their lives, he tried to be more outgoing. Eleanor's trip to Greece had torn him apart. He had let things go too far. He'd known he was being cruel but couldn't stop the silent treatment. When he and Jason got to Ithaca he wanted to call home but was afraid Eleanor would hang up on him. Instead, he canceled the camping trip and he and Jason headed for Riverton the minute the seminar ended.

Hannah told Eleanor he had gone bananas. He broke down in tears, crying like a baby on the phone. She couldn't imagine it, the Great Stone Face crying. He told her it was all his fault and if anything happened to her he would kill himself. Eleanor decided it served him right. He didn't know about the adoption and Eleanor vowed never to tell him.

When Hannah called him with the news of the baby's birth, he packed Jason in the car and drove down to the city. Hannah said he was like a caged beast, prowling around the apartment—and it was a huge apartment. Finally he was getting on her nerves so she sent the two of them off to the Bronx Zoo.

"I wish I'd been there when Luke first saw Bliss," Jessie said now.

Eleanor's eyes welled to overflowing. "You know, Jessie, I really toyed with the idea of leaving him. Going back to New York with the children. Let him have his damned trees. I was going to have manicures and go shopping at Bergdorf's with Rachel. But when I saw his face and how much he suffered and little Jason peeking out at me from behind him—" She could not go on.

"I know you talked about it, but I didn't really think you'd leave him. After all, Bliss needs her father."

All was well and good, Jessie thought. Eleanor seemed happy and content, even if Luke didn't seem to have changed that much. He was still undemonstrative. When she bear-hugged him on arrival, he stood stiff as a board in her embrace. He was still a man of few words, mainly reports on the weather, reminders to the children to finish their homework, and shorthand advisories on where he could be reached.

He had no curiosity whatever about Jessie. Her life in London. Her experiences as a photographer. Her plans for the future. Eleanor had not mentioned Jimmy Kolas. She simply said Jessie was overtired and needed a rest and that Hannah and Rachel weren't to know where she was until she felt up to it.

The local news agent ordered the *New York Times* for Jessie. No mention of the Kolas scandal appeared. Cliff was relieved to hear that when he phoned. The British press continued to milk the story until there was no milk left. Various sightings had Jimmy skin diving at the Great Barrier Reef, bartending in Juneau. One masterpiece of a composite print showed him go-go dancing at Chippendale's in Los Angeles. But eventually, in the wake of other, juicier scandals, Jimmy Kolas literally became yesterday's news.

Photographing Bliss began as a familial undertaking, a pleasant way for Jessie to repay hospitality and take some decent pictures for the family. From the very start, a special kind of synergy developed, a connection at once lyrical and spontaneous in which the sum was infinitely greater than the parts.

Soon Jessie was sleeping in Bliss's room in the matching twin bed with the matching Cinderella sheets and pillowcases. Jessie's ever-present camera became an extension of her arm, a projection beyond what her eyes could see and her mind could sense. Without having read Joseph Campbell, the ten-year-old followed the bliss for which she was named with a purpose that ranged from the quietly introspective to the wildly uproarious and zany.

Impervious to the camera, Bliss agonized over her school assignments and her glorious hair, suffering alternately frustration and triumph. She could concentrate on a geometric construction for hours or moonwalk to headphones while simultaneously ironing a shirt, polishing her cowboy boots, and rearranging her rock collection.

Out of doors, she raced wildly with the dogs until she fell panting to the ground while they licked her face barking for more, more, more. She filled the bird feeder and put seed on her lips for her regulars to swoop down for a snack. Ignoring the ladder, she shinnied up an apple tree and brought Jessie a choice specimen from the topmost branch.

She was still child enough to read to her dolls on a rainy afternoon, and grown up enough to set the table and start the potatoes and salad for dinner. When Jason brought home his schoolmates, Jessie could feel the bratty kid sister clashing with the incipient adolescent seeking male contact by getting in their way.

Much of the time, watching her daughter Jessie felt herself torn between tears and laughter. The girl had no guile. She didn't play to the gallery with a bag of proven tricks. She acted and reacted from a wellspring of honest and loving expectation. When Jessie's first set of prints came back from processing, Jessie examined the results with an emotion bordering on awe. What she had captured was beyond anything she had previously achieved, the images of Bliss so sweet, so radiant, so fierce in their unashamed joy that she wondered if she were seeing things that weren't there.

Cliff would set her straight. She sent the prints without comment and waited in an agony of suspense for his response.

"It's the book I've been wanting you to do," was how he began his phone call. No hyperbole. Stiff upper lip and all that.

"Does that mean you like them?"

Like them? Another man would say he loved them, they were the greatest thing since sliced bread or the Sistine Chapel. Not Cliff. You had to listen carefully and steer your way through the shoals of diffidence. "Jessie, dear."

"Yes, Cliff, dear."

"They are ravishing. Brilliant. Heartbreaking. Glorious. Just as I knew they would be. But—"

"But?" There was always a but.

"I want more. Half again as many. I want to make it the number-one book on my spring list. We'll call it, with your permission, *The World of Bliss.* Okay with you?"

She could only nod.

"Jessie? Are you there? Damn this phone."

"I'm here," she managed to say.

"One thing more. I thought I might toddle over and see you. Would that be convenient?"

Was he putting her on? He knew she liked to take the mickey out of his clenchjaw accent. Toddle over? "How about toddling to the travel agent as soon as you hang up, or 'ring off,' if you prefer."

Hannah had a four-star fit when Jessie told her she'd been staying at Eleanor's. "Three months and you never let me know? What am I, some kind of monster? I know you girls are close, but this is ridiculous."

"I'm sorry if I hurt your feelings, Mom."

"Not hurt! Disappointed, that's all." She was hurt.

"I had some things to work out. That's why I went to Eleanor's. For some peace and quiet."

"You can find peace and quiet here." Hurt to the core. "Anyway, how is Jimmy?" The question really meant *When are you getting married?* Clearly the scandal had not been juicy enough for the American papers.

"We've split, Mom."

"Why didn't you tell me?" *So I could say I told you so?*

"I didn't think you were interested."

"How dare you say that? I'm interested in everything that concerns you."

"That's not my impression. I've sent you copies of the magazines with my photographs in them. Have you ever bothered to say you liked them?"

"What is the matter with you? Of course I like them. I'm proud of you. How could you think otherwise? Jerry and I have them on the cocktail table. Show them to all our friends. I'm surprised at you."

She'd made her point. Time to change the subject. "How's Grandma?"

With Marcus now permanently institutionalized, a palace revolution was threatening Rachel's control of their real-estate empire. A group of officers and stock-holders were moving to have Marcus Salinko declared incompetent and his transfer of control to his wife declared invalid. To complicate matters, a group of take-over vultures were threatening to swoop down and suck the company dry before spinning it off to die.

Would Rachel lose everything?

"Not on your nelly. She's hired some of the new style corporate assassins to protect her. Lawyers. Financial sharks. I attended one stockholders' meeting and I can tell you this. Your grandmother managed to look like a pathetic waif and Marlene Dietrich in sables and diamonds, both at the same time."

Jessie waited until she got to New York to tell her mother about Clifford Smith-Avery.

"Are you going to marry him?"

"I'm not sure."

"Don't tell me he has a wife somewhere, too."

"*Mom!*"

"Well, at least don't tell Rachel. She's got a lot on her mind. I'm really worried about her."

She could have told Hannah there was no need to worry. Rachel was in high spirits when they arrived at the penthouse. At eighty-five, she looked more like sixty-five and would have been highly insulted to hear that. She had just come from an arbitration.

"The bastards tried to make me out to be a little old lady in tennis shoes. I showed them. I knocked them all out with my photographic memory. I recited every spreadsheet, every detail of every changeover from rental to condo since the year one. The bastards didn't know what hit them. They didn't know if I was lying and it'll take their Wharton school accountants a couple of years to find out."

Jessie couldn't help but grin. Clifford was going to love Rachel. "Did you lie, Grandma?"

"What do you think?"

"I think I'm going to take your picture, that's what I think." She'd brought her camera, as always. "Okay—say *cheese*."

"*Camembert*, okay?" Rachel sucked in her cheeks. "But seriously, Jessie, tell me. Are you making a living with your pictures or is that Greek paying your expenses? Not that it's any of my business. You're a grown woman. You can make your own decisions."

"Yes, I'm making a living. No, Jimmy Kolas is not paying my expenses. We've split."

"But she has a new man in her life!" Hannah defended her daughter's honor. "A publisher. He's going to publish a book of Jessie's pictures of Bliss. He says Jessie's an artist."

"I brought some of the pictures for you to see, Grandma."

Rachel paged through the portfolio with agonizing slowness and in unaccustomed silence until with tears in her eyes she embraced her granddaughter. With tactless disregard for Hannah, she assured Jessie, "You inherited your talent from me!"

She held up one of the portraits of Bliss to make another point. "Look at that face. She's going to be a great beauty just like her mother. Eleanor always was the pretty one, but you know something?" She propped her thumb under Jessie's chin and tipped her face into the light. "There's a little of Jessie, too. Beauty and brains. Bliss has it all.

"Remember how Eleanor was going to adopt a baby when the doctor said she couldn't have any more? I agreed with Luke two thousand percent. He was against adoption and so was I. Like he said, you never know what you'll get. Think about it. If they'd gone ahead and adopted a baby, Eleanor would never have had Bliss."

Turning to Jessie, she added, "And *you* wouldn't have a book coming out."

CHAPTER 32

1988

Jimmy

"A howling success," Clifford informed her. In less than a week after its British publication, *The World of Bliss* was about to go into a third printing. The Sunday supplements had been lavish in their praise. The fashion magazines ran photographs of Bliss with their reviews. Clifford's press officer arranged book signings and television appearances for Jessie. There had been some discussion of bringing Bliss herself to England. But Luke objected; he did not want her to miss school.

"It's actually a good thing she won't be here," Clifford said. "She's nearly two years older than the photographs. Better to be mysterious. Have the photographs stand on their own."

Despite all the kudos, Jessie couldn't bring herself to relax and enjoy it. Something was going to spoil it. Exactly what, she couldn't guess. But something.

Clifford heard the news flash from Athens first. Jimmy Kolas had turned himself in at the British Embassy. He told reporters he had been "vacationing" and finding spiritual renewal in a convent on a remote island in the Aegean called Helios. His long months of meditation had shown him the error of his dissolute life as a playboy. He had had a spiritual awakening and was now ready to pay his debt to society.

"It's not fair!" The old scandal would be raked up and plastered in the papers once again. Only now, Jessie had become an acclaimed artist, quite a different person from the one who had shared the house in Hill Street and disappeared after his arrest.

"We'll ride it out," Clifford promised. Instead of hiding from the media he called a press conference. In his remarks, he portrayed Jessie Lawrence as a young American who had been dazzled by the international lifestyle showered on her by Jimmy Kolas—the motor cars, private planes, jewels, servants. How many times she left him. How many times he lured her back with his charm and wealth.

"She knew she had more to offer society than to be an adornment on a rich man's arm and to take photographs of film stars and Eurotrash. In one of life's ironies, being abandoned by Jimmy Kolas was the making of this extremely talented artist."

He beckoned her to the podium and put his arm protectively around her. "Jimmy Kolas went into hiding to escape justice. Jessie Lawrence went into hiding in order to find her true self." He held up *The World of Bliss*. "And this, ladies and gentleman, is the exquisite result!"

The applause was deafening. Following Clifford's instructions, all Jessie said when they quieted down was a husky "Thank you from the bottom of my heart." In the hush that followed, Cliff spirited her out a back door. Whether it was Clifford's impassioned speech or the power of Jessie's photographs, the resulting media coverage was sympathetic in the extreme, warmly commending her for picking up her socks and going on with her life.

In any case, the Jimmy Kolas scandal was old news. All he'd actually done was steal some money and escape from prison. He had not murdered a rock star or had an affair with a royal. The stories about him were brief and in most instances neglected to mention Jessie Lawrence.

"You're a bloody genius," she told Clifford. "You saved my life. How can I thank you?"

"Marry me."

Marriage? Was he serious? One look at his face told her he was indeed serious. The subject had come up so suddenly and was so totally out of context with what they were discussing, she was at a loss for words.

"I'm asking you to marry me, Jessie."

"I know. I just don't know what to say."

"Yes would be pleasant."

She still couldn't think of anything to say.

"You do love me, Jessie, don't you?"

She nodded.

"But you're not *in* love with me, is that it?"

She turned away from him and murmured, "Can we discuss this some other time?"

A heavy silence hung over them until Clifford turned her around to face him. "There's something worrying you. Care to tell me?"

"It's nothing. I guess I'm just knocked out from all the excitement."

She put her arms around him and kissed his cheek. "You're right about one thing. I do love you. Let's wait 'til New York to talk about marriage."

He had been right about something else. There was something worrying her. To put it mildly, she was worried sick about Jimmy Kolas. If he'd been hiding all this time in the convent on Helios, he must know the truth about Bliss. There was nothing she could do except hope that Anna and the other nuns had died or been transferred. She couldn't bear to think about what would happen if he revealed the secret. It would destroy her family and ruin Bliss's life.

She did not have long to wait. A call from Jimmy's lawyers advised her that the government might call on her to give evidence against him.

"What evidence? I have no evidence to give. I was as surprised at what happened as anybody."

By some miracle, they had managed to have him released on bail. "Mr. Kolas respectfully asks to meet with you."

Clifford was furious. "There's no reason on earth to meet with him!" There was, of course, a reason.

He had not changed. In fact he looked better than ever. The simple life of sun and sea and olive oil and fresh fish had kept him slim and fit. "I understand my old friend's boots are under your bed," he began.

"What is it you want to see me about?"

"Money." He explained without apology about the money he had embezzled. Through various international monetary loopholes he had converted it into several different currencies and finally into American greenbacks, which he then stashed away in the convent on Helios "where a certain baby girl was born and adopted by a certain American woman. I can't prove it, of course. There are no records. But it's rather a good story, don't you think? Could be rather embarrassing."

"What's that got to do with me?"

"I admire your spirit. You are the only person I can trust to go to Helios and get me my money. If you refuse I will tell what I know."

What exactly he did know was beside the point. Once he opened his mouth, the secret would be out. "Can I trust you?"

"All I want is the money. I wouldn't harm you for the world. Besides, if I did betray you, you'd tell them about the money. That's your insurance."

"What, may I ask, are you planning to do with the money? You won't be able to spend it in prison."

"Don't laugh. I'm planning to make restitution."

"Then why can't you just say where the money is and turn it over to the authorities?"

"Because, my dear, the money is in Greece. I couldn't take it with me because I was under a police escort and they would have confiscated it. And if I say where I've hidden it now, the Greek government will confiscate it and that will be that."

Enroute to Helios, it occurred to her if she were caught smuggling currency *out* of Greece she could wind up in a Greek prison, and if she were caught smuggling it *into* Britain she could wind up in adjoining cells with Jimmy. She had no choice.

This time she traveled by commercial airliner to Athens and waited for the twice-weekly steamship to take her to Helios. Jimmy's grandiose plans for an island paradise had been abandoned. The house they had shared lay in ruins from a series of violent storms. The convent had been made much more comfortable during Jimmy's stay. Anna was still very much there and welcomed her like a long-lost friend.

The suitcase Anna gave her was almost too heavy to lift. When she opened it, it was empty. On examination it had an entirely false outer shell. She never dreamed money was so heavy. She had thought she would breeze casually through customs and immigration, swinging her suitcase as though it weighed next to nothing.

Dear God, this is for Bliss, not me. If you get me through this in one piece, I'll never do another dishonest thing as long as I live!

The power of prayer intervened. Because of a wildcat strike of government officials at the Athens airport, passengers were told with much apology to carry their own bags through the deserted customs and immigration stations. At Gatwick, her prayers were answered again. Storms had diverted several flights from Manchester and Liverpool. Thousands of disgruntled travelers crammed the immigration lines. When Jessie reached customs, the harried officials asked, "Anything to declare?" and scribbled the chalked okay without waiting for a reply.

Never again. To express her gratitude, she planned to give substantial donations to every religious denomination she could think of. She delivered the suitcase to Jimmy's lawyer and returned to Clifford's house. She had been gone less than three days on what she said was a fashion shoot.

"Have you heard the news about Jimmy Kolas?" Cliff asked a few days later when he arrived home, waving the *Evening Standard*. The lawyers had made full restitution on Jimmy's behalf, in light of which they were now petitioning for a suspended sentence, and would probably get it.

The day before Jessie and Clifford were to leave for New York, Jimmy showed up unannounced with a copy of *The World Of Bliss* for Jessie to autograph.

Jessie was alone. "You can only stay a minute."

"Just long enough to thank you. For everything." He indicated the book. "She's utterly glorious."

"What will you do?"

"I'm barred from doing business in Britain so I'm off to Argentina. My wife's lover was killed playing polo. He left her a fortune and she, poor darling, wants me back."

Jessie had to laugh in spite of herself.

"And you, Jessie?"

"I'm going to marry Clifford and live happily ever after," she said lightly, but tears filled her eyes.

"And so you should. By the way, don't forget it was I who introduced you."

She laughed again, pulling herself together. He reminded her of Rachel. Whatever happened, he managed to take the credit. And where Bliss was concerned, he did deserve half.

CHAPTER 33

1990

Jessie

For the fickle and famous, the Minkow Gallery on Madison Avenue was the current place to be. It stood a good chance of a long and healthy life because it gave the movers and shakers something they wanted more than art. A way to make a grand entrance. Taking a leaf from the films of the 1930s, where everyone wore dinner clothes and virtually lived in nightclubs, the interior designers had created a spectacular staircase leading down to the lavishly carpeted and softly lit pavilion below.

The beautiful people, male as well as female, could arrive at the top of stairs and pose for a moment before walking down the steps into the waiting arms of friends and the media, who were often one and the same. A quip making the rounds referred to a certain gossip columnist as *Rude Descending Staircase*.

Rachel made the most of her entrance. Encased in a silver sheath with a pinkish tinge that made her skin glow, diamonds and rubies rampant, she stood imperiously alone until her presence was felt and all conversation stopped. Only then did she beckon Jessie and Bliss to join her on either side as she made her regal descent. Eleanor, Hannah, Clifford, and Luke followed like palace retainers.

"She makes Marlene Dietrich look like a fishwife!" Clifford whispered loudly. Rather wide of the mark, of course, but that's what he thought the old girl would like to hear. He hoped flattery would get him somewhere. He needed her help in convincing Jessie to marry him. The reappearance of Jimmy Kolas last year had shaken her deeply and put her off marriage.

Although their professional relationship continued, Jessie avoided all talk of the personal. "Let's wait until after the American launch. Let's see how the book sells." And on and on.

Bliss had never seen Jessie's photographs of her blown up and mounted. Almost fourteen now, she was no longer the ten-year-old adorning the gallery walls. The preadolescent softness of her features and coltish angularity of her body had metamorphosed into the first intimations of womanhood.

Hands reached out to touch her. Faces beamed adoration. From everywhere in the crowd she could hear her name. *Bliss. Over here! . . . Bliss. Isn't she lovely! . . . Bliss! . . . Bliss! . . . BLISS!*

Dewey eyed with excitement, she clung fiercely to Jessie's arm, trying to accept the compliments and answer the myriad questions. *Was this what Madonna went through?* All those people with all those teeth, looking like they'd like to swallow her whole.

Walt Minkow was ecstatic. *The World of Bliss* was turning into the most successful opening in the history of the gallery. Photography was becoming big business. Almost half the prints had been sold and for prices Clifford called none too shabby. Jessie and Bliss had signed a hundred books and those too were mostly gone.

"Congratulations, Jessie." Jimmy Kolas had materialized among them. He kissed her hand before turning his attention to Bliss. "And this is the exquisite child?" Clifford stepped smoothly between Jessie and the intruder. Jimmy stood his ground. "Oh, come now, old man. I was passing through town. I didn't think you'd mind my coming."

"I mind," Clifford said mildly and with a single punch knocked him to the floor.

The entire family was on Clifford's side. Jessie didn't care. Her mind was made up—she never wanted to see Clifford again. Rachel tried to reason with her. Hannah talked to her for hours. Jessie refused to listen. A year had elapsed since she decided to remain in New York alone, giving Cliff no choice but to return to London without her.

"Jealousy is sick! It turns my stomach. I am not flattered by having a man fight over me. How dare he turn my opening into a brawl." In fact, Cliff's attack had gone virtually unnoticed. And to give him his due, Jimmy Kolas had behaved like a gentleman, insisting he had slipped on some spilled champagne, apologizing profusely, and leaving the gallery.

But Jessie was adamant, and Hannah and Rachel finally gave up.

Hannah had troubles of her own, with Rachel in trouble and refusing to admit it. Hannah knew that Rachel's real-estate empire was once again in danger of being stolen from her by the board of directors. Her holdings were in fact jointly owned by her and her husband. Rachel's lawyers were exasperated and beseeched Hannah to use her influence. What influence? Some go-between! Jessie refused to listen. Rachel turned a deaf ear. She was tempted to let her entire crazy family self-destruct, but the Salinko situation was seriously dangerous.

"You've got to have Marcus declared incompetent, Mom!" Hannah cried.

"It would break his heart," Rachel said coldly.

"But he won't know."

"The man has his pride."

He also had the power to sign away his portion of his holdings if some shyster got hold of him. Visitors were in and out of the sanitarium all the time. Stranger things had happened. Hannah's offer to accompany her mother on visits to Marcus were always turned down, yet another rejection Hannah learned to accept.

That didn't stop her from phoning regularly to check his condition. Marcus was not her real father but he had been kind and generous to her all her life. She also made it a point to make friends with one particular nurse, sending her little thank-you notes with a check enclosed, getting her theater tickets on her days off so that if anything odd happened Hannah would be notified at once.

Sure enough, two men with briefcases had visited Marcus and the nurse had seen him signing some papers. As Hannah might have expected, her mother turned on her for meddling when she alerted Rachel to the incident.

Hannah didn't back down. "Mother! God knows what they got him to sign. If you get thrown out on the street, it'll be up to Jerry and me to take care of you. Some fun."

In the end, with further prodding from Jerry, Rachel sat down with her lawyers and told them what Hannah had learned. They called an emergency meeting of the Salinko board and confronted them with proof of unethical behavior. Whatever Marcus signed would be challenged in court. Their chicanery when made public would reflect disastrously on the company's integrity.

The board saw the wisdom of their remarks. Rachel had Marcus declared incompetent and was accorded full power of attorney over his finances. During a private moment with Hannah she thanked her for butting in. "You're a good and patient girl. A good daughter. I wish I could be as good a mother to you."

"I'm sixty-four years old," Hannah said. "I've had two fathers, one brother, two husbands, two daughters, and two grandchildren. I've never had a mother. You loved Samuel more than you loved me. When he died, you told me to my face you wished it were me. You've never forgiven me for living, have you? Well, it's taken me all this time, but I can look you in the eye and tell you I've forgiven you."

Having got it off her chest, Hannah girded herself for some fancy histrionics. Instead of the expected tears or haughty denials, Rachel looked sadly at her only living child. "What can I say? I'm sorry? I did the best I knew how? You know I never knew my own mother. You know what it was like when you and Sam were growing up. I had to go out and do what I had to do to pay the rent and put food on the table. Remember the time with the chewing gum?"

Hannah remembered. It was shortly after Will's suicide. Rachel and she were buying fruit from a pushcart on Broadway. Hannah kept nagging her mother for a stick of gum, spearmint gum, her favorite. Driven to distraction, Rachel handed her the package from her coat pocket. There was one stick left. "Be a good girl and throw the wrapper in the basket."

When they got home, Rachel reached into her pocket for the last five-dollar bill she had in the world. It was gone. In giving Hannah the spearmint-green wrapper, she had inadvertently included the tightly folded five spot. Mother and daughter spent heartsick hours retracing their footsteps, covering every inch of sidewalk, questioning the fruit peddler, as if he would have told them if he had found it.

Her face hardened as she recalled in detail how she emptied the trash basket on the sidewalk, ignoring passersby, turning every bit of garbage over with her foot to no avail.

"That's what being a mother was like during the Depression." She looked squarely at her daughter. "Shall we try to be friends?" She extended her hand as if offering to clinch a deal.

Hannah shook her mother's hand. "I'd like that, Mom."

That settled, Rachel turned briskly to another family matter. "Let's talk about Jessie. She's a damn fool to give Cliff the heave-ho. Doesn't she realize he's the best thing that ever happened to her? You're her mother. Have you talked to her?"

"She told me to mind my own business."

"Well, we can't let her wreck her life. We've got to do something to get them back together."

Hannah knew if anyone could do it, Rachel could.

CHAPTER 34

1991

Rachel

Jessie could feel it in her bones. Rachel was up to something and not just getting Jessie to take her picture for free. "Now remember, Jessie. I insist. I expect you to bill me. Business is business. This is what you do for a living. I absolutely will not allow you to do it for nothing."

Grandma up to her old tricks. Jessie wondered what she would say if she actually got a bill, for a thousand dollars, maybe? Five thousand? "Don't be silly. I wouldn't dream of charging you. You're my glamorous grandma, aren't you? You gave me my first camera, didn't you? Where would I be without you? Flipping hamburgers at McDonald's? It's the least I can do."

Rachel managed to look troubled and then graciously gave in. "After all, it is for charity. You can declare your fee as a contribution on your income tax."

The idea for the fund raiser was Rachel's. A celebrity fashion auction. Well-known women from the arts and the professions would model a favorite item from their personal wardrobes. The guests would bid and the proceeds would go to a program for homeless mothers.

"Are you going to make them strip on the runway?" Jessie teased.

"Not a bad idea. I've still got the body for it, you know. Damned impressive for an old dame of eighty-nine!"

The outfit Rachel would be wearing was a 1947 Dior suit, the first example of the New Look. Its nipped-in sculptured waist and soft ballerina skirt had revolutionized fashion after the war.

"Are you sure you want to give this away?" Jessie knew of Rachel's collection but had never seen any of it. Bliss was the only one invited into that part of the penthouse.

Rachel smiled serenely. "Don't worry. I've told Hannah to bid on it."

"But Grandma, won't everyone know it's your own daughter?"

"What's the difference? The money will go to the shelter and I'll get my Dior back. Besides, who's going to know she's my daughter? Hannah always refused to serve on any of my committees. She says they're a lot of hot air. She'd rather teach a class in remedial reading to immigrants."

Jessie had created a setting reminiscent of Cecil Beaton with flowers, crystal, and a mirrored wall behind Rachel reflecting light and showing her back, which was as straight and slender as a girl's.

"Oh, by the way, darling . . ."

Here it was. She knew Rachel had more on her mind than the photograph. Jessie tried to guess. More copies of *The World of Bliss* to give to friends like Brooke Astor, who was not yet actually a friend but was on the way to becoming one if Rachel could help it.

"Yes?"

"I was talking to Clifford . . ."

Bloody hell! Why didn't he give up? How much clearer could she be? She did not wish to marry him. She did not wish to return to London. She wished to stay in New York and live in her mother's apartment and have no responsibilities except for the series on New York she was doing for *Harpers Queen*.

"Really?"

"Yes, really. Don't be so snotty. He said when all the foreign sales come in you stand to make close to six figures."

"Well, good for me. I don't care to discuss it."

"Well, it so happens I do. You're cutting off your nose to spite your face. Since you don't read his letters or take his calls, he wants me to tell you he would like to do another book with you. You owe him that contractually, you know."

"What's he going to do, sue me? He can't force me to take pictures."

Rachel swallowed her exasperation. "No, he's not going to hold you to your contract. He's not going to sue. He wants you to know he accepts your decision not to marry him, and now that so much time has gone by he would like to resume your professional relationship and publish your next book—but only if you want to. Not because you owe it to him."

"It's pointless to talk. I'm not going back to England."

"Oh, didn't I tell you?"

Rachel, I'm going to kill you! "Tell me what?"

"He's bought a small American publishing house, Gramercy Press. Charming premises in an old brownstone off Gramercy Park."

"When did he tell you that?"

"He says it reminds him of Hampstead."

"Grandma, what's going on?"

"Stop making a face. It will freeze that way."

"Tell me this minute. When did you talk to him!"

Rachel rose and kissed her granddaughter. "About five minutes ago. He was having a cup of tea in the kitchen."

1991

Clifford

"Let's see what you've got."

Clifford had set up the light box on the coffee table in the room he was temporarily using as an office. Jessie laid out the transparencies. They sat on the floor on cushions, close enough to touch yet not touching. The reunion in Rachel's kitchen had established certain ground rules for their reconciliation and the style of their professional relationship.

By a silent but mutually recognized agreement, they scrupulously avoided all physical contact. Not a handshake on meeting nor an arm taken while crossing the street, not a coat held nor an elbow steered through a restaurant. Even now they managed to pass the transparencies back and forth between them without fingers grazing, and to bend over the light box for closer inspection without touching foreheads.

The tension could be cut with a knife.

"Not too bad, are they?"

Cliff's highest compliment, British understatement.

"Not *too* bad."

All was silent except for the faint click of the transparencies in their plastic overcoats being moved around. These were the first shots of Rachel and Bliss together. The hope was that the chemistry between them would be as evident on film as it was in life.

"It's going to be all right, I think."

British understatement again. Translation: The pictures were terrific because Bliss and Rachel were terrific together. From the moment Rachel met Bliss's train at Grand Central, they were off and literally running through the station in an impromptu game of tag, their roles temporarily reversed. Rachel insisted on having an ice cream cone with sprinkles while Bliss sipped an Evian.

The theme for the day was Rachel taking Bliss shopping for something appropriate to wear for Thanksgiving dinner. A bantering battle of wits took them from the neon outrages of West Broadway to the cloistered dressing rooms of Saks Fifth Avenue, with stops along the way at sidewalk marts selling sunglasses, jewelry, and accessories designed to enhance every conceivable part of the human anatomy.

Jessie's camera captured the affection between the old woman and the adolescent girl while each fought to keep her temper in check. Facial expressions and body language told how they felt about each other's taste far better than shouting matches or threats to forget the whole thing.

When Bliss tried on the velvet party frock that Rachel simply adored, Bliss puffed out her cheeks and slouched to demonstrate how fat it made her look. She was a good sport, however, when Rachel insisted they buy it. It was a reciprocal gesture to thank Gransy for letting her have the mylar jumpsuit with the Elvis appliques.

"It's good to be working together again." There was no irony in Clifford's voice, no undertone of provocation or reproach.

The finale of the first day's shoot had Jessie's two subjects zapped out with fatigue on a bench in the Rockefeller Plaza gardens. Together yet separated by seven decades, Rachel sat still as a lovely piece of sculpture, her lifelong devotion to good posture evident, while Bliss simply sprawled. Jessie couldn't be sure, but it crossed her mind that Rachel's pose, with her lovely legs gracefully crossed and her chin tilted at the most flattering angle, was cleverly rehearsed.

In contrast, the camera caught Bliss yawning, digging into her backpack for some raisin energy, and feeding one to a passing pigeon.

Well? What are you waiting for. Say something! Anything! Jessie held her breath as Clifford examined the series of prints.

"You know what you've done, Jess?"

"What have I done?"

"I hope you don't mind me saying this?"

This was an aspect of Cliff that drove her mad. Why couldn't he stop waffling and just say it, for God's sake! "Of course I don't mind. You know how I value your opinion."

"The old woman taking the young woman shopping is banal in the extreme."

"Wait just a minute—"

"Kindly be quiet. As I started to say, a banal situation—but you, my dear, are doing what the great painters have done through the ages with street scenes and bowls of fruit. You have made life into art."

There wasn't much she could say to that. A faint glow of color suffused his cheeks. "Clifford?" He was fussing with his watch and seemed not to have heard.

"Clifford, I'm talking to you."

His eyes remained fixed on his watch. "I hear you."

"For God's sake, Cliff. Is there anything to drink?"

He looked at her at last and smiled. "There's some sherry, I think."

Sherry! He had once told her how the British discovered sherry in Spain, during the Napoleonic Wars. To her it tasted like cough syrup and made her feel worse. In old English movies, everyone sat around sipping tea or sherry. How could she consider herself a card-carrying Anglophile when she loathed and despised both?

"Lovely. I think we should have a toast."

The amber liquor was less revolting than she had remembered. Some ice cubes or maybe a scoop of vanilla ice cream would have improved it, but she was not about to spoil things.

"I've been an ingrate and a brat, a spoiled brat. I've never thanked you for all you've done for me, for encouraging me and inspiring me. If not for you, I would still be doing rock stars at home and families who won the pools. If not for you—" Emotion threatened her composure "—If not for you, there wouldn't have been a book." She raised her glass. "To you, my dearest."

His glass clinked against hers. "To us." This said, he became flustered at having transgressed. "That is, if you think we might try again."

Since he didn't seem ready to kiss her, she seized the initiative and kissed him—a long, luxuriant kiss that reminded her, if she needed reminding, that she had been faithful to him all these months by default, there being no one else she wanted to kiss.

They were alone in the brownstone, the carpet thick, the sofa cushions soft and welcoming to reconciled lovers. A cool breeze seeped through the cracks in the windowsill bringing with it an abiding sense of the optimism that is autumn in New York.

CHAPTER 36

1992

Jessie

With child. She liked the sound of that better than pregnant. A pause could be pregnant. A woman was with child. Jessie had known for sure before getting medical confirmation. The revealing symptom was an entirely uncharacteristic driving compulsion to clean out cupboards.

It had happened on Helios and here she was again. Emptying out the medicine chest, throwing away the petrified nail polish and dried-out creams and the left-over prescriptions with the warning labels, FINISH ALL MEDICATION. What survived was washed, dried, and returned to the empty shelves in carefully designed patterns.

She was preparing the nest. She was giddy with happiness.

"Cliff? Prepare to meet your fate. I've decided to make an honest man of you," she said to the medicine chest mirror.

The four generations of women in her family gathered in tribal jubilation, ignoring Jessie's protests that all she and Cliff wanted was to get hitched quietly and without a lot of fuss and bother. Fuss and bother they did. Hannah gave a combination bridal and baby shower. Rachel arrived with a layette extensive enough for triplets. Eleanor made a crib quilt and enough fruit pies for the freezer to last until the baby was born.

And Bliss? Never had such sweetness and love gone into a gift for her expected baby cousin. She had found an enormous straw trunk at a garage sale. After cleaning it up, she had painted it white and threaded it with yards of yellow ribbon before filling it with treasures of her own babyhood. Baby books. Baby toys. Rattles. Her Raggedy Ann that had sat patiently in the corner of her own crib until she was big enough to hug it. And, best for last, Teddy the Teddy Bear. "He was getting bored," she declared when Jessie hesitated to accept such a precious gift.

Clifford was incredulous at the outpouring of gifts. In Britain, diffidence would have dictated a more modest response. "Only in America!" he marveled when Luke and Jerry pooled resources on an incredibly lush terrycloth robe for him, for walking the floor with the newborn.

For the simple Valentine's Day wedding, Rachel turned the penthouse into a combination of the Taj Mahal, Versailles, and Radio City Music Hall. Her mother's friend Judge Latham performed the ceremony. The buffet lunch was a masterpiece of excess, with everything from the Beluga caviar to the three-tiered wedding cake presented in a heart shape.

Finally it was over and the newlyweds slipped away to see how far the workmen had progressed in converting Cliff's genteel shabby brownstone into a functioning family home.

As for the traditional toss of the bridal bouquet, Jessie had lobbed it directly at Bliss. Thrilled at being included in the company of adults, she nevertheless protested, "I'm not old enough to get married!"

Jessie clasped the girl to her. "Of course not, sweetheart. I just want you to press it in a book in memory of this day."

CHAPTER 37

1992

Chloe

Amniocentesis. Jessie refused to have it. She didn't want it. It sounded like a Greek movie star. *Starring Amnio Centesis in a new Greek tragedy.* She did not want to know whether the baby was a boy or a girl. *What else would it be?* As for physical deformity or mental retardation, she was nearly forty years old and she was keeping this child no matter what.

She had never realized how superstitious she was. *Hubris* was defying the gods, being smug, thinking you had the world on a string and nothing could hurt you. The gods didn't like that. She was happy, she was married, she was successful. Her next book about Bliss and Rachel was well under way.

The pregnancy had been difficult, she had come close to miscarrying several times, but now all was well. The baby was kicking as if it was auditioning for *A Chorus Line.*

"Less than two more months," she had reminded Cliff that morning. Why hadn't she kept her goddammed mouth shut? An hour later she was in an ambulance, screaming in duet with the siren, enroute to Mt. Sinai Hospital with her husband beside her. "It's going to be all right, darling. I promise. I love you. Trust me. I'm here."

Hannah raced to her daughter's side. Eleanor was on her way from Riverton. If Jessie should need blood, her mother and sister had the same "O" type. They agreed not to call Rachel. Not for the moment. She was nearly ninety and better off at home. The doctor conceded that the situation was serious but assured them it was not life threatening. "At least not to the mother," he added ominously.

When Eleanor arrived, Jessie was under sedation. The sight of her sister revived her sufficiently to insist on seeing Eleanor alone. "Oh God, El. Was this what it was like when you lost your baby? I can't bear the thought of another little grave under the apple tree."

Eleanor eased herself past the tubes and onto the bed, and took her sister's hand. "Shhh. You'll be fine. The baby will be fine. What they're trying to do is keep the baby in as long as they can. Every minute counts."

Four hundred and eighty-five minutes later, by Cliff's reckoning, they were told there was no choice. There was an obstruction in the birth canal but the baby was moving down. The only viable option, a Caesarean.

"My camera, Cliff. I want my camera! I'm not going into that operating room without my camera. Please, darling, my camera." Jessie had become hysterical with fear.

"Later," Hannah soothed. "They're ready for you now."

She clung desperately to her husband's hand. "You've got to get it. I've got to have my camera or else—or else I refuse to have the baby. I just won't have it."

Her camera! Of course. They had joked about what a lousy photographer he was and had made elaborate plans for Jessie somehow to smuggle her camera into the delivery room and photograph the child as it was born. All nonsense, of course.

"Clifford, please. My camera is my good-luck charm. If I don't have it something terrible is going to happen. It'll die. The baby will die!"

"I'll be back in ten minutes." Luck was with him. It

was two o'clock in the morning and the streets were deserted. The cabbie he flagged down was an old-timer who rode his steed like a bucking bronco. He made the roundtrip to Gramercy Park and back in eighteen minutes flat.

Jessie caressed the camera as if it were a Stradivarius. As the anesthesia took effect, she smiled at her husband and handed the camera to him. "I'll still be asleep when it's born. So it's up to you. Please remember to aim the camera at the baby and not at your chest. Is it loaded, by way?"

When the five-pound, four-ounce girl was placed in Clifford's arms, Jerry took the picture for posterity. C-section babies were always more beautifully formed than those who had to squeeze and struggle for life. This child was no exception. Her face was clear skinned rather than mottled, her expression sanguine from the ease with which her mother had been unzipped like a duffle bag. The doctor swiftly transferred her from her cosy prenatal cave to an incubator for preemies.

"Just as a preliminary precaution," he said. The infant was healthy and hungry. The floor nurse would take her back to the nursery until Jessie came out of the anesthesia and was alert enough to feed her.

Chloe was the name Jessie and Cliff had chosen for a girl. "And what a wonderful girl you are, Chloe," Jessie said when at last she held her daughter close.

"Something's wrong!" Cliff spotted it before Jessie did. "She's turning blue. Nurse! Nurse, come quick!" He pushed all the buttons on the bed console and ran into the corridor.

"Chloe! Dear God!" The baby was in spasm, the tiny limbs rigid and shaking, the little fists clenched.

The nurse ran in, followed by Cliff. He had found her chatting at the Coke machine. "It's convulsions!"

"No—no!" Jessie refused to let the nurse take her baby. "She'll die. I'll never see her again," she wailed.

Cliff pushed the nurse aside. "I won't let her die!" He held out his arms.

"You promise?"

"I promise."

She surrendered the tiny bundle. By now Chloe's eyes were closed; her skin was a grotesque blue, like mummified infants found in ancient tombs. The nurse led the way to the intensive care unit. The doctor had been roused from sleep and was on his way.

"I'm being punished." Her energies spent, Jessie stared into the middle distance, oblivious to the anxious faces of her family.

"Perhaps, if you will allow me," Clifford began politely. "I'd like to be alone with my wife. There's a visitor's lounge at the end of the corridor."

Hannah started to protest. Jerry took her by the arm. "He's her husband, dear." Eleanor followed them out with one helpless backward look at her sister.

When they were alone, Clifford took Jessie's hand. "No more of that nonsense. Everything's going to be fine."

"I'm being punished."

"Being punished for what?"

"For lying!" Her face crumpled.

"Everybody lies."

She refused to be consoled. The tears oozed from her eyes in salty rivers of fear. He dampened a towel and wiped her face.

"Shall I recite something while we're waiting?"

Her face brightened slightly. It had become their habit after making love for her to lie safely in her husband's arms while he recited some of the verses he had learned by rote as a schoolboy. She too had studied the sonnets in English Lit but barely recalled them until

Clifford's lyrical voice in the night stillness of their bed-room brought them thrillingly to life. There was no question about it, she had told him, love poems sounded better with an English accent. The Brownings especially. One day they would go to Florence.

" 'How do I love thee?' " Jessie smiled up at him. Her favorite.

"Close your eyes and try to relax. 'How do I love thee? Let me count the ways.' "

Her breathing became more regular as the tender words of love caressed and calmed her. In his desperate desire to soothe her, he did not anticipate the effects of the sonnet's final words. " 'I love thee with the breath, smiles, tears, all of my life!—and, if God choose, I shall but love thee better after death.' "

Death! "If she dies, I'll die, too!" Jessie cried.

All he could do then was rock her in his arms until the door opened and the doctor walked in. He was not smiling.

Chloe was suffering from some rare form of blood disease. They were making tests and sending the results by computer to blood specialists across the country. Until the opinions of the experts came back and could be evaluated they were keeping her alive with blood transfusions from the hospital blood bank.

"What about me? Why didn't you ask me for blood? I'm only the father," Clifford stormed, pacing about the room.

"You and Jessie have O-type blood," the doctor explained. "The baby's is AB/RH-negative." AB/RH-negative was a rare blood type present in less than eight percent of the population. The odds of anyone else in the family having it were miniscule.

"So where does that leave us?"

"The supply from the blood bank will keep Chloe stable until we get some answers."

The family gathered in the visitor's lounge to wait. At Eleanor's tearful behest, Luke had driven down with Jason and Bliss. After some painful discussion, Jerry was sent over to Riverside Drive to tell Rachel what was going on.

"Why didn't you call me? Didn't anybody have a quarter?" Rachel raged as she entered the waiting room.

"We didn't want to upset you," Hannah said.

"Upset *me*?" Her withering look of contempt could skin a cat. "That'll be the day!"

After two agonizing days, the expert medical consensus was that Chloe was suffering from a rare form of leukemia. The white cell cannibals were literally consuming the red cells. The only way to save her life would be a total blood replacement.

The technique involved draining the infant's tainted blood and replacing it with healthy blood of the same type. "There is a further complication," the doctor said gravely. "The healthy blood must come from a genetic family member with the same blood type or it will be rejected." Chloe's blood type as they knew was AB/RH-negative.

"What about me?" Rachel remembered that she was AB. Was that enough? A quick test proved it was not. The match had to be exact.

Clifford called his brother in Edinburgh and a first cousin in Norfolk, to no avail. Was there anyone they had forgotten, the doctor asked? Was Jerry the baby's grandfather, for instance?

Viktor! Hannah put aside her loathing and called telephone information in Munich. No listing. Jerry called the International Red Cross. She didn't know Viktor's blood type, but he was after all the baby's grandfather. The Red Cross promised to do their best to find him, but it might take several days.

Chloe did not have several days. She needed the blood *now*.

"What about me?" Bliss had been sitting quietly beside her mother. She rose shyly. "Maybe I'm AB/RH-negative."

"Right here. In our midst. How could we be so stupid?" Clifford hugged the girl. "Never fear. The test won't hurt a bit. I'll be right there with you."

"No!" Eleanor cried. "She's—" Distraught and groping for an excuse, any excuse, she protested, "She's too young!"

But Clifford and Bliss were on their way down the deserted hospital corridor to tell Jessie and the doctor. Luke tried to keep his wife from following them. "Please, Eleanor. She's sixteen and fully grown. She's strong. It's our last chance. She may save the baby's life!"

Eleanor wrenched free. "You don't understand!" She ran after them. "Please, Bliss! Wait." She caught up with them outside Jessie's room. "Jessie! We've got to tell them."

Eleanor had known all along that Bliss was AB/RH-negative. She had been told at the time Bliss had her tonsils out. The doctor had advised Eleanor to make a note of her daughter's blood type in the event of an emergency. Perfect. Except for one thing. The blood for Chloe had to come from a genetic family member. Otherwise, the baby would reject it and die.

Eleanor's cries had stopped Bliss and Clifford in their tracks. They turned around just as Eleanor sped past them and entered Jessie's room, slamming the door behind her. "We'd better see what's up," Cliff said.

The rest of the family came hurrying down the corridor right behind them.

Eleanor was whispering frantically in Jessie's ear when the entire family burst in and crowded apprehensively at the foot of the bed. Eleanor turned to face them.

"Please—everyone—listen to me. Luke, dear—I'm sorry—I never wanted you to know—" They all stared at Eleanor as if she had gone crazy. "Bliss can't save Chloe. Because you see—Bliss is—adopted!"

The story poured out. How desperately she had wanted a second child. How she had poked holes in her diaphragm. How she endured several miscarriages until at last she was pregnant again.

"Eleanor—" Jessie cautioned.

"Don't interrupt me, Jessie! I've got to explain what happened! I thought I'd made it. I thought the baby would be okay, but then—you were away, Luke, at that seminar, remember?" She described how she was all alone when the baby was born dead and how she had waited for Luke to call from Ithaca, and how Jessie had this crazy idea about adopting a baby on Helios and how Jessie had made all the arrangements and how she returned home with the sweetest, most loving baby girl in the entire world.

She collapsed in tears at the side of Jessie's bed. "It's not fair. You did everything for me. And now I can't do anything for you."

Jessie smoothed her sister's hair. "It's all right, Eleanor. It's going to be all right. Bliss?" She beckoned her niece, the girl she had immortalized with her camera. Her face was ashen. Jessie held her by her shoulders and stared deeply into her eyes before turning her attention to those watching.

"Bliss is mine. My baby. My sweet little girl. I vowed never to tell anyone. Ever. Not even you, Eleanor. I was the one who gave birth at the convent and I was trying to figure out what to do next. Tell Mom? Tell Grandma? Tell Jimmy Kolas? And then? The miracle! You called me, Eleanor, and the idea came to me in a flash!"

She smiled at Rachel. "You always said I was the smart one, Grandma. Well, I proved it, didn't I? I gave

my sister the baby she wanted and now, another miracle. Bliss is going to give my baby her chance to live."

Tensions mounted in the visitor's lounge as the family awaited the results. By common agreement, they
kept their emotions in check. Recriminations would
keep until, God willing, the crisis had passed and little
Chloe's life was saved, thanks to Bliss.

A suffocating silence filled the air, Jessie sat hollow-
eyed and ravaged with fear while Clifford rubbed her
hands and whispered reassurance. Rachel pretended to
need Hannah and Jerry's help with the crossword puzzle, a challenge they gratefully seized. Anything to pass
the time and to postpone dealing with the incredible
secret that was just beginning to sink in.

Eleanor sat in a patch of isolation of her own making, as far away as she could get from her sister and
from Luke, who paced up and back in the adjacent corridor. When Jessie gazed at her beseechingly, Eleanor
turned her head.

Bliss appeared finally, in a wheelchair pushed by a
nurse, but looking none the worse for the blood trans-
fusion. As the doctor had reassured her, they didn't
need that much for a newborn baby. A large glass of orange juice, a big jelly doughnut, and some hot sweet-
ened tea, and there she was, smiling in the doorway.

"Piece of cake. Nothing to it. Really cool," she said.
Everyone smiled back at her with delight except
Eleanor, who covered her face with her hands. Bliss
leapt up and went swiftly to her. "Am I still your
daughter?"

Eleanor sobbed. "Do you want to be?"

"Of course, I want to be."

The doctor chose that moment to appear. He was
smiling. "I think it's going to be all right." Chloe was
sleeping peacefully. Her color had returned. Her tem-

perature was normal. If there were no complications, she could be taken home in a few weeks.

In the ensuing outburst of relief, Bliss spotted Luke in the corridor and ran to him. "Isn't it wonderful, Daddy? Chloe's going to be okay. Now we can go home." When she tried to hug him, he held her away from his body, his hands digging into her shoulders like iron claws. "Stay away from me!"

"But, Daddy—"

"Don't call me Daddy."

"But *Daddy*!" She tried again to put her arms around his neck. He raised his hand as if to slap her, caught himself, and with the yelp of a wounded animal ran from the room.

"Daddy—?" She called after him as if her heart would break. "Daddy—?" She ran a few steps before turning back in tearful bewilderment. "Daddy—?" She sagged like a rag doll. Eleanor and Jessie sprang to help her, colliding in their haste. Bliss clutched them both in a convulsive embrace. When she released them, they were crying, too, and fell into each other's arms.

"I guess I'm pretty lucky to have two mothers," she said with a wavery smile. "Some kids don't even have one."

Hannah looked toward Rachel to see if she had heard. A flicker of regret passed between mother and daughter in acknowledgment of the intimacy they had missed. The strain of the day's events was taking its toll. For the first time that Hannah could remember, her mother looked old. Having nothing to lose, she squeezed Rachel's hand and kissed her cheek.

CHAPTER 38

1992

Rachel

As the seasons changed, so did all their lives.

Jessie's universe became the brownstone house off Gramercy Park, with Chloe and Clifford at the center. Clifford conducted his publishing venture from offices at street level. Jessie's studio and darkroom were on the top floor adjacent to the nursery. Her photographs of Bliss and Rachel were beginning to look like a book. She suffered from the photographer's disease, congenitally dissatisfied, compulsively wanting one more, ten more, a hundred more shots.

Cliff was more than satisfied and made plans for publication. "You do need one more shot, though," he conceded. "Bliss and Rachel at her ninetieth birthday party. The perfect endpiece and back cover."

Eleanor's universe did not fare as well as her sister's. After Luke fled from Mt. Sinai Hospital, he drove home to Riverton like a man possessed and spent the rest of the night hurling Bliss' and Eleanor's personal belongings into shipping crates. In the morning, he had all the locks changed and called Jason in his dorm to tell him what had happened.

Since he could not trust himself to call his wife or any of her family personally, he instructed his lawyer to inform them that their possessions were being shipped to Rachel's address and that the locks had been changed on the Riverton house. Within a week,

Eleanor was notified that she was being sued for divorce on the grounds of fraud and gross deception in the matter of the birth of the female child known as Bliss.

Rachel for one couldn't have been happier. She had always resented the Great Stone Face for taking Eleanor to the boondocks and turning her into a farm wife. Now she could have what she wanted. Bliss was living with her on Riverside Drive while Hannah welcomed the opportunity to have her elder daughter home again after nearly twenty years. Though the subject was never discussed, Hannah's relationship with Eleanor had been strained ever since the girls' trip to Europe with Viktor.

Something had happened, but they never told their mother what. Looking back, she reproached herself for not probing the matter. She was in the midst of falling in love with Jerry at the time and failed even to question her daughters' lame excuse for returning home from Germany sooner than expected. When Eleanor insisted on marrying Luke and going to live in the wilds of upstate New York, Rachel had managed to make Hannah feel that it was somehow her fault, that she had driven her daughter away.

Now the arrangement was ideal, Bliss living with Rachel and Eleanor back in the bedroom she and Jessie had shared as girls. It was wonderful having a daughter again. With Jerry on hand, Eleanor would soon see that there was such a thing as a witty, thoughtful, caring man. Not all men were rats like Viktor or Luke.

Eleanor and Jessie agreed to forgive and forget the past. One afternoon, Eleanor and Bliss paid a visit. "Is Chloe my sister or my cousin?" Bliss asked.

"Both!" the two women cried in unison and hugged with genuine affection. They still had a way to go before attaining their previous intimacy. There were still some questions for Eleanor to ask and for Jessie to answer. They knew they would reach a total reconciliation for one simple reason. They wanted to with all their hearts.

Rachel was in her glory when, one day Bliss made a solemn announcement. "I've changed my mind about wanting to be Donna Karan, Gransy. I've decided to be me. An original, not a knockoff. Just like you."

For months, Rachel had planned to have a ninetieth birthday party, a gala celebration of her longevity and a great way to get loads of presents. Now it would also be a launching pad for Bliss, rocketing her into the cultural and political life of the city. Rachel's invitation list included the fashion designers, models, buyers, and journalists with whom she regularly toiled on fund raisers. A Liz Smith here, a Barbara Walters there. A Democratic leader. A Republican insider. Movers and shakers from City Hall to real estate lobbyists. Brooke Astor, of course. In years to come, long after she was dead and buried, fashion historians would mark Rachel Salinko's ninetieth birthday as the start of Bliss Lawrence's meteoric rise.

The day of the party was crisp and clear, the city contributing its autumnal splendor as a backdrop for the event. Flowers, champagne, and packages from Tiffany, Cartier, and Steuben arrived in profusion. A decorating crew transformed the triplex apartment into an ocean-going liner, *The Queen Rachel*. Simulated portholes festooned the interior walls while huge murals covered the windows with stylized moonlit seas. Food and music heralded various ports of call. A Hawaiian luau. Texas barbecue. French omelettes and vichyssoise. Pizza and pesto. And Rachel's favorite, blinis with Beluga prepared by the Russian Tearoom.

Except for the rooms where she stored her private costume museum, the entire penthouse was open to guests. All the rooms were filled with flowers. The seating arrangements were designed for conversation. The more adventurous could explore her gymnasium or, as one couple did, recline in the magnificent black marble tub with a bottle of Moët Chandon.

Choreographed waiters circulated with trays of food and drink, followed by minions who whisked away empty glasses and plates and replaced dirty ashtrays with clean ones.

Rachel's bedroom was like a movie set, a blend of the Arabian Nights and Marie Antoinette. A pair of coromandel screens were positioned to hide the bed itself from view. Instead of making a grand entrance at a given moment and wending her majestic way through the throngs of well wishers, Rachel had decided to greet her guests from her bed like an empress of old holding court.

As the festivities got fully under way, the music suddenly stopped. A series of drum rolls signaled the removal of the coromandel screens. Wreathed in a cloud of chiffon, her diamonds sparkling like stars, Rachel Forsyth Lawrence Salinko reclined on a profusion of scented silken pillows. The French doors to the bedroom terrace admitted a cool breeze from the Hudson River far below, while the western sky above the Jersey palisades blazed crimson and gold.

Wild applause. Shouts of affection. Clifford's deep baritone voice led off the familiar "Happy Birthday to you" and was instantly joined by an exuberant chorale. At a signal, a birthday cake the size of a piano was wheeled in. It was decorated with Rachel's favorite gardenias in butter cream and ninety candles.

Hannah offered a lit taper, but Rachel made a charming show of declining to light the candles. "You want me to set off the smoke alarm?" she quipped.

She ordered the cake to be paraded through the

penthouse for all to see before being taken to the pantry to be sliced for serving with coffee and brandies.

"And now, my darlings—" She raised her fingers to her lips in a kiss of theatrical dismissal.

Jerry called out, "You promised me a dance, Rachel, How about it?"

"Me, too. A tango you said," a friend from the mayor's office added.

Rachel accepted their clamorous demands with the coquettish diplomacy of a debutante. "Give me a minute to change and I'll dance your feet off."

Protesting the delay, demanding she get a move on, they withdrew from the bedroom. Wesley closed the door after them and approached her mistress for further orders.

"Everything is ready, Ma'am."

Her plan was to change into the spectacular gown that showed off her youthful figure and Marlene Dietrich legs. People always said she should have been an actress. Didn't they realize life was a soap opera and everyone had to fight for a leading role?

She loved making an entrance. No slinking in quietly. No sidling anonymously on the sidelines. Whether arriving at the dentist's or the office or taking Bliss shopping at Saks, she stopped traffic. It had always embarrassed Marcus, poor thing, still gallantly clinging to life in Connecticut. Couldn't she just walk into a room like an ordinary person? he often lamented.

She was not an ordinary person. In a little while she would prove it once again. *My fans expect it.* Her dear friend and dancing partner George Abbott would be arriving in a little while. She couldn't wait to see everyone's face when she and the one-hundred-one-year-old Broadway producer sashayed out and broke into a fast foxtrot.

Meantime she would lie back and do the breathing

exercises Robert had taught her for restoring energy. "Wesley?"

"Yes, Madam."

This would be a good time to round up the family for a little private get-together.

"Yes, Madam." *Yes, Madam!* What a pill!

The generations filed in and gathered around her bed.

Chloe gurgled when Jessie placed her in Rachel's arms.

"See, Grandma? She likes you!"

"Good girl!" Jessie was the one she praised. Jessie knew she would be pleased to see the baby in the French couturier ensemble she had bought her.

"Clifford has something for you."

It was the mock-up of the cover for BLISS AND RACHEL with a photograph of the two of them trying on hats at a street fair. "What do you think?"

"We-ell—" She fought back tears. Besides, she had never cried in front of her family and wasn't about to start now; they would spoil her eye makeup. "Wouldn't it be better to have *RACHEL* AND BLISS?"

Jessie pretended to be hurt. "Grandma, what do you think about the photograph?"

Rachel sniffled to avoid blowing her nose. She dared not look directly at Jessie for fear of completely breaking down. To Clifford she said, "Tell your wife she is the greatest photographer in the entire world."

Hannah piped up, "And it's all because of you, Mother." With a wave of her hand she entreated the others to join in the familiar litany. "You gave Jessie her first camera!"

Rachel regained her composure. "Don't be such a wisenheimer!" To the astonishment of all, herself included, she kissed Hannah's cheek and then beckoned each of the others in turn for her benediction. Clifford,

Jessie, Chloe, Jerry, and last of all, Eleanor, hand in hand with Jason and Bliss.

"Never feel guilty," Rachel said quietly. "Guilt is for people who do bad things. You did a good thing. If you hadn't, we wouldn't have Bliss, would we? Now scram the hell out of here, all of you, so I can change."

Alone again, Rachel smiled at the thought of Chloe's tiny face. Her *great*-grandchild! Like so much of late, it was hard to believe. She despised being old, but as George Burns said, it was better than the alternative. There were still things to do. Clifford planned to send her and Bliss on a publicity tour with Jessie when the book came out. What's more, he said it was time for her to write her memoirs.

She closed her eyes in contemplation. She would begin at the beginning and tell it all. She would be dead and gone by the time Chloe was old enough to read the spicier parts.

She would discuss it with Clifford, of course. He was a bright boy. Jessie the smart one had been smart to marry him. But one thing was not negotiable. The title of the book would be *Rachel*. No arguments. There was only one Marilyn, one Liz, one Cher, one Madonna. Soon there would be one Rachel, and she was it!

The question, of course, was whether to tell the truth about Sam's real father and Will's real reason for jumping off the subway platform and what she really did to keep food on the table and a roof over their heads during the Depression. She might take Hannah into her confidence to consider the ramifications. Her daughter was after all not only a professional writer but a teacher of composition to immigrant children. In fact, she might just ask Hannah to do the actual writing, though naturally there could only be one byline— Rachel Forsyth Lawrence Salinko.

* * *

A little while later, when Wesley found them in the library and told them something was wrong, the women of Rachel's family hurried swiftly and discreetly to Rachel's bedroom. She lay against her silken pillows in graceful splendor, a slumbering Cinderella newly kissed by the prince of eternal sleep.

There was a smile of satisfaction on her face. Famous for her skill in making an entrance, she had made an exit people would talk about for years.